CEMETERY PICNICS

a novel

I0692787

Patricia L. Walsh

TOA PRESS LLC
Boulder, Colorado

TOA PRESS LLC, P.O. Box 2262, Boulder, Colorado 80306
ISBN-13: 978-0-9822989-2-3
ISBN-10: 0-9822989-2-7

Author's Note

RIVER CITY a nurse's year in Vietnam was a memoir. **CEMETERY PICNICS** is a work of fiction. But I returned from Vietnam in denial of severe Post Traumatic Stress Disorder (PTSD) and have given the protagonist my name.

CHAPTER ONE

I remember precisely the first time my mind took leave of my body, not to another place, but somewhere up near the ceiling where it could observe below what remained of my person struggling to appear normal. I remember the room, the time of day, who was on my left and my right. And I recall vividly the antiseptic smell and coolness of the tiled floor as my cheek pressed against it, my hip aching from falling dead weight onto its hard surface as the gun continued firing.

March 29, 1974, began as most did at Filmore Hospital, a Baltimore institution known around the world for its success in treating nature's mistakes, a gathering place for obscure diseases with difficult to pronounce names. Patients suffering from potentially fatal maladies such as Leptospirosis, carried by the urine of rats, mice and swine, were diagnosed and successfully treated at Filmore when lesser institutions had given up.

Kings, queens, dictators and others of great wealth or power flocked to its doors in search of miracles. Such dignitaries were housed in an elaborate private wing, far from the rabble of the city's surrounding slum who swarmed to Filmore's clinics and emergency rooms with common ailments of the disadvantaged, perforated ulcers, abscesses, pneumonia, complicated pregnancies and, of course, the Friday and Saturday night shootings and stabbings.

Filmore was not the first inner city hospital in which I had worked, but it was still unclear to me whether large teaching hospitals were purposely built in ghettos in order to provide young interns and residents ample subjects on which to practice, or if the hospitals were built in once high-class neighborhoods that only later deteriorated into slums. Of one thing I was certain, there were two very separate

1

standards of care.

The affluent were attended to by male professors in starched white coats with contingents of eager young students ready to carry out their every order. They swept like football squads down waxed corridors on grand rounds, darting off into private rooms to palpate, poke and listen while deliberating the best possible treatment.

The charity cases lay in multiple occupancy wards that smelled of body wastes, attended to by exhausted interns and junior residents who fumbled through various diagnoses with little supervision from their senior residents, let alone the professors. Unless, that is, they were lucky enough to have a disorder which defied all diagnosis.

Early in my year at Filmore, I discovered that in the absence of title or money one could still get the attention of the professors with a disease worthy of front page headlines. Those with mundane disorders such as gallstones or appendicitis, left in the hands of the inexperienced, were more inclined to end up on the obituary page.

On this particular Friday, always surgery's busiest day because both doctors and patients demanded to be done before the weekend, I had begun work at seven a.m. And being the anesthetist on duty until seven the following morning, I was assigned to an operating room which would run past the customary four o'clock quitting time.

The final case belonged to Dr. Fallis, the professor of plastic surgery, who would be doing a revision of eyelids.

I was wrapping a blood pressure cuff around the left arm of a pallid little man who had skin so translucent it looked like wax.

"You oughta come on down ta Fishback Ahlund and let me show y'all around," he said to me. "God's piece a' heaven raght here on earth."

Reba, the technician in the sterile field who would hand instruments to the surgeon, gave an audible humph.

"I've heard it's nice," I said.

Anyone living in Baltimore knew of Fishback Island's miles of wide, well kept beaches. But Filmore Hospital took care of enough vehicular carnage from the weekend traffic to and from the summer mecca to discourage me from making the bumper to bumper trip.

As I continued to work on the patient I became somewhat mollified about beginning the non-emergency case late on Friday. His eyelids were so slight they didn't cover his eyeballs even when closed as far as possible. As a result of having air and light constantly assaulting his corneas, he blinked and teared excessively.

Dr. Fallis was still scrubbing his hands just outside the O.R. while I pasted heart monitor leads to his patient's chest.

"Ah'm tellin' you for fact, oncet you come down you'd never

leave." A blink accentuated each word. "A nice young woman like yerself needs ta have some fun, not jest work." I wasn't sure if the patient winked at me or if it was a lopsided blink.

And it wasn't just his eyes that were peculiar; he was almost short enough to be classified as a little person, and as white as an albino. Henry Fishback was what the medical profession would have classified in his youth as an FLK, funny looking kid. The label was given to children who were not quite normal, yet failed to fit into any specific category of congenital anomaly.

"I hate anesthesia," he whined as I delicately threaded an IV needle into a spidery vein as stiff as uncooked macaroni. "You people and your needles are the worst part a' surgery." I wanted to ask if he would prefer to have his surgery awake.

"You're going to sleep now, Mr. Fishback," I said as I pushed on the Pentothal syringe.

The drug was barely in when he managed to rip one of his short arms free from the armboard I had taped it to, flapping it up and down like a wing. With his defective eyelids open, it was not clear whether he was still conscious when he grabbed hold of my breast while I leaned across him to restrain the loose arm.

"God, I've given this guy enough to knock out a horse," I said after prying his stubby fingers from my breast, securing the arm once more and injecting another 10 c.c.s of Pentothal.

"That's Hen for you, a drinker and a lady's man," Reba said with a laugh. "Won't know he's dead till he tries to move."

I looked at the wall clock indicating five PM and was once more annoyed by the case. "Why are we doing a non-emergency case this late?" I demanded of the circulating nurse as she cleansed the operative area with an antiseptic solution.

"Because he's rich," the nurse replied simply.

Reba turned from the sterile table where she expertly arranged instruments in neat rows. "I'd keep your voices down if I were you. Old Fallis hears you, he'll keep us here all night."

I glanced toward the windowed door where Dr. Fallis could be seen scrubbing his hands with a wide-eyed contingent of interns and residents. "I don't care if he does hear us. He knows it's Friday and we'll be up all night with the knife and gun club."

"That's just my point. He'll take twenty minutes a stitch if you make him mad. Then the bar brawls start and we have no supper, no coffee and no time to pee." Reba's eyes shone darkly from mahogany skin between her white surgical cap and mask.

I dropped my complaints about the professor. There were

important things to attend to.

Anesthesia is frequently compared to flying, with the induction and recovery periods being as critical as take-off and landing. The patient's blood pressure, pulse and respirations must be checked and recorded at least every five minutes. And the skin color must be watched closely now that I had knocked out the patient's respirations with anesthetic drugs and hooked him to a ventilator. It had alarms to indicate a malfunction, but I was too seasoned to rely solely on technology without a stethoscope taped to the chest to listen to actual breath sounds and the beating of his heart.

Mr. Fishback had such a beak-like nose I had failed to find any anesthesia mask to fit over it properly. So I had quickly inserted an endotracheal tube directly into the trachea to deliver oxygen and anesthesia gases. The tube would be necessary anyway since both my equipment and I would have to move down to the left side of the table to be out of the surgeon's way while he did the eyelid revision.

"How do you know this guy is a drinker?" I asked Reba.

"I grew up on Fishback Island. Hen's family got some kinda' charter from the king way back. He owns half the island."

"Hen?" I started to laugh but suppressed it when I remembered Dr. Fallis just outside the door at the scrub sink.

"His name's Henry," Reba said quietly. "But folks on the island all call him Hen." Reba was silent while I checked the patient's blood pressure. "I think he got the nickname when he went into the chicken business instead of becomin' a waterman like everybody else," she said when I finished. "Fishing, crabbing and oysterin' just wasn't for Hen."

She had finished arranging an array of delicate eye instruments and was presently threading needles. "Or maybe he got the name because he looks so much like a chicken," Reba added.

I looked more closely and was struck not only by Mr. Fishback's short, wing-like arms and beaked nose, but by a wattle of red flesh hanging at the front of his neck. His hair was so fluffy and white it could have been feathers, and he had a comb of bald, sunburned skin running from his forehead almost to the back of his head.

"Poor Hen was teased all his childhood," Reba continued. "The rest of his family's all normal looking, for Fishback Islanders that is, but he turned out all white and squatty."

She came over to the operating table and began arranging sterile towels over the patient's face, leaving only his eyes exposed.

"He started raisin' chickens as pets when he was just a boy. But you oughta see his set-up now, whole island covered with his hatcheries and processin' plants."

The towels were secured with sharp metal clips Reba snapped into place. "He's got more money than you or I'll ever see."

She then placed larger drapes over the entire body, leaving me with only the arm holding the I.V. to look at when checking skin color for adequate oxygen content.

"Course, that don't mean I'll never have me any money." Reba gave a nod toward the scrub sink and lowered her voice. "One day soon I'll be selling my properties to the same rich doctors I've been waitin' on all these years."

"Doctor Fallis says he needs these, too," the circulating nurse told Reba as she carried in a newly sterilized rack of instruments she dumped into a basin of sterile water. They sizzled and steamed from the intense heat of the autoclave.

"Honey, he needs every instrument in the whole place," Reba grumbled. "Even if he's removin' a mole."

The scrub technician was in her late fifties and had spent the past twenty-four years working in Filmore's operating rooms to support five children, now grown and moved away, and to pay for what she proudly referred to as her properties, the latter consisting of several hulks of dilapidated buildings overlooking Baltimore's run down harbor. The structures had been damaged by fire in the riots following Martin Luther King's assassination six years earlier, and Reba bought them from the city for a bargain price.

It was her dream that the harbor would one day be revitalized, and she could sell her properties to middle-class whites who fled the city during the race riots but were now returning to be closer to their jobs. Reba worked as many extra weekends as possible to pay for her investments.

I glanced at the patient's chart. "It's still ridiculous to be wasting time making an old gumper's eyelids look better when so many people around here aren't even getting basic medical care."

"That war you were in makes you think too much about people who don't get any doctorin', and not enough about all the ones that do."

I looked worriedly over the anesthesia screen and was relieved to see the circulating nurse was out of the room. Reba was the one person I talked to about Vietnam, and I only confided in her because we often worked together on the bloody Friday and Saturday nights that reminded me so much of the war.

We all fell silent as Doctor Fallis marched into the room with the exaggerated caution of one getting used to bifocals. His much younger students followed in the same high-stepping gait, all dripping water and orange antiseptic soap from hands held out in front of them. The circulating nurse trailed behind them, bobbing up and down like a sandpiper, cleaning up their slippery wake.

Absolutely no one was allowed to speak in Dr. Fallis' operating room but himself. "This is a fascinating individual," he began. The plastic surgery professor was in the habit of elevating each of his patients to the level of aristocrat, thereby making them worthy of his exalted attention.

Reba politely handed him a sterile towel to dry his hands, then slapped one into the waiting hands of the interns and residents she towered over. She had been showing young physicians their way around operating rooms so long, none of them dared object to the sting she left in their palms and fingers. Even Doctor Fallis had been guided from bumbling young intern to pompous professor by Reba, and he showed his respect by not swearing or throwing instruments at her as he did with less experienced personnel.

Dr. Fallis quickly gowned and gloved. "This shouldn't take too long. I don't know why the poor man waited so long to have it done."

The entire team brightened at the prospect of finishing in time to have dinner before the weekend warriors hit the E.R.

"Mr. Fishback has direct lineage to royalty and owns one of the largest poultry industries in the country," Dr. Fallis said.

The surgery was tedious, and so boring in the deadly quiet operating room, I found myself struggling to stay alert. I was having to administer heavy doses of anesthesia to compensate for Henry Fishback's alcohol abuse.

The up side was that Doctor Fallis stayed with his students throughout surgery, making sure everything was done as efficiently and perfectly as possible. Many other members of Filmore's teaching staff made only token visits to operating rooms, where the brunt of their cases were handled by interns and residents.

A tiny stitch was being precisely placed at the corner of Mr. Fishback's right eye when the circulating nurse entered to announce a genuine emergency, a ruptured appendix would be starting next door as soon as Dr. Fallis was finished. The legs of the student doctors, who had been on duty for as long as thirty-six hours, all sagged so they lost several inches of height. And you could see Dr. Fallis shift into a slower gear to remind us that his case dominated.

"Where's Dr. Rasheif?" the circulating nurse wrote to me on a piece of paper so she would not further break the code of silence. The anesthesiologist needed to see the emergency patient and get the equipment set up in the adjoining O.R.

"Try the dog lab," I wrote back.

"That stink hole?" she whispered.

"That's why it's a good place to hide," I wrote on her sheet of paper. She left without further comment.

Any physician licensed to practice medicine in the United States could call himself an anesthesiologist, whether or not he had taken the necessary training in the specialty or passed board exams. Dr. Rasheif had done neither.

Nurse anesthetists like myself were mandated by law to graduate from an accredited school of anesthesia, following completion of registered nurse's training, and to pass national boards in the specialty. I had resented the double standard even before I went to Vietnam, but after spending more than a year doing battlefield anesthesia without the help of a single anesthesiologist, I was not inclined to depend on them. That was particularly the case with Dr. Rasheif, who graduated from a Middle Eastern school of medicine of such questionable reputation he was hardly qualified to give anesthesia in the dog lab, where experimental surgery was performed.

I was helping Reba push Hen Fishback's stretcher to the recovery room when we passed the open door of the operating room next door. The appendectomy patient lay wincing while Dr. Rasheif tried unsuccessfully to start an I.V. The frazzled doctor waved to me.

"You come here do case."

"Let that camel jockey wait," Reba said before I could respond. "This is America, not some desert where he can order women around."

"Watch his arms," I told the recovery room nurse when I turned Mr. Fishback over to her. Hen was already awake enough to flap his stunted appendages up and down as if he was about to take flight.

We were leaving the recovery room when the telephone at the surgery desk down the corridor rang. "Gunshot wound to the head on its way into the E.R.," the nurse called to me. "They need anesthesia down there pronto, Pat."

"Crap. The midnight morons are already at it."

"Get set up for a craniotomy stat," the nurse told Reba as we reached the desk.

"I'm not gettin' into anyone's blown up brain 'til I empty my bladder," the scrub tech retorted and continued on down the corridor. "It's been holding Lake Michigan the last hour."

CHAPTER TWO

I had time for half a cigarette as I ran down six flights of stairs, not waiting for elevators. By the time I burst through the double doors of the E.R. my lungs sounded as if they were in need of my own ministering. The charge nurse greeted me.

"Gunshot wound isn't here yet but they need you in room five," she said. "Patient's raising such hell the doc can't stitch him up."

I stopped to give the German shepherd next to the policeman on emergency room duty a pat on the head. Filmore kept an armed canine patrolman on the premises at all times to deal with the locals.

"Hello, Dr. Jekyll," I said. "You keeping everyone in line down here?" The dog wagged his tail and licked my hand.

"Evening, Miss Walsh," the policeman said, tipping his hat.

"Please call me Pat," I said, as I had many times before.

"Yes, ma'am," the officer replied.

"He needs just enough anesthesia to let me finish putting his face back together," the intern said when I entered room five.

The patient, a scrawny white male in his late twenties, was handcuffed to the side rails of the stretcher on which he lay, but he kept his head in constant motion flipping it from side to side. Blood oozed from a number of deep lacerations on his cheeks and forehead.

"Careful, Miss," the policeman said when I stepped closer to the stretcher to get a better look. He and his dog had followed me into the room and stood near the door. "He's a junkie just held up a gas station and killed the kid working there."

"For a lousy sixty bucks," the intern added.

"Fuck you!" the patient screamed up at him. "Fuck all of you!" He arched his body up from his manacled wrists, trying to break free.

8

"You shut your mouth and lie down!" the policeman yelled at him as he moved swiftly across the room. The German shepherd raised his massive front paws onto the stretcher and added an impressive growl.

"How did his face get so cut up?" I asked at a safe distance from the junkie's flailing feet.

The intern looked to the policeman. "He resisted arrest, ma'am."

"Those fuckers beat me!" the junkie screamed. "Beat me with their fuckin' sticks!"

The officer's face remained coolly impassive.

"C'mon, give him something." The frustrated intern was holding his threaded needle away from the constantly moving head. "I want to finish so I can turn him over to the cops."

"I can't put him to sleep," I said. It was standing policy to treat people off the streets as if they possessed a stomach full of food or booze, most often both. Aspiration of stomach contents into the lungs was the number one cause of anesthesia deaths.

"You don't have to give him a full anesthetic," the intern pleaded. "Just a little to settle him down."

"Giving a little anesthesia is like being a little bit pregnant." The intern looked as if he was about to cry. "I can sedate him for you," I relented.

"I don't want no needles!" the junkie yelled as I drew a sedative into a syringe.

Both his arms had a series of dark tracks from drug use. "Yeah, like you've never had a needle stick," I said as I approached him.

He nearly caught me in the midsection with one of his motorcycle boots, and the cop was on him in an instant. "You settle it down or I set the dog on you!" he roared only inches from the patient's face. Doctor Jekyll, with the hair on his neck standing straight up, put his front paws back up on the stretcher and bared his teeth.

"And if you don't shut your mouth, I'll stitch that shut, too," the intern said.

The junkie quieted but squirmed as far as possible to the other side of the stretcher. "Down Jekyll," the policeman said to his dog. "Good boy, good boy." He gently petted the animal while keeping a 'no more bullshit' eye on the frightened junkie.

"Ambulance on the way in," the desk nurse said when I had the junkie sufficiently sedated to leave the room. "Seizure patient."

It was turning into the usual Friday night freak show before it was even dark. "What about the gunshot to the head?" I asked.

"On the way. Cops had trouble breaking up a fight in the bar so the ambulance crew could get to him."

9

While I sat at the desk waiting for the two ambulances, I watched the E.R. staff hurrying from room to room caring for broken bones, chest pain and children with high fevers. Over each of the examining rooms was a hand lettered sign designating it as M*A*S*H ONE, M*A*S*H TWO, and so on, after the Korean War film and popular television show.

A nurse led a man bleeding from a wound on his arm to the room labeled M*A*S*H TWO. "Incoming wounded!" she proclaimed. "Clear the deck for incoming wounded!" The remainder of the staff joined in the fun with calls for Doctor Hawkeye Pierce and Nurse Hot Lips.

I wondered how they could have so much fun playing war when I was having such a hard time forgetting it.

"Is this your idea of a joke?" the chief E.R. resident asked when the seizure patient, grey-haired and wino pale, was wheeled in. Sputum bubbled from his mouth and ran down his whiskered chin while his body twitched in a rather odd looking pattern.

"We picked him up down by the harbor," a police officer who looked as if he was still in his teens said. "Fell right down in front of my patrol car and started having this fit."

The chief resident gave the officer a look, then turned his attention to the man on the stretcher. "O.K., Jimmy, knock it off." The old man continued to shake and grunt.

"I said knock it off!" The resident slapped the patient's face.

As if a switch had been turned, the seizure stopped and he sat up rubbing his reddened cheek and looking around. "Shit," he said, and wiped at the drivel dripping from his chin with the sleeve of his dirty shirt. "Shit, shit, shit."

"That's right, Jimmy," the E.R. resident said with no mercy. "They brought you to Filmore so you might as well give up the act."

The older officer still standing guard over the junkie in room five called out to the resident. "He's just a rookie, sir. He doesn't know the fakers yet."

"But he fell down right in front of me." The junior officer protested. "I swear."

"I was closer to University Hospital," the patient scolded the ambulance crew. "You shoulda' took me to University!"

"They're full up," an attendant answered nonchalantly.

"He pulls this whenever he wants to get hauled in," the chief resident told the young officer while looking a little more kindly at Jimmy, now sitting on the stretcher clutching a spare bundle of grimy clothes to his bony chest. "He's just looking for a warm bed, three meals a day and whatever drugs he can con us out of."

"My nerves has been terrible," Jimmy said, holding out a trembling hand as evidence.

"That's what happens when you smoke cigarettes and throw booze at them twenty-four hours a day." The resident motioned for a nurse. "Check his vitals and give him five milligrams of Valium if they're O.K.," he told her. "But then you're back on the street," he said to Jimmy. "This joint's so full we're going to have to start setting up cots in the morgue."

"Maybe a little soup and toast," Jimmy said to the nurse as she wheeled him away.

They were barely out of sight when the gunshot patient arrived. The chief resident turned to hurry alongside the stretcher as it was rushed into the largest trauma room. "How long since the shot, was he conscious at any time, how much estimated blood loss...?"

The ambulance crew fired back answers while inflating the victim's lungs with a breathing bag and holding pressure dressings against spurting blood vessels in what was left of the right side of the patient's skull. "Twenty-six year old black male, shot during drug deal at Cozy Corner, no response to verbal or painful stimuli, massive blood loss, brain tissue evident on floor of bar...."

It took only a few minutes for me to get a tube into his trachea, hook the unconscious man to a ventilator, and put in an additional I.V. line. I was just out of the double E.R. doors, heading for the O.R. to set up for the craniotomy, when I heard loud shouting. When I turned back, staff members were gathering outside room five.

They made way for me as I moved to the room, thinking the junkie needed more sedation. But I found him on his feet, all stitched and bandaged, holding the terrified intern who treated him in front of his emaciated body as the two backed away from the E.R. police officer and his dog. The scalpel from the suture tray, now in the unsteady hands of the junkie, was coming very near the intern's jugular veins.

"He grabbed the knife the second I uncuffed him," the canine officer told the chief resident. "I thought the doc got rid of the blade when he finished."

"Get that fucking dog outta here!" the junkie yelled. He was taller than the intern, and his hand was quaking so badly the scalpel was intermittently touching the intern's shock white throat, leaving tiny droplets of blood.

"O.K., you got it," the chief resident said in a quietly controlled voice. He motioned the officer and the dog out of the room, then gave the head nurse standing with the onlookers orders in the same measured tone. "Call the neuro doc and tell him we have a train wreck down here.

He needs to come take over his gunshot case."

The nurse went to the desk to telephone, and the E.R. chief returned his attention to the junkie and his shaken hostage. "I want you to give me the knife," the resident said as he took a cautious step forward, his hand outstretched. "Put it here in my hand."

The junkie pulled quickly back, dragging the stricken intern with him. "Nothin' doing. This doc's gonna go for a ride with me." The junkie's eyes were wild and the intern's legs so weak they wobbled visibly. "You get everyone outta here an' a car pulled up to the door," the junkie demanded.

"Please do what he says," the intern croaked, trying to keep his Adam's apple away from the scalpel. "Please."

"Anyone tries to stop me and the doc gets sliced," the junkie warned. The intern's neck now had a necklace of red beads stretched across it.

"We'll get you the car," the chief resident said reassuringly. He motioned for the rest of us to step back, but not before we saw the door to a pass-through box, used to hand x-rays from the dark room next to room five, swing slowly and silently open.

There, framed in the square opening, was the head of Dr. Jekyll. His handler was beside him, giving silent hand commands as the dog moved up onto the ledge of the opening.

The junkie continued shouting demands, unaware of the scene unfolding behind him. There was a nurse on my left and an orderly on my right. We moved back in unison, watching expressionless as the cop raised his forty-five.

"Go!" he shouted and the growling dog leapt for the junkie.

"Hit the floor!" the chief resident screamed to the intern, who was already on his way due to legs that gave way completely.

The junkie reeled to confront the dog just as the officer fired.

A third sharp crack reverberated off the walls as I fell dead weight against the E.R.'s tiled floor.

Somewhere I hear a baby crying. A very small baby.

I watch myself searching for it, pausing at dimly lit doorways of a crowded, primitive hospital. The patients are all Vietnamese, lying two and three to a bed, or on the squalid floor. Their broken bodies are swathed in bandages or filthy plaster casts, and they fight futilely at swarms of flies crawling into their eyes and noses.

I come to a room that is white-hot bright. Several Vietnamese nurses are gathered around a wooden examining table where a baby with its skin charred by napalm lies whimpering. I move through the nurses and reach automatically for a pulse in the baby's neck. But my hand halts as I see a faint heart beat pulsating beneath a layer of raw muscle stretched across the baby's rib cage.

"Time to leave," another American nurse says from the doorway. She cannot see the baby because of the people gathered around it.

"In a sec," I reply.

I draw a pain killer into a syringe, then scan the baby's body for a place to inject it. There is no skin left, and when I try to gently turn the infant over to look at its backside, cooked flesh comes off in my hands.

"We'll be in the jeep," the waiting American nurse says from the doorway.

"Coming." I am trying to wipe my hands on a stiff cloth that refuses to cleanse me of the bloody flesh sticking to them.

The infant cries pitifully and I pick up the syringe again and inject the only unburned tissue I can find, its tiny pink tongue.

"Are you coming or staying?" a British nurse snaps from the door. "It's bloody broiling in that jeep."

I step back so she can see the baby. "Sorry," she says and walks away.

The baby is quieting from the drug. I am certain it will not live long.

I join my fellow nurses in the jeep and we drive to a crumbling French villa where I scrub my hands and eat lunch prepared by a Vietnamese cook. I rest on my bed for an hour afterwards, while all street activity ceases for siesta, then return to the hospital with the others to work until dark.

The baby is still there, crying its pathetic kitten cry. I feel the food I have consumed rising up my esophagus in a sour mass.

"Oh God," I moan as I wake to find myself lying on a cool, tiled floor. "How could I have done such a thing?"

"What the hell's the matter with her?" a young doctor inquires from where he helps doctors and nurses work on a hemorrhaging patient.

Someone is tugging at my arms, pulling me up from the floor. "C'mon, try standing. That's the way." The room is white-hot and my back and left hip are aching. "Are you O.K.?" It is the orderly looking into my face with a worried expression. "You fainted," he says. "When the gun went off."

I can hear each word being spoken to the me standing in the midst of a loud, bloodied emergency room. Yet the physical me has no connection to the mind hovering up near the ceiling.

"Get her over here or get someone else!" the resident in charge orders. "This guy needs an airway established stat!"

"We can't find the anesthesia resident on call," a nurse tells him from the door as more personnel pile into the room. "The anesthesiologist is in the O.R."

The orderly gently takes my shoulders, looking directly into my eyes. I am rubbing my sore hip as the part of me up near the ceiling wonders how I know all these people.

"You need to get yourself together," the orderly tells my body below. "The patient needs an endotracheal tube."

I look to where the junkie lies on the stretcher. His chest is awash in bright red blood and people frantically stuff sterile packs in to curb the flow.

"Next time you get rid of the goddamned scalpel blade before you let the guy loose!" the chief resident yells at an intern wearing a necklace of dried blood.

"Can you hear me?" the orderly asks the me below.

When I do not respond, he leans me up against a wall and moves into the midst of the bedlam. "I can put the tube in," he tells the angry chief resident.

"An orderly can't do intubations!"

"I was a medic in Nam." He picks up an endotracheal tube and lighted laryngoscope. "We invented shock trauma."

The physical me watches in silence as he expertly puts in the tube and hooks the patient to a ventilator. When he finishes he comes back to me.

"Let's get you a cup of coffee."

"Get her a new job while you're at it," the chief resident calls after us. "If she can't take a little blood she has no business being a gas passer."

"She's fine," the orderly says back. "Just a little shook up."

He leads me, limping from the pain in my back and hip, to a waiting room just outside the E.R. and gets a cup of coffee from a machine, but the physical me cannot hold onto it, and he throws it in a nearby trash can. Two black women with fretful, dehydrated children sit in worn chairs amid the refuge of candy wrappers and discarded coffee and soft-drink cups. They watch silently while the orderly helps me into a plastic chair, then lights a cigarette he puts in my trembling hand. The me below smokes mechanically as he lights one for himself and sits down.

"You want to tell me what happened in there?" he says after a moment.

"I don't know." My mind, which has somehow managed to

follow my body into the room, continues to observe from the ceiling. "I don't know," I say again, my body feeling very much like a wrecked and abandoned car.

The two children in the room fidget feverishly and their mothers try to comfort them. I want to talk with the orderly, but words sound strange coming from a body without me in it.

"Try to act normal," my wayward mind prompts from above. "Don't let on that anything's wrong."

"Do you always faint when you see blood?" His manner is teasing. "Or are you just gun-shy?"

"Say something," my mind tells my body. "Anything."

"Why did they shoot him?" my other self asks. "Why did they shoot him and then try to save him?"

The orderly laughs. "You asking me to make sense of this place?" He takes a puff on his cigarette and exhales. "It's as fucked up as Nam."

CHAPTER THREE

My mind was suddenly back where it belonged. The orderly sitting across from me was so new to Filmore's E.R. staff I had to look at his name tag to see his name was Andy.

"You were there," I said. "In Vietnam."

Andy's shoulders raised slightly and pulled back, as if getting ready for a confrontation. "What if I was?"

I looked into the same old soldier eyes I had seen in thousands of young faces, feeling a kinship I no longer felt even with members of my own family. But the eyelids suddenly snapped shut, like a shade being pulled in the face of a peeping Tom.

"I was there too."

The shades lifted cautiously. "No shit?"

"Danang, sixty-seven to sixty-eight."

"Whoa, the big stuff," he said with a smile. "Tet?"

I nodded. "And two months of mopping up casualties afterwards."

"Army?"

"Civilian, Agency for International Development."

Andy smiled. "Good old A.I.D."

His eyes were somewhere between blue and green, with tiny yellow flecks at the borders of the iris. His dark hair was straight and fell past his shoulders, but was pulled into a neat pony tail.

"Man, I don't envy you working in one of those civilian dung heaps," he said. "I hauled a lot of casualties in there; the stink almost knocked me out."

In my mind a movie was beginning in slow motion. It was of the junkie being shot and Andy inserting an endotracheal tube while my

16

body, minus my mind, watched.

"How long were you over there?" I wondered if he could see the trembling I felt in every inch of what I had to keep reminding myself was my person.

"Long enough," he said with a laugh devoid of humor. He tapped at his left leg, which gave off the dull thump of an artificial limb.

"I'm sorry."

He squinted while he blew smoke past his eyes. "No big deal."

"I signed up for eighteen months with the State Department," I said. "But I came home after fourteen."

"Told Uncle Sam to shove it, huh?" His smile was much nicer than his laugh.

"I met a Marine over there." Andy waited for me to go on, as did the mothers eavesdropping on our conversation now that their children were asleep. "He was killed in the Tet Offensive."

"Oh." Andy dropped his cigarette to the floor and took his time grinding it out where dozens of others had been discarded by patients and family waiting to be seen in the busy emergency room. The mothers were giving me sympathetic looks.

"I'd better get back," Andy said as he got up. "Although that junkie dude's probably cashed it in by now."

The entire frenzied scene in the E.R. was back in full sound and vivid color, as was the ghastly image of the burned baby. My mind had even returned enough to my body to remember the gunshot to the head that had been taken to the O.R. It was time to summon all of me into a cohesive unit and return to my duties.

Andy's limp was pronounced as he started for the double E.R. doors. I stepped on my cigarette and began to follow.

"I should explain to..."

"You don't have to explain to anyone," Andy interrupted. "I almost hit the deck myself when that gun went off."

He turned to flash his lovely smile, and for a moment I thought of confiding in him the strange separation of my mind and body. But I had a case waiting for me in surgery and was afraid even talking about the episode might make it happen again.

"You think you broke anything?" he asked as I rubbed a hand across my lower back.

"It's nothing new. I wrecked my back in Vietnam."

Andy smiled. "Old war wound, huh?"

Even though my back spasmed painfully I had to smile. "Yeah, old war wound."

"See you later, Danang," he said as he started for the E.R.

"Thanks for..."

He gave me a think nothing of it wave and was gone.

When I reached the O.R., Reba was cleaning instruments while the circulating nurse scooped up dozens of bloody sponges from the floor. A man's body with its skull half missing lay on the operating table.

"He was dead when they brought him up here," Reba groused in my direction. "Turned out to be nothin' but a damned expensive autopsy."

The junkie did not make it to surgery, nor did a stabbing victim brought in at about ten. I was free to go to the call room and get some sleep, an unheard of luxury on a Friday night.

But I could not stop thinking of the baby my mind had gone back to revisit in Vietnam, nor could I get the smell of cooked flesh out of my nostrils. For six years I had managed not to remember it, or many of the countless others I had seen suffer and die.

I did not watch the news on television, listen to the radio or read the papers. I lived alone, moving from state to state and committing myself to no one and no place, sleepwalking my way through life to the extent that I could not recall people I had met along the way, or even some of the places where I had worked. And now an unnamed baby on the other side of the world had come to haunt me.

I paced the tight confines of the call room, praying for the telephone to ring. But what if it did and my mind deserted me again in the midst of a case? What if I killed someone?

The sickening, dank smell of death filled my nostrils until I felt a sour mass rising up my esophagus.

I made it to the nearby restroom only seconds before it erupted, spewing forth what little food I had consumed, then bitter, green bile. When my legs became too weak to support me I sank to the floor, banging my head into the metal divider between stalls.

"I thought it would die soon," I heard myself cry. "I only went home to lunch because I thought it would die."

It was of little comfort that I had given it pain medication before I left. Or that I had tried to do whatever possible for the thousands of others I had attended for more than a year. I could see all of their faces now and hear their pleas for help. And above all their loud entreaties, I could hear that kitten cry.

"Oh, god," I said to the deserted restroom. "How could I have left a suffering child? How could I have left any of them?"

My legs and back were cramped and aching when I pulled myself upright after what might have been hours. All that time I had tried to find some justification for my actions and had found none.

It was true that we had to care for our patients with a fraction of the supplies our government sent us that we actually received and what we could beg from area military hospitals. It was also true that Washington did not care that our supply planes were unloaded by Vietnamese who diverted the majority to the black market. But none of that excused me from letting a helpless baby suffer alone.

With three spent bullets and a hemorrhaging junkie, I had been catapulted out of the numbness surrounding me since the war, and thrown into a frightening awareness of a past I preferred forgotten. I could no longer escape the wretchedness I had witnessed, nor continue doing my job with the emotionless confidence and skill one develops caring for mass trauma day after day.

I was either losing my mind or just finding it.

CHAPTER FOUR

I grabbed the telephone before it could ring a second time. "Anesthesia."

"What?"

"Anesthesia call room, what can I do for you?" I pulled myself up in bed, trying to shake off a dream I was having.

It was the same dream that began shortly after Dan was killed and still recurred on a regular basis. He had lost a leg in battle and I was sitting in the rain on a row of sandbags waiting for him to be brought out of surgery at Danang's Navy Hospital. I needed to tell him I still loved him and wanted to be married, that the loss of his leg did not affect my feelings for him. That's where the dream always ended, with me sitting in the rain outside surgery.

"Anesthesia call room?" the male voice on the other end of the line repeated with amusement. "Sounds like a rough night."

I rubbed a hand across my face and looked around a room so bare it looked as if nobody lived there. A bed and a suitcase on the floor, still packed and ready to go. Not even a picture on the chalk white walls. Somehow I had managed to leave Filmore Hospital, drive home and fall into my bed still dressed in my O.R. clothes. My lungs hurt from all the cigarettes I had smoked the night before. I had gotten up to one pack a day in the war and was now up to two.

"Are you there?" the voice on the other end asked.

"I'm here," I answered. "Who is this?"

"Andy." I didn't recognize the name. "The orderly from the E.R. Your Nam buddy."

"Oh, hi." I blinked at the bright sunlight invading through an uncurtained window. "What time is it?"

"Two. I thought you might like to take in a movie."

My antisocial life had kept me off the dating circuit so long I didn't know how to answer.

"A matinee if you're up for it," Andy continued.

I was definitely not up for it. But outside my bedroom window the early Spring sun shone through the delicate pink blossoms of a Dogwood tree and it didn't seem right to waste such a day sleeping.

"Sounds good," I said and gave directions to my apartment.

When I stepped out of the shower I caught sight of myself in the mirror over my apartment-style sink and vanity. My face was so puffy I looked as if I was on steroids.

"Twenty-eight and trapped in the body of Eleanor Roosevelt," I said to my reflection.

I splashed cold water against my skin, which did nothing to improve its condition, then rubbed in a moisturizer and moved on. By the time I finished drying my short brown hair the moisturizer had worked no miracles.

I had gone to Vietnam a young, naive farm girl and returned an old woman. Looking at myself in the mirror, I wondered if I would ever feel young again.

The precious time left was spent on my eyes, my best asset. My clothes closet presented a more perplexing problem. Shopping malls had sprouted up everywhere while I was gone, a nightmare I discovered I did not need when I was coaxed into one shortly after my return.

"I really don't need anything," I told my mother as she rummaged through sweaters on a sale table.

"Everything you own is either worn out or out of style." She held a sweater up to me. "You're so thin," she said, as she had every day since my return. "Skin and bones."

"I don't need any sweaters, Mom."

"You're home now," she said with the genuine concern of a parent with a child she no longer knows but wants to help. "You have to put that war behind you, buy some pretty clothes and go to parties."

"You make it sound like a bad virus. Like it was nothing more than a case of the flu I should just get over." I didn't intend the harshness in my voice.

"You're not the same." The sadness in her face made me look away.

I didn't know how to tell her I didn't want to be the same, that I had no desire to be like the people swarming past us, laughing, talking, eating and carrying bags of clothing they did not need.

Every night millions of televisions disgorged endless images of war, and Americans responded by going shopping. They had been sitting down to dinner with the fighting on television as background for so long it had become just that, a television war. One that could be turned on or off at will.

"I don't want to be in this mall, or whatever you call it," I told my mother in a kinder voice. "And I don't want to go to parties. Or the cleaners, or stand in line at the bank, or the grocery store."

My life in Vietnam had been reduced to staying alive and helping the injured do the same. And I missed that simplicity immensely.

People were looking our way as they passed, like motorists slowing to gawk at an accident.

"You didn't have to go," my mother said.

It was the same conversation we had had right up until I stepped onto the plane.

"Someone had to take care of the people caught in the crossfire."

"But that someone didn't have to be you."

It was my last shopping trip, and digging through my few articles of clothing I now regretted it. In the end, I chose a blue sweater that matched my eyes and a mini-skirt a sister had sent for Christmas.

Andy escorted me toward a gleaming Harley Davidson.

"You expect me to ride on that?" Besides the obvious danger, my back throbbed from my restless night.

"Come on, it'll be fun."

He revved the powerful engine, which blatted loudly in the quiet neighborhood. I debated for a moment, then climbed on behind him. He gunned the machine so abruptly I nearly fell off as we spurted out of the parking lot and down the street.

My arms were locked around Andy's waist as we raced up the entrance ramp of the interstate and merged into Saturday traffic, headed for the fast lane. My hair slapped against my face as he pushed the engine harder, weaving in and out of cars at a speed which would guarantee instant death with only the slightest miscalculation. But Andy was right, my initial reluctance was being replaced by a long ago feeling of youthful recklessness.

"Fuck you, Eleanor Roosevelt!" I screamed into the wind.

The movie was a disappointment. We had pizza for dinner and Andy invited me to his apartment for a beer.

"That's a lousy fitting prosthesis," I said as I followed his stiff-legged gait up two flights of stairs.

"That's why I took the job at Filmore. Need a new one."

"Doesn't the VA pay for it?"

He was fumbling with the lock on his door. "You know the government, take a number and wait five years." He limped to a sofa with a sheet sticking out from its hidden bed and began removing his prosthesis. "Besides, the VA's where I got this beauty." He dropped the artificial limb heavily to the floor with the shoe still on it. "Ahhh, nothing like coming home and taking off a tired foot."

I didn't mean to stare.

"Do you mind?" Andy said. The stump ended just above the knee and was red and swollen from the ill-fitting prosthesis. He rubbed it gingerly. "I thought a nurse wouldn't be squeamish."

"I'm not." I stood with my jacket still on.

"Hacked on by Uncle Sam's finest," Andy said as he pulled his jeans down over the stump. "Take off your coat and grab a couple beers from the fridge."

I went to the tiny kitchen off the main room. It was the first bachelor's place I had been in that did not have dirty dishes in the sink. There was even shelf paper on the boards mounted on the walls to serve as cupboards.

When I returned I tried not to look at the amputated limb resting on the sofa. Andy said nothing when I took a seat on the opposite end. He took a pack of cigarettes from his pocket and offered me one.

"No thanks," I said before my hand could snatch one. "I'm trying to quit."

He fell back into the crevice of the sofa, looking me over with an expression that I interpreted as paternal. "Don't be too hard on yourself, Danang, trying to give up cigarettes while you're working through so many other things."

"What other things?"

"For whatever it's worth, I see you just beginning to deal with the shit that happened to you over there."

I hated his calm. But I craved it for myself.

"Until last night, I tried to repress Vietnam." I made the same little humorless laughing sound I found so annoying in Andy. "I don't even communicate with the people I served with."

"My point exactly. You have every day for a whole year to work through," he said. "Over there you were just thinking about staying alive and pulling people back from the brink. And I happen to know it's not easy playing tug of war with God."

"Were you a medic over there or a shrink?"

"A little of both. And a guy learns a lot lying around a VA hospital for nearly a year."

When he leaned forward to set down his beer, his long hair separated at the back of his neck, revealing a huge purple crater just to the left of his spinal column. I moved toward him to touch it without thinking and he quickly pulled his hair back over it.

"Sorry."

"Forget it." He drained his beer and crushed the can.

"I'll get you another," I said anxiously. Andy was already pulling himself up on his good leg.

"I'll get it." He hopped out to the kitchen and returned with a beer for himself and another for me. "See, I get around just like a regular guy." He popped open his can and foam fizzed out. "But hopping shakes up beer something awful."

"Did you get the neck wound the same time as your leg?"

Andy nodded. "Messed up my spinal cord pretty good." He reached back to run his fingers around the periphery of the deep scar. "I was paralyzed almost a year; docs thought I'd never walk." He took a long drink of beer. "Guys who got their shit blown completely away would be damned grateful to trade places with me." He rubbed his inflamed stump. "At least pain lets you know you're still alive."

I did not resist when, after a third beer, Andy kissed me first on the forehead, then on the lips. Nor when he pulled me down beside him on the sofa.

The dream started the moment I fell asleep. I was sitting in the rain on a row of sandbags outside surgery at Danang's Navy Hospital. Dan had lost a leg and I wanted to tell him it didn't matter to me, that I still loved him and wanted to be married.

I woke with pain careening through my chest. When I discovered I was undressed, I looked frantically around, trying to remember where I was. Moonlight glimmered through a curtainless window, falling across the unclothed man sleeping next to me. In the grey-blue light I saw his amputated leg.

Somewhere a baby is crying, and I am in triage sorting through casualties. Most are napalm victims and they plead for something to ease their suffering.

I try to explain that I have no morphine, no burn dressings or penicillin. The patients keep begging, holding their charred hands and arms out entreating me to help. I back out of triage and run down a dimly lit corridor. The patients follow, and others come from crowded wards to join in the chase.

I run out of the hospital and through a courtyard teeming with people in bloody bandages and soiled casts. Those patients join the mob pursuing me as I flee out the gates of the hospital and into the busy streets.

On the bank of the Danang River I wave wildly to an old woman who propels her flat bottomed boat by standing at its stern, dipping a long pole in and out of the water. It is the same boat I always take with Dan to a small chapel on the other side of the river for Sunday Mass.

As the boat draws nearer I see that someone is already in it, an American Marine wearing a flak jacket and helmet. The patients are gaining on me and I call to the old woman to hurry. The boat reaches the shore just in time for me to jump aboard as my pursuers clamber down the slippery river bank.

As the boat moves out into the current, they stand there begging me to come back. "I can't help them," I tell the Marine. His helmeted head is lowered and an M16 is slung across one shoulder. "I saved as many as I could."

Slowly he raises his head and I find myself looking into the sunken eyes of my beloved Dan. Blood is running down one leg into an empty boot.

"You didn't save me," he says.

A hand reaches me the moment I scream. I turn, expecting to see Dan.

"You had a bad dream," Andy says as his arms encircle me. "Just a bad dream."

My mind, which is up near the ceiling, tells me to push Andy away. But I pull him closer, embedding my fingernails in the flesh of his back.

"Help me," I plead in the same voice as my patients.

"I'm here," Andy says. "I'll always be here."

My mind tells me it is not coming back. No matter how much I beg, it is not returning to the body lying below in Andy's arms.

The wrong man has been brought out of surgery.

CHAPTER FIVE

I am driving the sixty-seven Mustang I purchased before going to Vietnam. It is the only thing in my life that has remained the same, the only place I've felt comfortable since coming home. But today my sporty yellow car is neither comforting nor familiar.

It is easy enough to convince Andy I need time alone. My boss, Dr. Ware, is more difficult.

There is no way I can safely do anesthesia in my present state. But how does one call in sick for a mind which refuses to be part of its owner's body? In the end I simply tell my boss I am suffering from the flu, which is not entirely untrue. The bad virus my mother thinks I should be over is back in full flame.

"I hope it's not more than a day or two," Dr. Ware says over the phone. "We're short staffed all week."

"I'll be back as soon as I can," I reply, having no idea when that might be.

The beginning of spring is early for a trip to the beach, but I am not going for pleasure. I need to escape to a place where I will not be observed by Andy, or anyone else who knows me, while I try to figure out what is happening.

Bright yellow forsythia lines the road. "Don't be afraid," I tell myself aloud as I start up the steep incline of the bridge connecting the mainland of Maryland to Fishback Island. Enormous steel girders on either side of me arch up into the sky as if built from a giant erector set.

I glance at the ships passing below on their way to Baltimore's harbor. Near the top of the bridge a curtain of fog drops so suddenly I am having trouble keeping my car away from the guard rails. Dim headlights of oncoming cars appear only seconds before we meet in the thick vapor.

My car slows as I strain to see. But when it comes to a complete stop at the very top of the bridge it is for an unanticipated reason.

Everything can be over so fast, the nightmares about Dan, the guilt for not having done more for the Vietnamese. The crying baby.

With the dense fog I won't even see the water of the Chesapeake Bay far below as I fall toward it.

My door is slowly opening when I hear a shrill blast from behind. I look into my rear view mirror and see a tractor-trailer bearing down on me, its lights flashing from low beam to high and its horn blaring the message that it is stopping for no one. Let it come, my mind says from where it resides outside my body. Let it push me and my car over the side. What more fitting coffin than my Mustang?

But my reflexes overrule my mind and my foot tromps down on the accelerator, propelling me forward only moments before the eighteen-wheeler reaches the space I have just vacated.

The truck stays on my bumper, flashing its lights and sounding its air horn as it chases me along the bridge. Its grill is still in my mirror when I reach the down side, with my hands sweating so badly I have difficulty holding the wheel.

The fog has been replaced by a torrential rain falling straight down like a monsoon. The truck is pressing me faster and faster along the rain slicked highway, where the headlights of oncoming vehicles are now barely visible. I turn my windshield wipers to top speed, but they still cannot handle the torrential downpour. Mercifully, the truck gives a final blatt and swings around me, catapulting down the highway where it just escapes a head-on collision.

I slow down and wipe a wet palm against the leg of my slacks, then fumble in my purse for cigarettes before I remember there are none. My eyes scan the sides of the road for a filling station or restaurant, until another loud horn grabs my attention. A second truck, blinking its lights from low to high the same as the other, is playing a mating game with my rear bumper.

"Jesus, where am I supposed to go?" my body implores. My mind, riding along somewhere in the car, does not respond.

I soon find myself in the watery wake kicked up by the oversized mud flaps of the first truck. As I draw closer I can make out a large sign on its rear doors. THIS DRIVER IS A PROFESSIONAL. IF ANY COMPLAINTS CALL FISHBACK POULTRY AT.... I stop reading as the second truck pulls wildly around me and swings in front of me so closely my Mustang almost slides under its rear carriage. It has a sign on its back doors identical to the other.

Get off the road, my mind instructs my body, but I can see only a few feet ahead of me. Then, like a mirage, a small roadside diner appears on my right. My car careens into the drive and up to a rusted gas pump which is no longer in service. I push the shift into park, turn off the engine and sit there.

The diner is vintage fifties made to resemble a railway car. Pink and green neon lights run across its silver front, and a sign advertizing home cooked food is taped to a window. I watch a dog turn in circles before curling itself into a pile of old tires where it finds little refuge from the rain.

I sit for several minutes inspecting the red creases in my hands from gripping the steering wheel. To stop their trembling I clasp them together with fingers intertwined, like a game I played as a child; look at the church, look at the steeple, open the doors and see all the people.

Maybe a hot cup of tea, my mind ventures. And who can blame you for having just one cigarette?

I check my physical body in the mirror to see if there are any telltale signs of the hollowness I feel beneath my skin. My eyes are red, and so startled looking I pull a pair of sunglasses from my glove compartment and put them on.

"Quite a nor'easter we're havin' us," the waitress says when I blow into the diner. I stay at the entryway wiping off rivulets of rain my jacket has collected during the short sprint from my car. "When it does somethin' on the ahlund it does it right, not a thin little drizzle like y'all are used ta up in New York." The waitress emphasizes the new, as if it has just been colonized.

A male customer dressed in camouflage hunting jacket and red baseball cap sits carving a wooden duck decoy at the lunch counter the waitress leans across. He does not look up as I approach.

"I'm not from New York," I say.

The waitress takes a reserved sign from the counter and replaces it with a heavy mug of coffee, motioning me to a stool in front of it. The woman has widely set eyes and elongated lips that almost disappear when she closes her mouth, which she appears not to be in the habit of doing often.

"Fresh coffee's what y'all need on a day like this." I don't want the caffeine, but even though my mind has consented to follow me into the diner, I do not wish to speak any more than necessary.

As I pick up the cup of steaming liquid, my hands shake so badly I nearly drop it. "The fog and rain kind of got to my nerves," I say.

"Everone's nerves is bad up ta New York," the waitress says with the same emphasis on new. "Too many cars, too many people in 'em."

"I told you, I'm not from New York." Then in an immediately contrite voice, "Could I have a pack of cigarettes, please? Marlboros if you have them."

"We don't sell nothin' that's bad for people," the waitress proclaims.

"Praise the Lord," the male customer intones without looking up from his duck decoy.

It is difficult to imagine that the apron stretching across the wide expanse of the waitress' abdomen was once white. "Y'all from Baltmur?" she asks as she supports her weight on the counter in front of me.

"I grew up in Minnesota." My body sips at the coffee.

"Never had neither nor mind ta live in Minnasoda." The waitress straightens and gives the greasy counter a swipe with an even greasier rag. "It don't suit me."

"You've been there?" I ask.

"No, an' it ain't likely I ever will."

"Never did understand it," the man says from beneath the beak of his baseball cap. "People's always talkin' 'bout the places they come from, but thur sittin' raght here on Fishback Ahlund, God's own home, tellin' it." He sets the exquisitely carved decoy on the counter. "Turists don't seem able ta stay away anymore when summer's come an' gone. Or not near here yet."

"You said it there," the waitress agrees.

The male customer swivels his stool toward me. "No need for them dark glasses taday."

I raise a hand to remove them but stop when the waitress' busy eyes bear down on me. "I have an eye infection," I say. "Doctor's orders."

"People don't get infections in God's country," the man says as he takes the wooden duck back into his lap to add a few refinements to its wings.

"Though we might could start with the outsiders comin' mor'n more," the waitress says.

I feel like I did while trapped between the two trucks. "I've never been to the island before," I say in my defense. "I just need to get away awhile."

The waitress's entire demeanor changes. "Someone die?" she asks in a mournful tone.

"No."

The woman seems disappointed. But I must look in some kind of need.

She turns to pick up a plate piled high with toast, eggs and a congealed mixture of pork gristle known as scrapple, a Maryland delicacy for which I have never developed a taste.

"I fixed this for mahself, but a thin little thang like yerself needs it mor'n I do," the woman says as she slides the plate across the counter to me.

I feel my intestines cramp painfully. "Thank you, but I'm really not hungry." My mind is threatening to leave the diner without my body. "I just stopped to get out of the storm." I pull a dollar from my purse, begging my mind to wait for the rest of me.

"That'll take two, maybe three days." The male customer is now working on the eyes of the mallard duck with a minuscule knife he holds expertly. Other decoys sit around the diner in various stages of flight or rest, and pictures of ducks and geese adorn the walls and place mats. "Nor'easters take thur own sweet time movin' on through."

"Y'all are welcome ta get comfortable over there." The waitress points to a row of green, vinyl booths against the opposite wall. "Worst a' the storm oughta blow past; give, take an hour."

I look toward the booths. "But they all have reserved signs."

The waitress laughs so heartily her soiled apron moves up and down. "Honey hush, that don't mean y'all. The signs is for them civilian rights people keeps comin' down from Baltmur spyin' on us."

"If you've not got the room for culurds, you've not got ta serve 'em," the male customer says with the first smile I have seen on his taut face.

They both have faded beige hair, pale blue eyes, elongated frog lips and skin weathered by the elements.

I lay my dollar on the counter. "Keep the change."

"You never did tell us what kinda work y'all do up ta Baltmur." The waitress is not yet ready to give up her distraction from the cold, gloomy day.

"Anesthesia. I put people to sleep for surgery," I add when she appears not to understand.

"Honey hush, don't say no more!" She turns to a drawer behind the counter labeled pickles and olives and rummages frantically. "Lookie here," she says, holding up a jar of round dark objects. "Worst gallstones my docter said he ever took outta anyone." I do not take the jar extended across the counter. "Cut me clean acrost." The waitress makes a slicing motion across her abdomen.

"I really have to go," I say.

"Best ta put your troubles in the hands of Jesus," the waitress says as she picks up my money. She smacks her frog lips, perfect for catching flies.

"Praise the Lord," the male customer croaks.

I was driving away, laughing at the oddness of the islanders, when I was surprised to find my mind had reunited with my body. Fishback Island might be the antidote I needed.

"Two nights or a week?" the motel owner asked as I checked into one of the few motels open for business in the beach town of Seaport.

"Just one night," I replied. I was exhausted from driving hours in torrential rain.

"Two nights minimum." The owner looked like the people in the diner, with the same faded hair, elongated lips and weather beaten skin. Duck decoys and pictures of them decorated his motel lobby.

"But what if the storm keeps up?"

"Bound ta be weather this time a' year. Two nights minimum, order a' the city council; no dawgs on the beach, no men without shirts lest they's in the worter, no...."

I held up a hand to stop the litany. "All right, I'll stay two."

"The wife'll be happy ta cook up some supper," the owner offered while I signed the register. He nodded toward a windowless dining room adjoining the lobby. A frail looking woman appeared in the doorway holding a delicate doily she was crocheting.

"I reckin," she said, then disappeared back into the darkened room without further comment.

"I'll just take the key." I wanted the privacy of my room.

There was a cigarette vending machine crammed into a corner of the lobby. I paused briefly in front of it. "We keep it for turists, don't use it 'rselves," the owner said behind me. "Need change?"

"Yes." Then just as quickly, "No. No I don't." The owner gave me a suspicious look as I backed out the door.

My room overlooked the beach, although it was too dark to see. I turned on the T.V., but the black and white screen was a maze of zig-zagged lines which defied all attempts to straighten. I gave up and sat down on one of the beds to look at a map of the island the owner provided with my key.

Fishback Island was actually shaped like a fish, with its tapered head lying just off the coast of Delaware, its wider midsection off Maryland and the lower section, which narrowed before fanning out into a tail, off the coast of Virginia. I wondered if the island had gotten its name from its shape, but then remembered Hen Fishback, the little man who had his eyelids done at Filmore.

When the map no longer entertained me, I crawled beneath the covers to rest the spasming muscles of my back. But lying there in the cold made it hurt worse.

"Headin' for New York?" the man at the cash register of the liquor store asked as I paid for a bottle of Scotch. He emphasized new like the woman in the diner.

"Why does everyone think I'm from New York?"

"Cause y'all talk raght funny."

"My room doesn't have any heat," I complained to the motel owner. The Scotch was tucked discreetly beneath my jacket.

"Heat's turned off end a' March." His manner was the same as when he told me the motel had a two night minimum and no dogs on the beach. "Summer's near here."

"Not near enough."

Back in my room I piled the blankets from both beds on one and crawled in fully clothed except for shoes.

"At least I don't need ice," I said as I poured Scotch into a glass. My thoughts began with Andy, wondering how I had allowed myself to get so involved with him in such a short time. Was I trying to replace Dan with the first guy I met who had been in the war?

Daylight was sliding beneath the glass doors when I woke to the cry of sea gulls somewhere beyond the strange room in which I lay. There was an overturned glass next to a half empty bottle of Scotch on the bedside table. I forced myself out of bed even though my back was on fire, and pulled open the drapes.

Remnants of the storm remained, but I could see a slice of blue on the horizon. Sea gulls flew in circles, and wispy balls of foam whipped up by the surf skittered along the sand like tumbleweeds of beaten egg whites. My head ached and my stomach churned.

"Oh, Dan, I'm so scared," I said as I stood looking out at a beach that looked nothing like the white sand and aquamarine water where the two of us had walked along the South China Sea.

I found aspirin in my purse that I hoped would help my back, as well as my head. I wasted no time getting out of the bleak room and to my bright yellow Mustang with its black vinyl top.

The engine started on the first try, as it always did, and my hands on the familiar steering wheel did not tremble. I felt good, despite my hangover, but not good enough to return immediately to Baltimore. I needed more time to try to understand the strange spells I was having and what to do about them.

"I'll go back to work tomorrow," I told my car when a twinge of guilt reminded me that Dr. Ware was short staffed. I checked my watch, which read eight-thirty. "It's already too late to get there in time to do cases today." My Mustang's purring engine concurred.

I headed south, passing through a series of small towns. Each was comprised of a handful of white houses and a rundown general store and gas station combination selling bread, donuts and an assortment of odd-sized fan belts certain to rescue any stranded motorist. There was an elaborate firehall in each of the settlements, with more shiny firefighting equipment than there were buildings to protect. And in both town and countryside, there stood row upon row of one story chicken houses.

The buildings were covered with grey shingles and their roofs sagged in the middle, as if a giant had traversed the land using them as stepping stones. The houses people inhabited were weathered white clapboard and had open verandas with ceilings painted as blue as the sky should have been.

When I reached the southern tip of the island, where the fish's tail fanned out into a concaved marina, I parked my car and sat watching the harbor. Boats rolled and pitched on the choppy water as a few isolated figures in hooded rain slickers checked lines securing vessels to docks. Most were fishing boats, but there were sailboats too, their lines chinking against their masts in a frantic metallic cry. Large craft with flying bridges used for deep sea fishing sat so low, they moved little in the turbulent water.

I had come to the island to think, yet I thought about nothing as I sat there watching boats bob up and down. Within minutes I was lulled into a peaceful sleep.

"Two nights minimum," the motel owner said when I went back to the office some three hours later to check out.

"I only have to pay for two nights," I said. "I don't have to stay." I felt rested enough to return to work and wanted to cross the enormous bridge spanning the Chesapeake Bay before any evening fog had time to descend.

"Suit yerself," the motel owner said.

And from the back room his wife added, "I reckin'."

As I drove inland, a town I had not noticed in the storm of the previous day seemed to spring from nowhere. It had a small cemetery bordering the highway, and I stopped my car to view more closely the ornate headstones and thick concrete slabs covering the graves like protective blankets.

The sun had broken through the remaining clouds, and its warm rays on the wet earth created a mist that rose up between the various resting places. A small, white frame structure stood next to the cemetery with a sign reading HIGHWAY HOLINESS CHURCH.

I got out of my car and stood at the edge of the cemetery, not eager to pass through its iron gates, yet drawn to it in a way that was as mysterious as the mist swirling between the graves.

Because we met in Vietnam I did not know Dan's family, yet I felt compelled to visit them to answer any questions they might have about his death, as well as to tell them about our time together. They assumed I would like to see where he was buried and took me to a vast national cemetery.

His little sister pointed out the grave site while his weeping mother waited in the car. I placed white roses on the grass, but laying them beneath the plain white marker made me feel as if I was placing them on the grave of a stranger. The information was correct: name, date of birth and date of death, but it was still all wrong. My life with Dan had been far from this manicured grass, shade trees and neat paths intersecting a sea of precisely placed white headstones.

I was standing over the grave, trying to convince myself Dan was there, when suddenly there was a sharp volley of gunfire, then another, and another, twenty-one shots in all. There then followed a sound so sorrowful my chest tightened to where I could not breathe.

I looked across an expanse of white and green to where another soldier was being laid to rest while his loved ones wept. A lone trumpeter stood on a hill above the burial site playing Taps as the flag draping the coffin was folded into precise triangles by Marines in dress uniform, then handed to a woman with two young children.

The mournful strain of the trumpet followed as I fled, lost in a maze of dead Dans.

"It's this way!" his little sister called as she waved toward her mother's car.

"You could stay with us awhile," Dan's now composed mother said while slowly following a perfectly paved road through the trees and headstones. "The family will all be home for the weekend."

I exchanged with her the haunted looks of mother and lover left alone. "I think it's best that I leave."

Her smile was one of gratitude. There was no need to continue the terrible grief, the only thing we had in common.

As she drove me to the airport I debated whether I should tell her the truth about how her son died, abandoned by the Vietnamese troops he trained and left to bleed to death. By the time we pulled up to the terminal, I decided to leave her with the story the officer on funeral detail described about his heroic death. Perhaps it was easier to mourn the loss of a hero than that of a victim.

I was just inside the iron gates when I became aware of voices.

Through the mist I saw a woman and a girl in her teens sitting together at a low table placed next to one of the blanketed graves. The table was spread with a picnic lunch.

"Some day we'll be happy again," the elder of the two said as I stood eavesdropping in a veil of mist. "Happy and free."

"You know that can never happen, Mother." The young girl's bird-song voice was high and clear, and her hair a mantle of gold that fanned out around her face and down her back.

"Your father will find a way to help us." The woman rearranged flowers spread over the concrete slab next to them while she talked. "Won't you, Adam Lee?"

Her voice was as smooth as her ivory skin, and a coronet of stunning copper braids wrapped majestically around her head. Her long-sleeved jacket and slacks were of the same color.

"He always hated arranged flowers, especially gladiolus," she said as she lovingly scattered forsythia and lilacs across the grey concrete. "He said they reminded him of funerals." She looked back at her daughter, who turned quickly away to hide her tears. "Don't be sad, Allison. You know your father still loves you."

"Tell me how we danced together," Allison said in a child-like voice. "And how he sang to me."

The woman got up, moving to music only she could hear. "He used to go into your room every morning," she said, as if repeating an oft told story. "He would take you out of your crib and dance with you, holding you right up next to his cheek like this." She demonstrated, smiling dreamily as she danced with the imaginary child. "While singing all your favorite songs."

"And he took me out on his boat," Allison prompted.

"Every Sunday he took us on his fishing boat, and he let you help pilot it up and down the waterways looking for the perfect spot for a picnic. We would spend the whole day there, eating, napping and playing with you." The expression on the young girl's face was ethereal as she listened to the soft cadence of her mother's voice. "He loved you so, Allison. He still loves both of us."

"Then why did he leave us?" Allison asked with such sorrow I could feel the ripple of its sadness from where I secretly watched.

"He didn't want to die, Allison. It was an accident."

The young girl and her mother continued talking as I quietly left the cemetery and drove straight through to Baltimore.

CHAPTER SIX

Doctor Ware met me in the O.R. corridor. "Got over the flu all right?" My boss was middle-aged and had a round paunch that hung over the drawstring waist of his O.R. scrub pants.

"It was just a two day thing," I said, but something in my voice caused him to look at me with a concerned expression.

"You're sure?"

He was a physician as born to medicine as Picasso was to painting. If anyone would know what the strange spells I was having were, it would be him.

"Actually, I would like to discuss something with you." The words were difficult, especially in an O.R. corridor with people rushing by with respirators, stretchers and tables of instruments. "I mean I'd like to get your professional ..."

Another member of the anesthesia staff interrupted us. I excused myself and started down the corridor in the direction of the anesthesia work room to check my assignment for the day.

"Hold on a minute," Doctor Ware called after me. "We can go down to my office and talk."

"Later," I said, with a wave over my shoulder. "I'll get my cases done first." I had lost my nerve.

The assignment sheet, tacked to a bulletin board in the workroom, had my name penciled under ECT, Electro-Convulsive Therapy. That meant I would spend the day administering anesthesia for electroshock treatments in a lab on the psychiatric ward, totally separate from the O.R.s where I usually worked.

"I hate this place," I said while I checked my machine to make sure it had full oxygen tanks and was in good working order. The ECT lab was small and contained only the anesthesia machine, a stretcher and the monstrous contraption with wires and dials that delivered an electrical jolt to malfunctioning brains. Psychiatry was housed in the oldest section of the hospital and had dreary tan walls and high ceilings crisscrossed by pipes.

"I don't expect anyone likes it here," the male nurse in charge of the lab said. "The patients least of all."

"I'm sorry, Al." And I truly was.

Al treated all patients with equal respect, from wealthy to wino. "I have nothing against the patients," I said. "I just don't like turning people into zombies who shuffle around with blank faces."

Al was about to comment when a young psychiatric resident bounded into the room. "Everybody ready for Shake and Bake?" he asked as he rubbed his hands together in anticipation. It was the irreverent name given shock treatments because of the violent seizures induced by the hot electrical current delivered to brain cells.

The resident put one hand on the ECT machine and mimicked a profound body convulsion. "Man, you can almost see the smoke coming out their ears."

"Don't talk like that in here," Al said to him.

"Oh, come on, Al." The young doctor nudged playfully at one of Al's lumberjack shoulders. "What's wrong with a little levity to get you through the day?"

"Don't say Shake and Bake here," Al repeated in a voice that was quietly unyielding.

"O.K., O.K."

The resident left the room and returned with a confused looking old man who wore most of his last meal on the front of his shirt. I looked at the patient's chart and handed it back to the resident. "He needs an EKG, blood work and a urinalysis to start," I said. "And it looks like he's eaten." I indicated the food on the old man's shirt while he stared straight ahead, oblivious to his surroundings or the people discussing him.

"Doctor Frankfurt said to get him done first thing this morning," the resident told me. "It'll only take a few minutes."

Physicians could be as naive as patients in thinking a short anesthetic was not as risky as a long one, when the opposite was true. "He doesn't get put to sleep until he's been properly worked up and had no food for eight hours," I said. "Aspiration of stomach contents into the lungs isn't much fun. For anyone."

"But Frankfurt gave orders to do him now," the resident insisted.

"Then get Doctor Frankfurt and I'll tell him myself." I was relieved to hear the confidence in my voice; I could still do my job.

"He's testifying at that big murder case in D.C.," the resident said of his professor. The case, involving a wealthy businessman who was pleading innocent by reason of insanity for having bumped off his business partner, was the talk of Washington and Baltimore. And testifying in court as an expert on insanity pleas was one of Doctor Frankfurt's favorite pastimes.

"Then this case is cancelled," I said. "Get the next patient."

"You can't do that," the resident asserted.

Al already had the old man on the stretcher, but he stopped connecting the electrodes to his head and requested that the resident and I step next door, away from the patient, while we argued.

"That patient is suicidal," the resident said before Al had time to close the door between the lab and the small recovery room where we talked. "If we don't zap him right now he might kill himself."

"If I put him to sleep without a decent workup he won't have to," I retorted. "I'll do it for him."

"Listen, you two," Al intervened. "Either we do the case or cancel it. We have other patients waiting."

"It's cancelled," I said.

"I'll call Doctor Frankfurt," the resident threatened.

"Go ahead."

I returned to the lab with Al, and the resident took the patient and went off to call his professor. The next patient was accompanied by another psychiatric resident.

"Hello, Mr. Ryan," Al said to the man in his late fifties. "How are you doing today?" The question was genuine, giving the terrified looking patient time to respond.

"I'm pretty good," he said in a voice that trembled as much as his body. "But I hate these things, hate these things." He looked in the direction of the electroshock machine.

"It'll only take a few minutes, Mr. Ryan," Al assured. "And we'll take real good care of you."

I introduced myself while I wrapped a blood pressure cuff around the man's frail arm. "I hate these things," he told me.

"I understand."

"No you don't."

Al gave a small laugh. "You're right," I confessed. "I don't know how it feels at all." And I did not wish to find out.

When I began injecting the anesthetic, the patient looked up at Al with entreating eyes. "You're a nice colored man, Al. Please don't let me wet myself."

Al took hold of one of the patient's hands, secured by sturdy leather restraints. "I won't, Mr. Ryan."

"Why do all these patients remember your name?" the new resident asked when the patient was unconscious.

"Because I remember theirs," Al answered.

Mr. Ryan's fragile body arched upward into a rigid seizure when the resident hit the button. It stayed suspended there for a few seconds before collapsing into a mound of twitching muscles.

He came out of the anesthetic like all the others, completely disoriented and fighting the gag I had placed in his mouth to prevent him from biting his tongue during the convulsion. I removed it and suctioned the mucous bubbling from his mouth and down his chin.

His eyes opened but he stared vacantly at the ceiling, not even recognizing Al, who was checking to see if the patient had been incontinent during the treatment. Al put the spare clothes he kept in the lab away when he saw that Mr. Ryan's trousers were dry.

The patient was wheeled out of the room and I began to set up for the next case. I stopped when Dr. Frankfurt entered the room leading the old man I had previously cancelled.

The first resident followed, smiling triumphantly. "He finished with court yesterday," he told me with obvious delight.

"I'm sorry," I told the psychiatry professor. "This patient hasn't been worked up or been NPO."

"He's had nothing to eat or drink since he was admitted," the professor said testily. "I gave the order."

"And when was that?"

"The police picked him up on the street sometime during the night," the junior resident said. "I'm not sure when, but the E.R. sent him over to psych around four a.m."

I went to the phone and called Dr. Ware, who listened to only part of my story before telling me to postpone the case until the following day. "Would you like to tell Doctor Frankfurt yourself?" I asked. "He's right here." Doctor Frankfurt moved toward me.

"Don't put that sanctimonious jackass on!" Dr. Ware shouted into the phone. Then in a frustrated tone, "I'll come over."

"Yes sir," I said as Dr. Frankfurt reached for the phone. "I'll tell him you'll be right over."

Al had the subject of the interdepartmental feud lying on the stretcher again, and I checked the old man's vital signs while we waited for my boss. Dr. Ware did not come but sent Dr. Rasheif.

"What you need?" he asked Dr. Frankfurt.

"I need my patient put to sleep so I can give him a treatment," Dr. Frankfurt answered in the respectful manner physicians reserved for one another.

"Put sleep," Dr. Rasheif ordered me.

I gave him all of the reasons the case had been cancelled. "Put sleep," he repeated while admiring Dr. Frankfurt's handsome suit.

I was so indignant I could feel my pulse in every part of my body. Putting a patient to sleep in my present state would be like an impaired pilot taking a jet off with a load of unsuspecting passengers.

"No, you put sleep," I said to Dr. Rasheif. I left the room before anyone could stop me and headed for the general surgery suite.

Dr. Ware was in the habit of acting as if he was having chest pain whenever he had to discuss something unpleasant.

"You can't leave Rasheif over there giving anesthesia alone," he said when I told him what had transpired. "I don't trust him alone in the dog lab."

"I'm not going back."

The professor rubbed his chest and let out a loud belch. He was about to resume the debate over me leaving Rasheif in the electroshock lab when the beeper attached to his scrub shirt went off.

"Anesthesia to 3B, stat!" it said. "Anesthesia, 3B stat!"

"Get that," Dr. Ware said to me.

I took off down the corridor at a run, despite my lousy back. A stat page for anesthesia to a medical ward meant either a cardiac arrest or some sort of respiratory emergency.

"Which room?" I asked breathlessly of the desk nurse on 3B.

She pointed in the direction of a crowd gathered at one end of the corridor. I fought my way through the throng to a sight I found difficult to believe even in Filmore Hospital.

Two beds had been chained together to accommodate a single mass of humanity. The side rails were up but could not contain the bloated flesh protruding through the bars like dough overflowing a pan.

"Get a tube in her," a medical resident said when he saw me. "She's barely moving air."

I stepped to the head of the two beds, where I found a bloodied endotracheal tube and laryngoscope. "Looks like somebody's already tried."

A baby-faced intern spoke for the group. "We all did."

Blood and mucous sputtered from a mouth tucked down between two beach ball sized breasts. There was no visible neck, and her head looked as if it was being swallowed by the rest of her body.

An intern hoisted me up to where I hung over the two

headboards. It felt as if my back would break hanging there struggling to put a tube down the woman's throat.

"Christ, even her tonsils are overweight," I said while advancing the metal blade of the laryngoscope that had a bright light at the tip to show me the way to the trachea.

I assumed the unconscious patient was not aware of anything, until she bit down on the laryngoscope like a giant snapping turtle. I could neither advance nor retract the blade, which dangled from her mouth as if she was having it for lunch.

"Hurry, she's going to arrest!" an intern watching a heart monitor said. I couldn't imagine doing CPR on the mass of protoplasm towering above me.

"O.K., we'll do it another way," I said when I could not pry the laryngoscope blade free of the woman's locked jaw. I inserted the breathing tube into one of her nostrils and slowly advanced it down the back of her throat with nothing but experience to guide it blindly along. When it was several inches in, I gently lifted the patient's head and waited until she took a breath. The moment she did, I slipped the tube through her open vocal cords.

"It's in," I said when I held a hand over the opening of the tube and felt air coming through it. The patient was coughing and choking so badly I had to suction the tube before hooking it to a breathing bag and oxygen.

"It can't be in," the senior resident objected. "I don't see any chest movement."

I was pushing oxygenated air into the massive chest with supreme effort. "She's got too much fat over her muscles to show chest movement."

Several young doctors held stethoscopes to the expansive chest, listening intently. "I hear breath sounds!" one of them said as I squeezed the breathing bag. "Big Ruby lives!"

The woman's jaw bones were relaxed now that she was getting enough oxygen, and I looked down the lighted laryngoscope to confirm proper placement of the tube. The opening to her esophagus, just below the trachea, was so distended from all the food forced down it that it looked like a train tunnel.

"It's in," I confirmed as I retracted the laryngoscope. "Vocal cords are clearly visible on each side of it." The woman's skin color was already beginning to pink up.

"I'm impressed," the senior medical resident said. "Where'd you learn how to put a tube in like that?"

"In...another hospital." I was not about to reveal my tainted past, where we were required to do blind intubations on a regular basis because of a constant shortage of laryngoscopes and the batteries to light them. I had quickly learned to be cautious about letting people know I had served in Vietnam. Even though I cared for civilian casualties I was told more than once, "If you were there, you were part of the problem."

CHAPTER SEVEN

Coming here was a mistake, I told myself on my second visit to Andy's apartment. He sat on his thrift store sofa with his amputated extremity exposed.

"Are you going to stay over there all night?" he asked. I was looking through piles of books stacked against an otherwise bare wall.

"These are all medical books," I said as I perused the stacks. "I didn't know you were planning to be a doctor."

"I was in med school before I went to Nam; had to drop out a year to earn money and the Army got me." Because of his background he was put through medic training and sent to Southeast Asia.

"When do you plan to finish?"

"Never." He hopped out to the kitchen for a beer to replace the empty can he crushed between his hands.

"Why not?" I called after him. "I should think your combat experience would make you a shoo-in for med school."

Andy hopped back to the sofa and sucked up the foam that fizzed from his beer when he popped it open. "I had enough doctor shit in Nam, ten guys screaming all at once. Doc, Doc! I'm hit Doc!" He sounded as if he was hearing them even now. "I don't want anyone calling me doc. Not ever again."

I continued to look through books a few minutes before joining Andy on the sofa. "I couldn't stand it when they cried for their mothers," he said. "The ones who were dying always cried for their mothers." His eyes held that numbed, faraway look known in the war as the thousand-yard stare.

While I went to the kitchen to get a beer, I thought back to a mother who lost her son in the war.

He was an only child and the parents lived on a farm adjoining the one my family moved to after I had already left home. They were only passing acquaintances to me, but my mother, without first asking my permission, told them I would visit upon my return.

"It would mean so much to them," she said after breaking the news. "They want to know how he died and who was with him."

"But I didn't take care of their son, I didn't even work in a military hospital." I had been home only a few days and was annoyed she would make such a commitment without my consent.

"But you were there. They've never talked to anyone who was actually there. They hardly go off the place anymore."

It was a clear summer afternoon when I drove into the yard, a day when a farm should be bustling with the labor of mowing hay and storing bails in the barn. But the place looked abandoned, the lawn unmowed and flower beds untended. Shades were drawn over each window of the house, which looked uninhabited. I was about to drive away when one of the shades rose halfway and a woman peered out.

"I made coffee cake," she said when I was seated at the kitchen table. She poured coffee and put a saucer containing a fresh stick of butter next to the cake in the center of the table. Her husband came in dressed in overalls and sat down after a silent nod in my direction. He did not remove his hat and seemed anxious to have the ordeal over with. The woman remained standing, nervously wiping her hands on her apron. A clock ticked loudly on the wall.

"Get the things," her husband said gruffly. He was a big man, and his voice boomed through the quiet house. "You wanted to know, now go get the things."

He said nothing while the woman was upstairs, preferring to examine his large misshapen hands. The house was July hot and flies droned and thumped against the screen door. The coffee cake sat untouched while the butter next to it began to soften and lose shape.

The woman returned with a sealed plastic bag. "I keep all of his things in his room upstairs." Her manner was timid, almost apologetic. "People say I'm living in the past, but everything's just the way he left it."

She sat down at the table and I watched a mother, who was a mother no more, carefully remove each item from the plastic bag: a worn wallet, a comb, a Purple Heart still in its case, and a packet of letters from her son's commanding officer and buddies. She handed the letters to me and I read them one by one, some scrawled by boys still in the field and soiled by red dirt and sweat. They told of how a medic had gotten to the young man as soon as he was wounded, and of how he was medevaced by helicopter to a nearby field hospital for emergency care, then transferred to a larger facility where he could receive more sophisticated treatment for his severe head and neck injuries. Reviewing the odyssey of medevacs and hospitals was like following the flight of a wounded bird, one I knew could never fly home again.

I explained to the patiently waiting couple what the various medical facilities were and assured them everything possible had been done. But their son was still dead, and nothing I could say or do would change that. Or eradicate the pain in their stricken faces.

"I'm sorry," I said as I handed the letters back to the woman.

"No need for you to be sorry," the man said in his same gruff voice. "You at least told us what all those damned words meant, medevac, field hospital and all." It was the first he had spoken since he ordered his wife to get the things, and he rubbed a calloused hand across his face and sighed so deeply I thought he was about to pass out.

"I used to get after the men in town for talking about the war," he began in a voice now painfully subdued. "I cussed them out and told them not to keep bringing it up." He let out a long, weary breath. "Then one day in the middle of yelling at them I realized I was the one who had brought it up. It was me who'd been bringing it up all along, and they'd been letting me cuss at them without ever saying a word."

His wife looked at him with an expression of both surprise and betrayal. "But you never said anything to me. You won't even let me talk about it."

"I know," her husband said shamefully. "Then I was going off to the feed store and talking to anyone who would put up with me." He avoided her eyes. "I don't know why," he said in a voice which still did not understand.

The butter was melted into a yellow pool in its saucer. I wanted to escape the stuffy house, closed up to keep out the world.

"I should be going."

"One more thing," the man said looking directly into my eyes. "Tell me honestly, was it worth it?"

I took hold of the back of the chair I had vacated, feeling as if I was losing all shape and form, turning to liquid the same as the butter. "I don't think any war is," I said. "Especially this one."

The woman burst into tears and I regretted my candor. "That's all right," the father said when I tried to console her. "I asked you to be honest." He reached a tentative hand across the table to take one of his wife's hands. "We needed someone to tell us straight out what went on with our boy, not that big-word letter the bastards in Washington sent us."

"He's right," the woman said as she dried her eyes with the hem of her apron. "You helped us more than you could know." A mother's hand lovingly caressed the worn wallet on the table. "I wanted to be sure everything was done to save him," she said. "Losing him so far away like that." She was crying once more.

They were the common concerns people voiced in any ordinary hospital when they learned of the unexpected death of a loved one. Being reassured that the patient received prompt and competent care was at least something to cling to in the early stages of grief, a luxury those left behind by war seldom had. Their loved ones died in faraway places in the arms of strangers, and still more strangers brought them the terrible news.

The woman carefully replaced each of her son's belongings and sealed the plastic bag tightly, as if trying to protect what was left of him from the world that killed him.

"I'll come again," I said, knowing I would not.

"There's one thing the wife can't seem to get over," the father said while walking me to my Mustang. "Our Tommy's Army picture and the notice of his death were in the paper. The next day some guy called the house." He paused a moment to look out over a cornfield I felt certain he did not see. "When my wife answered the phone he told her Tommy got what he asked for, going over there killing innocent people." He looked back toward the house. "She won't answer the phone anymore, won't hardly step outside."

Andy's voice startled me. "Hey, Danang. I didn't mean to scare you off," he called to me in the kitchen.

"You didn't scare me off," I said when I returned without the beer I went to get.

"You're the only person I've ever told those things to," Andy said. "The shrinks at the VA were always trying to get me to spill my guts, but I never would. What the hell do Stateside docs know about the shit happening over there? They wouldn't know a bullet from a bedbug."

"Maybe it's better not to talk about it at all." I was afraid further conversation would trigger one of the disquieting spells.

"You can't do that forever." Andy used his arms to hoist himself closer to me on the sofa. "I think I might be falling in love with you." I didn't mean to pull away when he tried to kiss me. "But then, I fell in love with every nurse who took care of me," he said with his nervous laugh.

"Andy...."

"It's O.K. I know you're not over that marine you were in love with." He ran a fingertip lightly across one of my cheeks. "You have the saddest eyes."

"I have to get up early for work," I said and got up abruptly.

Andy sat watching while I put on my coat, making no effort to dissuade me. "Take it easy, Danang," he said when I reached the door.

"Why do you keep calling me that!" I hated the hurt it caused in his face. And I hated the stump of his amputated leg lying there so helplessly. "My name is Pat!"

I tried to convince myself he had asked for it all the way back to my apartment, but I could see his injured expression even after I turned off the light in my bedroom. It wasn't his fault he lost a leg, nor was he to blame for me constantly dreaming that Dan lost his instead of his life. I had put myself in the surreal world between them, and it was up to me to bring it to an end.

CHAPTER EIGHT

Reba was in the cafeteria when I went in for lunch, seated with a blond woman I had seen her with before. When I joined them Reba introduced her as Lori Donlin, a Filmore midwifery student.

"Lori came here from Fishback Island, same as me," Reba said.

"But I'm not <u>from</u> the island," Lori clarified. "I just married a guy from there." Her hair was a silvery blond, and her eyes matched the green of her O.B. scrub gown. "After twelve years of living there," she said to me, "I was still considered an outsider."

"Honey, if you were born anywhere else and moved to that island ten minutes later, you'd still be an outsider," Reba proclaimed.

Out of habit I wolfed down my sandwich so I would have time for a cigarette or two before returning to work. But when I reached for them, my pocket was empty. A cigarette machine nearby looked as if it was walking toward me, but I resisted by listening to Reba and her friend discuss details of caring for Lori's three children that night.

"Reba watches them when I have to cover call in O.B.," Lori told me. "We live in the same neighborhood so it works out well."

I knew Reba lived in the surrounding ghetto, where she purchased her burned out buildings, and was surprised Lori would live there with children. "Does your husband work around here?" I asked.

"Ex-husband," Lori corrected. "He still lives on the island. I came to Baltimore to get my degree in midwifery after we divorced." She looked fondly at Reba. "Reba offered to help with the children until I get through school and can afford to move somewhere else."

"I don't mind earnin' a little extra babysittin' money for my properties," Reba said in a manner that could be described as haughty.

While my idle hands shredded my paper napkin, Lori told me of

48

her house on Fishback Island that was part of her divorce settlement, but she did not plan to return there when she finished school the end of May. "My children love the beach," she said. "And it would be more economical to live in a house I already own, such as it is. But I can't bear the thought of returning to that backward island."

"Those children don't just like the beach," Reba scolded. "They want to be near their father."

"I don't know why. He never spent any time with them when we were married."

"No doctors do."

"I didn't mind the time he spent at the hospital," Lori defended. "It was his extracurricular activities I resented."

"He's a doctor?" I couldn't imagine a physician allowing his children to live in Baltimore's worst neighborhood.

"An anesthesiologist," Lori replied. "Maybe you've met him at an anesthesia meeting."

"I don't think so." I didn't tell her I avoided them as much as I did most social gatherings.

Lori and Reba continued their discussion of Lori's situation, leaving me to shred each piece of my already decimated napkin. I learned that Lori's ex-husband refused to pay child support unless his children lived on Fishback Island, where he had been born and raised. The only time he was off the island were the years he spent at Harvard getting a medical degree, then completing an internship and anesthesia residency at Massachusetts General Hospital. Lori lived in the ghetto out of financial necessity while she worked for the midwifery degree she hoped would better support her children than her R.N.

"I raised five children begging bones for soup," Reba said in my direction. "Now I'm doing the same for three more."

"Why don't you come over sometime?" Lori said to me before leaving for the O.B. department.

"Sure," Reba said. "Come have some soup."

Lori was sitting along in the cafeteria when I went in for dinner that evening. She motioned me over to her table.

"Not much to get you through a night of call," she said when she saw my tray. It contained only cheese and crackers.

"I'm not very hungry." I had spent the weekend trying to make myself call Andy to apologize. Now I was obsessing over whether I should stop by the E.R. to see if he was on duty.

"I was starved," Lori said. Her tray contained a plate stained with the remnants of lasagna. Lori rubbed a hand over a stomach that was as well proportioned as the rest of her. "I ate too much. But I've delivered five babies today and have two to go."

While I nibbled like a gerbil at my crackers, she told me they were all welfare patients, many of them in their early teens. And that midwifery students and obstetrical residents were completely responsible for whatever the ghetto presented at the labor room door.

"It wouldn't hurt our sanctimonious O.B. professors to give us a hand once in awhile," she complained. "It's a nightmare taking care of twelve year olds having babies."

"Twelve year old mothers?" Obstetrics had its own anesthesia staff, making it unnecessary for me to do cases there.

"We had an eleven year old a month ago."

I had worked in another third world country besides Vietnam. But even within the poverty and illiteracy of Haiti, men were not impregnating children.

"Eleven years old," I said incredulously.

"She kept telling us she was almost twelve. Between screams." Lori pushed her tray away and rested her chin tiredly in her hand. "It was the same on Fishback Island."

"Hey, I went there last week." I was pleased to have something less somber to talk about. "It's really quaint for the Seventies."

"I've always said people should be required to have a visa to cross that bridge." Lori had the ability to be cynical and likable at the same time. "They like to consider themselves part of the South's Bible Belt. Reba and I call it the Bastard Belt."

"I saw a mother and daughter in a cemetery." It sounded strange even to me when I added, "They were having a picnic."

"Hope and Allison Taylor," Lori said nonchalantly. "Adam Lee, the husband and father, was killed when his fishing boat blew up."

"How long ago?"

She had to stop and think. "It was before I moved to the island after marrying Earl Roy." She counted on her fingers. "I'd say about fourteen years. Allison was two; Hope remarried a year later."

The simplicity of idle chatter was calming. "Do you know her?"

"You mean Hope?" I nodded. "We were actually pretty good friends before I started divorce proceedings against Earl Roy." Lori gave a small laugh. "Zebediah, that's Hope's present husband, refused to let her associate with me after that; fine, upstanding Christian that he is."

"That's too bad."

"Not really. Hope got kind of strange; her daughter too."

"You mean the picnics?"

"Not just that," Lori said getting up. "I have to get going. How about a cup of coffee at Bullwinkle's in the morning? I need a fresh muffin after twenty-four hours of eating hospital food."

My first impulse was to decline, but Lori made me feel as much at ease as when I was with Reba. "Sounds good," I said.

"I'm off call at seven," Lori said before we parted in the corridor. "Meet you by Jesus."

Filmore Hospital had a monumental statue of Christ in its main lobby. Whether American, Asian, Jew or Moslem, you'd hear staff members telling one another they would meet by Jesus.

CHAPTER NINE

"I'm going back to Fishback Island," I said as Lori and I sat over coffee and blueberry muffins at Bullwinkle's, a popular bar across the street from Filmore that sold cheap pitchers of beer at night, and fresh muffins for the exhausted staff getting off call in the morning.

"The beach is wonderful this time of year," Lori said. "It's warm, but the tourist season hasn't started yet."

"I don't mind tourists, but the motel was Dracula's castle."

"You were just on the wrong end of the beach." Lori scribbled information on a paper napkin and slid it across the table. "Here's the name of a place that rents cottages."

"Thanks." I tucked it into my purse.

"Reba tells me you were in Vietnam."

It was as unanticipated as a thank you from a member of the knife and gun club. "She did?"

"I'd really like to hear about it." Lori brushed the last crumbs of her muffin from the table and pushed aside her empty coffee cup to give me her undistracted attention. "I was so busy trying to deal with three children, then getting a divorce. I don't understand how America even got in there."

"I don't think anybody understands that." I glanced around to see who was sitting near us. Bullwinkle's still smelled of beer.

"Then tell me why you went and what you did?"

She sat back, waiting for my response. The waitress came to refill our coffee cups, which brought only a temporary reprieve.

"There's a lot to tell, I was there more than a year." Although I liked Lori, I really didn't know her.

"We could do it in installments," she said affably.

I told her the worst part first, the part about Dan. But it did not seem to dampen her curiosity.

"He believed in the people," I continued. "Even built a clinic and school on an island he helped pacify."

"That's wonderful."

"They hid the Viet Cong who killed him."

"How awful. You must have hated them."

"The Viet Cong would have killed them and their children if they didn't cooperate."

Lori listened quietly while I told her of the primitive hospital I worked in, how we had to use outdated blood the military threw away because it was all we had for our patients. It was painful to describe triage and what it was like to decide who could be saved and who had to be set aside as unsalvageable because we didn't have the supplies or time to save them. When she asked about napalm victims I concentrated on the frustration of not having burn dressings or morphine to give them. I did not tell her about the baby.

"But why didn't you have burn dressings?" Lori demanded. "We've been sending billions in humanitarian aid over there."

She grew even angrier when I described how most of it went to the black market. And how Washington ignored us when we complained.

"But why didn't you get it in the papers back here? People would be furious. I'm furious!"

"The press didn't give a damn. They were too busy making our troops look like Nazis."

I described how we peeled skin off cadavers to lay over napalm wounds to seal in precious body fluids and try to stave off infection. "That's what most of them died of. They lost fluids and electrolytes faster than we could pump them in. If we had any to give them."

Lori was turning as green as her O.B. gown. "I think that's maybe enough of the medical side," she said. "But I still want to hear about you, how you felt about what you saw and how you coped."

I told her things I had never told anyone, not even my family. Sitting there in a dim, smelly bar, halfway around the world from my risky venture, made me feel as if I was describing a movie I had seen and Lori had not.

Before either of us noticed, the lunch crowd was beginning to filter in dressed in hospital uniforms.

I began gathering up my belongings. "I'd better take off if I'm going to get to the beach before sundown."

Lori dabbed at tears that suddenly appeared. "Me too. I have to go to the grocery store, clean house and try to catch some sleep before my children get home from school."

She insisted on paying for our breakfast. "Careful driving," she said outside Bullwinkle's, where we both blinked from the sudden change to bright sunlight. "And stay clear of the local rednecks."

"I will."

We started off in opposite directions, but I heard Lori call to me after only a few steps. "I need to say something," she said as she came back to where I waited.

Here it comes, I thought. And you asked for it unloading all the shit you've hidden for years.

"Thank you for going over there and doing what you did," she said as she gave me a tight hug. "Especially for the children."

I was so astonished I could not have responded even if she had not hurried off. She was the first person who had ever thanked me for my service in the misery that was Vietnam. And only now did I realize how much I had been longing for such recognition.

"I don't know why I got so angry at you," I told Andy in the shabby E.R. waiting room. I couldn't bring myself to leave for Fishback Island without first making peace.

"That's O.K., Dana....I mean, Pat."

"You can call me Danang," I said apologetically.

"I have to get back to work," Andy said as he gestured toward the double E.R. doors. I wondered if he just wanted to be rid of me.

"See you when I get back from the beach?"

"I'll be here." He gave me a quick kiss on the cheek before returning to work.

I carried it with me all the way to Seaport, even though I chastised myself for doing so.

After paying a property manager rent for three days, I found the isolated cottage and went immediately to the single bedroom to rest my painful back. Road construction had increased the already tedious drive to the island, so it was again too dark to see the ocean. But I heard it just outside the open window above the bed.

As I lay there in the humble but charming beach house, I tried to look honestly at the day to day existence I had become accustomed to before the E.R. shooting of the junkie jolted me out of my daze. I had told Lori about Dan and our plans to marry as soon as we returned home. And how all of that ended in the time it took one bullet to cross a remote patch of jungle.

War was said to change everyone, but people returning from

Vietnam had the additional hardship of trying to fit back into a country which had changed as much as we had. Martin Luther King had been assassinated, as well as Robert Kennedy. Whole sections of cities were torn by riots and buildings torched. College campuses were no longer places of learning but battlefields where unarmed students could be gunned down by jittery national guardsmen.

And then there was the fiasco of Watergate, symbolizing the total disintegration of a government we once respected. The question I wanted to ask Lori but had not was, how did one come home from a war when the home you knew no longer existed?

I woke to the music of gulls and stepped out into a world I had not envisioned when I decided to revisit the island. There were only a few cottages in sight, all of them small and sided in weather-beaten, wooden shingles like the one in which I resided. The beach was wider than I remembered, and the sky a cloudless blue.

I made myself a cup of tea, which I drank on the porch that jutted out onto the dunes of sand. Afterward I walked barefoot for miles, my feet tingling in the sharp coolness of the surf.

With the rain on my earlier trip, I had not noticed the nearly solid wall of towering condominiums I found when I ventured to the tourist end of Seaport. Nor had I seen the boardwalk running along in front of them, ending at an amusement park built on a huge pier out over the water. The roller coaster and dozens of other rides sat silent now, awaiting the Baltimore and Washington residents who would flood into the small town beginning Memorial weekend.

As Lori predicted, it was a perfect time to be at the beach, warm and breezy with only an occasional person flying a kite or surf fishing. And best of all, no nightmares.

The three days passed too quickly. I took a final look at the diminutive cottage after backing my car out onto the highway, and it appeared to be waving good-bye with several loose shingles flapping in a brisk afternoon wind.

As soon as I entered Muskrat Marsh, the town thirty miles inland, I came upon the frame church I had seen on my earlier trip. I looked instinctively toward the cemetery and there, among the slabbed graves and headstones, were Hope and Allison Taylor.

A large building under construction sat just behind the small church, but workers were nowhere in sight. I stopped my car and walked to its framed skeleton, where I stood watching the mother and daughter, wondering what inexplicable compulsion drew me to them.

"Tell me how we danced," the daughter said as she had before.

The mother got up dutifully and danced to music she hummed

aloud. "He held you up close to his cheek like this." She pantomimed the action as she moved gracefully. "Sometimes you fell asleep, but if he stopped singing or dancing you woke immediately and cried for more."

The young girl laughed her high, bird-song trill, then prompted her mother to continue. "And he let me steer the boat..."

Her mother picked up on cue. "Little as you were, he would hold you on his lap and let you pilot the boat in and out of the waterways."

She stopped dancing and rearranged the fresh flowers scattered over the concrete slab of her departed husband. "He loved you so."

While I watched, the dreamy look in the daughter's face was transformed to one of such despair she went from teenager to hopeless elder in one brief moment. "We'll never get away from here," she said morosely.

"Yes we will, Allison. And I'll send you to college just as Adam Lee would have wanted."

"I wish we had all been on the boat when it blew up."

"Allison, what a thing to say!"

"You know you've thought it, Mother! We both think it all the time!"

I was so engrossed in what was going on, I wasn't sure if I coughed or made some other kind of noise that caused the mother to jerk her head my way. Her expression was one of a frightened doe ready to defend her fawn from an intruder in their forest.

"I just stopped to stretch," I said, pointing to my car. "On my way back to Baltimore."

The woman's face relaxed. She had a regal manner as we moved toward one another. But the hand she offered was rough and surprisingly strong compared to the porcelain texture of her face. "Hope Taylor," she said with a lovely smile.

"I know," I said. Both Hope and Allison reacted. "I mean I know someone who knows you. Lori Donlin."

Hope was pleased. "Oh Lori, I haven't seen her in so long."

"She's in midwifery school. In Baltimore."

"Yes, I heard." I couldn't take my eyes from Hope's majestic crown of copper braids. "We were friends before...she moved away."

Allison watched me with an expression somewhere between curiosity and contempt as I walked with her mother to their picnic site. I indicated the building under construction, now behind me. "Looks like they're building a new church, or something."

"Church," Allison said. She remained seated at the checked tablecloth spread on the ground, covered with a simple but elegant lunch.

"Please join us," Hope said. Neither of them looked like islanders.

Allison was giving me a don't you dare look. I held up my arm with my watch on it. "I'm already late getting home."

"Then you might as well be good and late," Hope said in her soft, persuasive manner. "Please, we have plenty."

Despite Allison's obvious displeasure I wanted to stay. It was something in Hope's brown eyes, a private and terrible pain that made me feel somewhere in her past she might also have a burned baby.

The construction crew gave us disapproving looks when they returned to work on the new church, but I was enjoying myself too much to let them destroy my pleasant encounter. Hope was in the midst of explaining to me how she began the practice of having picnics among the dead, after growing up in an orphanage.

"The nun's cemetery was just behind the orphanage," she said as she passed me a wedge of apple topped with almond cheese. "They made us go out there every Sunday after Mass to pull weeds and put fresh flowers on all the graves. Those dreadful gladiolus they grew in their garden," she added with a frown.

Allison was no longer trying to drill holes in me with her eyes. Although it was clear she was not overjoyed by my presence.

"Afterwards we had a marvelous picnic," her mother continued. "The only food they managed not to ruin." She looked in my direction. "I truly believe that's why those women end up in convents, no one would marry them because they're such dreadful cooks."

Allison's laugh sounded like the birds in the surrounding trees. When her mother looked at her it was with sheer adoration.

"On All Soul's Day we had a really elaborate celebration." Hope's voice was as smooth and delicate as her complexion, but strangely audible above the sounds of hammering and sawing coming from the construction site. "They had an enormous picnic, then a candlelight service after dark." Her expression was winsomely nostalgic. "All those wavering little flames in a procession of nuns and children that seemed to stretch forever into the night."

We didn't notice when the hammering ceased, nor see the dark clouds overhead until the skies opened up on us. We shrieked with laughter as we grabbed up the remnants of the picnic and ran for our cars. The building crew, gathered under a tarpaulin stretched across beams of the new church, stood regarding us as if we were escapees from an asylum.

"Please come again if you're down this way!" Hope called to me from the partially rolled down window of her car.

"I will!"

Allison turned to look in my direction as her mother steered her worn Volvo out the cemetery gates. I thought I detected an ever so slight smile.

Why Hope wanted to maintain a relationship with a deceased spouse when she was already married to another was beyond my comprehension. Especially when she encouraged the same behavior in her impressionable young daughter. And why were they talking about the island as if it were a prison?

CHAPTER TEN

I wondered what was wrong as soon as I saw Dr. Ware coming down the O.R. corridor rubbing his chest.

"You're pretty good friends with Reba, aren't you?" I couldn't imagine what Reba could have done to have him looking so distressed.

"Sure, why?"

"There's been an accident. Well not actually an accident."

"Is she O.K.?" My heart was already accelerating.

My boss calmly related how the elderly O.R. tech was attacked as she walked to her car the previous night after work. "You know how she parks on the damned back streets around here to save money for those worthless properties she's always going on about."

"Tell me how she is," I said, fearing the worst.

"She's in ICU." I started for the intensive care unit but Dr. Ware stopped me. "No visitors. She's in bad shape." He pulled a slip of paper from the pocket of his white lab coat. "A Lori Donlin in O.B. asked me to give this to you."

The message had been scrawled by a hand so shaky I had difficulty making out the words. But I managed to follow the hastily drawn map to Lori's residence near the hospital.

Lori's ex-husband, Earl Roy Donlin, opened the door of the rented row house. Their three children, Billy aged twelve, Peggy nine and Brendan seven, were watching cartoons on a black and white television set in a sparsely furnished living room.

"How's Reba?" I asked the moment Lori entered from another room. "Have you seen her?"

"She didn't come home from work," Billy said from a sofa missing a cushion. "I tried calling her at work but nobody knew where

59

she was."

"The children were alone all evening," Earl Roy said with a look in Lori's direction. "I only found out in the middle of the night and drove all the way from Fishback Island."

"I was in the delivery room when Billy called," Lori told me, after first returning her ex-husband's glare. "The nurses forgot to give me the message."

"Would somebody please tell me how Reba is?" I said impatiently.

"She appears to have suffered an M.I.," Earl Roy said in a clinical manner befitting his physician status.

Lori looked worriedly in my direction. A myocardial infarction could mean significant damage to the muscle of Reba's heart.

"But Dr. Ware told me she was attacked."

"She got beat up too," Billy offered. "And she almost got...." His father signaled for him to stop and Billy did so immediately.

"We'll discuss that later," Earl Roy said in a formal manner. Billy's face flushed crimson as he returned to the television.

The adolescent was tall and thin like his father. He had the same faded beige hair and pale blue eyes I had been looking at for the past three days on Fishback Island. The two younger children were shorter, rounder and as blond and green-eyed as their mother.

"We already know Reba got raped," Peggy said. "We heard Billy talking to Dad on the telephone."

"Raped?" The story was as incredulous as it was confusing.

"Attempted rape," Lori's ex corrected. "When she had the heart attack the guy thought she was dying and took off."

"I called Dad when I couldn't get Mom," Billy said. Peggy was half listening to the conversation, but Brendan was completely absorbed in the fate of two cartoon chipmunks on T.V.

"You did fine," Lori said to Billy in a voice filled with worry.

"It's a good thing he had the sense to call me," Earl Roy persisted. The children were dressed haphazardly, but he wore an expensive suit with a pastel shirt and matching tie.

"I gave Billy explicit instructions to call you if there was ever an emergency and I could not be reached," Lori snapped.

"She did, Dad," Billy said anxiously.

Earl Roy went over to pat Billy's shoulder in his stiff, formal fashion. "And you did right, William James."

"I still don't know how Reba is," I said when I could no longer stand the family drama taking center stage. "Has anyone seen her?"

"I only got as far as the corridor outside her ICU cubicle this morning," Lori answered. "She's on every monitor possible, but they said I could see her later today."

"The man was colored like Reba," Peggy said.

"Black," Lori corrected.

"You're changing their vocabulary as well as raising them in a dump?" Earl Roy looked around the living room as if he wouldn't consider sitting down in it.

"It's nineteen seventy-four," Lori said. "You don't refer to people as colored anymore."

"They've bin culurd as long as Ah've bin talkin' an' I don't plan ta change now." No one but me seemed to notice the change in Earl Roy's speech pattern. Or his reversal when he turned to me.

"I don't believe we've been introduced." He rearranged several seaweed strands of hair he had grown long enough to sweep up over his head from a part just above his left ear. Like so many balding men, he felt the need to demonstrate he could grow hair some place, and the patchy beginnings of a beard clung unevenly to his face.

"This is Pat Walsh. An anesthetist who works with Reba."

Earl Roy was smiling as if we were being introduced at a cocktail party. When he shook my hand he didn't let go. "Have I seen you before? Maybe at an anesthesia conference?"

"I don't think so," I said, retrieving my hand.

"If we're going to the hospital we need to leave," Lori said.

"I'll drive." Earl Roy walked toward the door with the slightly bowlegged waddle of a child kept in thick diapers too long. Billy followed just behind.

"They won't let us see Reba," Peggy told me when we were all squeezed into Earl Roy's sport car. She had tried to braid her yellow hair, but it looked more twisted than braided.

"I'll tell Reba you're all thinking of her," Lori said to her children. "And that you want her to get better real soon."

Peggy and Brendan tried to fill their mother in on everything that happened during the scary night.

"Dad says we can't stay in Baltimore anymore 'cause we're living in the slums," Peggy told her. The nine year old sat between Billy and me in the back seat.

"That is not for Dad to decide." Lori, in the front passenger seat, looked toward Earl Roy, who kept his eyes on the road.

"But we want to go back to the island," Brendan whined from Lori's lap. "We want to live in our real house."

"We are not moving back to that island." Lori spoke so sharply Brendan began to cry and Earl Roy turned to her with a see-what-you've-done-now expression. Lori cuddled her seven year old to her breast and spoke in a motherly tone. "Mom's just upset about Reba. We'll decide what to do about us after I see how she is."

"I refuse to let my children grow up in a ghetto." Earl Roy was driving at an unsafe speed in the narrow streets.

"Give me some support money and I'll move to the suburbs tomorrow," Lori shot back.

"You have a perfectly good home on the island that's being ruined by renters. That's where my children belong." Earl Roy pushed the car even harder, weaving in and out of traffic.

"I'm staying in Baltimore until I finish school and my children are staying with me. Or have you forgotten that I have custody?"

I was embarrassed by the squabbling, and the children had all fallen silent. I put an arm around Peggy, who leaned into me. "They always fight," she said.

Lori heard and turned to the back seat. "I'm sorry."

"It's all right," I said. "Everybody's upset."

Brendan ran to the towering statue of Jesus as soon as we entered Filmore Hospital's lobby. While he climbed over its giant feet, kicking at each of the marble toes, Peggy begged to see Reba. She cried when her mother insisted she would have to wait until Reba was moved out of intensive care.

"You stay here with me," Earl Roy said to his daughter. "We can have ice cream while we wait."

"Ice cream and candy time," Lori said as she walked with me to the elevator. "The only interaction he ever has with them is over some syrupy mess."

"How did the two of you meet?" I asked while we waited for the elevator. They were so different I couldn't conceive of them ever being married.

"He was with some friends from Harvard at a little gin mill down by the Charles River in Boston. I was there with girlfriends from my college in Pennsylvania." Lori's voice softened. "I thought he was cute with his double name and island accent. I always told him he learned a second language at Harvard, English."

The wistfulness disappeared as she glanced back toward Earl Roy and jabbed impatiently at the elevator button. "Then I married him and we moved to his precious little island. It wasn't so cute when I found out how bigoted and backward the people are."

The elevator arrived and I pushed the button for the third floor, where the coronary intensive care unit was located.

"Would Earl Roy try taking the children back to the island with him?" The elevator stopped on the second floor to pick up a full load of interns and residents.

"His new wife doesn't want anything to do with them."

"I didn't realize he was remarried."

"Married her ten minutes after our divorce was final. Although I've never quite understood why he felt he had to make it official when he'd been sleeping with her for years." The young physicians all looked at Lori but she did not appear to notice.

We asked at the desk for Reba's room number, and the nurse gave it without taking her eyes off the bank of monitors she was watching, each attached to a different patient.

We were about to enter Reba's cubicle when another nurse stopped us. "Family only," she said.

"I am family," Lori said. The nurse's eyebrows raised. "I mean we're like family. Reba takes care of my children."

"Immediate family only." The nurse pronounced each word as if addressing a toddler. "And the patient's children are unable to travel here from Chicago at this time."

"But the doctors told me I could see her. I'm the only one she has in Baltimore."

The nurse remained territorial; this is my unit and I run it the way I choose. She started to walk away, then unexpectedly gave in. "You can page the nursing supervisor and ask if you can see her. If she says it's O.K., it's all right with me."

A high-pitched alarm sounded and the nurse hurried into the next cubicle. While Lori paged the supervisor, the nurse expertly handled a malfunctioning ventilator. Nurses were expected to operate and repair almost every machine invented, as well as understand the data they provided. Physicians concentrated only on machines within their areas of expertise, and had technicians responsible for the mechanics.

When the nursing supervisor arrived she recognized me from my frequent visits to the ICU to resuscitate patients. She advised Lori and me to simply put labcoats over our clothing and pretend we were on official business whenever we wished to see Reba.

"I saw the patient," the supervisor said before she left. "It's terrible what that man did to her."

Even with the warning, I was totally unprepared for the battered heap that once was Reba. Only her unusual height, which left her feet dangling over the end of the bed, gave a clue that it was the same woman I watched work twenty-four hour shifts in the O.R., slapping instruments as accurately at the end as the beginning.

"Oh God." Lori stood immobilized at the door.

I approached the bed. "Reba?"

From somewhere beneath the bruises and stitched-up lacerations, a narrow slit appeared. Slowly it widened until there was a glimmer of eye. "Pat?" The word was barely audible through swollen lips.

Lori came to the bed and leaned over the side rail to touch her friend. "Oh, Reba."

"Don't cry over me." Reba's voice was so raspy it was difficult to understand. "Where's the children? I've bin worrying the whole time over them."

"They're with their father," Lori said, choked with emotion.

"He left me for dead." There were finger print bruises on Reba's neck, and a raised welt encircled it almost completely. "Police say he tried to strangle me." She moved a hand with an I.V. in it part way to her puffy neck, then dropped it weakly back to the bed. "Might's well killed me as leave me like this."

"You're going to be fine," Lori said in a stronger voice. "We'll get you well and I'll take you home and look after you."

"Five children I raised with no help from their father, and now this happens," Reba said hoarsely. "I fought my whole life, fought him too till my heart gave out." She sighed so deeply the alarm went off on her monitor and a nurse came running.

"You'll have to leave now," she told us while putting a stethoscope to Reba's chest.

"We'll come back later," I said as I gently touched one of Reba's bruised arms.

"There's no later." She stared up at the ceiling with her one eye. "He killed me just like he thought he did." Lori leaned over the side rail to kiss her forehead. "It wasn't worth all the bones," Reba whispered up to her.

I had to help Lori from the room. When we reached a secluded spot, she leaned against the wall crying. "She raised her own children making soup from bones the butcher gave her," she said when she could speak. "And now she's doing the same for mine."

"Parking on back streets instead of paying to park in the hospital ramp is what put her in the hospital," I said, feeling angry at Reba for putting herself in such jeopardy. "Saving money for those damned properties of hers."

Lori's voice was quiet. "Her properties and my ridiculous attempt to get through school. None of it is worth all the bones."

CHAPTER ELEVEN

After a night of boring cases and little sleep, I went to the intensive care unit to check on Reba. Lori was in the waiting room.

"How is she?" I asked.

"About the same. The cardiologists are with her now."

"And how are you?" Lori looked exhausted.

"Terrible. Earl Roy and I have already had our daily battle."

"I thought he went back to the island."

"We're fighting long distance." She pulled herself up in her chair, only to slump back down again. "He has graciously allowed the children to stay in Baltimore, if I find a better place to live. How am I supposed to do that when I'm flat broke, have no one to baby-sit and don't finish school for another six weeks? If I finish at all."

"If he insists you move, make him pay half the rent."

"I already tried that." She got up to move about the small room. "I can't force him unless I take him to court and have our ridiculous divorce settlement changed." She sighed wearily. "I was so desperate to get away from Earl Roy I settled for nothing but the house, and it's no mansion. The rent I get barely pays my rent here."

"What about your family? Can't they help?"

Lori's laugh was as humorless as Andy's. "They still haven't forgiven me for divorcing a doctor." She sat down again and twisted at a loose strand of blond hair that trailed down from where the remainder was wound into a disheveled bun at the back of her neck. "I don't want to give up midwifery school, but without Reba to watch the children on the nights I have call there's no way I can make it."

"I wish I could help, but I'm on call two nights a week myself."

"I should never have depended on her so much." Lori spoke as if she were alone in the room.

The professor and his squadron of residents and interns came out from Reba, but they immediately went into another patient's cubicle.

"Do you think you might be able to arrange your call schedule so I could help with your children?"

It took her a moment to comprehend. "Do you mean it?"

My head nodded yes before my mouth could say no. Had I just offered to look after three children in knife and gun territory?

"Billy's old enough to get the younger ones off to school, so it's really just being with them during the night." The color was back in her face and her voice had lost its desperation. She pulled a folded sheet of paper from her scrub gown pocket and handed it to me. "Here're my call nights this week and next. If they conflict with yours I'm sure my supervisor would let me change them."

"What about Earl Roy's demand that you move?"

"If he pushes me I'll take him to court. No judge in Baltimore would uphold a stipulation that I have to live on that stinking island in order to get child support." Lori got up. "Let's go see Reba."

She was several yards ahead of me when she turned. "You're sure about this?" she asked, her voice anxious. "I want to tell Reba so she'll stop worrying, but you can back out before I do."

It was my chance, but Lori's face told how disappointed she would be if I did. "I'm sure. At least until Reba's back on her feet."

When we reached Reba's cubicle, we both knew that would take a long time. Our friend's lower legs and feet hung over the end of the short bed, and her upper torso had slipped down into a crevasse made by the bed's elevated knee and head rest. "You'll get pneumonia all slumped down like that," Lori said while we pulled her back up in bed.

"What does it matter?" Reba's voice was despondent.

"It matters because my children are moping around like they've lost their best friend in the world," Lori told her.

"You don't have to worry about the children anymore," I told Reba. "I'm going to watch them the nights Lori's on call."

Reba smiled despite swollen lips. "That's fine, real fine."

Earl Roy Donlin's concern for his children was understandable when I got a closer look at where they lived. Their rented row house was crumbling red brick, boxed in on both sides by identical units sharing common walls. Designed to take maximum advantage of the limited land on which they were built, the units were two or three stories high and deep and narrow. Their facades sat flush with the sidewalks, with long narrow windows upstairs and down facing the street. The front doors were battered from years of abuse, and the streets and sidewalks were littered with refuse. Oddly, all the steps to the dwellings were white marble that looked freshly scrubbed.

Lori found parking for both our cars some distance down the street from her row house. I was concerned about leaving my cherished Mustang to anyone who happened along, and took several furtive glances over my shoulder as I walked away from it. Lori's battered station wagon was in little danger of being stolen or stripped.

We were attracting openly hostile looks from black neighbors sitting on their stoops. "When we first moved here, everyone was friendly," Lori said quietly. "Now white developers are buying up rental buildings to convert them to condominiums." A group of women took time from their neighborhood gossip to watch silently as we passed. "They've taken a dislike to all whites. You can't blame them when they're being forced out of their homes with nowhere to go."

Mothers called occasional admonishments to children playing in the street, or plaited the hair of young girls sitting a step lower than them on the marble stages of their community. With the exception of male children, the landscape was entirely female.

"Reba's properties are over there." Lori pointed to a sizeable chunk of real estate which sloped downward to Baltimore's seedy harbor. All but a few of the buildings were burned out hulks, their white marble stoops still blackened by smoke. "They were set on fire in the riots after Martin Luther King was assassinated," Lori said. "Reba thinks they can be refurbished but I can't see how."

"Get back here!" a woman shouted from a doorway.

Two small children who had been following us ran back down the street and up the steps to where their mother stood watching us. I was relieved when Lori started up a set of identical stairs.

"There're people here who've rented for generations," Lori said as she unlocked her battered door. "They don't know any other way."

I looked back at the street before going inside. It didn't strike me as prime real estate for developers.

Lori dropped her purse and keys just inside the door. The row house was like a tunnel, one dark room opening to another until we reached the kitchen in the rear. A small window in the back door provided a glimmer of daylight that filtered down between Lori's row of buildings and its neighbor across a miserly strip of alley. A patch of ground which might have served as a yard was filled with a rusting kitchen stove, a sofa with the stuffing popping out and an assortment of sinks and bathtubs. The neighboring yards were similar.

"Mom's home," Lori called up a set of stairs when we returned to the front portion of the house. Her two younger children thundered down the uncarpeted steps to greet her. "Where's Billy?" she asked.

"Seven Eleven," Brendan said. "He told us not to tell."

Peggy gave the seven year old an exasperated look. "You just did, dummy."

"I'll have to go get him," Lori said to me. "Peggy can finish showing you around."

"Reba has a garden." Lori's nine year old and I stood amongst the junk in the backyard. "She lets me pick beans and tomatoes in the summer." Having been raised on a farm, I found it difficult to believe anything could grow in the midst of so much concrete and rubble.

"Does Reba live close by?" I asked. Peggy was pulling tufts of stuffing from the abandoned sofa and launching them on an early evening breeze. They floated toward a sky so leaden it looked as if it would fall on us at any moment.

"Her apartment's that way," Peggy said, pointing eastward. The child kicked at the claw feet on one of the bathtubs. "Our mean old landlord won't haul his junk away so I can have my own garden." She returned to plucking stuffing from the sofa. "Nobody likes us here. Mom won't hardly let us play outside anymore."

"I'm back," Lori called from the kitchen door.

I went inside and found her trying to clean up a stack of dishes in the kitchen sink. The sleeves of her coat were getting wet.

"I can do that," I told her. "I have all night."

Lori abandoned the dishes. "I got hamburger at the store," she said. "I thought it would be easy for you to fix for dinner."

"We always have hamburgers," said Peggy. She twisted absently at her thick yellow braids. "Or soup."

"I guess we do." Lori opened a cupboard with boxes of cereal. "The children fix their own breakfast and Billy walks them to school," she said. "You don't need to do anything before leaving for work."

She walked ahead of me through the dining room, stooping to pick up comic books and tennis shoes. The windowless room was depressingly dark, but a red and white checked table cloth and large travel posters tacked to dingy walls gave hope. "I couldn't find Billy. I'll take a drive around on my way to the hospital to see if I can spot him."

"Come see my room." Peggy pulled me toward a steep staircase clinging to one side of the living room.

It was too dark to see clearly the framed school pictures lining the walls as we climbed to the second floor and walked along a darker corridor to a room overlooking the street. "This is Ginger," Peggy said, picking up an orange cat from her bed. "I got her last year for my birthday." She stroked the pet and it stretched lazily in her arms. "She's my best friend," she said, burying her face in its fur.

"She's pretty." I petted the pampered cat and it purred.

The room had two skinny windows facing the street, through which the siren of a passing police cruiser could be heard. Flowered curtains were tied back to allow as much light as possible inside.

I peered out to where my Mustang sat blessedly untouched. The women and children were still on their glistening doorsteps.

"I'll be glad when we move away from here." Peggy lay on her single bed with her cat draped across her chest. "I wish we could go back to our house on the island. That's where I like it best." Ginger jumped to the floor and disappeared down the dark corridor. "Billy calls this the slums the same as Dad."

"It looks like your mother has worked pretty hard to fix things up." A multicolored afghan hung on one of the water stained walls.

"It used to at least smell good when Reba baked yummy things."

"I can bake." I was anxious to please on my first night as housemother. "We could make cookies."

"I don't know if we have the stuff." It was said in the voice of a child stung by the shame of poverty. "Reba mostly made bread."

"I know how to make that too."

"I have to get going," Lori called up the stairs. "I need to show you how to work the stove, Pat."

My eyes had accommodated enough to the dark to make out two additional bedrooms on our way back along the corridor. One had twin beds for the boys and the other was Lori's, where I would sleep.

"I've given up trying to get this thing fixed." Lori tightly wound newspaper into a long baton she lit with a match, then stood back while she lit the outdated stove. "Our landlord would rather have us blow up than spend a few bucks." The torch ignited the gas spewing from the burner with a burst of yellow flame.

"Reba swears at it," Peggy said.

"Could you show me how to light the oven?" I asked.

Lori opened the back door before turning on the oven, which hissed putrid gas before lighting with a bang. "Don't turn it off," I said when she reached for the knob. "We're going to bake bread."

The front door slammed. "Billy, is that you!" Lori demanded. There was no answer, but the television came on.

Brendan, who had shown little interest in my presence until now, came to the doorway of the kitchen. "Is Pat going to make cinnamon rolls?" The seven year old had an uneven kitchen haircut.

"Uh-huh," Peggy said without first consulting me.

"With sticky stuff on the bottom?"

"As sticky as you want," I said to the small boy.

Lori was looking through cupboards so high only Reba could have reached them without a chair. "I'm not sure I have all the ingredients," she said in the same embarrassed tone Peggy had used.

"That's all right," I said. "We can go to the store."

"We don't go outside at night," Peggy said.

I looked at my watch. "It's only five-thirty."

"Yeah," Brendan said. "But someone might beat us up and take our money."

"I don't let them out after five," Lori told me. "And they're not supposed to go out alone at all," she added when Billy came to the kitchen and leaned against the doorjamb with the arrogance of one approaching his teens. "It really isn't safe," Lori said to him. "I've told you that enough times."

"What's for dinner?" Billy asked as if his mother hadn't spoken. "Soup or hamburgers?"

"Hamburgers," Peggy said.

"Big surprise." Lori ignored the sarcasm.

"Call me at work if you need anything," Lori told me as she prepared to leave. She kissed Brendan and Peggy good-bye but Billy dodged the kiss intended for his cheek.

"Be good and help Pat," she told them as she headed for the door. "And be sure to check the locks on all the windows and doors."

"I'll check them," I said.

"That's my job." Billy gave me a side-wise look that made it clear I was not about to invade his turf.

"And you do a good job," Lori said to Billy before hurrying out the door.

I stood in the doorway watching her car until it was out of sight. A group of children played a spirited game of kick ball in the street.

Most of the women had left their stoops and I could smell the varied odors of cooking dinners; hotdogs, hamburgers, and what smelled like spaghetti from next door. A few men filtered through the neighborhood, most of them coming and going from Cozy Corner, a bar just down the block. Loud laughter and music could be heard each time the door was opened to allow someone in or out. I thought about Reba and the man who attacked her. The incident had taken place not far away and the police were doing little to find the perpetrator.

"I'd better get some dinner going," I said after closing the door and starting back toward the kitchen.

"Don't forget the bread," Brendan said. He sat on the end of the sofa that was missing a cushion, giving his older brother the two remaining while they watched T.V.

"I can fry the hamburgers," Peggy offered. "And you can make the bread."

She took a package of ground beef from the refrigerator, which contained a gallon of milk, a carton of eggs, several partially used bottles of catsup and mustard, and a limp bunch of celery. A piece of unwrapped cheese had a layer of green mold on it and Peggy noticed me looking at it.

"It's Billy's turn to unfuzz the fridge," she said. "I did it last time."

The comment made me laugh and Peggy laughed with me. "We only have fancy dinners on Sundays," she told me while she shaped the hamburger patties in her small hands.

"It was the same for me when I was growing up."

"Really?" She interrupted her work to look up at me. "Mom says when she finishes school we'll have lots of money."

"That won't be long now." I was on a kitchen chair collecting salt, sugar, yeast and flour from one of the high cupboards.

I scalded milk and set it aside to cool while the yeast dissolved in lukewarm water. Brendan came into the kitchen with an expectant look on his face. "Are the cinnamon rolls ready yet?"

"It'll be past your bedtime when they're done," I told him. He had round cheeks perfect for kissing. "You can have them for breakfast."

"Can't we stay up till they're done for a special treat?" Peggy asked. "Because it's your first time staying with us?"

"Your mother said to get you to bed by eight."

"Pleeeeze." Brendan was bent over holding his upturned palms toward me like a street beggar. I laughed as I had with Peggy, that long forgotten laugh that begins down in your midsection. I really was not looking forward to sitting alone in a drafty old house waiting for bread to bake.

"I guess maybe this one time," I relented.

The two children celebrated their victory so loudly Billy came into the kitchen to investigate. "Mom won't like you letting them stay up late," he warned when they revealed the source of their excitement.

"I'll talk to her." Billy rolled his eyes and returned to the television.

A fight erupted in the row house next door just after I went to bed at ten. I listened to the thump of furniture hitting walls, glass breaking and the cries of a woman. When I heard a child scream, I got out of Lori's bed and stood debating whether or not I should go downstairs and call the police.

I thought I heard someone talking and went to the children's rooms to see if the noise had awakened them. They were all sleeping peacefully despite the racket on the other side of the communal wall.

The man eventually stopped shouting and the child quieted, but the woman was still crying when I returned to bed. I lay there listening until it subsided.

Billy got downstairs to the ringing phone first. I heard him say, "She knows how to make cinnamon rolls. They're good as Reba's."

I allowed myself a smile. My first night was a success.

"Pat, Mom says it's time to get up for work!" Billy bellowed.

"O.K." I tried not to wake the other children with my response, if Billy hadn't already. I heard rummaging in the kitchen as I went into the bathroom to shower. The hot water relieved some of the back pain from Lori's saggy mattress. When I went to the boys' room to say good-bye, Billy was asleep with a half eaten cinnamon roll in hand.

"Are you sure I can't do anything for breakfast?" I whispered when he half-opened his eyes. "Maybe put some cereal and bowls out?"

"I do that," he said groggily. He rolled onto his side and fell promptly back to sleep.

I checked his clock to make sure his alarm button was out, covered Brendan, fast asleep in the next bed, and went to check on Peggy. Her room was cooler than the rest of the house, but she looked comfortable enough with Ginger sprawled across her chest. The cat regarded me a few moments, then yawned and closed her eyes.

CHAPTER TWELVE

Reba was recovered enough to be discharged within two weeks. Lori put a rented hospital bed and commode on the first floor so Reba did not have to climb stairs. And we squeezed a single bed in next to Peggy's so I could be there whenever Lori or Reba needed me.

I had stopped by the E.R. more than once to say hello to Andy but never found him on duty. And without any attempt to contact me, I was left to believe he was not as interested in me as I thought.

But when I answered a call for anesthesia in the E.R. I ran into him. "I'm only working part time," he said when I asked where he had been. "I'm back in school."

"Studying what?"

"My pre-med and medical school credits transferred to a physician's assistant program."

"I thought you told me you had enough of medicine in Vietnam."

"I said I had enough of people calling me doc. I'll be doing physicals and routine office care with physician back-up. And I'm sure as hell not going to be responsible for saving ten lives at one time while I'm being shot at."

He walked me through the waiting room on my way back to the O.R.

"So, how was the beach?" Andy asked.

"Wonderful. I stayed in the greatest little cottage where I could hear the surf right outside the bedroom window."

"Sounds nice."

"I hated leaving."

"Then why did you?"

"I don't know," I said after a few moments. "I guess because I have a job back here. But it's good that I did come back."

I told Andy about Reba and that I was helping Lori with her children. "Reba's still too frail to be alone with them."

"How long do you plan to play housemother?" Andy asked.

"Just until Reba's better."

It sounded like a sacrifice, but the time with Lori's family was the happiest I had felt since the war. It was fun to be part of the day to day bustle of a family, doing laundry, cooking, helping with homework and listening to the children's tales of school and friends.

Andy stopped at the door to the corridor. "Time for me to get back to work." I noticed that his limp was far less pronounced.

"What's different with your leg?" I asked.

Andy held it out in front of him and pulled up his pant leg to display a gleaming prosthesis which made no pretense of looking like a real leg. "New butt kicker." He stepped up and down on it. "See that? They put a spring in the foot so it feels more natural when you're walking." He lowered his pant leg. "Cost me a bundle."

"You really didn't pay for it yourself?"

"I told you, the VA is out of my life for good."

He began to walk back toward the E.R., but stopped. "How about a beer at Bullwinkle's later?" he said.

"I'm off at three."

"O.K., Bullwinkle's at three-thirty," he said.

I returned to the GYN surgery suite, where Dr. Ware had assigned me for a full week. I was administering anesthesia for a number of abortions, a procedure that was becoming routine since the Supreme Court's ruling making it legal a year earlier.

"Have you had an anesthetic in the past?" I asked my current patient while I started her I.V.

"You mean for one of these?" She was eighteen and had avoided the word abortion whenever it came up in my pre-anesthetic interview.

"An anesthetic for any reason. I just need to know if you've had any complications I should be aware of before I put you to sleep."

"I had my tonsils out when I was little, but I don't know if I had any trouble." She looked up from the stretcher with frightened eyes. "My mother would remember, but she doesn't know I'm here." She wiped perspiring palms on her sheet. "Please don't call her."

"Don't worry," I said, reading over her chart. "You look pretty healthy."

"Yes. Very healthy."

This was my fourth abortion of the day, with two more to go. I hunched down behind the anesthesia screen when the surgeon began scraping the girl's uterus with a metal curette that sounded like a rake being dragged across gravel. That was followed by the slurping of the suction machine as it extracted bloody remnants of the fetus.

The young girl was crying when I pushed her into the recovery room. "Give her five milligrams of Valium if her vital signs stay stable," I told the nurse taking care of her.

The next patient was in her mid-thirties. "My doctor promised I would be out of the hospital by five," she said as I readied her for surgery. "I'm a realtor and have lots of work to catch up on."

"That will depend on how you do," I said.

"I had one before and was back in the office the next morning."

I paused from starting her I.V. to look at her. "You mean another abortion?"

"Yes. Why do you ask?"

"I only need to know how long ago it was," I said too quickly. "Some anesthetic gases can cause liver problems if they're given too closely together."

The woman was placated. "The other one was about ten months ago," she replied. "Does that meet your requirements?"

"Yes, any anesthetic over six months ago is fine," I said as I pushed her into the operating room.

The case did not go as smoothly as doctor and patient had wished. "I can't find the goddamned skull," the surgeon groused as he probed the uterus with a suction tip that gurgled and hissed. The pregnancy was so advanced it had been necessary to sever the fetus head in order to remove the body from the uterus, but then he couldn't find it.

He tossed the suction tip aside and hunted through an assortment of instruments until he found the one he wanted. He inserted it and scraped for a while, then probed for the head with a gloved hand.

"Open the suction bottle and see if you can see any of it in there," he ordered when he still could not locate the elusive skull.

I turned away while the circulating nurse stirred the bloody contents of a tall bottle attached by a long plastic hose to the suction tip in the doctor's hand. The patient was losing more blood than usual, and I increased the rate of her I.V to compensate.

"Never mind," he said to the nurse. "I think I have it." The surgeon had his whole hand inside the woman's pelvis. When he pulled out a bloody glob of tissue and dropped it into a metal basin there was a discernible ping. "Hot damn! I hear bone!"

He did another manual exam of the uterus to make sure everything had been removed. "When you wake her up, tell her she won't be able to go home today," he told me. "She's lost too much blood."

"Life has its disappointments," I said into my mask.

"What did you say?"

"I said I would tell her."

He snapped off his bloody gloves and tossed them onto the messy instrument table. "Women have the right to abortion now," he said as he walked to the head of the table, where I was administering an I.V. drug to make the boggy uterus contract and decrease the blood loss. "Or haven't you heard about Roe versus Wade?"

"Yes sir, I have."

"Too bad it wasn't the law when his mother found out she was pregnant with him," the circulating nurse said when he left the room. "He's had a curette in one hand and a suction tip in the other ever since that court case was decided. And he doesn't want anyone interfering with his gold mine."

I pushed the patient to recovery, where she was complaining about being hospitalized overnight, and returned to the O.R. to set up equipment for my final case. "I don't think the Court intended these to be done for birth control," I said to the nurse cleaning the room.

"It's the ones done for sex preference that make me sick," she said. "Here we are thinking women have made so much progress, and we're scraping out ten times more female fetuses than male."

"You could probably get out of doing them by claiming religious preference," I suggested as I checked the oxygen tanks on my anesthesia machine.

"I tried the religious route," the nurse told me. "My punishment was to be assigned the longest and hardest cases on the schedule every day. I gave up after a month."

Her back was to me as she fished through the suction bottle contents with a large sieve-like spoon. After scooping out several pieces of tissue, she turned to show me the open laboratory container she had put them in. "She was a lot further along than he said."

I could clearly see body parts of a tiny baby, missing its head.

Somewhere I hear a baby crying.

I am trying to comfort it, but it will not be consoled by anyone but its mother, who lies dying on a field stretcher. The woman has been planting land mines for the Viet Cong when one of them goes off, mortally wounding her and injuring the baby strapped to her back. I try everything, rocking the child, singing to it, and finally a sedative. Its breathing slows and I worry that I have given it too much.

I shake one of its legs to stimulate it, then snap the bottom of its foot. The baby's skin washes a ghostly white and I run with it to the surgery suite.

"I just gave it a drop," I insist as I push oxygen into the infant's lungs with the anesthesia machine.

The surgeon working with me turns the baby over, inspecting it for an injury other than the obvious lacerations and bits of shrapnel imbedded under its skin from the exploding land mine. On its back, just below the left scapula, the doctor locates a cut so small it is difficult to see even when pointed out. Frothy pink fluid bubbles from it each time I push air into the baby's lungs.

"Sucking chest wound."

"I didn't see it," I say. "I wouldn't have given it sedation if I'd seen it."

"You learn to turn them over with experience," the surgeon tells me while he works quickly. "They can have an entry wound anywhere."

He puts a tube into the chest of the baby to drain off the air that has leaked through the wound and collapsed a lung. But the child's heart stops.

We immediately begin compressing the small breast bone, trying to restart the heart. "Keep going!" I order when the surgeon finally gives up. "We have to get it back!"

The surgeon gently pulls my hands away from the lifeless body. "There's nothing else we can do," he says kindly.

"I shouldn't have given it anything," I say again. "I pushed it over the edge with the sedation." Tears run down my face and into my dangling surgical mask.

"You did what you thought was right." The surgeon picks up the tiny body and carries it toward the door of the O.R. "We have patients waiting in triage."

"Miss Walsh, do you hear me? Miss Walsh?" I looked up into the face of a nurse who seemed familiar.

"What?"

"You passed out or something." I was lying on the floor, while the nurse knelt to hold a cold compress to my forehead. "You just went white and hit the floor. I called for Doctor Rasheif." She looked worried. "The surgeon is outside pacing the floor to get his next abortion started."

Now I knew who she was. "I'm so sorry," I said, trying to get up. The nurse only allowed me to sit.

"You hit your head."

Dr. Rasheif, the anesthesiologist in charge of GYN for the day, hurried into the room. "Give big breath," he said to me.

He helped the nurse get me up from the floor. "You O.K.?" the nurse asked while still holding onto me. I nodded even though I had to lean against the wall because of a spasm in my back from the fall.

Dr. Rasheif was looking into my face with actual concern. "You will go home." I knew I must look terrible to warrant such sympathy. "I call Doctor Ware and tell him you go home rest."

"I don't know what happened," I said.

Then I caught sight of a specimen container sitting near the suction machine. FEMALE FETUS was printed in bold letters across it.

A sour mass moved up my esophagus as I ran for a kick bucket and vomited up my lunch. It had happened again, my mind had so totally left my body it had rendered me unconscious.

Even out in the fresh air I knew I could not drive to my apartment in the suburbs. I had enough difficulty making it the few blocks to Lori's row house.

Reba was in her plaid, flannel bathrobe watching television. Lori was in the kitchen making a special dinner of spaghetti.

Somehow I made an excuse for coming home so early in the day, especially on Lori's day off when I was not needed. "I'm going to take a little nap," I said and headed for the stairs.

"Is the front door locked?" Reba asked.

I went back to check and found I had not locked it behind me. "Sorry, it is now," I said as I threw the heavy bolt Lori kept on it since Reba's attack.

Reba returned to watching her game show in the wooden rocker Lori had brought from her apartment. It was the one she rocked five babies in, who somehow all ended up in Chicago, and the only piece of furniture she cherished. It squeaked each time she rocked forward.

Lori came from the kitchen and followed me upstairs. "You look pale," she said as she touched a hand to my forehead.

"I'm just tired."

I was grateful when she left. I felt like I was on a railway platform with my whole body trembling as trains thundered by.

The sounds of Reba's game show floated up the stairway as I lay on my bed next to Peggy's. "YOU ARE THE WINNER OF AN ALL EXPENSE PAID TRIP TO HAWAI-EEEEEE!" the announcer shouted gleefully. "FIVE WONDERFUL DAYS IN BE-UUU-TI-FULLL HAWAI-EEEEEE!"

I managed to get up and close the door, but it did not completely block out the noise. I lay back down with my hands over my ears, my head tucked down toward my middle and my knees drawn up. Peggy found me the same way when she came home from school.

CHAPTER THIRTEEN

"Pat, have you seen Ginger?" The child whispered it directly into my ear, startling me from sleep.

I looked around the room, unsure of where I was. "No," I said when I realized I was at Lori's. "Maybe she's under one of the beds."

Peggy lifted the spread on hers and looked beneath, then did the same with mine. Ginger was not in the room.

"I asked Reba if she let her out, but she didn't open the door all day." Peggy's voice was as forlorn as her expression. "She said to ask if maybe Ginger got out when you came home from the hospital."

I got up from my bed. "I don't think so Peggy." But I knew a lion could have slipped past me in the state I was in when I came through the door. "Don't worry," I said. "I'll help you find her."

Billy and Brendan joined in a search of the neighborhood, as did their mother when she had the dinner dishes washed. It was well past dark when we gave up until morning.

"She'll probably be sitting on the doorstep waiting for us when we get back to the house," Lori told her disheartened daughter.

As we walked back to the row house I noticed curtains at a number of windows being pulled back just enough for the occupants to see out. Lori's children asked a few people passing by if they had seen Ginger.

"Your cat wouldn't be lost if you weren't living where you don't belong," a woman said as she looked to where Lori and I stood.

Lori was not in the mood for being reproached. She put an arm across Peggy's shoulders. "She's just a little girl! She has nothing to do with what's going on in this neighborhood, none of us do!"

"Then why're you here?"

"Cause we're poor," Brendan said before his mother could reply.

Lori smiled at her young son, and after a few moments so did the woman. "I didn't see no yellow cat," she said as she climbed her marble steps. "If I do I know where it belongs."

"Thank you," Peggy said.

Ginger was not waiting on the doorstep when we reached Lori's house. Andy was. "I thought we had a date after work," he said when the others had gone inside. "Anesthesia said you went home sick."

"I'm sorry, I didn't even think to call you. Did you wait long?" I had forgotten completely about going to Bullwinkle's for a drink with him after work. And it was the last thing I wanted to do now.

"It's O.K.," he said. "I went to O.B. and got Lori's address."

I was about to tell him I would take a rain check on the drink when I heard Peggy crying inside and Lori admonishing her for not taking better care of her pet. I went in to tell Lori it was me who probably let the cat out, and Andy went with me.

"She'll come home when she gets hungry," Andy said after I confessed my crime. "Cats can take care of themselves."

Peggy said through tears, "But Ginger's not used to being out."

"Maybe it's time she used that fur coat of hers," Andy told her. "It's not just for decoration, you know."

It coaxed a small smile. Reba took Peggy on her lap in her rocking chair to comfort her.

"I'm glad you came," Andy said when we were seated in a booth at the rear of Bullwinkle's. I wasn't glad to be there, but I wanted to be at Lori's even less.

"I feel terrible. I'm usually so careful not to let Ginger out."

"A cat deserves a little foray into the real world once in awhile," Andy said after ordering drinks.

"Not in Lori's neighborhood. Whites aren't very popular right now." I told him about the developers buying up the neighborhood to convert rentals to expensive condos and town houses.

"Dumb jerks," Andy laughed. "Who the hell do they think is going to want to live in that slum?"

"Reba seems to think a lot of people will. She owns several buildings."

"That's nuts."

I was still shaken by the episode at work and badly in need of someone to confide in. But I did not know how to tell Andy without sounding as crazy as he thought Reba was.

"Andy, do you ever feel like you're back in the war?" I asked after drinking half my Scotch and water. "I mean really back, not just remembering."

"Like how?"

"I see things that happened over there, and sometimes things that didn't." Andy waited for me to continue. "There are times when it seems like my mind isn't even part of my body."

Andy took his time lighting a cigarette. "I knew guys in the VA who had spells that came and went like that. Depended on what was happening in their lives to trigger them."

"It doesn't happen to you?"

"No." He toyed with the empty beer glass in his hands. "At least not since I came home."

"There was a guy in my platoon, a big dumb guy we called Ox." He smiled at the memory. "He was always telling us how he got it on with his old lady whenever he could, twice a day, three times; it got more frequent the longer Ox was in-country."

Andy paused to signal the bartender for another beer.

"Every time we went out on patrol he told me how he didn't care what got shot off, just so his credentials didn't take a hit. If his balls were gone, he made me promise not to save him."

Andy's hands pressed tightly around his empty glass.

"Then one day he took a piece of shrapnel in the belly. I got to him as soon as I could, and all I could find was this one tiny slit." He held up two fingers to show how small it was. "His whole body was perfect except for that one little buttonhole in his big old belly, but everything had just fucking stopped." Andy's eyes held the amazement they must have as he looked at Ox. "I did CPR, shot of Adrenalin to the heart, plasma. No dice. Greased. Blown away."

We listened to Joan Baez on the jukebox. "I was kneeling over him with shit flying all around us," Andy said suddenly, "telling him he didn't have to worry because his credentials were O.K. A couple of guys grabbed me and hauled me to cover or I wouldn't be sitting here."

He said nothing while the waiter took his empty glass and replaced it with a full one. Andy took a long drink.

"Dust-off chopper came in as soon as the landing pad was secured. Next thing I know my men are loading me in it along with Ox." He took another drink. "I kept trying to convince the fuckers I was just telling Ox his balls were alright, but they wouldn't hear it."

"But, Ox was dead."

"Yeah," he said with his short, humorless laugh. "I figured that out having to ride next to his body all the way to the hospital."

A group of interns and residents were engaged in a noisy game of darts on the other side of Bullwinkle's. My stomach was beginning to object to the alcohol I was dumping on it.

"What did they do to you at the hospital?" I asked when it looked as if Andy was not going to reveal anymore.

"A shrink gave me a few talks," he said with a shrug. "I was back in the field in less than a week."

"Why so fast?"

"Medics were getting blown away at a pretty good clip. They needed everyone they could get."

"And nothing like that ever happened again?"

"Nope. Not that it couldn't, I guess."

My head was hurting as much as my stomach. "I didn't have any spells while I was in Vietnam, only bad dreams after Dan was killed."

"The mind takes its own sweet time digesting all the crap we throw at it. And Nam was one huge piece of shit."

I thought of Peggy's cat when he asked if I would go with him to his apartment. "I should help look for Ginger in the morning," I said. "Lori's taking them out to search before school."

"I get up early."

"I really should go back to Lori's."

Andy got up. "I'll drop you off."

I had wanted to escape Peggy's tears so badly, I had no reluctance climbing onto Andy's motorcycle to come to Bullwinkle's. But when we were standing by his Harley, I had to say something. "Do you know the O.R. calls these donorcycles because that's …"

Andy held a hand up to stop me. "That's because they get their transplant organs from people like me who squash their brains on the pavement. The E.R. crew calls them donorcycles too." He got on the bike but did not start it. "I promise to drive slowly."

Everyone was asleep when he left me at Lori's. I slipped quietly past Reba's hospital bed and up the stairs. Peggy kept me awake tossing and talking in her sleep, calling for Ginger.

I finally got up at five a.m. and left the row house. I wandered the sidewalks and back alleys, calling for Ginger and stopping each time I heard a rustle of paper or the rattle of a garbage can.

Lights were coming on in the neighborhood when I started back to Lori's empty handed. I ducked to clear a low branch on the only evergreen tree in the area, the one the neighborhood referred to as the Christmas tree. I hit a low hanging branch and the dew on its needles trickled down the inside of my collar. I put a hand back to wipe it away and when I finished I found my fingers stained red. "What the...?" I looked up at the tree and there, just above my head, swung Ginger's lifeless body. Her throat slit completely open.

Reba let me in the house, after first peering out to see who was there. "Girl, you almost scared me to death tapping on the window. What're you doing prowling around in the middle of the night?"

I motioned for her to keep her voice down so she wouldn't wake the children. "I found Ginger," I whispered. Reba smiled widely. "It's not good news." I didn't know whether I should tell her with her bad heart.

"Say what you mean," she said as if speaking to a new intern.

"She was hanging in a tree down the block with her throat cut."

"Oh Lord." I made Reba go sit in her rocking chair, where I checked her pulse. "Peggy's going to die when she hears this."

"She doesn't need to know the details," I whispered. "We can bury Ginger before anyone is awake."

I started for the back door, where I had left Ginger's body in the cluttered back yard. "It was probably someone in the neighborhood who resents Lori living here."

"That gives them the right to kill a little girl's kitten?" Reba whispered indignantly as she followed behind in her flannel robe.

"What happened is my fault."

"It's nobody's fault but the people who did it, plain and simple." Reba stepped cautiously down the steps. "The children's been telling me how people yell honky at them on their way to school."

"Do you think we should wake Lori?" I asked amid the junk.

"Best we take care of it ourselves," Reba said after a moment of contemplation. "Maybe tell them Ginger got hit by a car."

The soil had not been turned in so many years it resisted the shovel I tried to sink into it. Reba stood in the early morning light holding the body wrapped in a bath towel.

"Break it up a little first," she suggested.

I chipped away at the surface, trying to be as quiet as possible. Once I got past the first couple of inches the earth began to yield.

I almost had the hole deep enough when the kitchen door opened and Lori stuck her head out. "What in God's name is going on?"

Reba turned so abruptly she dropped Ginger out of the towel. Lori let out a small cry before we could stop her. I grabbed the towel and threw it over Ginger, fearing the children were behind her. But the house remained blessedly silent while Reba filled Lori in.

We sat at the dining room table after the burial, drinking coffee and discussing what we would tell the children. "The truth is better coming from us than hearing it in the street or school," Reba said.

"If people can do that to a poor cat that never hurt anyone, who knows what else they might do?" Lori said as she got up to refill our cups. "I've got to get them out of here, but I've sent resumes to every state and not one job offer." Obstetricians had convinced hospitals not to hire midwives because of the malpractice risk, even though both groups had the same success rate with deliveries.

"I spend two years knocking myself out in midwifery school, making my children live in a ghetto," Lori said. "And what do I have to show for it? A piece of paper that won't even get me a job."

"Mom?" It was Peggy.

"I don't think I can tell her," Lori whispered in a sudden panic.

"Let me." Reba went to her rocking chair in the living room and put her arms out to Peggy. "Come here baby, Reba needs some sugar." Peggy sat on her lap, rocking with her head on Reba's shoulder. I thought she had fallen asleep when she suddenly sat straight up.

"Did Ginger come home?" she asked in her mother's direction. Lori stood with me just inside the door separating living and dining rooms.

"We have some very sad news for you," Reba began. "Pat found Ginger, but she was hurt real bad."

Lori went to her daughter but Peggy pushed her away. "Is Ginger going to be O.K.?" she demanded. "Where is she?"

"Ginger died," Lori said tenderly. "We buried her in a nice soft towel."

"Ginger can't die!" The yelling brought Billy and Brendan down the stairs. "Ginger's mine and she's not dead!"

Peggy was upstairs crying when I left. Lori and Reba were crying downstairs, and the boys were in the back yard inspecting the grave. I was so distressed about my role in the family tragedy I had stopped worrying about having another of the disquieting spells.

The day passed without incident, and I reluctantly returned to the row house in the afternoon to once more tell Peggy how sorry I was. I found Reba sitting in the living room dressed in a worn man's suit, shirt and tie, topped off with a hat pulled down over closely cropped hair. "We bought them at the Salvation Army," Billy told me proudly. "I think she looks cool."

"Reba's too tall and skinny to be a lady," Brendan decided as he scrutinized her new image. "She looks better being a man."

"I walked the children the few blocks home from school," Reba said in the voice of a woman once more in charge of her life. "I figure no one's gonna mess with a black man."

Lori agreed to let Reba escort the children to and from school until her graduation from midwifery school. Everyone settled into the routine except Peggy, who spent most of her time in her room.

"If I could just find a position in a nice small town." Lori was washing dishes with Reba and me while Billy and Brendan watched T.V. "I could sell the island house and buy us something to start over in."

"Why not just move back to that house?" I asked.

Lori and Reba groaned. "Move back to the Bastard Belt?"

"I don't even go back there to visit my mama's grave," Reba told me as she put dishes away in the high cupboards. "Fishback Islanders don't know slaves got freed."

Lori continued to have no luck finding a position, even though she made long distance calls to check out each of the few jobs advertised in a professional midwifery journal the moment it arrived. I continued on at Filmore Hospital, where Dr. Ware still rotated me through GYN surgery despite my request not to. But I avoided the two operating rooms now devoted entirely to abortions by trading assignments with other anesthetists. That meant doing longer and more complicated cases, but I had not had another of the episodes.

Peggy would no longer talk to me as she used to while we lay in our beds listening to night sounds in the street below. But when I was awake at two or three, after dreaming about Dan, I still found her presence comforting.

Children did not make the deep, despairing sighs of sleeping adults. Their sounds were soft and wistful, with little humming noises as if they were about to burst into song.

I had become more a part of Lori's extended family than I ever intended, and with it came an unexpected concern. Every time Lori telephoned a distant state I worried that she and her children would disappear from my life. And each time she was rejected, I felt guilty for the part of me which secretly rejoiced. Even though it remained unspoken, I suspected Reba did the same.

Lori, however, grew more desperate the closer she got to graduation. When there were only two days to go, she gathered all of us in the living room for a family meeting. Only Peggy was missing.

"I've finally landed a job," she announced. Reba and I applauded politely and Brendan cheered. Billy was waiting for more information.

"It's only temporary." Maybe that could explain Lori's less than enthusiastic demeanor. "Just for the summer, actually."

Reba sat in her male attire, her rocking chair giving off its small squeak. Even though she walked the children to school, she could not climb a flight of stairs without becoming short of breath.

"I tried everywhere," Lori said as if apologizing. "There's just nothing out there."

Reba was giving her a strange look. "Are you going to say what

I think you are?"

"I have a house there," Lori defended. "It doesn't make sense to move somewhere I don't have a job or a place to live when I have a perfectly good place that I already own."

Billy jumped from the battered sofa with a loud whoop. "We're going back to the island!"

That brought Peggy down the stairs just far enough to see what was going on without joining in. Billy was so excited he ran to embrace her, forgetting for the moment this was the sister he barely tolerated. "Mom's taking us back to Fishback Island!"

Brendan ran to hug Peggy also, thinking it the appropriate thing to do. "Are you really?" Peggy asked from where she stood.

"Just for the summer," Lori answered.

Her daughter bestowed upon the three adults below a smile that was truly beatific. It was the first any of us had seen since Ginger's death.

"You're going with us, aren't you?" Peggy asked when she came down to stand next to Reba's rocking chair.

"Uh-uh, not me," Reba said. "They hang worse than cats down there." Peggy's eyes widened. "Oh sweet Jesus, I'm sorry, baby." Reba pulled Peggy into her lap. "I never should have said that. That's not what happened to Ginger." Peggy leaned into Reba's neck.

"It wouldn't be so bad just for the summer," Lori said to Reba. "I can't leave you here all by yourself."

"If I go anywhere it'll be Chicago with my children." Reba continued rocking and smoothing Peggy's yellow hair.

"Chicago's a long way from your properties," Lori reminded. "Or are you planning to sell them to those white developers grabbing up everything else around here?"

Reba sat up so fast Peggy slid off her lap. "No honky developers are gettin' their hands on what I worked for all these years. If anyone makes money off those properties it's going to be me." Her voice was back to its full timbre.

I felt abandoned standing off to one side listening to my adopted family making plans to leave. I could not imagine living alone in an apartment again.

"How about you?" Lori asked as if reading my mind. "Are you planning to stay on at Filmore?"

"I've been giving some thought to working in a third world country again." The idea was totally impulsive.

"With your lousy back?" Lori said. "They would never take you."

Peggy addressed me like old times. "Why don't you come live with us on the island, Pat? Our house is big enough for you and Reba."

I didn't know a nine year old could make an adult feel so loved. "Thanks, Peggy, but I don't have a job to go to like your mom."

"That's easy enough to arrange," Lori said. "The hospital always needs extra help during the tourist season."

"Would I have to work for Earl Roy?" Billy flinched at the disapproval in my voice.

"He's hardly ever there," Lori said. "There's a male nurse anesthetist who's been running the anesthesia department for years. You'll love him."

She went to the telephone, dialed the only hospital on Fishback Island, and asked for personnel. "Most of the summer surgery cases are just beach trauma," she told me while she was on hold.

I was still hesitant, until I remembered the GYN surgical suite was planning to open a third abortion room because of demand. That would make it almost impossible to avoid giving anesthesia for them.

Lori looked to where Reba now dozed in her rocking chair. "If you go with us, it'll be a lot easier convincing her," she whispered to me. Peggy nodded her agreement.

"Yes, I'm here," Lori said into the phone. She told the personnel director why she was calling and handed me the phone. "Come on, it's only for the summer," she cajoled when I did not immediately take it.

CHAPTER FOURTEEN

The caravan left Baltimore one day before the start of Memorial weekend, 1974. Lori did not look back when we pulled away from the decrepit dwelling where she had lived, mothered and studied for two years. Peggy, sitting next to me in my Mustang, turned to take a final look up at her room, where curtains flapped out a window we forgot to close. Ginger's grave was visible only in her face.

Reba had agreed to return to Fishback Island at the eleventh hour, with the express understanding that she would move back to Baltimore and her properties as soon as she was strong enough to live alone. She sat in the front seat of Lori's weighted down station wagon with her man's hat pulled so low over her brow, and the collar of her suit jacket up so high, she looked as neckless as Big Ruby. Her precious rocking chair rode in the seat just behind her, and Brendan and Billy sat in the very rear watching the U-haul to make sure it did not pull loose from the station wagon's rusted bumper.

As we drove past Filmore Hospital, I looked to see if Dr. Ware's car was in the doctor's parking lot. He was the only reason I regretted leaving.

Andy had been nothing but encouraging. "It'll give me a place to stay when I come to the beach on breaks from school," he told me while he helped load the U-haul.

"Watch what you're doing there," Reba admonished when he accidentally knocked her rocking chair against the door frame of the station wagon. "That's the only thing in my life not worn out or pulled out from under me, my apartment, my health, even my job."

"Nobody's pulling anything out from under you," Lori said with an edge of impatience. She carried a stack of pillows and blankets she balanced like a circus clown. "You know you're not up to living alone yet, just like you know you can't go back to standing in an operating room all day."

Filmore Hospital had not seen fit to grant Reba the twenty-five year retirement pension she missed by just months. She received only a percentage, which was about equal to that of a ten year employee.

"Over twenty-four years I give them," she said as she finished supervising the loading of her rocker, "and they hand me a measly check that wouldn't keep a whore in G-strings."

The weather was clear, and the view from the bridge spanning the Chesapeake Bay spectacular. But when we came down on the Fishback Island side, I was again amazed by the flatness of the land.

Tidewaters from numerous inlets and rivers seeped over the farmland bordering them, and water from a recent nor'easter stood in fields and ditches. Pools the size of small lakes surrounded chicken houses, where mounds of drowned chicken lay steaming in the sun.

Trucks loaded with crates of squawking fowl on their way to slaughter whisked past us on the two lane highway, trailing a wake of feathers, dust and noise. I rolled up my car window to muffle the frantic squawking of the victims hunched in their cramped prisons. A few that managed to escape lay on the highway, their feathers a dirty grey and their red combs and yellow feet flattened into the asphalt.

Peggy told me the chickens went from hatchery to processing plant in only seven weeks using a system developed by Hen Fishback to accelerate their growth. By keeping the lights on in the houses around the clock, the chickens were tricked into believing it was always daytime. As a result they fed constantly, literally eating themselves to an early death.

I asked Lori about the sickening stench hanging in the humid air when we stopped for lunch. "Chicken smog," she said. "It's from all the feathers and dust emitted into the humid air."

"The guts from the processing plants stink the worst," Billy told me. "They dump them in the rivers."

"Yeah, and the water gets all pink when a boat goes by and stirs up the blood," Brendan added delightedly.

"Boys," Lori scolded when she saw me put down my chicken sandwich. "You're making Pat sick."

"How's Reba?" I asked. She sat in Lori's car eating her lunch, even though there were no reserved signs on the outdoor tables where we sat.

"Pretty quiet." Lori looked toward the car. "She must be roasting in that heavy suit."

"Maybe she'll give it up now that she's out of Baltimore."

"I think Reba looks nice," Peggy said. Her face had regained its youthful optimism, and Lori smiled lovingly at her.

The landscape became flatter and duller the further we traveled. White clapboard houses, rundown grey-shingled chicken houses and desolate beige marshes made the scene look like a huge unused coloring book. The only relief from the sameness was the mammoth roadside billboards for Seaport motels and restaurants on the beach. Or the ones advertising Fishback Poultry that urged motorists to visit Muskrat Marsh, the settlement just west of Seaport where we would be living. It was the home base of Hen Fishback's empire.

"Is the town named after those hairy animals that look like overgrown rats?" I asked. My brothers had trapped them in Minnesota and sold the pelts to furriers.

"Sure, muskrats," Peggy said as if the answer was obvious. "My dad goes to the muskrat feast every year at the firehall."

"They eat them?" .

Peggy looked hurt. "It's a real important party."

"Tell me about it," I said with as much enthusiasm as I could summon.

"They have it in the firehall and it's real secret," Peggy said dramatically. "The women cook the muskrats, but they don't get to stay when the party starts. Only the men can."

She was still describing the annual affair when Lori put on her right directional signal. I followed her off the highway near a billboard reading: MUSKRAT MARSH, MUSKRAT CAPITOL OF THE WORLD. And underneath, Population, 36,418. The Highway Holiness Church and cemetery were just visible in the distance.

Peggy leaned up against the dashboard. "There it is!" She pointed to a white clapboard house sitting in an untended lawn.

Lori already stood against her station wagon scrutinizing the structure and its peeling paint when I pulled up behind the U-Haul. A sagging front porch was covered with trash left behind by renters.

"It looks worse than I remembered," she said when I joined her. "Earl Roy thought it was fine for us, but he built his new woman a mansion in the swanky section of town."

It was the first time Brendan had been allowed out of the house to play since Ginger's death, and he ran wildly around the yard, stopping to turn occasional cartwheels or try standing on his hands. Peggy squinted at the house through bright afternoon sun.

"Let's paint it," she said.

"It could certainly use it," Lori agreed.

Brendan ran by with his arms held out at his sides, dipping and gliding as he pretended to be an airplane. "Paint it red!" he shouted and kept on running.

"I'm not living in a red house." Billy, recently turned thirteen, disagreed with any and everything his mother or siblings said. "Dad wouldn't like it if we painted it red."

It was the wrong thing to say to Lori. She looked around at the neighboring houses, all sided with white clapboard. "This neighborhood could use a little color."

Reba nodded toward faces pressed to windows as she came to stand by us. "Looks to me like you've already accomplished that."

CHAPTER FIFTEEN

Muskrat Marsh's hospital, located in the center of town, was constructed of red brick, the only building material the island appeared to allow besides grey shingles and white clapboard. CHRISTIAN HOSPITAL was etched above the main doors, and a portrait of its main benefactor hung in the lobby. I stopped to read a plaque beneath it: Henry Fishback, Mayor and Chicken King.

The likeness to the little man I anesthetized at Filmore Hospital was there, but the artist had omitted the strip of bald, red skin running down the middle of his feather white hair. And there was no wattle of skin at the neck.

"He doesn't look as much like a chicken in this as he does in person," I said while studying the portrait.

"Shhhh, don't say that here." Lori scanned the lobby to see if anyone might have heard. "They don't like anyone saying Hen looks like a chicken."

"Even if he does?"

We started toward a stairwell off to one side of the lobby, but someone called to Lori before she could open the door. "Oh no, it's her." She indicated a woman waving to her from the information desk. "My ex-mother-in-law."

"Why Lori, y'all weren't goin' ta walk right on past without as much as a hello?" the woman asked in a pouting manner. She wore a lavender silk dress under her pink volunteer smock and a heavy choker of pearls. Her hair was a series of lifeless henna sprouts scattered sparsely over pink scalp, like a wheat crop devastated by drought.

"I didn't see you, Lovey." Lori introduced me to the woman. "It's Pat's first day; I'm showing her around."

Lovey Donlin tried to smile at me, but her facial muscles were so restricted the effort succeeded only in drawing her upper lip back into a snarl. "So you're goin' ta be one of my Earl Roy's little nurses?" she said. She pronounced Roy as if it had two syllables, Ro-eee.

"I'm an anesthetist," I said. And I don't belong to your son, I added silently.

"We need to get to surgery." Lori was edging away from the desk. "Pat's already late."

"But y'all didn't tell me when I'm goin' ta see my grandbabies," Lovey said with her childish pout. The action made her tightened skin pull her carefully penciled eyebrows almost off her face.

"As soon as we're settled."

"Where did she get her facelifts?" I asked when we were in the stairwell. "Her skin's been stretched so tight she has no facial movement left."

"Her husband was a plastic surgeon," Lori said as I followed her down the stairs. "He died a couple of years ago."

"Too bad he didn't live long enough to give her a hair transplant."

Lori giggled like a naughty school girl. "You'll get both of us in trouble if you keep making cracks like that."

We parted at a set of wide automatic doors. Once inside I followed the sound of chattering women to a locker room. The surgery nurses, all in various stages of undress, fell silent the moment I entered. They remained so even when I introduced myself.

"Could you tell me where I could find some scrub pants and a top?" I asked. Operating rooms were kept cool so staff could work under hot lights. But Fishback's surgery suite was like a meat locker.

"Nurses here don't wear pants," one of the women said.

"Pants is for men," another added.

The latter indicated a pile of scrub dresses on a shelf, which I dug through looking for one my size. They were all large or extra large, the same as the women in the room, but I managed to fold the excess fabric back and forth on itself and secure it at my waist with a belt sewn into the dress. When I asked the location of the anesthesia office, I was pointed in the direction of a room at the opposite end of the small O.R. suite. Conversation in the locker room resumed the moment I left.

The nurse anesthetist I found sitting in the anesthesia office looked nothing like the islanders, and appeared genuinely happy to see me. "Hi, Cal Roberts," he said as he stood to shake hands. "But everyone calls me Skipper."

He told me Memorial weekend was when the hospital got crazy,

94

and that it didn't settle down until after Labor Day. "You're just in time for opening season."

Skipper was older than me, perhaps in his fifties by his graying hair, and had the perennial tan of one who spends a good deal of time on the water. I associated his nickname with the sailor's knots he tied in the drawstring of his scrub pants while we talked.

Another anesthetist came into the room and Skipper introduced her as Getta Mae Fishback. She looked like the nurses in the locker room. "Well, I reckin," she said after acknowledging Skipper's introduction. "Best git Docter Donlin's room set up."

"Is she related to Henry Fishback?" I asked when she pushed a cart with drugs and equipment out of the room.

"Everyone on Fishback Island is related in some way," Skipper replied. "Until they built the bridge across the bay back in the fifties they were so isolated they had nobody to marry but one another."

He showed me to a cart I could use for my cases. I began checking the items on it while he did the same with a cart displaying a bumper sticker which read, OLD ANESTHETISTS NEVER DIE, THEY JUST RUN OUT OF GAS.

"Getta Mae likes to pamper Earl Roy," he said while we worked. "I don't believe in waiting on anesthesiologists."

Lori was right. I already liked my new colleague.

The surgery suite consisted of four operating rooms, rather than the twenty-seven at Filmore. The O.R. nurses setting up cases in the various rooms Skipper took me to were only slightly more friendly to him than they were me.

"Unless you were born on the island, you're always considered an outsider," he told me as we concluded our tour. "It's a price I'm willing to pay to have a boat and a house right on the water."

Back in the anesthesia office Skipper informed me I would be on call with him the entire holiday weekend. "I figured it would be a good time to break you into the beach trauma we get from Seaport."

Other than a few surfboard injuries I had encountered while working in California during my past years of wandering, I had no idea what such a designation entailed. "You'll see," Skipper answered rather ominously when I inquired.

The rain began early Friday morning. Lori and Reba were stuck in a dirty house filled with boxes and three children complaining about not being able to go to the beach. And I was stuck at the hospital caring for an endless stream of victims from rain-drenched Seaport: fractured noses, hands and legs, lacerated tendons from fists going through windows, and perforated ulcers from too much alcohol.

"They'll keep coming as long as it keeps raining," Skipper predicted as we prepared for our fifth case of the day. "The GDTs get ticked off because they've laid out two or three hundred bucks rent for a place at the beach, then have to spend the whole time listening to their kids whine. Out comes the booze and they start falling down stairs, getting into fights and generally abusing themselves and anyone else who gets in their way."

"What are GDTs?"

"Goddamned tourists," Skipper said with amused eyes above his surgical mask. "The locals gave them the name, but they abbreviate it so it doesn't sound like they're swearing."

He told me the island's population swelled dramatically when the tourist season began each spring, but vacationers provided only part of the summer influx. Migrant workers also flocked to the island to work on huge produce farms where melons, strawberries and cucumbers thrived on its sandy soil. They were called stoopers because of the nature of their work.

An emergency laparotomy on one such worker was to follow the fracture case we were presently doing, and the surgeon came into the operating room to ask Skipper how soon he could start. "I'm sure it's a hot appendix," the physician said. "Shouldn't take more than an hour."

"What's the white count?" Skipper asked.

"Well, it was normal early this mornin'. Although it's surely elevated by now," the island surgeon quickly added. "I'm fixin' ta have the lab draw another blood right soon."

"Get me an elevated white count and I'm ready to go when we finish here," Skipper told him. The physician left without comment, let alone one of the temper tantrums I had become accustomed to at Filmore if anyone dared to question the validity of a case.

The patient must have had a normal white count, since he was not brought to the O.R., but several others were. "We're in for it now," Skipper said of the accident victim we were currently working on. "They've taken to their cars."

The rained-out vacationers were cruising the streets of Seaport looking for entertainment but finding nothing but traffic jams of people doing the same. The result was a series of wrecks as they took out their frustration by pressing accelerators to the floor. When two days passed with little sleep, I began calling them GDTs too.

"Go get some rest," Skipper told me. It was two a.m. on Sunday and we were still working.

"But you must be tired, too." The present case was a drunk who cut the tendons in his right wrist when he put it through the plate glass window of a seafood restaurant where he and several dozen others were trying to get seated.

"I'll finish up this one," Skipper said. "You get whatever comes in next."

The hospital provided no call room so I went to the nurses' locker room and curled up on its orange plastic sofa. After turning this way and that, trying to get comfortable on the cold surface, I went to the recovery room and got blankets out of the warmer. They were made of white flannel and kept in a large, heated cupboard to be put over shivering patients brought out of frigid operating rooms.

I continued to toss and turn on the sofa, unable to fall asleep despite the blankets. My back was killing me and the room reeked of sweaty shoes in lockers with just enough ventilation to let out the stink. In desperation, I pulled the surgical mask still dangling around my neck up over my mouth and nose.

Four hours later I woke and pulled myself out of the valley I had created in the pliable sofa. I shuffled into the surgery corridor, holding my back, and found the O.R.s deserted. Skipper was sleeping in the anesthesia office on a love seat so short his feet dangled over the arm on one end and his neck leaned at a right angle against the other.

I got a pillow from the recovery room and attempted to ease it under his head. He jumped the moment I touched him.

"I was afraid you'd get a stiff neck," I apologized.

"Oh hell, I've had a stiff neck for the last twenty years." He sat up and rubbed his reddened eyes. "What time is it?"

"Seven a.m. Monday, if you've lost track of the days."

"Good, the drunks should let up now." He got up to splash cold water in his face at the sink used for washing dirty anesthesia equipment. "Now we'll just have the pile-ups when they start racing one another back to Baltimore and Washington." The work had been hectic, but it was the first time I had gone through a Friday and Saturday night of call without one gunshot wound or stabbing.

"Have you lived here long?" I asked while Skipper dried his face with paper towels.

"Too long," he said with a yawn. "My wife and I came down for a vacation one summer and just never left."

He sank back down to the loveseat and began tying sailor's knots in the drawstring of his wrinkled scrub pants. There were white crow's feet at the corners of his eyes where the sun had not turned the skin as brown as the rest of him.

"It was nice when we first came here," he said. "I did all the anesthesia and still had plenty of time to fish. The beach was sand dunes and a few cottages, not those godawful condominiums they're throwing up all over."

I was drawing Sodium Pentothal into syringes and setting up equipment for any kind of emergency that might come in.

Skipper stood and stretched. "I'd like to get in a few hours of fishing before the chase to the mainland starts. Do you think you can handle things for awhile?"

I looked around the office, wondering if I could find everything I might need. "Can I call Doctor Donlin if I need to?"

"There's something you ought to know right up front. Earl Roy doesn't spend much time around here, especially at night or on weekends." It was stated as fact, not complaint. "I give him his freedom to hang out in the bars in Seaport, or wherever he's currently womanizing, and he gives me the freedom to run things the way I like."

Skipper went on to tell me Earl Roy had come to Fishback Hospital following an anesthesia residency at Massachusetts General Hospital in Boston. "I already had the department established and we agreed to just keep it my way." He laughed good naturedly. "Except I do most of the cases and he gets most of the money."

"Sounds like every job I've had so far." I looked over the shelves of drugs and equipment, which were all marked with neat labels. "I guess I can find my way around."

"Just don't kill anybody." He winked at me and left.

CHAPTER SIXTEEN

At the conclusion of the marathon weekend I was awarded two days off. "Who wants to go to the beach?" I asked at breakfast. The rain had stopped just as the disgruntled tourists were heading home.

"Me! Me!" Peggy and Brendan shouted in unison. They raced out of the kitchen with no further thought of breakfast.

Billy remained seated, looking as unhappy as he hoped he was making his mother. "I'm goin' on over ta dad's," he said. "Thur ain't neither nor thang ta do 'round here."

"Stop talking like an islander," Lori said sharply.

"I am an ahlunder," Billy retorted. "Bein' born here makes me one." The implication was clear that his mother did not enjoy equal status. He got up and walked heavily across the kitchen. "See y'all later," he said, banging out the back door. Lori started after him.

"He's talking that way just to make you mad," Reba said.

"He's succeeding." Lori returned to the table and sat ripping at a strip of yellowed wallpaper that had come loose from where it bordered a window, the stress evident in her face. "Billy wanted to spend the weekend with his father. But as usual, Earl Roy didn't have any time for him. Now he goes running back first thing this morning."

"That suits me fine," Reba said. "No sense him sittin' around here sulking all day." She was still in her robe and looked as if she could use a break from the children.

"We all got off to a bad start," I said as I got up to pour more coffee. "I'll take the little ones to the beach, you start your new job, Lori, and Reba can have a good rest."

Lori seemed not to hear. "The younger children took the divorce

99

in stride," she said as she continued to peel at the wallpaper. "But Billy has always resented me for leaving his father."

"He was older," Reba said. "And besides, he's a teenager."

"What does that have to do with it?" Lori asked irritably.

"God made toddlers cute so you won't kill them when they're runnin' wild, and teenagers ornery so you're glad to get rid of 'em when it comes time to leave the nest. Just the law of nature."

"More like the law of the jungle if you ask me." Lori yanked the strip of brittle paper free, exposing an even more yellowed pattern beneath. "Three months," she said. "Then I'm off this island and away from Earl Roy for good." She took a final sip of coffee and picked up her medical bag. "I need to get to work."

"Doctor Donlin didn't want Billy around him this weekend 'cause he's having woman troubles," Reba said. Lori stopped at the door. "He's got himself a new girlfriend the missus just found out about."

"Who told you that?"

"Billy."

"But he didn't tell me." Lori sounded betrayed.

"You were upstairs unpacking boxes when he came in and blurted it out. I didn't see any sense making a big fuss over it." Reba turned her attention to the window next to the table to watch a neighbor setting out strawberry plants in her back yard. "We should plant us a garden," she said. "Give me somethin' to do."

Lori lingered in the middle of the kitchen. "I just don't want Billy to end up hating his father. And that's exactly what will happen if he finds out what Earl Roy is really like."

"You can't do anything about that," Reba said. "He has to see it with his own eyes."

Brendan and Peggy returned in bathing suits, their arms filled with beach toys. "Where did you find all that?" their mother asked.

"In the garage," Peggy answered. "Dad saved it for us."

"How nice of him. He always was better at looking after objects than people." Peggy's face sagged and Lori was immediately contrite. "It truly was nice of dad," she said as she put down her medical bag to hug her daughter, then Brendan. She dug in her purse and gave each of them two dollars to spend at the beach. "You have a good time and mind Pat. No going in the water unless she's watching."

The children looked wide-eyed at the fortune Lori had handed them. "I'm getting a giant box of caramel corn," Peggy said.

Lori smiled and started again for the door, but Reba called after her. "Don't forget, we're going to my mama's grave sometime soon."

"My first day off," Lori promised.

I wondered where Reba's mother was buried in the cemetery. It could be right around the spot where I had enjoyed a picnic.

"Use plenty of lotion so you don't burn," Reba cautioned.

It was the first time I noticed she used little of the dialect so evident in the speech of others born and raised on the island. I wondered if it was due to the many years she had been away, or a desire to rid herself of anything reminding her of the island.

I felt a small twinge of guilt driving away from the house and its heaps of boxes. The old dwelling, smelling of dust and renters when we arrived, now also smelled of mildew from three days of rain.

We were headed toward the highway leading to Seaport when Billy came riding his bicycle wildly across lawns calling for us to stop.

"I want to go with you," he said breathlessly. "Will you wait til I take my bike home and get my suit?"

"Good grief, you scared me half to death," I said.

"I bet Dad's new wife chased him away again," Peggy said when Billy was gone. "She doesn't like him."

"She doesn't like all of us," Brendan said from the rear seat.

Billy began complaining the moment he got in the car. "What's all this junk?" he groused, pushing a plastic inner tube aside.

"Beach stuff," Brendan said.

"You mean beach toys," Billy chided. "You're eight years old now, not a baby." He punched his younger brother in the arm.

Brendan punched him back. "You're just mad 'cause you couldn't stay at Dad's."

"Boys," I said, looking in the rear view mirror.

"I could have stayed at Dad's if I wanted to," Billy contended. "But he had to go to work, and Adella Dawn had shopping to do."

"Adella Dawn?" I repeated. "That's an unusual name."

"All the people here have two names," Peggy told me.

"People everywhere have two names, but Dad says they're too dumb to use them," Billy said from the rear. "From now on I want everyone to call me William James, the way Dad does." Brendan laughed and Billy gave him an elbow.

"I wish my name was Earl Roy," Billy said after a minute. He pronounced it Ro-ee, the same as Earl Roy's mother.

"I met your grandmother," I said.

"Mom-mom gives us lots of presents at Christmas," Peggy said.

"Pop-pop died," Brendan informed solemnly. "Mom-mom says it killed him when we moved to Baltimore."

"Oh, I'm sure that's not true."

"It is so," Billy asserted. "He died right afterwards."

We were passing the Highway Holiness Church and its adjoining cemetery. The new church now had a roof. I looked toward the spot where I sat with Hope and Allison. There was no one there.

"Why do the graves have those big slabs over them?" I asked.

"Floaters," Billy said. "There's water not far down, and the coffins would float to the surface if they weren't weighted down."

"Yeah, and skeletons would jump out," Brendan chortled.

Further along the highway was another burial plot, but this one had a split rail fence and lush green grass. A marble headstone in the shape of a horse's head stood in the center of the enclosure.

"Horse graves," Peggy said when she saw me looking.

"They have cemeteries for horses?" It was much better kept than the one for humans.

"They're special horses," Billy said in the manner of a teenager burdened with an ignorant adult. "Lots of people on the island have expensive jumpers." There was a horse farm just up the road with green pastures bordered by a white fence.

"Mom-mom says never touch the stamps on letters you get in the mail," Brendan said incongruously.

I looked at him in the rear view mirror. "Why?"

"Because you can get germs," Peggy said before her younger brother could answer. "Mom-mom says you never know who's been licking on them to make them stick."

"Maybe even culurd people," Brendan added.

There appeared to be even more condos in Seaport than on my last visit, all competing for a strip of beach that was being steadily eroded by waves washing around huge pilings driven into the sand to support the encroaching development. It looked as if one good hurricane could knock down the wall of buildings like dominos.

It was my wish to spend the day on the section of beach near the cottage I had stayed in. But I was outvoted by the children, who wanted to be right in the middle of the boardwalk honky tonk.

"Who wants to bet I can't hit every duck?" Billy said as he squinted down the sight of a rifle at a shooting gallery.

"I'll bet you don't hit one," Brendan challenged.

"Hah!" Billy yelled when he hit the first duck dead center, then another and another. "Dad taught me how to shoot when I was little."

But Billy had hit more than the targets. The gun fire made me feel as if I were going to be abandoned by my legs, or my mind.

"Why don't we get some sun," I suggested. There were other customers on both sides, and I startled each time they pulled the triggers of their guns.

"I still have three more quarters," Billy said.

"O.K. You finish while we find a good place on the beach."

"You're cruising with Jesus on WGOD," the radio announcer said. I turned down the volume so it wouldn't wake the children, who had fallen asleep the moment we left Seaport. "Remember, you've not got but one life to live and it passes with the tides," a Reverend Taylor said. "Best start preparin' now ta meet the Lord Jesus Christ."

A nasal chorus sang JESUS MAKE US CLEAN. "And what better way ta make us clean than by joining together to build a temple to His greatness?" Reverend Taylor said when the singers finished. "Our fund raisin' is way behind, my friends, and the Lord is not happy about it." He paused a moment to let the reprimand find its mark.

"This is the chance of a lifetime. Buy a brick for Jesus, buy two, three, four, even ten! We etch your name on each and everone of 'em before they go into the holy temple growing toward the sky." The preacher sucked in a quick supply of air. "Watch your name goin' higher and higher, until the Lord God Almighty Hisself can reach right out from heaven and touch it!"

I turned the dial and found nothing but static until I reached the opposite end of the panel, where an announcer was giving the times for high and low tides. "Rat Radio's latest in fishin' and duck huntin' will be right along following this word from Fishback Poultry," the announcer said when he finished with the tides.

Hen Fishback did the commercial for the fattest chickens this side of the Mississippi. "Our competitors like ta claim their chickins are fresh," Hen said in his high-pitched voice. "But I ask you folks, what's fresh about chickins that's been kept cooped up for months on end, years for all we know, before goin' ta slaughter? Why if the truth be known, they probably died a' old age." Hen cackled.

"Now when Fishback Poultry says fresh, it means fresh," Hen continued. "Our chickins go from biddies ta slaughter in jest seven short weeks. They're on your table before they even have time to lose their innocence." Another cackle. "And now I turn y'all over ta that lucky angler and duck hunter hisself, Windy Duckman." A duck call sounded in the background.

"Good evenin' folks, this is Windy H. Duckman with the fishin' story of the day." I wondered if his name was real or an advertising gimmick. "The annual Blue Fish contest finally got underway this morning, an' what a day it turned out ta be." He spoke with the passion of a poet reading his finest work. "The sun was there in bountiful abundance to shine on happy anglers pullin' in Blues as if there was no ta-mar-ah. And who do you thank pulled in the biggest?" There was a pause during which I swore I heard someone passing gas, followed by muffled laughter. "Why none other than our own Hen Fishback." Applause.

"Yessiree, Hen's talents don't lay only in raisin' the finest chickins this side a' the Mississippi, and probably the other side too. Which brings me to the next topic of the show, Hen's annual chickin plucking contest jest three weeks away."

"It's not too late to get your entry in for Miss Spring Chickin; the young lady need be only fifteen or older. Not too much older, though. This is a spring chickin contest, not your layin' hen kind."

Windy paused to toot his duck call. His studio crew added whistles and catcalls.

"Get her name in and be sure to have her get herself a nice little bikini, emphasis on little." There were more whoops and whistles. "The winner gets an all expenses paid vacation ta New York City, compliments a' Hen Fishback." Windy's emphasis was on new, an island peculiarity that seemed to be universal. "Hen will personally escort the lucky young lady ta New York, as he does ever year. Though I don't know who's luckier, the winner of the contest or Hen gettin' to go with her ta New York. Ha, ha, ha. You listenin', Hen?"

Reba fussed over the children and admonished me for letting them get sunburned. Rather than spending the day resting, she had scrubbed much of the mildew out of the first floor.

I got up early the next morning to tackle the remainder of the house. The curtains were in the washing machine when Reba came into the kitchen for breakfast.

"I don't know if they'll hold up through a washing," she said when she saw what I was doing. "They looked pretty sun rotted to me."

I assured her I had washed curtains many times before, but I soon found I had underestimated the island's intense sun. The curtains came out of the machine in shreds.

"Now those nosey neighbors can look in all they want," Reba said as she examined the tattered remains. "I don't see how to mend them."

I offered to buy new ones. "It can be my contribution to the household."

Reba had to be talked into going with me to pick them out, while Peggy and Brendan piled into my car before even being asked. Reba, still wearing her men's attire, brought faces to the windows of neighboring houses.

"Can we buy pink curtains for our room?" Peggy asked. We were sharing an upstairs room the same as we had in Baltimore. "Pink is my favorite color."

"It's fine with me." I was still trying to make up for Ginger.

"I want Spiderman ones," Brendan said. His sunburned face was shiny beneath his blond bangs.

"I don't know if Billy would go for Spiderman," Reba said.

"But he wants ducks on everything," Brendan lamented. "And he's not here to pick, so I should get to." Billy had left for his father's house before even eating breakfast.

Reba stayed in the background while I talked Brendan into blue curtains with matching spreads for his and Billy's room, along with a plastic spiderman to set on his dresser. Peggy fell in love with filmy white curtains covered with tiny pink flowers, which she matched with brilliant pink bedspreads.

We found white Cape Cods for the kitchen, and yellow sheers to brighten the dark bedroom Reba occupied on the first floor so she wouldn't have to climb stairs. Lori's bedroom and the other rooms would have plain off-white drapes that would hopefully freshen some of the drabness of the old house.

When we finished we wandered through the cavernous shopping mall, Reba staying a few steps behind even though I stopped often to allow her to catch up. Slippery French fries were mashed into the floor, and food wrappers and popcorn were dropped everywhere. Scores of stands sold fried apple fritters, fried chicken and fried okra, all of which were first dipped in a heavy batter.

"What's that weird smell?" I asked as we neared the mall's central court. It mingled with the greasy smell of food to produce a heavy, pungent odor.

"Biddies!" Brendan shouted and sprinted ahead of us.

"They show all the different baby chicks each spring," Peggy informed me. She clutched her flowered curtains to her breast, ignoring her younger brother's pleas for her to hurry. But when an assortment of wire pens came into view, Peggy tossed the curtains to me and ran off behind Brendan.

When Reba and I caught up, the two were hanging over a wire fence watching yellow balls of fuzz darting about. The pen was divided into separate sections with a sign over each telling what breed it contained. Troughs of feed and water sat in layers of shredded newspaper fouled with droppings.

"It's hard to believe they'll be full grown in only seven weeks," I said as I observed the small chicks. Reba stood back from the pens, appearing not to be interested.

"Jew chickins don't go to processin' in seven weeks," a woman standing next to me said. "They havta put more fat on for them folks in New York City."

"Jew chickens?"

The woman pointed to a pen that had a sign over it with only a J. "They can't write it out no more," she told me. "Someone pitched a fit up ta Baltmur. Probably a GDT."

"But why do you call them Jew chickens?"

"Hen sells 'em ta the Jews up there. They like 'em nice and fat so's they can use the drippin's for other cooking."

"I'm surprised he would have a special processing plant for Kosher chickens."

The woman eyed me narrowly. "You from New York?" I shook my head no. "They aren't for them old timey Jews," she said. "They're for the ones who don't care about all that clean stuff."

"Well, I reckin," a woman on the other side of me said as she pushed her considerable bulk away from the fence. "I got chickins goin' out tanaght and biddies comin' in first thang the mornin'. No time ta stand here talking."

"Them biddies is troublesome," the woman who had told me about the Jew chickens said. "Oncet you get 'em you're stuck to 'em."

"Lor-dee, yes," the second woman empathized. "And we got worter half a leg deep 'round all the houses." She held a hand to the height the water reached on her voluminous legs.

"You lose 'em any way you try," the first woman said. "We got neighbors hired a catcher kilt near three hunert."

"Three hunert chickins!" The woman spoke so loudly she attracted the attention of several others around the pen. "Land A'mighty, how'd he find a way ta do that?"

The story teller positioned herself against a pole supporting the pens to address her audience. "He hired a head catcher who went out an' gathered up a bunch more catchers," she began. "They weren't near done catchin' and cratin' when they got to fussin' over how much they was ta earn. The owner told the head catcher ta break it up."

She paused to let her eyes travel over her audience, drawing

106

them in. "Damned if that fool nigger didn't shoot off a gun right there in the house. Scart them chickins so bad they piled up faster'n anyone could get to 'em. Three hunert suffocated, jest like that." She snapped her sausage fingers to demonstrate how little time the catastrophe had taken.

"And what about the nigger that shot the gun?" someone in the crowd asked. "I hope he got what he had comin'."

"He was gone before the owner knew ta look after him," the woman said sadly. "And he carried the rest a' the culurds with 'im." The listeners clucked their tongues. "There worn't no one ta lay into, jest dead chickins pi-ilt near to the ceiling," the woman concluded.

The story over, the people began to disperse. I turned and saw Reba with her head bowed and her body shaking. "I'll get the car," I said worriedly.

"I don't need the car," she said with some difficulty. Only when I was next to her did I realize she was shaking from suppressed laughter. "I wish I'da been there to see the look on the face of that owner," she said quietly as we left the mall. "Three hunert dead chickins an' not one culurd ta beat for it."

On the way to the car she told me how blacks were hired to catch and crate chickens for slaughter because Hen Fishback thought they were better able to sneak up on the unsuspecting fowl in houses darkened for the event.

"Does he give them a piece of watermelon if they remember not to smile?" I asked as we crossed the parking lot. Reba was walking alongside me, as she had not done in the mall.

"Well, would ya look at that?" a passing man said to his wife. "Near arm in arm with a culurd man right out in the light a' day." Brendon thought it funny, but Peggy hurried ahead to the car.

CHAPTER SEVENTEEN

Working with surgeons who could do cases in a fraction of the time it took inexperienced interns and residents was a welcomed change. Having to do obstetrical anesthesia was not.

"Don't bother calling Earl Roy even for complicated deliveries or C/sections," Skipper said before my first solo weekend of call. "He has his wife tell you he isn't home, which is probably true."

At quarter past ten on Sunday night I was summoned to the O.B. department for a patient in active labor. I hurried to the hospital, expecting a quick delivery. But when I entered the labor and delivery suite, I found a child screaming in pain while her mother and grandmother tried to comfort her.

"How old is she?" I asked Mrs. Critchfield, the nurse on duty.

"Thirteen." The nurse, well into her fifties or early sixties, sat at a desk outside the labor rooms knitting a fluorescent orange sweater. "Culurds start ta messin' early," she said as she paused to count stitches. "I hadn't even fell off the roof by the time I was her age." My expression must have conveyed my bewilderment. "Started menstratin'," the nurse translated.

We could see into the occupied labor room. "See those two in there with 'er?" Mrs. Critchfield said, pointing a knitting needle. "I remember when the patient herself was delivered to the mama there holdin' her hand. The mom-mom, soon to be great mom-mom, was holding the mama's hand." She scratched her head with the needle before returning it to her sweater. "Land, it's tahm I retire when I start deliverin' fourth generation babies. An' everone of 'em on welfare."

"Where's the doctor?" I asked later when the patient's screams were coming closer together.

"She's not near ready to call 'im yet." Mrs. Critchfield held up the sweater to check her progress. "I might could have this finished by the time she squeezes that baby out." She smiled and dropped the sweater back into her lap. "I promised my husbin' a good warm sweater for duck hunten' this fall. But honey hush, if I didn't have me a time findin' the right orange so's some GDT don't shoot him dead."

"Could you check to see how far she's dilated?" I asked.

The nurse stabbed her needles into her ball of yarn and went dutifully into the labor room. "Y'all will havta leave now," she told the mother and grandmother as I followed. "Visitors aren't supposed ta be in here; I only let you 'cause there's no one else in labor."

The young patient grabbed at her mother's arm and begged her not to leave. With the exception of her distended abdomen, she was no larger than Peggy, sleeping peacefully in our shared room dreaming little girl dreams instead of going through the agony of childbirth.

"Can't I jest sit with her?" the mother asked.

"Y'all shoulda' been sittin' with her nine months ago," Mrs. Critchfield said, and waved her and the grandmother out of the room.

The child's cries changed to shrieks as her uterus contracted into a taut balloon which left her frail arms and legs sticking out from under her bloated belly like a woodtick filled to capacity. Strands of loose hair were matted to her perspiring face and her lips were cracked and bleeding.

Mrs. Critchfield slipped a gloved hand into the girl's vagina as soon as the contraction was over. "She's right small in here," she said as she examined the cervix and felt for the baby's head. "Goin' ta have her a time pushing this youngin' out." The child's abdomen tightened in another contraction and she screamed even louder than before. The nurse retracted her hand and pulled off the bloodied glove. "No sense layin' here yellin' like a mashed cat," she told the girl. "Won't bring that baby no sooner."

I had taken the child's hand during the last contraction, and her fingernails were embedded in my flesh. When I managed to pull myself free, I went out to the desk where the nurse had returned to her knitting. "What is she?" I asked.

"Fahv, maybe six centimeters. Long way ta go."

"Her contractions are pretty strong. Do you think we could give her something for pain?"

"Docter Arst won't give her nothin' till she's raght ready." Mrs. Critchfield continued knitting. "Slows 'em down too much."

The child let out another air raid siren shriek. "I'll get her mother," I offered.

"This ain't Baltmur," Mrs. Critchfield began. But her expression softened as she looked to where the patient now lay weeping like a little girl who had fallen off her bicycle. "I guess it can't hurt ta let them sit with her," she conceded.

After summoning the mother and grandmother, I went into the delivery room we would be using to see that the anesthesia machine was functioning properly and had full tanks of oxygen and nitrous oxide. I also set up emergency equipment I might need for the baby or mother.

When I returned to the labor area, I found the patient trying to climb over the side rails while her mother and grandmother fought to keep her in bed.

"We have to give her something," I said to Mrs. Critchfield.

"Docter Arst don't give nothing till they're ready ta pop," she said emphatically. "She's welfare."

"You mean only private patients get pain medication?"

Mrs. Critchfield did not appreciate my inference. "Call him yerself," she said. "I don't make the rules." She handed me a Rolodex with physician phone numbers.

"Docter Arst's residence," a woman answered sweetly. There was laughter and music in the background.

"Doctor Arst please," I said. "Delivery room calling." The receiver banged onto a hard surface.

"Docter Arst," a man barked into the phone after several minutes. "What the hell's the problem?" I explained my reason for calling as briefly as possible. "No she can't have anything for pain! It'll slow her down!" The receiver was slammed down so hard even Mrs. Critchfield heard it.

"Let me go home! Let me go home!" The patient was trying to climb over the rails again, as if escaping the hospital would make what was happening go away.

Ignoring Skipper's advice, I dialed Earl Roy Donlin's number. "He's out," his wife told me.

"Could you tell me where?"

"The hospital." She took a long drag on a cigarette and forced the smoke out of her lungs so angrily I could almost smell it. "Least ways that's where he told me he was goin' five hours ago."

"I'll have him paged," I said when I could come up with a reply. "I'm sure he's around here somewhere."

Mrs. Critchfield was enjoying my dilemma. "Looks like you got yerself in the middle of a little somethin'," she said when I hung up.

After three more vaginal exams, and much screaming, she pronounced the patient ready to be moved to the delivery room. The child was so exhausted we had to lift her over to the table.

The situation was beginning to make me so nervous I drew a blood sample so the lab could prepare in case I needed to transfuse her. I also started an I.V. with the large needle I used to draw the blood sample to be ready for anything, with the exception of my mind deserting me. I briefly considered calling Skipper but vetoed the idea; this was my first weekend on O.B. call and I wanted to prove I could handle it, not only to Skipper but to myself. I wished it wasn't Lori's weekend off for welfare patients.

Mrs. Critchfield prepared the delivery room with practiced ease, flipping open sterile packs, splashing antiseptic solution over the patient's perineum, and readying a bassinet for the baby, all within minutes. "She's raght ready," she said from the foot of the table as the patient continued to grunt and push.

I went to take a look and saw the head about to rip its way through a very small opening. "Where's the doctor?" I demanded.

"He'll be here," Mrs. Critchfield answered confidently.

The elderly doctor hurried into the room still tying the drawstring on his scrub pants. "You sure know how ta time 'em," he told Mrs. Critchfield after a quick glance at the patient's bulging perineum. He did not bother to scrub before donning a sterile gown and gloves.

"Could you listen to the heart tones?" I asked the nurse.

"This baby's gonna be out here in a second where you can check 'em yourself," the doctor said as he sat down on a stool at the foot of the table. "Put her ta sleep."

Putting a patient under general anesthesia for delivery in the seventies was as archaic as not allowing family to be part of the birthing process. But I doubted Dr. Arst even knew how to put in local anesthesia.

"I need to know the heart tones before I put her down." I was giving the patient oxygen to get as much as possible across the placenta and into the baby while the umbilical cord was still intact.

"She's tearin' from stem ta stern down here an' the baby's hung up!" the physician yelled. "Put her ta sleep so I can get it out!"

I turned on an anesthetic gas but the child choked and coughed, making the situation at the other end of the table even more perilous. "Goddamn it all!" Dr. Arst screamed. "She's gonna spit this baby clean acrost the room if you don't cut that out!"

I adjusted the settings on my machine to give the young girl a dose lower than ordinary for delivery. "I'm sorry," I said. "I've never given pediatric anesthesia in the delivery room before."

I was glad the patient was unconscious when I heard a snap that sounded like a dry twig breaking. "Damn it to hell," Dr. Arst yelled at no one in particular. "Collar bone jest broke."

He was struggling so hard to deliver the baby he was pulling the patient nearly off the end of the table. A few more seconds passed before a limp blue infant slithered into the world. Dr. Arst clamped the cord and handed the infant to Mrs. Critchfield.

"Bring it up here," I said, making room at the head of the table.

Mrs. Critchfield splashed cold water on the baby and snapped the bottoms of its feet in an attempt to make it take a breath.

"Bring it here," I ordered and she carried the cyanotic baby to me, placing it on the table next to the mother's head. I inserted a tiny tube into the trachea and hooked it up to oxygen, pumping air gently but rapidly into the chest. It was a nightmare everyone in anesthesia dreaded, two unconscious patients and only one pair of hands.

"Call Skipper," I told Mrs. Critchfield. "Tell him I need help right away."

She was out of the room for several lifetimes. "Wife says he's out for the naght on his boat," she told me when she finally returned. "Won't be back till six in the mornin'."

Several more minutes of managing the mother while frantically inflating the baby's lungs, compressing its chest, and praying that my mind would not desert me brought no response from the limp infant. And I could see bright red blood dripping from the other end of the table to a clotted pool on the floor.

I increased the rate of the I.V., but the girl's blood pressure, whenever I managed to take it, was steadily declining. "I have to wake her up," I told Dr. Arst. "She's going into shock."

Mrs. Critchfield came to the head of the table to offer her assistance and I sent her to the lab for blood. "I'm not getting anything here," I said of the baby. "No pulse, no respirations."

I was worried that I might lose the mother, too. Children, particularly children having babies, had little resilience when suffering major blood loss.

"Better let the baby go and pay attention to the girl," Dr. Arst told me. "She's about ta bleed out down here." His face above his surgical mask was ashen, and damp tufts of silver hair stuck out from beneath his perspiration soaked scrub cap.

I reluctantly abandoned the baby. When Mrs. Critchfield returned from the lab she wrapped it entirely in a white sheet and placed it in the bassinet.

The young patient was receiving her second unit of blood when Dr. Arst finally got the hemorrhage under control and began sewing the lacerated perineum back together. "Damned if I know why she bled like a decapitated chickin," he said while he worked.

"That's one good-sized baby," Mrs. Critchfield said.

Dr. Arst examined the infant when he finished suturing and pronounced it dead. "Are you going to tell her family?" I asked.

The physician removed his cap and mask and ran a hand through his wet hair. "Mrs. Critchfield can take care of that."

Speaking without his surgical mask, the sweet odor of whiskey wafted heavily in my direction. The girl opened her eyes and looked up at me. "Mama?" Dr. Arst left without saying a word to her.

"We'll let you see your mama in a few minutes," I said.

"Not till we're sure she won't take ta bleedin' again," Mrs. Critchfield warned. She was busy mopping the bloody floor.

"Where's mama?" the child asked. And as if an afterthought, "Did I get me a baby?"

Mrs. Critchfield came to the head of the table, mop in hand. "Your baby dahed," she said. "It was the Lord's will."

The young girl looked more confused than sad. "What was it?"

The nurse went to the bassinet and unwrapped the body. "Boy." She rewrapped it without offering to let the patient see him and returned to her cleaning.

The patient was shivering violently from the trauma her young body had undergone, as well as from the cold blood I had not had time to warm before transfusing. The O.B. nurse stopped mopping long enough to bring blankets from the warmer and wrap them around the girl after helping me move her to a stretcher. The patient fell promptly into an exhausted sleep with her legs drawn up against her like the child she was.

When I passed the waiting room intended for fathers, I saw the mother and grandmother holding one another crying. "My poor baby," the child's mother wailed. I didn't know if she meant her daughter, or the baby boy presently on its way to the morgue.

From the corridor I stood witness to the suffering of four generations. And not one male representative of the wandering sperm banks that had so affected their lives was anywhere in attendance.

CHAPTER EIGHTEEN

I slept in the O.R. nurse's lounge so I would be available if the patient should start hemorrhaging again. At six a.m. I dislodged myself from the plastic sofa and started the large coffee pot the nurses took turns keeping filled throughout the day.

"That's raght nice of y'all," one of them said when she came in to dress for work. "I need a cup a' coffee something fierce." She was younger than the other nurses, and although her hair was the same island beige, she did not feel obligated to tease and spray it into a pile of stiff Grecian curls on top of her head.

"I don't think I've seen you before," I said when she sat down next to me on the sofa. "Are you new?"

"Carol Faye Critchfield," she said cheerfully. "Jest finished nursin' school."

The other women who had joined us were talking among themselves as they dressed for work. But I had the feeling they were aware of every word Carol Faye and I exchanged.

"Are you related to Mrs. Critchfield in O.B.?"

"Cousins. Most people on the ahlund are cousins," she added with a laugh. "First, second or at least third." She put down her coffee and got up to begin removing her street clothes.

"Did you go to nursing school in Baltimore?"

"Lor-dee! I wouldn't go up ta Baltmur for a weekend, much lest three years a' school." Carol Faye was island plump but pretty. The brief satin underwear stretched over her stripper figure was attracting disapproving looks from her fellow nurses. "We have our own nursin' school right here at Fishback Colleech."

114

"I didn't know there was a college here."

"If y'all would like, I might could show you around after work." The other nurses stopped their conversations in mid-sentence.

"I'll buy dinner," I suggested. The silence continued and Carol Faye glanced nervously around the room. "Unless you have family to get home to."

"I'm not married." It was a cross between an apology and a confession.

"Neither am I."

Carol Faye looked at me in disbelief. "Y'all have never bin married even oncet?"

"No. Not once."

"Honey hush, there's one more a' us!" she said as she did a little cheerleader jig. "I hate bein' the only old maid."

The others were filing out of the room. "Well, at least she's not a dee-vorce-say," I heard one of them say.

"They don't like sangle wimin," Carol Faye said as she wound her long hair up on top of her head and pinned it in place before covering it with a scrub cap. "They think we're after their husbins."

"I don't even know their husbands."

"Then y'all haven't been ta Seaport," Carol Faye said secretively. "They hang out in the turist bars lookin' for loose ladies, if ya know what I mean."

Her breasts were so large her name tag looked like a hood ornament on a Buick when she pinned it to her scrub gown bodice.

Earl Roy Donlin and Skipper were both in the anesthesia office when I entered. "We lost a baby in O.B. last night," I told them. "And came close to losing the mother."

Skipper listened while I related the story, but Earl Roy was more interested in an apple fritter he was dunking in his coffee. "The patient was only thirteen," I said in his direction. "Doctor Arst should have come in a lot sooner than he did."

"Arst is incompetent," Skipper said. "It wouldn't have mattered if he'd been there when she conceived."

Earl Roy still said nothing, dunking his fritter.

"She should have had a C/section," I said. "She was too small to deliver a full term baby."

"She should have had an abortion," Skipper countered.

It took me a moment to reply. "You're right."

We now had Earl Roy's attention. "This ahlund's almost one hundert percent Christian Republican. No baby killin' allowed."

Skipper laughed. "Yeah, right." Earl Roy gave him a look that returned Skipper to arranging equipment on his cart.

I had requested on my employment application that I be excused from giving anesthesia for abortions. But until now I had not noticed there were never any on the surgery schedule.

"I'm not for wholesale abortion," I said to Earl Roy. "But what sense does it make to have a child go through the ordeal of labor and delivery, only to have the baby die?"

"That's an opinion you had best keep to yerself." He switched to his Harvard English to further make the point. "There's a movement originating right here in Muskrat Marsh to challenge Roe versus Wade. It's a matter of time until it's overturned."

I could not forget the suffering child and her dead baby. Nor Dr. Arst's indifference to her pain. "But why would you want the law overturned?" I asked Earl Roy. "I would think all your Republican Christian friends would be happy about it."

Earl Roy looked at me as if I were speaking in tongues.

"Surely only Democrats have abortions. Just think of how many you're getting rid of before they're even old enough to vote."

Skipper laughed so hard he had to lean on his anesthesia cart. My boss was not amused as he got up to leave the room.

"You've been living with my ex-wife too long," he said.

"That's great," Skipper said when Earl Roy was gone. "Republicans getting rid of Democrats in the O.R.s." He laughed again. "If only that was the way it really..."

The other anesthetist came into the room to get Earl Roy's cases set up and Skipper fell silent. He took drugs from our locked narcotic cabinet, drew them into syringes and pushed his cart out of the room. But not before putting a finger to his lips behind Getta Mae's back to warn me not to say any more. And to be very sure, he put his hands together in prayer to indicate her Christian status.

I exchanged a few polite sentences with Getta Mae, then followed Skipper down the corridor.

"There's another thing you need to know about last night," I said when I caught up with him. "Doctor Arst had been drinking."

Skipper said nothing while an O.R. nurse passed in the opposite direction. "He's been drinking every night," he said when she was gone. "Maybe you'll have better luck convincing his colleagues they should do something about it. I've tried for years."

"Have you gone to the state medical board?"

Skipper was anxious to get his cases started, or to get rid of me.

"Look, Pat, I admit we have some problems around here, but I like my job, and in another five years I can retire and fish all day long. Don't make waves that could sink both of us."

Carol Faye wanted to have dinner before the tour of Muskrat Marsh, so we drove in her red Firebird to a plain brick building with faded awnings over its windows. "Do we darest have a drink?" Carol Faye asked when we were seated.

"You're not twenty-one?"

"Jest turned. But my family would flat out die if someone saw and told on me." She was checking out the other patrons in the restaurant while partially hiding her face behind a menu. "We're Christian." Her knit shirt was stretched across her considerable mammaries in a most unchristian fashion. "Aren't you?"

"I'm Catholic."

Carol Faye dropped the menu to look eye to eye. "Y'all have never bin born again?"

"Why should I? I haven't died yet."

She looked bewildered for a moment, then laughed. "Honey hush, y'all do have the funniest way a' jokin'."

A waitress came and Carol Faye ordered us steamed crabs from the Chesapeake Bay. "And a screwdriver," she added quietly. "You should order somethin' ta drink too," she said. "Those crabs are right spicy." She fanned herself with her menu to illustrate. "I never take alcohol 'cept ta cool my throat," she said up to the waitress.

"What church to you belong to?" I asked when I had ordered a beer and the waitress departed.

"Highway Holiness. It's the only one in Muskrat Marsh, plus the culurd church, a' course." I had been driving to Seaport for Mass.

The waitress brought our drinks and Carol Faye took a heady pull on hers. "Whew, that's a little strong when you're not used to it." She set the glass down with more than half its contents gone. "Ahlunders used ta all be Methodists before we embraced the Lord Jesus Christ and got born again."

Her body took on an attitude which raised her gaze heavenward, along with her Buick bosom. "The bible says, 'I tell you the truth, unless a man is born again, he cannot see the kingdom of God.'" It was said so loudly several customers turned toward us.

"Amen," said a woman at a nearby table.

Carol Faye smiled and swallowed the rest of her screwdriver. "If y'all want ta be saved I can introduce you to Reverend Taylor," she told me. "He does baptisms oncet a month."

The woman at the next table appeared to be waiting for my reply. "Thank you for asking," I said. "I'll let you know."

Two dozen steamed crabs arrived, and my dinner companion delighted in showing me how to break them open and peel the hard shell and innards away from the tender white meat. We used wooden mallets to crack open the legs, which held a juicier, firmer meat.

Maryland Blue Crabs turned bright orange when cooked, and were covered with spices as hot as Carol Faye predicted. They were served on layers of newspapers, so the waitress had only to fold up the entire mess when we were finished and throw it in the garbage.

"I'm bein' flat out wicked," Carol Faye whispered as she sucked up a second screwdriver. "Although anyone watching would think this was jest plain old orange juice." She held up the glass as evidence to the woman who looked our way whenever we spoke.

The air was heavy with chicken smog when we left the restaurant. "I'm feelin' right silly," Carol Faye told me with an appropriate giggle. "You're a bad influence, Miss Pat."

I felt somewhat silly myself, and it wasn't from one beer. I was having fun with Carol Faye.

She drove her sporty car fast to an outlying section of town, stopping at a set of ornate gates that had the words HEAVENLY ACRES woven into their wrought iron filigree design. "This is where the docters and other rich people lives," she said as she pulled up to a guard house and gave a telephone number. "I figure it's the best place ta start the tour." The armed guard made a call. "I went ta nursing school with Doris Yvonne Arst," Carol Faye said. "She lets me use her name to get in here whenever I want, sometimes jest ta drive up an' down the streets dreamin' I might could live here someday." The guard pushed a button and the gates swung open.

"I thought you were taking me to a cemetery," I said as we drove through the majestic entrance.

Carol Faye laughed. "See, there you go agin."

"Is Doris Yvonne Doctor Arst's daughter?" I asked.

Carol Faye broke into spasms of laughter, slapping her steering wheel. "Honey hush, she's his wife!" She settled down and drove along the wide, curving street. "Caught him jest after his wife died a' cancer and married him whilst we were still in nursin' school." She sighed wistfully. "Doris Yvonne always was lucky in love."

Large leafy trees arched over the pleasant street, which wound between rows of two-story, brick colonials with tall, white columns in front. The lawns were as identical as the houses, and crushed white stone driveways curved up to each of the front doors. Elaborate bird baths and lacy white furniture sat on manicured lawns.

"The docters take turns givin' New Year's Eve parties an' invite all the nurses. "Docter Donlin always has the best ones."

"He lives here?" The lavish development was a stark contrast to the rundown house where Earl Roy's children lived.

"Right over there." Carol Faye pointed to a red brick colonial like all the others. "Don't go tellin' anyone at the hospital this, but I wish I'da caught him in between his wife divorcin' him and his marryin' Adella Dawn." I wondered if Carol Faye knew Earl Roy already had a girlfriend on the side.

There were other doctors' names on many of the fancy mailboxes along the street. At the very end of the wide boulevard, sitting on an oversized lot that was higher than the others, was the home of Henry Fishback. A white Cadillac with a red roof sat in the drive with a personalized license plate reading HEN ONE.

"He has a whole raft a' cars," Carol Faye said. "Hen Two, Hen Three; I don't know how many in all. They're all made ta look like roosters and the horns go Err-er-err-er-errrr!" Her high-pitched crowing was so unexpected I jumped. Carol Faye howled. "I told you I was feelin' silly."

The Lincoln Continental parked in the drive of the house next to Hen's also had a unique license plate. There were only three numbers, preceded by the letters POW. "That's Senator Zebediah Taylor's place," Carol Faye said reverently. "Muskrat Marsh's very own war hero."

"Which war?"

"Kor-rea."

I had said nothing about my Vietnam experience at Fishback Hospital. And I intended to keep it that way.

Carol Faye turned her car back toward the gates of the exclusive enclave while telling me how Zebediah Taylor, who was presently a state senator, had been captured and held prisoner during the Korean War. "When he got out he come back to the ahlund an' started the farms where they grow melons and strawberries an' all."

We passed back through the gates, where the guard gave us a military salute. "Zebediah worshipped money as his God until he embraced the Lord Jesus Christ. After that he went into politics and run for senator a' Maralund." Both her voice and facial expression reflected the pride she felt in her fellow islander. "He's flat out committed ta bringin' the Lord's Word ta Washington."

We were approaching Fishback College. "Only bad thing, he tangled hisself up with a raght strange woman whose husbin got kilt in an explosion on his boat.

I did not mention that I knew Hope and Allison. "His wife's not an islander?" I asked, curious to see what she would say.

"Lor-dee, no! Her first husbin was, and a fine worterman too, though he was a bit strange for bein' an ahlunder and all." We were driving through the campus of Fishback College. "They had them a daughter, who's an ahlunder, but she's near queer as her mother."

We circled the modest campus, named after its benefactor, Hen Fishback. I noticed that none of the students wore the ragged clothing or long hair popular just across the bridge. They were dressed more like Carol Faye, without the physical attributes.

The next part of the tour was the heart of the town, where a large banner was strung across Main Street between Henry Fishback Bank and the post office on the other side. A construction crew hammered at a campaign-style platform being erected beneath the banner which read: TWENTY-THIRD ANNUAL CHICKEN PLUCKING FESTIVAL.

"I was runner up for Miss Spring Chickin two years ago." Then sadly, "Back when I really was a spring chickin."

The men constructing the platform provided Carol Faye a distraction from her spinsterhood, and she excitedly filled me in on the details of the chicken plucking contest. "Hen's a pistol at pluckin'," she said. "Wins ever year."

"Are there many contestants?"

"With Hen puttin' up five hundert dollars prize money?" she said in disbelief. "Why, people practice all year long ta win."

She pulled up in front of a dark brick building that looked authentically colonial. "How beautiful," I said.

"It's the courthouse. I thought y'all would like it."

The sun was just beginning to set and speckles of sunlight glinted off the building's copper dome, spattering the courthouse lawn with coins of golden light. "The best part's the story that goes with it." I could see myself becoming friends with Carol Faye, and I relaxed into the seat of her car to hear an historic tale of early settlers.

"See that tree over there?" She pointed to a gnarled White Oak whose vast branches reached every corner of the courthouse lawn.

"I've never seen anything so magnificent." I got out of the car for a better look and Carol Faye did too. "All of that is just one tree?"

"Yes, ma'am. And that's where the last nigger got lynched."

My head snapped in her direction.

"I mean legal like." Carol Faye's face took on an expression of genuine pride. "Folks think Baltmur and Washington's got all the turist attractions, but right on that spot is where the last culurd in the whole U-nited States was hanged by the people he wronged."

I looked again at the courthouse, now falling into shades of violet, then to the massive oak. I wondered which of its majestic branches had the misfortune of holding the rope.

"Why did they hang him?" I asked as we got back into the car.

"For rapin' a white woman," Carol Faye said with an air of absolute justification. "After he was dead the town folks tied him behind a pickup truck and drug him through Culurd Town ta show the rest what would happen if they tried what he did."

It was a story she appeared to have repeated many times. "I'll tell you for certain, those niggers didn't show their faces for one en-tire week. An' then it was only because they were hungry." We headed back toward the hospital lot where my car was, and I could not wait to get in it. "The store owners wouldn't sell 'em anything for another two days, jest so's they got the message real good."

"Who was it he supposedly raped?"

"There's so supposed about it, honey, he done it. An' it was Zebediah Taylor's own sister, Joanetta Jean." She pulled up next to my car, but I made no move to get out.

"Where is she now?" I asked. "Is she still on the island?"

"Well sort a'. She's out in the cemetery next to the church."

Carol Faye's face reflected a combination of sorrow and titillation. "She got pregnant from the rape and the doctor give her some pills for her nerves. She took too many one night and jest never woke up." She shivered in the warm evening air. "Can you imagine, carryin' a nigger baby around in your belly?"

"The autopsy showed the fetus was fathered by the man they hanged?"

"Oh, there worn't no autopsy. The judge said poor Joanetta Jean suffered enough already without cutting her open after she was dead an' gone." Carol Faye turned off the ignition of her car. "It tore the whole family up; mother and father would have nothin' ta do with no one an' dahed not long afterwards. Zebediah joined the Marines and went off and got hisself captured."

"Where is this Colored Town where they dragged the body?"

"Not far. But we daren't go down there this time a' night."

It was the furthest thing from my mind when I asked the question, yet I now found myself compelled to go there. "It's not that late," I said. "Not even completely dark."

Carol Faye was hesitant. "Well, I reckin," she said after some contemplation. "I swear, y'all are turnin' me into a raght naughty girl." She started her car and revved its oversized engine. "I guess this baby can barrel us through Culurd Town fast enough to get away from anyone wants ta do us dirty."

We sped southward through Muskrat Marsh and crossed a single lane bridge spanning a tidewater inlet on the outskirts of town. Kerosene lamps glowed in some windows, illuminating porches occupied by old furniture and wringer washing machines. There were no street lights or sidewalks, and from the outhouses evident in backyards, no indoor plumbing. Even a small, white church in desperate need of a fresh coat of paint had two outhouses in back, one for men and one for women. And the cemetery next to the humble church had only wooden crosses marking the graves.

We passed what looked in the twilight to be a mountain, but a sign further along the dirt road designated it as the municipal dump. Plastic and paper blew from heaps of garbage and hung in trees as if a band of Halloween pranksters had passed through. Screeching sea gulls foraged for food in the mounds of putrid waste.

"Honey hush! Roll up your window!" Carol Faye shouted. But it was too late, the stench of the dump permeated her car. "Shoot! If my family smells the trash heap they'll know I was in Culurd Town."

We travelled the length of the settlement's single dirt road, then turned and started back for the bridge. Smoke spiraled from the chimneys of shanties, and smells of cooking mingled with the rot of the dump. Scrawny chickens scratched in the dirt for food, and people wandering along the road looked toward us in Carol Faye's flashy car. But not with the same hostility Lori and her children had encountered in Baltimore. They looked afraid of us.

"Culurds were a lot better off when they lived on plantations and had someone lookin' out for 'em," Carol Faye said. "But no use tryin' ta tell them that." Colored Town disappeared in a cloud of dust kicked up by her speeding car.

When I got back into my Mustang it seemed determined to go to the cemetery. Hope and Allison were not there, but I could see fresh flowers strewn across Adam Lee's grave in the gathering dusk.

A grave only four plots from it bore the inscription:

JOANETTA JEAN TAYLOR
Gone to Jesus before her time

Lori was in the kitchen cleaning up after dinner, and I sat down at the table to tell her about my evening. "Did you know they brag about this being the last place a black person was hanged?"

Lori shushed me and peeked into the next room where Reba sat in her rocking chair watching television with the children. "Reba was living in Colored Town when that happened," she said quietly. "That's why she left the island."

"Is her mother buried in Colored Town?"

"You don't actually believe the rednecks would let her near their Highway Holiness cemetery, do you?"

CHAPTER NINETEEN

"You're going to be killed on that thing," I heard Lori say when Andy rode his noisy motorcycle into her driveway. She was on the lawn trying to coax grass to grow in the bald spots. "Pat's inside."

I watched from the upstairs window I looked out when I awakened from dreams about Dan. Over the months on the island the dreams were becoming so infrequent, I had hope they would go away altogether. But then Dan would too, and I was not sure I wanted that. I worried that I was becoming like Hope, with whom I had been sharing picnics.

And while I clung to my ghost, Andy appeared to be leaving Vietnam behind. He walked with such a slight limp one would never guess he had an artificial leg beneath his jeans. His long hair was tied carefully at the back of his neck.

I pulled a shirt over my bathing suit and threw the items I was taking to the beach into a straw bag. "I'll be there in a minute," I called out. "But I'm not riding a donorcycle through beach traffic."

Reba was in the kitchen when I came down, feeding Andy chocolate chip cookies straight from the oven. She wore her man's attire, minus the hat and tie.

"You put on suntan lotion this time," she lectured me. "It's not healthy letting your skin get all burned up."

Andy took my bag. "Are we taking the kids?"

"They're visiting their grandmother today," I told him.

"God help them," Reba said. "My own mother worked for the Donlin family for years. Started when Earl Roy was a boy." She used a pancake turner to lift hot cookies onto a wire rack to cool. "Mama never could stand the way they doted on him, buyin' anything he wanted and sending him off to Harvard like he was some sort of king. Smartest thing Lori ever did was get away from the whole bunch of 'em."

Lori came into the kitchen while Reba was talking and washed her hands in the sink. "And the dumbest thing I ever did was to marry into their family to begin with." She picked up a cookie as Andy and I started for the door. "See you for dinner? I'm making spaghetti."

Spaghetti and chicken were our inexpensive staples, along with an occasional feast of Chesapeake Blue crabs.

"We'll be here," Andy answered for both of us.

Andy drove my Mustang, and the beach was the nicest I had seen it since moving to the island. We walked for miles in the warm sun on soft sand and water that cooled our feet as it rolled gently ashore. Andy paid no attention to the looks his stick-like artificial leg attracted in his bathing suit.

"So, how's the old noggin been, Danang?"

We were on our blanket, where I watched children haul buckets of water to pour into holes they dug in the sand. Andy was lying on his back looking at the sky. "Have you had anymore flashbacks?"

"Where'd you get that fifty dollar word?"

"The government finds a sanitized label for everything."

"Like bodycounts instead of number of human beings blown to hell?" A woman sunning herself in a nearby lounge chair gave me a disapproving look. "I haven't had one since I left Baltimore."

I didn't count dreams; my mind was free to go wherever it wanted while I slept. Just so it came back when I opened my eyes.

"Island life agrees with you."

"Not all of it." I told him about Joanetta Jean and the black man who was hanged.

"Are you shitting me?" he said when I concluded with the part about dragging the body through Colored Town. The woman got up and moved her chair several yards from us.

"I like my job," I said as I lay on my back next to Andy, looking up at an unblemished summer sky. "But I can't get it out of my mind that people I'm working with would brag about such a thing."

"People are people. You're never going to find that perfect world you keep looking for."

"I'm not looking for a perfect world," I said indignantly.

Andy was weary of the conversation. He rolled onto his stomach and closed his eyes as he settled lazily into the sand. I thought he was doing it to shut me up, but within seconds he was sound asleep.

I lay there looking at the many shrapnel scars on his back, in addition to the red and purple pit now apparent at the base of his neck. It astounded me that he could have gone through so much and still be so accepting.

Andy lingered after dinner talking with Reba in the living room while Lori and I did the dishes.

"You're lucky to have such a nice guy," Lori said while she rubbed spaghetti sauce from plates. "I've given up on meeting anyone I can respect and love at the same time."

"That's because Earl Roy convinced you you're not worthy of a decent man's attention."

"Maybe so." She pulled the plug in the sink and let the tomato-tinted water run down the drain. "You and Andy have any plans?"

"We're more friends than a couple," I said quietly.

"You still think about that guy in Vietnam, don't you?"

"Sometimes," I said as a pain worked its way through my chest.

"You don't have to forget about him," Lori said kindly. "Just move on."

"Like you coming back to this island?"

"Touche."

We finished the remainder of the clean-up in the silence of friends with enough history to make constant conversation unnecessary.

"I'll wake you in the morning," Lori told me when Andy left for Baltimore and we climbed the stairs. "The festival starts at ten."

It was noon before we arrived at the crowded downtown area on the hottest day recorded. I was glad Reba elected not to come when I saw the crowd jamming a considerable length of Main Street, which was closed to vehicular traffic. Even in such an immense gathering whites managed to stay separate from blacks.

"The islanders have their protocol even at a chicken plucking contest," Lori had told me as soon as we were out of the house. "People would talk if Reba was with us."

"The neighbors talk about Reba already," Peggy said as Lori backed her station wagon out of the driveway.

"Who cares?" I said irritably. The car's air-conditioner was broken and I was already sweating like a work horse.

"Tell them she takes care of the house," Lori told her daughter as she pointed the car toward the center of town.

"Only rich people have coloreds to clean and cook for them."

"Don't call them coloreds."

"But people think Reba's a man," Peggy complained. "And she won't stop wearing those stupid clothes."

"I don't care what people think," Lori said sternly. "Reba is happy the way she is, and that's the way things will be until she feels comfortable being a woman again."

"She hardly goes out of the house," I said. "She's not bothering anyone." Peggy shriveled into a corner of the rear seat.

We drove silently a few minutes.

"I know it's hard for you to understand," Lori said to Peggy in a repentant voice. "But dressing like a man makes Reba feel safer." She did not respond. "Women and girls have to think about being safe."

"Don't boys have to be safe too?" Brendan asked.

"Of course," Lori answered.

"But boys don't get hurt like girls do," Peggy told her younger brother. "We have to be specially careful we don't get raped."

Her candor caused Lori to slow the car to look back at her. "Nine years old," she said in my direction. "And already she knows the shit women have to put up with."

"Mom said a pepper word," Brendan chided.

Lori opened her mouth to defend herself but what came out was a laugh. "Yeah, mom said a pepper word." Lori's punishment for bad words was a shake of pepper on the tongue of the offender.

The crowd on Main Street was so dense we had to hold hands to stay together as we worked our way through. I could see little over the heads of people, but the stink of wet feathers and the squawks of chickens waiting to be killed guided us to the spot in front of Henry Fishback Bank where the chicken plucking contest would take place.

Lori managed to find a pocket of space close enough for us to see a wire strung across the platform's forward section. There were several decapitated chickens hanging from it by what was left of their bloody necks, and an executioner stood nearby with his hatchet ready to provide more from the chicken crates under the platform.

Bikini-clad girls, all white, vying for the Miss Spring Chicken title, sat on a row of folding chairs about four feet back from the wire. Town dignitaries and the judges who would choose the winning beauty sat behind, their chairs on an elevated section high enough to give them a good view of the bosoms in the front row. Earl Roy Donlin was a judge and Billy, who had left for his father's at the crack of dawn, stood near the platform watching him. Lori waved to her son, but he was too busy watching his father watch the beauty contestants.

I was surprised to see Hope and Allison sitting to one side of the platform. Hope wore a silk, long sleeved blouse that complimented her copper braids, but it and her slacks looked far too warm for the scorching day. Allison's mane of golden hair shone like the light glinting off the dome of the courthouse in the background. Both she and her mother looked as if they would rather be anyplace else.

I tried to get their attention, but they could not see me in the press of people. Actually, they seemed not to see anyone as they stared straight ahead.

"That's Zebediah Taylor, Hope's husband." Lori indicated a large man with a florid complexion and white-wall, Marine crew cut who swaggered to and fro on the crowded platform. "Hen Fishback put up most of the money to get him elected to Maryland's state senate," she said. "Now they're trying to get him into Congress."

"He's the guy who was a prisoner of war in Korea?"

Lori nodded. "I really should try to see Hope again."

Lori didn't know I shared picnics with Hope and her daughter since our move to the island, nor did Andy. My relationship with Hope did not seem relevant to my other life.

Zebediah was not oggling the beauty contestants like the other men. His attention was on his wife and stepdaughter, who looked neither left nor right as he paced back and forth in front of them.

Their hair was striking next to the faded beige of the islanders around them, and their skin alabaster instead of weather beaten. Both appeared acutely aware of Senator Taylor's presence at all times.

"Somehow I can't see Hope married to him," I said to Lori. "Or to any other islander, for that matter."

"Adam Lee was an exception," Lori said.

"Do you think Hope and Allison are afraid of him?"

"Who?"

"Senator Taylor."

Lori was getting nervous about our conversation in the midst of islanders, even though we spoke in hushed tones. "No, I don't think they're afraid of him," she said as she watched Senator Taylor strut across the stage once more. "More like embarrassed."

Peggy and Brendan talked Lori out of five dollars and ran off to buy something from the dozens of stalls selling fried chicken, spicy chicken and miniature chicken pot pies.

The volunteer firemen had the town's prime spot for their food concession in the shade of the giant White Oak on the courthouse lawn. Stacks of cinder blocks contained the fire and supported a large wire grate the sweltering firemen labored over. People with faces reddened by the heat crowded around the smoky fire waiting to buy charred halves of chicken as fast as the men could cook them.

"Here comes Hen," Lori said when a roar went up from the crowd. Hen's white Cadillac moved slowly through the exuberant gathering with its horn blaring: Err-er-err-er-errrh! The car was polished to perfection, its red roof dazzling in the bright sunlight.

The little man got out of his car and marched up to the stage, stopping to shake hands eagerly offered along the way. The trousers of his polyester leisure suit had a five inch hem in them, as if he hoped to grow beyond his slight stature.

"Lord A'mighty, this is the finest lookin' bunch a' young chicks I ever did see," he said as he walked along the front section of the platform looking over the Miss Spring Chicken hopefuls. The girls tittered and wiggled in their chairs while the crowd cheered.

Hen signaled the high school band, seated next to the platform in uniforms that had the members looking on the verge of heat stroke, and it struck up a dissonant version of GOD BLESS AMERICA, to which many in the crowd sang along. When the band finished, unfortunately not all at the same time, Hen stepped to the microphone.

"Before we get down ta the business of pluckin' we'll have a few words from our own Reverend Taylor, who has graciously offered to bless this celebration." I thought Hen's eyes looked as beady and blinked as rapidly as they had before his plastic surgery at Filmore. He would have been better off having his beaked nose worked on.

A middle-aged man came to the microphone and heads bowed all around. Reverend Taylor was unusually slim for an islander but had the same hair and skin. He turned to the scantily clothed beauty contestants, sitting with their heads lowered to bared bosoms and their hands folded reverently in front.

"I see the Lord has blessed us with another fine bunch a' His children." The reverend's eyes wandered first over the contestants' bosoms then their legs, held chastely together. "And everone of these fine young ladies is in church ever Sunday, plus bible meetin'."

Lori poked me when I started to laugh. "He's Zebediah Taylor's cousin," she said directly into my ear. "And best friends with Hen Fishback." Lori was as cautious as other members of Christian Hospital's staff not to offend its generous benefactor.

"Let us thank the Lord for his bountiful blessings," the reverend prayed with his eyes closed. "And ask him to continue smilin' down on Fishback Ahlund, His piece a' heaven right here on earth."

The reverend opened his eyes and looked out over the crowd.

"And we ask you, Lord, to help with our fund raisin' so's we can finish the temple we are building in thy holy name."

Construction on the church had slowed, which made our picnics more pleasant. During our last, Hope told me how she had met Adam Lee while he was stationed in Illinois in the Navy. They were married there, and he brought her to the island after his four year hitch.

"Buy a brick for Jesus!" the reverend shouted with arms raised.

"Praise the Lord!" the crowd shouted back.

Hats were passed in all directions, including the black section, whose members parted reluctantly with coins to build a church in which they could not worship. "I thank you dear friends!" the beaming reverend shouted out over the crowd as the full hats were passed up to him. "And the Lord thanks you!"

He stuffed the loot into a plastic bag readily pulled from inside his suit jacket. The people went back to eating greasy chicken they had held in their folded hands during the prayer.

So much time had elapsed, the decapitated chickens had to be taken down from the wire and given another dunk in a huge caldron of boiling water to loosen their feathers. The first group of pluckers, including blacks, stepped up to the wire, preparing themselves for the task by cracking their knuckles and swinging their arms in wide circles. A cheer went up when Hen peeled off his suit jacket, rolled up his shirt sleeves and took his place at the center of the line.

"He always wins," Peggy said as she hopped up and down to see.

Lori told me that chickens were no longer plucked by hand in the island's processing plants. But Hen liked to demonstrate at the festival how things were done when he started his poultry business.

"On your mark, get set, go!" A shot was fired at such close range I ducked down into the crowd. Peggy and Brendan found my reaction uproariously funny.

"That sounded like a real gun," I said when I recovered sufficiently to stand upright.

"It was." Lori pointed to a small table at the side of the platform that was covered with polished weapons. "Zebediah's a collector."

The senator, still holding the fired weapon, was looking over an array of additional firearms with an enraptured expression, while his wife and daughter watched with undisguised horror. He chose a new gun and waited to fire the shot signaling the end of the first round. Wet feathers flew everywhere as the spectators clapped, whistled and cheered their encouragement.

Zebediah shot off another round, and the crowd broke into

ecstatic applause when Hen was announced the winner. The little man, covered with wet feathers, danced around the platform flapping his short arms and cackling joyfully.

A bunch of freshly decapitated chickens were dipped into the boiling caldron and suspended from the wire. Their defrocked predecessors were handed to the volunteer firemen at the barbecue pit.

A new set of challengers approached the wire, with Hen Fishback again in the center, and Zebediah selected a third weapon from his gleaming arsenal. His military stance was ramrod straight as he prepared to fire into the air. I plugged my ears.

Hen won the second contest and had even more feathers stuck to him when he did his wing-flapping victory dance. Feathers covered the beauty contestants as well, and they frantically tried to brush or pick them off. But the feathers were so wet and their bikini clad flesh so sticky from the intense midday heat, it was an impossible task. The more feathers they collected, the more appropriate they looked for the title of Miss Spring Chicken.

"Do we have to stay for the whole thing?" I asked Lori. My back was hurting from standing on the hard pavement, and I was eager to escape Zebediah's guns.

Lori looked at Peggy and Brendan, who chomped barbecued chicken as happily as the rest of the crowd. "They'd be disappointed if we left early."

As Zebediah began raising his latest weapon skyward my mind sent out an all points bulletin. Get out of here or I get out.

"Let's all go to the beach," I almost shouted. "I'll treat for rides and food." Peggy and Brendan were working their way back to the car before their mother could respond.

"I forgot Billy," Lori said when we were almost to the car. "I can't leave him there watching his father and looking so miserable."

It took half an hour for her to wind her way back to the platform and return. "He refuses to leave, even though Earl Roy is completely ignoring him." Damp hair hung down her flushed forehead. "I don't want to go without him."

"Billy spoils everything," Brendan said in a defeated voice.

Lori looked down at her two younger children wilting in the hot sun. "Not today," she declared.

Reba was in her rocking chair taking an afternoon nap in front of the television when we quietly entered the house to collect bathing suits and towels. She was still sleeping when we tiptoed out, leaving the game show host announcing to no one that a contestant had just won a

NEWWWWW CARRRRR!

CHAPTER TWENTY

"I hope you realize I only agreed to help you teach," I said as I entered the town's cavernous firehouse, awash with the stench of cooking wild meat. "I refuse to eat muskrat."

Skipper laughed. "You don't need to worry, they chase all the women out before the dinner begins."

Both of us carried large cases containing life-like manikins used to teach CPR. For the next six hours we would be instructing more than fifty volunteer firemen how to revive someone once they got them out of a burning house or the ocean.

Lori followed us into the hall with two smaller cases containing infant manikins. It was her job to teach the all-male ambulance crews how to save children and babies, especially those they might be called upon to deliver enroute to the hospital.

"You'd think Earl Roy would at least put in an appearance," I said when we began setting up equipment in the empty hall. "Since he volunteered our services without even asking."

"He's too busy lining up entertainment for after the dinner," Lori said of her ex-husband. "He has the distinction of being the man in charge of fun for the Muskrat Feast each year." I could tell from her expression it was not a subject I should pursue.

"Lord, if that muskrat don't smell good," one of the firemen I was teaching said. He looked toward the kitchen attached to the cavernous firehall, where women's voices could be heard as they prepared the vile feast. "It's got my mouth worterin' so bad I can't keep it on this rubber woman."

He wiped a hand across his lips and went back to doing mouth-

133

to-mouth resuscitation on the CPR manikin. But he had given only a few breaths when his partner, who was compressing the chest, decided to take a break.

"I hear Doc Donlin's got Cajuns comin' in," he said. "Nice soft ones the color of coffee with lots of cream. Um-umm."

"You need to pay attention," I said impatiently. It was already late afternoon, and I was tired of trying to instruct grown men with the attention span of children on Christmas Eve.

"The longer it takes you to learn this, the less time you have for your dinner," Skipper called to the men from where he taught. "Doctor Donlin says no one rides ambulance without passing this."

Riding the fire trucks and ambulance, all polished to perfection and presently parked out front to make room for our class, was the pinnacle of island life. And there was nothing the all male volunteer force would not do to enable them to race around town with sirens blaring.

We were still at it when Earl Roy arrived at five P.M. "All raght boys, we've not got all night." He clapped as he walked among his fellow islanders like a scout leader. "Let's get this over with an' move on ta what we're really here for." The men whistled.

I was impressed with how quickly Earl Roy could turn his island accent on and off depending upon with whom he was interacting.

The men went diligently to work so they could clear the hall and get tables and chairs set up for the dinner. As soon as I finished with those assigned to me, I packed my manikin in its carrying case and went in search of something cold to drink. And to take a pain pill for the spasms the long day had produced in my back.

When I could find no vending machines, I entered the steamy kitchen filled with women wearing long white aprons over striped and flowered dresses. Some tended enormous iron skillets of crackling chicken, and others watched over the gamey smelling muskrats roasting in industrial sized ovens.

"These are gettin' right ready," one of the women said as she pulled a large pan from one of the ovens and stuck a fork into a mound of dark meat. "Best get the corn fritters in the fat."

Those not working over the hot stoves shredded heads of cabbage for coleslaw. Or sliced cucumbers and fresh red tomatoes harvested on Zebediah's farms.

"I've not got enough cukes over here," a woman called from a sink where she stood peeling and slicing. A bushel basket of cucumbers was promptly hauled to her by a migrant worker from a truck backed up to the rear door of the kitchen.

"Pat, I didn't expect to see you here." I turned to look into the mink brown eyes of Hope.

"I didn't expect you either," I said with the same surprise.

She wore an oversized white apron like the other women, but rather than a dress she wore her customary blouse and slacks. That and her unteased hair made her appear as out of place in the hectic kitchen as I felt.

"I was looking for something to drink," I said.

"Let me get it for you." I watched Hope move through the crowd of bustling women, who stepped aside as if she was Typhoid Mary.

"Lori and I got roped into helping teach the volunteer firemen CPR.," I told her after swallowing a pain capsule. "My back is killing me."

"I'm so sorry," Hope said. "Would you like to sit down?"

She motioned to a straight backed, wooden chair, which was guaranteed to make things worse. "No, thanks," I said. "Lori's waiting for me."

"I really must visit her sometime." Hope's formal manner was nothing like our casual conversations in the cemetery. But out there we had only birds to eavesdrop on us, not dozens of island women.

I indicated the hall where the CPR course was concluding. "Lori's right out there. I'm sure she would love to see you."

Hope waved to someone behind me, and I turned to see her daughter coming toward us. Allison acknowledged me with a smile.

"Are you ready to leave, mother?" she asked in her bird-song voice. She looked disapprovingly around the room, jangling a set of car keys.

"I'll get my purse," Hope said.

Lori spotted us as we moved from kitchen to firehall. "Hope! I'll be there in a minute," she called as she packed the last manikin.

Some of the firemen were setting up long tables and folding chairs while others hung crepe paper streamers from the ceiling, as if preparing for prom night.

Hope smiled as Lori started across the room to where we stood. Then suddenly her expression changed to one of dread. Zebediah Taylor had entered the hall and was following right behind Lori.

"I have to go," Hope said to me as she turned away. She moved like a gazelle as her husband bore down on her, his florid face set as rigidly as his back and shoulders.

"Hope." His voice stopped her cold and she turned to face him. Lori also froze.

"I didn't expect you home from Annapolis so early," Hope said. Her vocal cords were so tight her voice was as high as her daughter's.

Zebediah looked from Hope to Allison, the latter's face a cross between loathing and defiance as she turned away from him. "It's time the both of you were out of here," he said to them. "Ah'll drive you home."

Allison held up the keys in her hand. "I have mother's car," she said in a manner that was strangely timid.

"We were just about to leave," Hope said. "I helped in the kitchen all day." She sounded like a little girl seeking the approval of a parent.

Zebediah was staring at me, but I didn't know whether I should say anything, or what that would be. I felt exactly as Hope and Allison appeared on the platform at the chicken festival. He had the uncanny ability to create an invisible corral around people with only his eyes.

"This is Pat Walsh," Hope said. "She helped teach the firemen CPR."

Zebediah scrutinized me so intently, my skin felt as hot as the roasting muskrats. "I've seen her before," he said while he continued to look me over. "Out there in the cemetery actin' as spacey as you."

Now it was Hope's turn to blush. "We're friends, Zebediah."

He suddenly smiled at me, a politician's stiff, phony smile. "Well, I guess the cemetery is better'n spendin' time in those junk stores where ya used ta throw away my money." He put a hand out to me, but I was so locked into his gaze I did not respond. "Glad ta make your acquaintance."

Allison pushed my hand forward as she pretended to bump into me. "Happy to meet you also," I said to Zebediah as I took his hot, sweaty hand.

He turned to look where Lori still stood like a statue. "It's nice ta see my wife has found her a friend worth knowin'."

I held my breath, waiting for Lori's reaction. But she stayed in her corral until Zebediah shifted his gaze to his gold wrist watch. "Time all of you were outta' here," he declared.

Hope hurried to the door before his last word was out. I followed with Allison, but Lori went back to get a notebook she had forgotten

"Can't have us spying on their fun," Allison said as we passed two firemen taping heavy black paper over windows.

Hope waited for us just outside the hall. "It's all rather silly," she said in an embarrassed tone.

"Silly?" Allison taunted. "You call a bunch of grown men

fucking imported whores silly?"

"Allison!"

"Oh please, don't pretend for Pat's benefit." Allison turned to look back at the firehall. "They hold everything in that sacred temple of theirs," she said to me. "Wedding receptions, graduations, church suppers, even orgies." She let out a laugh. "I can't wait until they start using it for funerals."

Hope moved on to her worn Volvo and got inside without another word. Allison followed her mother to the car.

"I guess Zebediah still wants me to keep my distance from his wife." Lori had come up beside me as I watched the Volvo drive away. "He's probably afraid she'll divorce him like I did Earl Roy."

"She's afraid of him, Lori. Allison is, too."

"You may be right, but she stays with him." Lori loaded CPR equipment into her station wagon, insisting that I not lift anything because of my back.

"Hope and Zebediah spoil Allison rotten with expensive horses and riding lessons. They live in one of those fancy houses in Heavenly Acres, but none of them seems very happy."

CHAPTER TWENTY-ONE

It was mid-August, and despite Lori passing her midwifery boards with exceptional scores, she was having no luck finding a permanent position off Fishback Island. "I've applied everywhere," she told me while she dropped Chesapeake blue crabs into boiling water that would turn them bright orange. The kitchen was fragrant with the spices of Old Bay seasoning. "The A.M.A. has all the hospitals afraid of lawsuits if they even allow midwives on their staffs."

"You'll find something," I said.

Billy and Brendan were having an escalating argument in their room. Lori stomped to the stairs and ordered them to the kitchen.

"He won't let me keep my turtle in our room," Brendan whined. "And it's already crawled away two times."

"What turtle?" Lori looked apprehensively around the kitchen.

"I found him down by the pond," the eight year old said. "I put him in a box in my room till I can get wire and boards to build a pen." Brendan took the opportunity to hit Lori up for the necessary funds. "I only need six dollars. I can make it all by myself."

"I can't be worrying about building a home for a turtle when I'm having trouble providing one for humans." Lori put a lid on the deep crab pot to allow it to steam.

"I've not got ta put up with a turtle in my room," Billy said.

"It's my room too," Brendan retorted.

Lori pounded her hand onto the stove top with such ferocity the lid on the crab pot did a little dance. "Brendan, you get that turtle out of this house immediately! And Billy, you stop talking like a goddamned local!"

Brendan looked at his mother with frightened eyes before silently slipping out of the room. Billy stood regarding her from a safe distance near the back door. "Ah'm an ahlunder, and Ah'll always be an ahlunder" he said. "An' ma name is William James."

In one motion Lori made it across the kitchen and slapped his face. Billy looked startled at first, then took on a look of disdain and slammed out the door. Lori went to the table, dropped into a chair and sat with her head in her hands.

Peggy peered into the kitchen, twisting at her yellow braids, before retreating back to the living room to watch television. Reba's rocker squeaked rhythmically as she watched the evening news and engaged in what she referred to as 'minding her own troubles'.

"You're tired," I said when I sat down across from Lori. "You've been working long hours, taking care of complicated pregnancies, then spending almost as much time filling out job applications."

"I can't believe I gave two years of my life and my children's to make me fair game for any doctor who wants to hang out his shingle."

A new doctor on the staff, Dr. Wells, was not only handling all medical and surgical care for welfare patients, he had recently gone to the hospital administration to ask if he could take over some of the O.B. patients Lori saw in her welfare clinic. The maternity fee paid to doctors by the state was not nearly what private insurance companies paid, but along with his patients from Colored Town, Dr. Wells could make a living without having to rely on referrals from islander staff. Although happy to give up impoverished patients, no island doctor was about to give paying customers to an outsider.

The hospital had not yet granted the new doctor's request to take over Lori's O.B. patients. But she felt it was a matter of time.

"There have to be jobs somewhere," I said. "You just haven't hit the right places yet."

"I'm not going to some backward hole with crummy schools," Lori said emphatically. "I refuse to raise my children in East Jesus."

I looked out the window at the white clapboard houses squatting in the gathering dusk. "I thought this was East Jesus." It elicited not even a smile from Lori.

"I think about all the nights I came home from Filmore with no energy left for them," she said while tearing at a strip of yellowed wallpaper next to the table. "And how I left them to get their own breakfast and walk to school alone in that awful neighborhood."

Reba changed the channel from news to a game show.

"I kept telling myself it would all be worth it when I graduated

139

and got a decent job." Lori yanked loose the strip of aged wallpaper and threw it onto the table. "And here I am, yelling at them worse than I ever did in Baltimore."

The stove's burner beneath the crab pot glowed blue in the darkening kitchen.

"WHICH DOOR DO YOU CHOOSE!" the game show host asked in the next room. "DOOR ONE, DOOR TWO, OR DOOR THREE!"

"Take two, take two!" Peggy yelled. "The prize is behind two!"

"It's three," Reba said confidently.

"Why did I put myself and my children through all that, Pat?"

"Because you were trying to provide a good life for them," I said firmly. "And you will if you'll just give yourself time."

"I hit Billy." It sounded as if she just realized it.

"He only talks that way to annoy you. He doesn't use his islander dialect when you're not around."

"COME ON NOW, DOOR ONE, DOOR TWO, OR DOOR THREE! YOU HAVE TO MAKE A CHOICE!" The audience yelled out various numbers while Peggy stuck to door two.

"Maybe it's door one," Reba said.

"Billy's eyes looked so hurt," Lori continued in her downward spiral. I switched on the kitchen light. "Look how late it is!" Lori said when she saw the clock. She gave a frantic glance out the window as she got up from her chair. "It's already dark!"

"This isn't Baltimore," I reminded. "The boys are O.K."

She went to the door and called to them but got no response. After clicking the porch light on and off several times, Brendan came dragging in without his turtle.

Lori fell to her knees to embrace her young son. "I didn't mean to yell at you, honey. I truly didn't."

"It took a long time for my turtle to crawl away," Brendan said. The wet and muddied knees of his jeans attested to the lengthy vigil.

"That turtle probably wanted to go back to the pond where it came from anyway," Lori told him. "How about if Mom lets you buy one in a pet store and we build a nice pen for it?"

Brendan considered for a moment, playing his guilt-ridden mother like a virtuoso. "Could I buy a rabbit instead?"

Lori kissed him. "O.K., but only one."

"Can I have a pet too?" Door two had lost and Peggy had come into the kitchen to spread newspapers over the table and get out wooden mallets to crack open crab claws.

"Sure you can." There was no limit to Lori's generosity. "Maybe we can find a cat like Ginger."

"I don't want a cat!" Peggy banged the mallets down onto the table. "I don't ever want another cat, never, ever!" The outburst was so unexpected even Reba came to the door.

"All right," Lori said calmly. "You don't have to get a cat if you don't want to."

"Could I have fish instead?" Peggy asked with all eyes on her. "And an aquarium that lights up so I can see them at night?"

"We'll have to see how much it would cost," Lori said. "Maybe next payday." Reba sighed her disapproval and returned to the T.V.

Lori went out to find Billy, returning with him nearly an hour later. The rest of us already had a pile of empty crab shells in the center of the table.

"Mom's going to pay me to paint the house," Billy announced as he passed through the kitchen on his way to clean up for dinner. "And I get to use the money to buy a boat."

"A small second-hand one," Lori said when Reba gave her a look. "The painting will give him something to do, and the house really does need it." Reba attacked a crab leg with her wooden mallet and pulled out the juicy white meat. "I can't sell it the way it looks," Lori continued while Reba gave all of her attention to savoring the delicacy. "And I certainly can't afford to have it painted professionally."

"I guess it's as good as spending his time hanging around his father's place waiting to be noticed," Reba allowed when she finished her crab claw. "But how do you expect a thirteen year old boy to paint a two story house?"

"I'll help him."

Reba's eyebrows raised. "With your work schedule?"

"Do we still get to paint it red?" Brendan asked his mother as Billy returned to the kitchen.

Billy gave Brendan a big brother look of superiority. "Houses are painted white," he declared. "Except the pretty brick ones like Dad's in Heavenly Acres."

"You promised ours could be painted red," Brendon said to Lori.

"I like red myself," Reba said.

Lori looked across the table at her friend dressed in her Salvation Army suit. Although she was strong enough to tend the small garden she had in the backyard, each time she went outside hostile stares came from neighboring windows.

"Red it shall be," proclaimed Lori.

CHAPTER TWENTY-TWO

"I never knew my father." Hope handed me a delicate cucumber sandwich. "The nuns told me my mother cared for me until I was three. Then she took me to the orphanage and never returned."

It was the first I had seen Hope and Allison since the awkward encounter with Zebediah at the firehall. I was glad he was back to his Senatorial duties in Annapolis so our picnics could resume.

"I was in a convent for a year," I said. Hope's mouth opened in surprise and Allison looked my way with genuine interest. "My mother was determined to have a nun or priest in the family, and I was it. At least for awhile."

"I can't imagined you in a convent." Hope poured me a cup of tea from the outdated thermos she brought to every picnic. I was sure it was the same one she had used with Adam Lee.

"Neither could the nuns, that's why they threw me out."

Hope laughed and the sadness that seemed always to be lingering in her eyes left for a moment. "What did you do?"

"Nothing so terrible, now that I look back at it."

"Tell me," Hope said with the excitement of Brendan or Peggy.

"It was so long ago. I was only fifteen."

Both Hope and Allison leaned back against the concrete slab of Adam Lee's grave like children settling in around a campfire to hear ghost stories. There were daisies, black-eyed Susans and other summer flowers scattered over it. In the background workers were adding bricks to the new Highway Holiness Church.

"The convent my mother stuck me in didn't embalm its dead. I was assigned to help keep the bodies cold while they lay in state in the chapel." A tiny gasp escaped Allison. "We did it by filling quart jars with ice, then packing them around the body in its pine box."

Hope shivered in spite of her slacks and long sleeved blouse. "It was the same where I was."

"You never told me that," Allison said. "How gruesome."

"I hated going into that eerie chapel all alone to ice them down," I continued. "So one night I took a friend along." I laughed at the memory. "She was in her first year, same as me, and usually in trouble." I had Allison's complete attention now.

"My friend started telling me the body wasn't cold enough and I should touch it to see, like she was doing. I didn't at first, but she kept insisting until I took a quick jab at the nose. Since the body wasn't embalmed, the tip caved in and refused to come back out."

Allison and Hope squealed in unison.

"I patted it, coaxed it, and even said three Hail Marys for it to pop back to its former shape, but it wouldn't budge."

"What about the girl that got you into it?" Allison asked.

"She took off as fast as she could. I stayed there trying to fix it until I had to report to my dorm for evening prayer."

"But what happened to the nun?" Hope asked.

"When the other nuns saw her the next morning, they all wondered why they had never noticed the dimple in Sister Josepha's nose."

Allison clapped her hands together and laughed with the abandon one expected in a young girl.

"And they never found out?" Hope asked.

"Oh, they found out. The Mother Superior had me in for a little talk, and we both agreed it would be best if I returned home for a year or two to see if I had a true vocation."

Allison offered me a plate of homemade macaroon cookies. "What a marvelous story."

"Did they ring the bells when a nun died at your convent?" Hope asked.

"Always, even if they died at three a.m. To this day I have never heard bells so loud."

Perhaps it was the cemetery that precipitated the dream, or Peggy. She was already asleep when I got into my bed, and I lay there watching her in the light of her new aquarium. Her yellow hair fanned out over her pillow, shimmering like silver in the fish tank's iridescent glow, making her look like an angel.

The dream started the same way. I was sitting on a row of sandbags waiting for Dan to be brought out of surgery after losing his leg. But it did not end there, as it usually did. The surgeons came out to tell me Dan died because he lost too much blood before a helicopter could get to him, which was what actually happened.

My chest felt as it had back then, like ribs cut and spread apart on someone about to have heart surgery. Only nobody repaired my broken heart once it was exposed.

In the next moment I was back in the United States. Music played and people drank, danced and laughed. I wore a blue silk dress, Dan's favorite, and sat on the sidelines watching.

Dan was standing next to a long table covered with food and drink when I first spotted him.

He saw me, I was sure of it, but he turned away with no acknowledgment and moved quickly into the crowd. I followed, pushing people out of my way and calling his name. But when I reached the other side of the throng, I found nothing but empty space. Dan had vanished where there was no place to go, no doors or windows, not even a chair to hide behind.

I looked back at the others, who were all watching me. "The doctors told me he died in Vietnam, but he was here," I said to them. When they didn't respond I went to stand next to the long table. "He stood right in this spot."

"He didn't die," a woman told me. "He didn't even exist."

I realized she was one of my sisters. We were at a family party for my brother-in-law who was drafted for Vietnam, and then judged 4F and discharged. There had been no party on my return, but we were celebrating for one who didn't have to go.

"Dan existed." I backed away, moving into the empty space where he had disappeared. "He loved me, and I loved him."

"You made him up," someone chided.

"No."

A baby began crying somewhere in the room, and I ran frantically around looking for it while the other partiers laughed. "Help me," I pleaded. "I have to find it so I can save it." They kept laughing.

I am sitting straight up in bed. In the iridescent glow of flares used in nighttime battle, I see a child lying so still she must be badly wounded. Silver hair radiates around her like a halo.

I want to go to her, but my body refuses to move. I try to call to the child, but I do not know her name. Call your own name, I tell myself. But I do not know that either.

"Help me," I manage to get out. "Help me save the child."

A hand touches my arm. "Are you alright?" I look up at a

woman. "You were having a bad dream."

I look across the room to where I saw the child. A young girl sits on the edge of a bed watching me intently, a girl with loose yellow hair.

"Are you O.K. now?" the woman asks. I do not know her name, and I can barely hear her above the hissing of a giant suction machine.

It is sucking up dismembered pieces of babies and depositing them in a large bottle that bubbles with foam and blood. Torsos, arms and legs bob about in its pinkish froth.

There are no heads.

"I heard you yelling about a child or something," the woman says. She sits down next to me on the bed. "You scared me; you scared Peggy too."

A name. A name I know.

Peggy was watching me from her bed when I came out of the flashback. Her pale face was made even whiter by an iridescent glow in the otherwise darkened room.

I am living with Lori on Fishback Island, I told myself silently. The glow is from the aquarium Lori bought Peggy.

Things came back in sections, like boxcars of a train emerging one by one from a tunnel.

"Go back to sleep, everything's all right," Lori said towards the door. I turned and saw Billy and Brendan. "I'll go back to bed now," Lori said when the boys were gone. "If you're O.K.?"

"I'm fine."

I watched Lori tuck Peggy back into bed while I apologized for waking her. Peggy fell quickly back to sleep in the silvery glow.

I am not fine, I told myself as I laid back down. A few minutes ago I didn't even know my own name.

I had been lulled into believing the odd episodes were gone now that I lived on the island. But this one frightened me more than any of the others had.

Fish chased one another in Peggy's aquarium, and while I watched I realized it was the noise of the bubbling filter that triggered the suction machine memory from Filmore Hospital.

The party for my brother-in-law had actually happened shortly after my return from the war, but I held no resentment toward my family. It was just another crazy facet of Vietnam, partying for one who didn't go while ignoring one who returned safely.

Lori stood in my doorway dressed for the hospital. "Aren't you going to work?"

I didn't want to tell her I was afraid to. "My back's acting up." And it truly was from every muscle in my body being tightened to the max. "Could you call Skipper for me?"

Lori looked concerned. "Maybe you should see a doctor."

"I'll be O.K. with a day or two of bed rest."

"That's the end of painting for you," she said before she left. "Billy and I can finish."

Lori and I had both been helping Billy with the house in our off hours. Enough paint had already been applied to make the rambling structure stick out from its white clapboard neighbors like a cherry in a bowl full of marshmallows.

Reba stayed downstairs watching T.V. except to bring tea and homemade soup at lunch time. "You need your strength," she said when I showed no interest.

She put a hand to my forehead. Her palm felt wonderfully cool and calm. "I'd better check your temperature."

"It's just my back," I objected. But Reba was already on her way to the bathroom.

It was difficult to hold the glass thermometer under my tongue without clamping my trembling jaw down on it. I felt as if I was on a vibrating railway platform with dozens of trains thundering by.

"Normal," Reba said when she removed the thermometer.

"Told you."

"Eat your soup," she said before going back downstairs.

I heard her rocker squeaking during a commercial, but it was drowned out when the game show host came back on.

CHAPTER TWENTY-THREE

I returned to work with a promise from Skipper that I would not take call for two weeks. My back was the excuse but I was afraid to work alone in case I had an episode with a patient under anesthesia.

I returned home at four P.M. at the end of the first week to find Andy sitting in the kitchen with Reba. "Whose car is that?" I asked. A Ford Falcon with much of its body given to rust sat in the driveway.

"Mine," Andy answered.

"Where's your donorcycle?"

"I decided I didn't like people waiting for my spare parts."

"It's about time," Reba said.

Andy grabbed playfully at her necktie and led her toward the door. "Come on," he said. "I'll take you ladies for a ride."

Reba could not be coaxed out of the house, but I accepted. We drove south through Muskrat Marsh, neither of us paying much attention to where we were going. I wasn't aware of crossing the bridge into Colored Town until noticing the unmistakable odor of the dump.

"Where the hell are we?" Andy said as he drove the dirt road.

"Colored Town," I said. "Where the black man they hanged was from."

Andy was looking around in wonderment. "Shit, man, this is a whole other country."

Colored Town was even more depressing in daylight. I pointed out the shabby cemetery where Reba's mother was buried, and told him how Reba vowed she would one day buy her a pure white, marble head stone.

Andy didn't appear to hear me. He drove slowly, taking time to look at the shanties and the people going in and out of a general store that looked like the heart of the settlement. "It reminds me of a village in Nam where I used to run a clinic for the locals."

He did not sound as detached as he usually was about the war.

"Andy, how did you get over Vietnam?" The dream about Dan, with me waking up not knowing my name, was still frightening.

His car was barely moving now. "Who says I'm over it?"

"You've been screwed by the government to the point of buying your own prosthesis. You should be screaming in their faces."

He reached a hand across the seat to box playfully at me. "Always ready to fight, huh Danang?"

"I'd really like to be normal again, to sleep without nightmares or my mind deserting me." I told him of the dream and its aftermath.

He pulled his car to a stop near the general store. "So you want to be normal like me?"

"I wish I could go to sleep with a strap tied to me and looped over the bedpost so I wouldn't fall into Vietnam every night."

Andy smiled. It was getting dark and kerosene lamps were being lit in the dilapidated houses surrounding us. The proprietor of the general store lit a gas lantern hanging over the cash register.

Andy opened the car door. "I need some smokes."

When he returned he held the open pack out to me, and I thought of a dozen justifications for taking one.

"No, thanks," I said steadfastly.

Andy started to take one, then tossed the full pack into his car's glove box, which was minus a door. "I'm trying to quit myself. In fact, I set a goal to be off them when I graduate next spring."

"Where do you plan to work?"

"No idea."

The sun was down and gulls screeched over the garbage dump, now silhouetted by twilight. Andy abruptly reached for the glove box, retrieved the pack of cigarettes and lit one.

"When I stepped on that mine I felt like I was blown into a time warp," he said as he exhaled. "I mean I was blasted way the hell up into the air and just seemed to hang there, suspended in space and time." His manner was mystical, disbelieving. "I could see the beach, the jungle, the guys down below, yet there was no feeling, no pain, nothing. All I could think of was what a fucking view!"

He laughed loudly and a woman entering the store looked in our direction. "I said to myself, Fuckin' A, you are flying, man! Then I fell back to earth," Andy said with the euphoria gone. "And reality hit." He looked down at his prosthesis.

The woman came out of the store and hurried past us.

"I could see my leg was gone, blown away clean as a whistle. Well, not that clean," he said with his humorless laugh. "There was a chunk of bone sticking out next to what was left of my knee. Lots of torn up muscle and one hell of a lot of blood. Jesus, I didn't think I had that much blood in me."

"Was there another medic to take care of you?"

He shook his head. "No such luck." He flicked ashes from his cigarette out the window. "I put a tourniquet on it myself and got the bleeding under pretty good control. The pain was getting bad."

"It was so numb up in the air," he said with the same wonder he expressed earlier. "It was like I was a character in a cartoon. I could see these dialogue balloons above my head with words like BANG! ZAP! POW!" He laughed again. "Pretty wild, huh?"

"I don't know how you managed to get a tourniquet on. I don't think I could have done that."

"I didn't have much choice." He forced cigarette smoke from his lungs with an impatient hiss. "Every guy in the platoon was either dead or on the way."

The screeching of the gulls filled the void until he went on.

"I haven't been exactly honest with you Danang." He mashed out his cigarette with deliberate little stabs in the car's battered ashtray. "My platoon was tracking North Vietnamese." He lit another cigarette. "I stepped on the mine and gave away our position. The North opened up on us with AK47s, RPGs and everything else they had."

"When it was over, every one of my men was greased, just lying there dead or on their way. And me, the big heroic medic, what was I doing? Why I was saving my own ass, man, that's what."

"Andy, you shouldn't...."

"Shouldn't what? You've wanted to know why I'm not pissed at the government for not providing me with a decent leg. Well I'm telling you why, I'm too fuckin' ashamed to be pissed!"

We were quiet while the proprietor of the general store came out and looked our way. Then went back inside and locked the door.

"A so-called doc who puts a tourniquet on his own leg while his men are dying all around him deserves nothing," Andy said while he watched the store owner watching him through the window.

"Maybe we should go," I suggested.

Andy made no move, but when I got out of his car and came around to the driver's side he slid over on the seat to let me behind the wheel. He said nothing while I drove out of Colored Town, or during the drive to Seaport. When I pulled the car to a stop on a dead end street facing the ocean he still said nothing.

"Andy, you were trained to put a tourniquet on a severed limb. You did it out of instinct." He would not look at me. "There was nothing wrong with saving your own life."

He looked out over the ocean. "The guys were yelling, doc! doc!" His voice dropped to a whisper. "Then it got real quiet."

He faced me for the first time since Colored Town. "The gooks came slipping in to make sure we were all finished off. I played dead, but one of them put a round through my neck just in case." He reached a hand to the crater at the back of his neck.

"How did you get out of there?"

"Dust off chopper." He took his hand from the scar and lit another of his steady succession of cigarettes. "I came to with the bodies of my men stacked all around me, some on top. The chopper crew assumed all of us were greased; and I couldn't move or talk."

"When did they discover you were alive?"

"I lay in the expectant area of a hospital for who knows how long. You know, the place where they put the ones they expect to check-out before they can get to them. I wasn't so sure I was alive myself," he said with his short laugh. "I kept passing out and coming to with bodies all around me and docs and nurses running in every direction yelling for blood, tourniquets, the usual triage mad-house." He paused a moment. "If I wasn't already gone I knew I soon would be, lying there bleeding to death with guys who already had."

"Then the funniest damned thing happened," he said with a laugh that was genuinely humorous. "This dumb shit corporal was putting everyone in bags, and I couldn't move a muscle or turn my head to see him because of the round through my neck. I couldn't see anyway 'cause my eyes were crusted shut with dried blood from my men bleeding out on top of me in the chopper. But I could hear, and I knew the sound of zippers on body bags after all the guys I'd stuffed in them."

"But didn't somebody first pronounce them dead?" It shocked me to consider a live casualty being sent to the morgue.

"He wasn't closing the bags completely," Andy explained. "We used to leave them open at the top so the docs could get a stethoscope in to pronounce them when they had time."

"So this guy moves on to me, and I'm completely paralyzed. And I'm thinking, Jesus, how do I let this bastard know I'm not dead when I can't talk and can't even blink my fucking eyes."

"I tried moving my mouth but couldn't make a sound," he said. "And the dip shit didn't notice my lips moving 'cause he's so busy trying to get me into the bag. Then I discovered the one thing that worked. No shit," he said laughing. "The only part of my whole fuckin' body that I could still control was my tongue."

"You stuck it out at him?" The gallows humor made me laugh.

"Worse!" He said it so loudly people taking an evening stroll on the beach paused for a moment before going on. "I rolled my tongue around and somehow managed to work up the last glob of spit my dehydrated body possessed. I mean the absolute last drop."

"Oh, Andy."

"So just as he's pulling the body bag up around me I let him have it right in the face." The two of us howled, the same as we had in the war when something happened to break the morbid monotony of more wounded and more dead. "He ran off screaming his fucking head off!"

When we stopped laughing he told me how medics and nurses came running and hauled him into receiving for evaluation. He pulled down his shirt to reveal a ragged scar near the base of his throat and described undergoing an emergency tracheotomy while fully awake. "I listened to them talking about the gunshot wound in my neck while they worked, debating what they should do about it. Then they started discussing how high they should amputate what was left of my leg."

"Did they know you could hear?"

"Hell, there was such a shitload of casualties in there, I guess they didn't have time to worry about feelings." A pale moon was coming up over the ocean and he focused on it while he spoke. "The worst part was not being able to talk," he said. "I wanted to be able to tell them just one thing." His voice wavered. "I wanted to say...that I would rather be dead than paralyzed."

I took his hand, but he pulled free of my grasp.

"The surgery in Nam and Japan wasn't so bad," he said while continuing to watch the ascending moon. "It was easy to pretend it was someone else they were carving on over there, and someone else trying to move his arms and legs."

He lit yet another cigarette. "Things were different when I got back to the world and my family could visit me in the hospital; the pretending was over. At least that kind of pretending," he added with his hollow laugh. "The new kind was making believe everything was going to be hunky dory for the sake of my mom and dad, and for all the stateside docs and physical therapists giving me their rah-rah pep talks about how I could make it if I really tried."

"Did they know what happened to you in Vietnam? That you lost all your men and were put in a dead pile with them?"

"I tried to tell them, but they told me I had to quit dwelling on the past." A sigh rose from deep within him. "My folks had a pretty hard time because I got hurt during my second tour. They never could understand why I wanted to go back after making it home in one piece the first time."

"You did a second tour?"

"Yup. The action junkie went back for more."

"I knew medics and corpsmen who signed up for three and four tours," I said. "They were afraid to leave their men with someone who wasn't as experienced."

"Exactly. But then I go back over there and step on a land mine that gets them all blown away," he said bitterly. "They would have had a better chance without me."

He moved away when I tried to put an arm around him. "You saved a lot of lives over there, Andy." He waved a dismissing hand.

"Andy, would you have blamed any one of your men for what happened if they stepped on that mine?"

He looked out over the ocean to where the moon drifted behind a bank of clouds that turned silver in its backlight. I could see the glint of tears on his cheeks. We sat for several minutes, existing within our own thoughts. "You know what I think of heroes?" I said finally. "I think there's no such thing."

Andy listened without comment.

"There are only heroic challenges, most of which last only a few seconds. You either take on the challenge, running into a burning house to rescue someone, or maybe throw yourself on a grenade to save your buddies. Or you exercise very good common sense and run as fast as you can in the opposite direction."

"Whichever you choose," I said when Andy remained silent, "does not make you a hero forever, or a coward." I knew he was hearing me by the way his breathing started and stopped in small spurts.

"War hero should be kicked out of our vocabulary. It's too easy to bang the drums and wave the flag marching off to battle, thinking it's going to make you a hero, instead of turning you into a bloody piece of pain. Or a specimen in a body bag."

I thought of my mother, and how she wept when my uncle's body was shipped back from Normandy years after the war was over. It was a sealed coffin containing the decayed remains of her baby brother that came home, not a hero as the War Department stated in its telegram.

"It's like claiming God is on our side to justify the slaughter," I said. "When war is the most godless act in which we participate."

The rusted old car shook with Andy's sobs.

CHAPTER TWENTY-FOUR

"Where the hell have you been?" Dr. Arst stood at the door to the operating room where I was assigned. "We have another abdominal hyst after this one, and I have office hours startin' at one."

"I'm sorry, I had some problems with the last patient's I.V. in the recovery room," I said as I went to the patient on the table. We had already completed three hysterectomies and it wasn't even noon.

Doctor Arst paced the room, stopping occasionally to remove his scrub cap and run a liver spotted hand through his silver hair while I started an I.V. on the young woman. Only when I began injecting the Pentothal did he go out to the sink to scrub.

"Isn't twenty-nine a little young to be having a hysterectomy?" I asked while the scrub tech and Carol Faye, who was the circulating nurse, arranged sterile drapes over the unconscious patient.

"Ahlund wimin have thur babies young an' get it over with," said the scrub tech. "Had my uterus out when I was not but twenty-seven."

"Honey hush, I'm near twenty-two and haven't even used mine yet," Carol Faye lamented.

Dr. Arst came into the room at the tail end of the discussion. "If you're not growin' babies in there, you're growin' weeds," he said while he dried his hands on a sterile towel. "Might's well let the pathologists carve on it."

"Lor-dee, Lord!" Carol Faye put a hand over her abdomen as if he was about to snatch hers.

Dr. Arst laughed. "I didn't mean you, Big Knocks."

The room was quiet while the surgeon made his incision and screwed in place a large retractor that stretched the woman's abdominal muscles apart as far as possible to provide him a clear shot at the uterus. Her postoperative pain would be dramatically increased by the heavy-handed tactic, but time was of the essence in the elderly gynecologist's operating room.

"Men don't have their privates lopped off when they're done havin' babies," Carol Faye ventured when the case was comfortably underway. "Why should women get castrated?"

"Castrated?" Dr. Arst was so taken aback he quit cutting. "I don't want ta hear that damned wimin's lib talk comin' from anyone with a nice set a' knockers like yours."

Carol Faye blushed behind her surgical mask. "Thank you."

"Men don't have periods ta put up with," Dr. Arst lectured as he made quick little cuts around the base of the uterus. "Wimin are glad ta get rid of cramps an' all that mess."

"A hysterectomy's pretty radical treatment for menstrual cramps," I said over the anesthesia screen.

"That's enough! I don't want ta hear another word till I get this thang out!"

The surgeon considered it a personal defeat if it took more than an hour, skin to skin, to do an abdominal hysterectomy. As a result, he spent little time clamping cut vessels and patients lost far more blood than necessary.

"Damn it to hell, look at the clock," he said as he lifted the trophy free of the pelvic cavity fifty minutes after the initial incision. "All this blathering's put me behind." The scrub tech had difficulty threading needles fast enough as he tied off bleeders and whipped the various layers of tissue back together. "I don't know what's wrong with wimin anymore, havin' ta go to colleech an' all," he groused. "Why can't those wimin's libbers be happy takin' care a' their husbins, playin' cards an' shoppin' like my Doris Yvonne?"

"But your wife went ta nursin' school," Carol Faye objected.

"That's different. At least nurses learn how ta keep a man's bathroom clean."

I was finishing my pre-op rounds my first evening back on call, making sure every patient to be operated on the following day had orders written for sleep medication and a pre-operative sedative, when I was paged to the delivery suite. Lori was on call.

"Twins," she said when I entered the labor room where she sat timing a young migrant woman's contractions. "I already called Doctor Wells to help with the delivery."

154

Even though the new doctor was after Lori's O.B. patients, she did not hesitate to consult him for complicated cases.

While she did a vaginal exam to see how far along the patient was, the young woman breathed calmly. A result of the natural childbirth training Lori gave each patient in the welfare clinic.

"She's ready to move to delivery," Lori said when she completed the exam. "I hope Doctor Wells gets here soon."

I helped Lori and Mrs. Critchfield move the patient onto a delivery room table and put oxygen on her to build up as much as possible in the blood circulating through the unborn twins.

Lori injected a local anesthetic into her patient's perineum and cervix to make her more comfortable while waiting for Dr. Wells.

The first of the twins was being delivered when Dr. Wells hurried into the room pulling a cap over a head of thick, sandy hair that, in combination with his freckles, made him appear too young to be a practicing physician. He took the healthy looking baby from Lori while she went after the second.

"It's small, high and breech," she told Dr. Wells. "Maybe you should check her."

The physician was doing a deep, pelvic exam when the heart tones on the second twin dropped precipitously, activating an alarm on the fetal monitor Dr. Wells had talked the hospital into buying. "Give me some relaxation," he said to me. "We have to go after it."

I turned on a potent anesthetic that would relax the uterus and began counting off seconds in intervals of fifteen. The baby must be delivered and the umbilical cord clamped within two minutes of the start of the anesthetic, otherwise the drug would cross the placenta from mother to infant and cause serious complications, or even death.

"Forty-five seconds," I called out as I watched the red hand on the wall clock.

Dr. Wells was struggling to pull the baby down into the birth canal. Lori pushed on the patient's abdomen to help.

"One minute."

"Give me more fundal pressure." Lori pushed even harder.

"One minute, fifteen." I could hear the anxiety in my own voice.

"More!" Dr. Wells ordered.

Lori's face was red. "I'm pushing as hard as I can."

"One minute, thirty," I called just as Dr. Wells delivered a tiny baby that was a bluish hue because of the cord wrapped around its neck. The physician skillfully slipped the cord free and clamped it to stop the flow of anesthesia via the cord.

I had visions of the fiasco with Dr. Arst recurring, and began waking up the mother so I could care for the baby. But Lori was already suctioning the infant and inflating its lungs with an airbag hooked to oxygen. It let out a weak cry.

"You'd better get a helicopter down here," Dr. Wells told Mrs. Critchfield when she came into the room to check on the progress of the delivery. "The small one needs to get to Baltimore as fast as possible. And we might as well send the other one, too."

He was massaging the mother's boggy uterus to make it firm up and stop bleeding. I was giving I.V. Pitocin to do the same.

"Ain't neither nor helicopter coming down here tanaght," Mrs. Critchfield told him. "It's stormin' something turble out there." The delivery rooms had no windows so we were unaware of the storm. "Lightnin' hitting everwhere last time I looked."

"Then get an ambulance," Dr. Wells said. "They need a neonatal ICU."

Christian Hospital had only five beds in its intensive care unit, and they were all for adults. Any child needing specialized care was transferred to Baltimore.

"Our ambulance takes four hours ta Baltmur in a storm," Mrs. Critchfield said. "And it's already out on a call."

Dr. Wells expertly inserted a breathing tube into the smaller twin while Lori stitched the mother's perineum back together. Mrs. Critchfield went to call the island's only pediatrician.

"Ambulance bringin' in a bad one," she announced when she returned. "Welfare O.B. from Erystchur Ahlund."

"Where the hell is that?" Dr. Wells asked while he assisted the breathing of the smaller twin with a miniature air bag.

"'Bout ten miles southwest a' Fishback Ahlund," Mrs. Critchfield said before leaving to prepare for the new admission.

"And fifty years back in time," Lori added. "It's Oyster Island," she said to Jeff Wells. "Used to be part of Fishback until a hurricane separated them years ago."

The new patient had delivered at home and was bleeding profusely. I started two I.V.s on her while Lori checked her vital signs and assessed the hemorrhage from the uterus. Dr. Wells was still waiting for the pediatrician so he could relinquish care of the newborn twins.

"Have you ever been in the hospital before?" I asked the ashen faced woman. She would have to go to surgery to stop the hemorrhage.

"No, ma'am, I ain't never bin sick but this oncet." Her voice was muffled under the plastic oxygen mask over her mouth and nose. "I birthed all my babies with no trouble till this one. Suppin' went wrong with my virginya."

"Vagina," Mrs. Critchfield clarified.

"The mail boat was since come an' gone when I took ta' bleedin'," the woman said weakly. "They had ta carry me over on a trawler."

"They mostly use the mail boat to get back an' forth between Erystchur Ahlund an' Fishback," Mrs. Critchfield said. "Though some folks live thur whole lives out there without ever oncet leavin'."

The blood I ordered arrived and I pumped it into the patient.

"It was pitchin' a storm like I never seen," the woman said. "I got ta vomickin' somethin' turble on the boat."

"It's the Lord's miracle y'all didn't go down on that trawler," Mrs. Critchfield told her. Lightning flashed outside the windows of the labor room where we worked, and thunder rolled over the island like barrels rolling down a ramp.

"It looks like she has some retained placenta and a cervical tear," Lori told Dr. Wells when he joined us.

"Who in the world does the deliveries on that island?" the physician asked after examining the patient.

"Wimin folk," Mrs. Critchfield replied. "They never had neither nor docter over there." The O.B. nurse helped us lift the patient to a stretcher. "They've not got but a store an' church," she said as we headed for surgery. "An' neither nor school."

On the trip down in the elevator to surgery, Mrs. Critchfield gave us the details of how the remote island had been detached from Fishback when a violent hurricane dug a wide channel across the southern section of what was once a single land mass. The inhabitants had chosen to stay on their marooned piece of real estate, living without benefit of the progress most Americans took for granted.

Babies were delivered by housewives and raised without medical care or education, Mrs. Critchfield told us, except for those who crossed the channel on the daily mailboat to attend school on Fishback Island. Most boys chose to ignore formal education, beginning work on their family's boat when they were seven or eight. Young girls worked alongside their mothers in seafood processing plants.

"Shuckin' erystchurs an' havin' babies is thur life," Mrs. Critchfield concluded when we reached the O.R. suite.

Lori offered to assist Dr. Wells in surgery. They removed fragments of retained placenta under a local anesthetic while I administered a mild sedative, oxygen and blood. "What's the name of that place she comes from?" Dr. Wells asked as he put in the final sutures. The patient dozed peacefully, exhausted from her ordeal.

"Oyster Island," Lori answered.

"Sounds like a good place to stay away from."

"Thur a strange bunch, all right," the scrub tech handing instruments said. "They've married one another till they all look the same." A piece of island beige hair stuck out from under her scrub cap. "They do things against the bible too, like sangin' and dancin'. And they won't allow neither nor new preacher." The expression in her pale blue eyes was grave. "Not one of them's goin' ta be saved if they don't change their ways an' embrace the Lord Jesus Christ."

Dr. Wells gave her a look that was a mixture of amusement and curiosity. He got up and pulled off his gloves. "I'll let you get her settled in ICU," he said to Lori. He started for the door but paused. "That was good work with the twins."

Lori sounded like a teenager. "Really? Thanks."

It was after midnight when Lori and I left the hospital and drove home through remnants of the storm. The only sound in her old house was the droning of the refrigerator, whose compressor threatened to quit despite Lori's daily invocations that it last the summer.

"Have you ever been to that island?" I asked over a cup of tea.

"I was always going to go over there but never did."

"We should do it sometime."

"You heard Doctor Wells, it's a good place to stay away from."

"It certainly sounds like it could use a midwife."

Lori set down her cup. "I'm trying to get off Fishback Island, Pat. I'm not about to move to one even more remote."

"I didn't say move there. Maybe you could do deliveries on your free weekends."

"And how would they pay me, with oysters?"

"Or crabs."

Lori laughed. "I have been thinking of starting some natural childbirth classes outside the hospital. If Doctor Wells gets his way and I'm without a job, it could at least bring in money til I get the house sold."

"You think these islanders are ready for natural childbirth?"

"The nurses are coming around. They're finally using the fetal monitor." She stood and stretched. "Come on, time for bed."

"I think I'll make a trip to Oyster Island," I said as we climbed the stairs. "It might be a fun place to take the children."

"He's a pretty nice guy, isn't he?" Lori said.

"You mean Wells?"

"I think I may have been unfair assuming that he's only out for the bucks."

CHAPTER TWENTY-FIVE

The staff of Christian Hospital was always quick to point out that Hen Fishback provided most of the jobs on the island. But he was also responsible for a great deal of suffering.

The most common malady we saw was a condition known locally as chicken hand, caused by the nerves and tendons of the wrist becoming inflamed and scarred from working in Hen's processing plants. There was severe pain associated with the disorder, and movement of the hand and wrist became so restricted the victims had difficulty performing simple tasks such as dressing and combing their hair.

Surgical intervention could relieve the symptoms, but if the patient returned to the same work the problem recurred, resulting in more surgery and more scarring. The hand eventually pulled up on itself in contractures so pronounced it looked more like the claw of a chicken than a human appendage. At that point, as far as the island surgeons were concerned, the condition was irreversible.

"The docters operated on it oncet," the elderly black woman told me. She was not having surgery on her crippled hand, she had an intestinal obstruction and I happened to notice the chicken hand while starting her I.V. "I went back ta work as a gutter after the operation," she said. "But them lines run so fast, before I knew it I had to have it fixed all over again." She held up the contracted talon for my closer inspection. "It worn't no good after that."

Cutters were responsible for slitting open plucked and decapitated chickens which hung from an automated line. From there the chickens moved on to the gutters, who removed the entrails.

To keep pace with the fast moving line, cutters held their knives in a cramped position ready to cut the chickens open in one swift slash.

The gutters constantly held their hands in a rake-like position to insure efficiency as they yanked out the slippery innards.

But the gutters had the additional hardship of having to work with their hands submerged in ice cold water used to begin cooling down the freshly slaughtered fowl. Many of the cutters, and almost all of the gutters, eventually developed chicken hand. And each of them had to retire from the line long before the usual retirement age.

"My husbin' and me were both put off the line the same time for chickin hand," the patient told me. "But Mister Fishback was good ta us, he give us jobs in the houses, me haulin' out manure and my man pickin' up chickins what suffocated or dahed from vaccinations, or from pilin' up when they got scaret by electric storms."

It was Saturday and we had been waiting over an hour for the surgeon who would be doing the intestinal surgery, Dr. Wells.

Welfare patients were accustomed to waiting, and the old woman seemed happy just having someone to talk to. "When we went off the line we made us only fifty dollars a week each," she told me, "workin' three months tendin' chickens, then a week off with no pay whilst we waited for the little biddies ta come in an' start all over." She flinched from a sudden pain in her distended abdomen. "It worn't like now when they do the whole business in jest seven weeks."

"Take a deep breath please." I had my stethoscope on a chest that rattled and wheezed like someone in the terminal stages of emphysema.

"Them biddies growed up fast," she said. "We fed 'em corn and medicines the last couple a' weeks, an' give 'em Marigold petals to make their skin nice and yella."

She hacked for a full minute while I tried to help her by suctioning the thick crud in her airway. "People like thur chickins yella 'cause they think that's a sign thur good an' healthy," she said when the coughing fit was over. "'Course, they really was healthy with all the medicines we fed 'em."

She paused to catch her breath and rub a hand across her taut abdomen. "Lor-dee, the fit my husbin' pitched when he had ta mix up them medicines. He couldn't read di-rections on the bags n' I worn't much help since I never learnt ta read neither."

She stopped talking and her eyes became so vacant I reached down to check her pulse. She shook herself to attention and picked up right where she left off. "They was good chickins even though they was troublesome," she said. "We loved 'em ta death."

I busied myself getting out additional instruments I might need. The patient was so stooped over from osteoporosis she needed two pillows to fill the gap between her rigid upper torso and the operating table. I was certain I would have trouble getting a tube down her trachea once I had her asleep. Even if I managed to get past her anatomical problems, her lungs were so bad I would be struggling the whole time to get enough oxygen to her.

"My man an' me sure did eat us a lot a' chickin," she continued. "Mister Fishback give us all the sick ones we wanted ta eat." She started to laugh. "I used ta tell my husbin' I didn't never want ta eat another piece of chickin as long as I lived. But I would dearly love a good drumstick nowadays."

"It's probably just as well you don't eat it anymore with all the drugs you're telling me they get." And mixed by people who can't read instructions, I thought to myself.

"Oh, us folks in Colored Town mostly eat crabs an' fish we get free outta the bay." She worked her gums together. "Can't chew chickin so good anyways since I lost my teeth."

I pulled a stool up next to the table so I could sit while we waited for the surgeon, who was held up in the emergency room.

"How long ago did your husband die?"

"Let me see now," she said. And after a long pause, "You lose track a' time not workin'. I mean not workin' reglar with the chickins; I do washin' and ironin' for folks in Heavenly Acres."

She brought up mucous that looked as if it had been in her lungs for twenty years. "Both 'r lungs went bad working in them dusty houses after we couldn't work the line no more. My husbin' dahed a' stuffocation when his lungs give out completely, and mine ain't much behind." She looked at me with eyes almost occluded by cataracts. "He was a good man; give his whole life ta chickins."

I could not understand why she didn't hate Hen Fishback. He had a fleet of cadillacs, lived in a mansion and owned what parts of the island Zebediah Taylor did not. Yet he gave no compensation to people suffering crippling disabilities they developed while in his employ.

"You should sue Fishback Poultry," I said to her. "There must be thousands of you with chicken hand and bad lungs."

"Honey hush!" the patient shouted in a voice I thought impossible. "No one's ever gonna go against Mister Fishback!"

Andy's advice about not trying to right every injustice in the world flashed to mind but did not take root.

"But you could at least get worker's compensation." The patient did not comprehend. "Do you have any children who could help you?"

"Had me a son," she wheezed. "But he got hit by a chickin truck and died a' e-ternal injuries."

Dr. Wells came into the room apologizing for holding everyone up. "I just had a kid scream in my face the whole time I stitched him up." He patted the patient's arm. "This ought to be a piece of cake."

The physician was in his late thirties, and it was rumored he was single. But he had not lived on the island long enough for Carol Faye to have compiled all the data yet. Even an outsider was acceptable marriage material, as long as he could provide her a home in Heavenly Acres.

"You're pretty tight here," the surgeon said as he palpated his patient's bloated abdomen.

"'Deed I am," she replied with her toothless smile. "My stomick's harder than a preacher's prick at a June weddin'."

The scrub nurse's eyes widened to where I thought they would pop out of their sockets. The surgeon roared so hard he had to take down his mask to catch his breath. And you could hear him laughing all while he scrubbed his hands out at the sink.

I had to get oxygen flowing into the old woman as a precaution before putting her to sleep to give me some grace time while fighting her arthritic spine and decrepit lungs. She didn't object to the mask I placed over her face, or to the cool oxygen blowing into it.

Despite her hardships, she seemed fairly content. Her chickens had taught her not to ask much of life. She mumbled something as I was about to inject the Pentothal. I lifted the mask. "What did you say?"

"I say my husbin' an' me had us some kinda' plans before we lost 'r boy." Tears brimmed her clouded eyes. "Seems like hard work an' hard luck done wore out all 'r dreams."

CHAPTER TWENTY-SIX

It was cool but pleasant as we walked along the marina situated at the southern end of Fishback Island. Instead of chicken smog, the morning air was heavy with the smell of fish and crabs that watermen unloaded from boats bobbing at their moorings. Most displayed a female name across its stern: THE SALLY ANN, THE BETTY JO, and so on.

Fishing nets hung from ropes strung along the docks like clotheslines, and old men and boys mended them with wooden fishermen's needles. Worn bushel baskets were stacked in pyramids waiting to be loaded onto boats and filled with yet another catch. And swooping and screeching above were flocks of gulls looking for a handout.

A section of marina opposite the fishing docks was reserved for sleek pleasure craft. Sailboat lines chinked like a xylophone in the wind against their masts, and large cabin cruisers with flying bridges rocked slowly from side to side.

"We belong over there," Lori said, indicating a platform jutting out over the water. A faded United States Postal Service sign hung above it from a set of poles which leaned away from a brisk wind.

"It isn't very fancy," Peggy said when she saw the boxy old mail boat making its way toward the landing.

"It sure is big!" Brendan had to be restrained when he tried to board the boat before it had finished pulling alongside the pier.

Lori found life jackets for all of us and insisted that Billy put one on when he resisted. "The water's cold in this channel," she lectured. "You wouldn't survive ten minutes."

"Oh yes he would," Peggy said. "In cold water you can live longer 'cause your body doesn't need as much oxygen."

"Smart girl," Jeff said with a smile.

Lori had to be talked into visiting Oyster Island, and finally agreed because we could ride free on the mail boat. Jeff became part of the adventure when he heard us discussing details in O.B. and said he would like to tag along. Lori was pleased, but Billy was not.

"I can't keep up with them anymore," Lori said of her children. "They're turning into regular islanders."

"There are worse things." Jeff's easy stance on the rocking boat made him appear to belong on the water.

Billy went to watch the skipper rev up the engines and turn the lumbering craft toward Oyster Island. Lori and Jeff took the two younger children to the railing to watch over the side. I retreated to the cabin to escape the chill wind gusting off the water.

A bus with SMILING JESUS CHURCH painted on its side had pulled into the parking lot while we waited for the mail boat, and its passengers were now crowded into the cabin. Most were women with tight grey curls and bunion slits in their shoes.

The white meat of Chesapeake blue crabs was a delicacy shipped around the world, and a contest to see who could pick it from its shells the fastest was coming up. The church people talked excitedly about their prospects while I sat between two members listening.

"I can pick crabs faster'n any a' my youngins," a woman said. "They can't come close ta the meat I can pile up oncet I get going."

"Y'all be careful what kinda meat yer talkin' about," the driver of the church bus said. The women laughed and the bus driver pulled a comb from his shirt pocket, running it through his oiled hair. The comb was missing almost as many teeth as its owner.

"I'm goin' ta sit next ta Cleta," he said, squeezing in next to a large woman. "She's got anuf insulation ta keep both us warm."

"Y'all stop that," Cleta said when he draped an arm across her rounded shoulders. "I got me a man ta home keeps me plenty company."

The bus driver continued his flirting until Cleta announced she had to go outside for some fresh air. But the boat was now rocking so vigorously she fell back to the bench when she attempted to get up.

"Try 'er again," the driver encouraged. Cleta gave a tremendous heave, and with the assistance of the bus driver's hands applied to her broad backside, finally was upright.

"Honey hush, if y'all ain't somethin'," she said, slapping coquettishly at his hands.

I had some concern that she would become stuck in the narrow passageway leading to the deck. But she managed to coax her bulk through it after turning this way and that.

"That Cleta's a pistol," the driver said as he took out his comb and rearranged his hair. "I only devil her 'cause she gets so riled up." He turned his attentions to another woman, and I went out onto the deck so I wouldn't miss the approach to Oyster Island.

Jeff and the two younger children were throwing potato chips to gulls that followed the boat. Peggy and Brendan squealed with delight when the gulls swooped down to catch each chip.

Lori stood watching fondly. Her blond hair was loose and blew out behind her, attracting the attention of several male passengers.

"There she is," someone said when a strip of land appeared on the horizon. I was intrigued by the female gender that islanders used for inanimate objects such as boats, cars and even islands. It gave the impression that possessions were female, and vice versa.

Watermen in flat bottomed boats made their way through the shallows bordering Oyster Island while holding long tongs over the sides, working the handles to and fro as they dredged the bottom for oysters. Mechanized dredges worked the deeper waters offshore.

A series of hand lettered signs anchored in the water along the route we traveled read like Burma Shave ads.

DON'T FORGET JESUS

AND HE WON'T FORGET YOU.

HAVE YOU THANKED THE LORD

FOR BEING ALIVE?

Buildings used for unloading and processing oysters and crabs were suspended above the water on tall poles. They reminded me of the Bamboo Hut, a small restaurant built out over the Danang River where Dan and I went for French onion soup on Sunday mornings after church.

"Look at all the wrecked cars!" Brendan pointed excitedly to an enormous sculpture of rusted cars rising surreally out of the water.

"They brought 'em here over the years," a man near me said. "There's nowhere ta put 'em but the worter oncet they stop running."

"Never did understand why they carried 'em over in the first place," another passenger said. "You can walk anywheres on the ahlund in not but thirty minutes."

The mail boat lumbered along a canal dug into the island like a road. Buildings on poles were now replaced by houses, some appearing to be built on nothing more than layer upon layer of oyster shells so dense they had become an extension of the land.

Tidewaters lapped at the doors of the houses, which had strategically placed stepping stones leading from one to another. Mounds of oyster shells stood next to each of the dwellings, as if the inhabitants merely opened the door and tossed them outside.

"I'm near starved ta death," Cleta said as she made her way along the rail. As soon as the boat docked, she waddled toward a house that had a sign advertising home cooking.

"It looks like most of the people came here to eat," Jeff said when the remainder of the church group hurried after Cleta.

"I'm hungry too," Brendan said.

"Then we'd better get a move on." Jeff grabbed the eight year old's hand and they galloped down the ramp laughing.

The restaurant was a private home with a long room added next to the kitchen to accommodate visiting diners. Waitresses bustled about calling out the day's specialties: crab cakes, oysters, clam fritters, corn fritters and chicken. Everything fried.

"No wonder I'm taking out so many gallbladders," Jeff observed.

Billy ordered a soft shell crab sandwich, a Chesapeake Bay delicacy. The crabs were referred to as peelers by watermen because they were caught after they peeled off their hard shells in order to grow, and before the soft one beneath had time to harden. The crabs were fried whole, shell and all, and served between two slices of bread with their crooked legs hanging out the sides.

"It looks like you're eating a squashed spider," Brendan said.

"And it looks like you're eating fried turds." Billy pointed to Brendan's corn fritters.

"Boys," Lori warned. Jeff turned his head to hide a smile.

The church group passed platters heaped with oysters, fritters and crab cakes until every morsel was gone. They topped off the meal with sweet potato pie, then prepared for a tour of the island. Billy decided to join them on an antique bus while the rest of us walked.

Large puddles from high tide stood everywhere, and Brendan jumped in them until his sneakers were soaked. Jeff served as lookout for battered cars, which veered recklessly around curves in the single lane road we walked. The island had one church, a plain structure set among simple but pretty houses. Discarded appliances were everywhere.

"What a depressing place," Lori said.

"Oh, I don't know," Jeff said. "It could be pretty if someone took the time to clean it up." The children ran ahead chasing sea gulls, and Jeff tentatively took Lori's hand in his as she smiled up at him. I walked behind, remembering another island where I walked hand in hand with Dan to a school and clinic he built for the Vietnamese inhabitants. It was the same island where he was killed.

"I think I'll go back to the restaurant and have a cup of coffee," I said. "The cold is getting to my back."

"Do you want us to go back with you?" Lori asked.

"No, go and explore with the children." Watching them walk away hand in hand made my body feel as hollow as when my mind deserted it.

The proprietor and chief cook of the restaurant came to sit with me while her waitresses cleaned up. "Where y'all from?" I expected her to assume it was New York, but she left it open-ended.

"I'm living in Muskrat Marsh. But just for the summer."

"Summer's near gone." The woman looked to be in her sixties, but she was eating one of her corn fritters and the grease ran down fingers as straight and strong as a person half her age.

"I know." Labor day was one week away, and I still had not found a position that seemed right. "How do you like living in such an isolated place?" I asked.

"Child, we aren't isolated," the woman retorted. "We got our homes, our families, our boats an' God. What more could we want?"

"Amen," a woman sweeping the floor said. "Though we might could use a docter an' a teacher."

"You ask me, that hurricane did us a favor," the proprietor said. "Folks on Fishback Ahlund give up their good Methodist upbringin' and turned right spacey about religion." She finished her corn fritter and wiped her hands on a kitchen towel tucked into the waist of her apron. "We run them preachers right off our ahlund, comin' here with all their talk a' gettin' birthed again."

I was finding Oyster Island more and more appealing.

The waitresses finished their work and gathered around the table as if I were a celebrity. They asked about movies and shared magazines so outdated and smelling of mildew they made me sneeze.

"Y'all sound like you're takin' a cold," one of them said.

"Just allergies," I said between sneezes. "I'm a nurse."

"Thank you, Lord! Y'all were sent to us," the proprietor said without the slightest concern of my outsider status. "We'd be right grateful ta have a nurse when sickness an' babies come along."

The whistle blew on the boat to announce its imminent departure, and I left the restaurant somewhat reluctantly.

"This wouldn't be a bad place to live," Jeff said. We stood at the back of the boat watching the receding island sink into the water like the lost city of Atlantis.

"I like it lots," Peggy said. And Brendan nodded his agreement.

"It sure would be a nice place for a boat," Billy said.

I looked at Lori. "I know what you're thinking," she said. "It's too far from Fishback Island for me to do deliveries. And I have to have physician back-up in case someone needs a C/Section."

"The two of you could set up a joint practice," I said, looking from her to Jeff Wells. "Jeff could take out gallbags and you could deliver babies with him as your back-up."

"Not a bad idea if they built an appropriate facility," Jeff said. "It would be a nice place to paint."

"You paint?" It was the first time Billy had spoken to Jeff.

"Mostly watercolor," Jeff said.

Billy looked confused. "He doesn't paint houses," his mother said, a bit embarrassed. "He paints pictures."

"I should have known." Billy sauntered off to watch the captain guide the mail boat back across the water.

CHAPTER TWENTY-SEVEN

I wasn't sure whether fate dealt me a good hand or bad when Getta Mae, the island anesthetist who played servant to Earl Roy, made an announcement. She had tried for years to have a baby and was finally pregnant. And she did not want the fetus exposed to the anesthetic gases and x-rays one encountered daily in surgery.

"She's requested an eleven month leave of absence," Earl Roy told me. "If you're willing to stay over the winter the job is yours."

"Will my duties change?" If it meant becoming his handmaiden, he knew my answer would be no.

"This place practically closes down when the GDTs and stoopers leave. As long as you keep my billing straight, you and Skipper can run the place any way you want."

Earl Roy charged every surgical and obstetrical patient a hefty fee for anesthesia supervision, whether or not he was in the hospital. It was up to Skipper and me to see that a bill for his services was submitted on every case, no matter how much it bothered us to do so.

"Can I let you know later?" I had been doing fine with my cases, but I was still troubled by the ethical implications of taking patient's lives into my hands if my mind decided to go wandering.

"I need to know by tomorrow morning," Earl Roy said as he got ready to leave. It was almost noon, long past his quitting time.

Skipper encouraged me to stay. "The work's easy over the winter. Mostly Chicken Hand, hysterectomies and gallbladders."

"It's not the cases. It's the nights and weekends on call." Practicing the only profession I knew while doing right by my patients was becoming as trying as working with the constant pain in my back. "You know how things can go to hell when you don't have any backup."

Quite by accident, I had happened upon the perfect thing to say.

"If an extra pair of hands is all you need, stop worrying. I'm not out on my boat much during winter, you can call me anytime."

Lori, Reba and the children thought it was a good idea to stay. "You're better off not changing jobs with your back acting up so much," Lori told me. "You'd be a sitting duck for the insurance mafia's pre-existing condition baloney."

What lingering doubt I had disappeared when she added, "I've been thinking of staying on over the winter myself. The children need to get enrolled in school, and I haven't found work anywhere else."

The two of us were sitting at the kitchen table. Lori was ripping at another layer of yellowed wallpaper next to it.

"The hospital wants me to stay," she said. "And Jeff does too."

"Oh, really?"

Lori said quickly, "I don't mean personally. He just wants me to keep running the clinic and assisting him when I can."

Jeff was so impressed with Lori, he had her assist on nearly all his surgeries. They lingered over coffee in the hospital cafeteria enough that Carol Faye scratched him off her list of possible suitors.

The children were ecstatic when they were enrolled in Muskrat Marsh's public school, Zebediah Taylor's private Freedom School being too far away, too expensive, and too white. Lori told me he founded it when integration was ordered on the island.

"I guess I'll stay put awhile myself," Reba said at dinner, after refusing for days to discuss the subject. "But come the first a' the year I'm headed back to Baltimore to make me some money."

A push to revitalize Baltimore's seedy harbor was on, making her properties ripe for development. Newspapers were running photographs of luxury condos and hotels going up all around her burned out hulks.

Lori was happier than I had ever seen her, but her relationship with Jeff was causing turmoil with Billy. That is, until Jeff volunteered to help finish painting the house.

When the job was completed, Lori, Jeff and the children began spending their free weekends on Oyster Island. They went over on the mail boat Saturday mornings, and returned on one of the islander's fishing boats on Sunday afternoon, after spending the night in the home of the woman who owned the restaurant. While the children explored the small island, Jeff did his water colors and acted as physician backup for Lori so she could deliver an occasional baby, or teach the locals how to do it correctly when she was not available.

Lori was also conducting natural childbirth classes for any interested patients on Fishback Island. Dr. Arst was initially opposed, but word spread to his patients, who began insisting on the newer method. Lori received a fee to train his patients and their spouses, then turn them back to Dr. Arst for delivery.

We now had a new refrigerator, Reba's mother's grave had a white, marble headstone, and life went smoothly, despite our neighbors' constant monitoring of the comings and goings in the red house.

"Would y'all like ta learn how ta do ceramics?" Dolly, a recovery room nurse, asked me. "My cousin owns a shop jest outside a' town."

I had seen things Dolly painted when she brought them to the hospital to sell to other nurses, or to doctors for their wives. I wasn't inclined to want any ceramic ducks or geese, but there was little to do on the island when the beach season was over. And I did not wish to discourage any islander's overture of friendliness.

Dolly had been part of the recovery room staff for years, and received her nickname before her body ballooned to its present proportions. Because of her bulk, she had developed a unique way of getting around the recovery room, where speed was often essential.

Each morning she eased herself onto a stool with heavy-duty legs and wheels, then propelled herself sideways across the tiled floor in a crab-like motion. Her dainty feet provided both power and steering as she navigated among stretchers and staff. She assumed duties at the lower end of the recovery room stretchers, sailing across the room with bedpans brimming and returning them clean and shiny, never complaining about her work. At day's end, Dolly left her mobility and painstakingly made her way to the elevator and out to her car.

The ceramics shop was located down a dirt lane running parallel to a sulfurous swamp, home to the muskrats that ended up in the firehall ovens. Tidewaters crept over the road and I worried we would sink into the swamp's murky depths with Dolly weighing down the car.

"My husbin' figured out how ta customize my car an' did all the work hisself," she told me as she drove at an uneven speed down the road. "Had me a time gettin' around before."

Dolly's husband had cut out the front seat of a station wagon, except for a narrow perch on the passenger side where I presently sat. She rested in a wide, armless wooden lawn chair bolted to the floor a good distance back from the steering wheel. Unfortunately, it left her tiny feet a considerable distance from the floor pedals. The result was a lurching motion as she intermittently tapped at the accelerator, then let the car coast until she had to goose it again.

"Is it much further?" I asked. It was after dark and we were surrounded by odoriferous marshlands without a building in sight. The car rode at a lopsided angle because of Dolly's weight.

"Yonder." Dolly pointed to a ramshackle building with windows so dirty it was difficult to see light behind them.

When we went inside, Hope Taylor, whom I had seen less since winter curtailed our picnics, sat at the back of a room filled with women applying layers of glaze to objects that would later be fired in a kiln. Allison was there as well, sitting with a group of girls.

"They're her classmates from the Freedom School," Hope explained after inviting me to join her at the table she occupied alone. "She enjoys being with them so much I try to bring her out once a week."

Hope was spreading a grey glaze onto a small ceramic Christmas tree that would come out of the kiln a shiny green. Then small plastic colored bulbs would be glued into the many small holes in it to glow from an electric light bulb wired into the hollow inside.

"Pick out whatever ya like," the owner of the shop called to me. She and her cousin Dolly sat with a group of island women up front near a wood stove, which did little to ward off the swampy chill.

Most of the customers were painting ducks and geese, but a few worked on life sized hands clasped in prayer that rested on a flat base. Several pair of already completed hands, painted in a rainbow assortment of colors, sat on tables next to their owners.

"They paint them to match the rooms they put them it," Hope said when she saw me staring at a set of lavender hands on a table near us. Her soft voice was respectful, but her eyes betrayed her amusement.

"Thur's more in the back room if nothin' out here fits your fancy," the owner said as I wandered shelves containing waterfowl and praying hands. "My husbin Odie Luke's out there ta help."

Her name was Iris Irene, and she had a six year old daughter who was presently tormenting a cat. "Crystal Lou, you stop worryin' that cat!" her mother ordered. The child picked up the animal by its tail and it yowled. "Let it go," Iris Irene insisted. Crystal Lou drop-kicked the cat across the shop to the delight of the customers.

"That child's a pistol," Dolly said. "Jest like her daddy before he gave up womanizin' and embraced the Lord Jesus Christ."

"Praise the Lord," Iris Irene said. "The bible says 'For all have sinned and fall short of the glory of God.'"

"Amen," a customer intoned.

I was headed for the back room when Hope motioned me over to her. "Watch out for Odie," she whispered. "He likes to embrace more than the Lord in that back room."

I found Iris Irene's spouse mixing a powdery substance with water, which he then poured into a mold in the shape of Elvis Presley's head. The thick liquid would be left to harden into clay-like greenware, which could then be sanded smooth, painted and fired into a texture close to porcelain.

"I'm doing some raght nice pieces for Christmas," Odie told me. His face, hair and clothes were covered with grey powder. "Everone's orderin' this one a' Ev-vis that jest come in."

"I'll look around," I said.

I walked between high shelves filled with more ducks and praying hands, but also mermaid soap dishes, light houses and one-legged sea captains. There were additional pieces on the very top, but when I leaned back to look up I felt Odie's arms come around me from behind. It startled me so I jumped forward, banging into the shelves and nearly bringing down hundreds of pieces of fragile greenware.

"Y'all got ta be more careful," Odie said when I turned to face him. "Almost stepped right back inta that hot kiln." He indicated a kiln in the process of firing painted objects at an extremely high temperature. But I did not recall stepping backward.

"Thank you," I said haltingly.

"That's what I'm here for." He smiled through the dust covering his face. "You're right choicey about pickin' something out."

I quickly chose a lamp in the shape of a football to make for Lori's boys for Christmas, a few weeks away, and a ballerina for Peggy. My last selections were two small Christmas trees like the one Hope was painting that I would give Lori and Reba. Odie helped me carry them out to Hope's table, then went back to get a third Christmas tree for Andy to brighten his apartment in Baltimore.

Allison and her classmates kept up a lively conversation at the table next to the one where Hope and I worked. "I like ta dahed when she went ta bed with her own mother's fee-ance-say," one said. "She don't give neither nor mind ta who she falls into the feathers with."

"I say she's not one bit in love with him," Allison said. "She's jest tryin' ta get back at her mama 'cause she left her an' her daddy for another man." Allison's use of island dialect did not appear to register with her mother.

"That child can pick up men faster'n a boat picks up barnacles," another girl declared.

"I guess there's a part of Fishback Island I haven't seen," I said to Hope. "Where do those people they're talking about live?"

Hope laughed. "They're discussing soap operas."

Allison brushed back a long section of wavy golden hair that had slipped forward while she painted. "We aren't even allowed to date at the Freedom School," she said to me in her non-islander voice.

"Nor dance or roller skate," one of her classmates added. "Lor-dee, we're all fixin' to be old maids when we're not near eighteen."

"We all ride," Allison said. "Most of us compete in jumping."

"Allison is quite an accomplished equestrian," Hope said. The comment elicited a look of contempt from her daughter. Hope blushed. "You know you're good," she said to her daughter.

Allison got up to carry her finished greenware to the back room to be fired. "Yes, mother," she said, pausing at our table to speak in a voice only we could hear. "We both know what a good little girl I am." The cruelty in her voice made me want to slap her.

"Teenagers," Hope said when she left, and bent over her work.

The evening passed at the pace of a child on his way to school on Monday morning. "I don't know if I'll come again," I said when Dolly lumbered back to tell me she was ready to leave. "Leaning over this work really kills my back."

"Oh, please do come," Hope said with such desperation that others turned to look. "It was so nice having someone to talk to."

"You've not got to talk ta that strange one," Dolly told me as she hoisted herself into her customized car. "Her first husbin' was near balmy as her, even though he was born an' raised an ahlunder."

She tapped at the accelerator and we spurted forward. "The two of 'em made a right good pair, off in the woods havin' picnics and laughing like they didn't have the sense God gave a cuke."

I held my breath while she navigated a large tidal pool, gripping the door handle in case a hasty escape became necessary.

"She takes that youngin a' hers out ta the cemetery and the two of 'em sit raght there, next to the place Adam Lee lays dead, eatin' and carryin' on like they were at a circus." She made a shuddering motion, setting her bulk into oscillation. "It's flat out peculiar."

"Her new husband doesn't seem to mind," I said in Hope's defense.

"Senator Taylor minds plenty." Dolly looked my way. "But he found out too late he married a woman won't even go ta church or do nothin' else Christian. And him first cousins with the Reverend Taylor." Dolly sighed deeply. "Honey hush, the ahlund girls that woulda married him an' made him happy."

We had left the marshlands behind and were now on the highway leading into Muskrat Marsh. The car was making noise beneath Dolly's chair, but she drove on as if the groaning and banging were normal.

"Zebediah fell for that widow woman with neither nor thought ta what he was gettin' into." Dolly made a tight turn, which shifted her perilously in my direction. "Anyone on the ahlund will tell you, he never got over what happened to his family; mama, daddy and sister all dead 'cause a' one fool nigger."

In spite of my reservations, I returned to the shop the following week to finish the Christmas gifts. Hope was there without Allison.

"She wanted to spend some time at home," Hope said when I inquired. "And I needed to finish up my pieces for Christmas."

"Is her father home from Annapolis?"

"Oh, no," Hope said in a startled manner, then, "Zebediah is too busy with his senate duties to spend much time in Muskrat Marsh."

We turned our attention to Odie, who was telling the customers up front about a man and woman who lived next to him and Iris Irene.

"They're cocky as a rooster about it," he was saying. "She sittin' right alongside him in the car, proud as can be. An' her hair as yella' and straight as his is black an' kinky."

"I say she come here jest ta make us trouble," Iris Irene said. "She didn't tell no one she was livin' with a culurd man when she took the job a' French teacher at the Freedom School."

"Why doesn't the Senator jest fire her?" another customer asked.

"'Cause she's threatened ta go to them civilian rights people up ta Baltmur," said Odie. Ceramic dust made him look like a grey ghost.

"Ain't no white woman layin' with no culurd man then comin' in ta teach my child," Iris Irene stated flatly. She went to where her young daughter teased the shop cat and put an arm around her. The cat took the opportunity to jump up onto a shelf filled with greenware.

Crystal Lou broke free of her mother and jabbed at the cat with a broom she grabbed. Ducks, geese, Elvis busts and praying hands crashed to the floor as the cat ran along the back of the shelf.

"Now look what y'all done!" Odie yelled. He batted Crystal Lou with the cap he removed and she disappeared in a cloud of dust.

When it settled she ran crying into the back room while her mother used the broom she abandoned to clean up the mess. Odie continued with the tale of the wayward Freedom School teacher.

"The nigger's supposed ta be some kinda' artist," he said. "But he ain't gonna be around here long anuf to paint anything but the signs headin' outta town." Several customers voiced their agreement.

"The Bible says, 'You that are righteous, be glad and rejoice,'" one woman said.

Crystal Lou came back into the room wiping her wet, dusty gray eyes. "Come here, daughter," Odie said tenderly. "Daddy's got a treat." He pulled a guitar from behind the counter that held the cash register. "You can go ta practice with me an' give your mama a rest." He looked toward his wife, still sweeping.

"Can I sang too?" Crystal Lou asked.

Odie smiled at her. "I guess, but only during practice. Come Sunday, The Lord's Messengers are the only ones can sang."

"He belongs to a gospel group," Hope told me when Odie and his daughter had departed. "Zebediah started it some years ago, but he had to give it up when he went into politics, except for special occasions." She kept her voice low. "He was happier back then," she said wistfully. "We all were."

I finished gluing plastic lights onto my Christmas trees and was ready to leave. But Dolly was working on a pair of orange hands she wanted to finish for a Christmas gift.

"I can give you a ride," Hope offered. "Lori's house is right on my way." Dolly gave me a disapproving look when I accepted.

It was high tide and the water encroaching on the road made me glad I was not riding with Dolly.

"Are you going to tell your husband about the French teacher?" I asked. "It sounds like she and her friend might be in for trouble."

Hope looked straight ahead. "I don't give my husband any advice on his school." We drove on in silence a few minutes.

"Why did you come to this island?" she asked suddenly.

"I came with Lori for the summer and just stayed on." It worried me to hear how much I sounded like Skipper.

When we left the marshlands for paved road, Hope turned to look at me. "This is an evil place," she said. "You should leave, and Lori too. She never should have come back."

"Evil how?"

Hope looked straight ahead. "You don't want to stay long enough to find out."

Nothing more was said until we reached Lori's. She stopped in front of the house, which remained bright red even in the dark, and I started to get out.

"Wait a minute." Hope's voice was soft once more. "I hate the way the school is run. I just can't do anything about it." I sat with the car door open, my right foot out on the pavement. "Please, Pat. It's important that you believe me."

There was such sorrow in the face illuminated by the dome light I regretted even raising the issue. "I believe you," I said.

CHAPTER TWENTY-EIGHT

All surgical patients well enough to be sent home were discharged by Christmas Eve. Babies had no respect for holidays, however, and I was called for a delivery in the middle of a late dinner of oyster stew and steamed crabs, compliments of Oyster Islanders who provided Lori and Jeff with a steady supply.

The patient's labor slowed, and what looked like a quick case dragged on until midnight. But there was something special about bringing a child into the world on a night when people felt at peace with one another, and were foolish enough to believe it would last.

The lights were turned off on the tree the children had chosen that took up most of the dining-living room when I returned to Lori's house. I bumped into Reba's rocking chair trying to make it to the staircase, but it woke no one.

Andy would be driving down the next day for a late Christmas dinner, to be held after Lori and her children attended an earlier one at Lovey Donlin's. I had agreed to accompany them so Lori wouldn't have to face her ex-husband and his new wife without moral support.

Despite the late hour, memories of a past Christmas Eve, when Dan asked me to marry him, kept me from sleep. I lay there watching Peggy in the light of her bubbling aquarium, remembering how we went to midnight Mass together at Navy Hospital's chapel.

Nurses and corpsman wheeled in G.I.s missing legs and parked them near the altar. Others made their way on crutches and canes. Those with bandages covering their eyes were led by their fellow patients.

But it was the silent head injuries on stretchers pushed in last that affected Dan the most. Their wounds were covered with bandages and paper surgical masks were over their mouths. More than once I saw his eyes wander toward the motionless forms whose only sign of life was the movement of the masks as they sucked air in and out.

"How wonderful to see a happy couple," the Chaplain said when he wished us a Merry Christmas at the end of the service. "I noticed you looking at one another with such love. Did you meet over here?"

"Yes, sir," Dan replied.

"Such a blessing for two people to find happiness in the midst of such sorrow." The Chaplain watched the stretchers being pushed out. "Enjoy the peace of the Christmas truce," he said returning to us.

"Thank you, Father," I replied.

Dan was quiet as we drove back to town in his jeep. "Look up there," I said. "Stars instead of flares and gunfire."

Dan looked skyward. "I'd forgotten how bright they are."

I kept watching the sky. "I finally know what that song means."

"What song?"

"Silent Night."

Dan pulled something white from the back seat of his jeep when we reached my rundown villa. "Don't come into your bedroom until I tell you to," he said as he held the bundle behind him.

"What do you have there?" I grabbed playfully at it.

"It's a surprise."

I was not prepared for how long the surprise would take. After an hour, I knocked on the door to my room. "Can I come in now?"

"Almost."

"What are you doing in there?"

"You'll see in a minute."

I returned to reading Christmas cards from my family and friends. Another twenty minutes passed before Dan called to me. He reached a hand out of the room. "Close your eyes."

I took his hand and he guided me into the room. Christmas carols played softly on my tape player.

"O.K., open them," Dan said with the excitement of a child.

There was white fabric hanging down all of my walls, but I did not see the full surprise until Dan pointed to my high ceiling.

My body moved about the room in slow circles as I gazed up into a billowing cloud of white pinned to the center of the ceiling, then out to each corner and draping down the walls like a majestic tent.

"It's a silk parachute," Dan said. "Do you like it?"

I kept moving silently beneath it trying to take it all in. "It's like the Arabian Nights," I said in a hushed voice.

"I got tired of watching gekkos run across your ceiling."

"It's beautiful." My musty bedroom of crumbling plaster had become the most enchanting place on earth.

"I'll buy you a real Christmas present when we go on R&R."

"No, this is perfect." Dan took my hand.

"I was thinking of a ring. Will you marry me, Patty?"

"Let's go back and find that chaplain," I said as I jumped into his arms.

Dan carried me to my bed, where we made love, then laid in each others arms looking up at our enchanted sanctuary. "Let's make this our special place," I said. "No war allowed."

We talked about our life together when we returned home. And the little boy Dan and I had taken to an orphanage out at China Beach after his mother had died at my hospital. Dan was the first to suggest what I secretly hoped, that we adopt him and take him home.

The dream began the instant I fell asleep, the old familiar one of me waiting for Dan at Navy Hospital while doctors worked on his severed leg. But from there it took a bizarre turn into a world of Viet Cong in black uniforms who overran the orphanage. The children screamed in terror as machetes sliced open their tiny bodies, spilling their blood in torrents. Those old enough to run tried escaping, but their legs were cut out from under them as they fled. Helpless infants in cribs had their fragile skulls split by rifle butts swinging savagely. Blood was spattered over the children, the walls, the floors, and the white habits of nuns trying to stop the massacre.

Some of the nuns knelt, begging for mercy. All were struck down, their white habits turning to crimson as they lay dying.

I was somewhere up near the ceiling, watching the slaughter without attempting to intervene. Streams of blood from ravaged bodies joined together to create a red river that made a bubbling sound as it ran down the beach to the South China Sea.

One nun remained alive, the mother superior I had come to know so well. Her usually spotless habit was stained with her own blood, and that of the children she tried so valiantly to save.

"Let me help you." I reached down from the ceiling to where she lay next to the river, but she did not take my hand.

"You let them kill the children," she said up to me.

"No," I cried. "I loved the children."

My last words were apparently said aloud, and Peggy was at my side shaking me. "Wake up, Pat. You're having another bad dream."

I sat up looking for the nuns and children. But there was only Peggy and her bubbling aquarium. I knew where I was. And better yet, who I was.

"Go back to sleep," I said to Peggy. "I'm alright now."

But I lay awake, afraid if I closed my eyes the dream would recur. Somewhere near dawn, when it was safest to sleep in the war, I fell into an exhausted slumber.

"Are you going to sleep through Christmas?" Lori was standing in my doorway. "Breakfast is almost ready; Reba's making waffles."

I could not bear the thought of food dumped into a stomach that felt like a caldron of acid. "I'm still tired."

"What time did you get back from the hospital?"

"Late."

"Sleep as long as you want," Lori said. "Just so you're up in time to go with me to the Donlins."

"Go where?"

"My ex-mother-in-law's house, where you promised to have Christmas dinner with my dear ex-husband and the zucchini he married."

I groaned and turned over. Lori left, but I was kept awake by the clatter of dishes and pans downstairs, and the smell of waffles drifting up the stairs.

"Come on, it's time for the freak show," Lori said in what seemed like only minutes.

I covered my eyes, wanting to shut out Christmas and everything else. "You wouldn't be alone without me. You'll have the children."

"Are you kidding? Earl Roy and his mother will bury them in so many gifts they'll forget they even have a mother.

The guard looked suspiciously at Lori's battered station wagon while he telephoned Mrs. Donlin to make sure she was expecting us. Peggy stuck her tongue out at him when he turned to the button in the guard house that made the gates to Heavenly Acres swing open.

"Mom-mom's soooo glad to see you," Mrs. Donlin said as she scooped her grandchildren into her arms at the front entrance.

Adella Dawn, standing next to Earl Roy, avoided speaking to Lori by herding the children inside as soon as their grandmother released them. "Come see what your dad-day and me bought y'all." Their stepmother indicated a mountain of gifts under a tree sprayed the same blue as the flocked wallpaper in the spacious foyer. "I spent near a month pickin' it all out." I knew from Lori that Earl Roy's new wife was in her twenties, which was hard to believe with her island beige hair sculpted into a lacquered beehive atop her head.

"Adella Dawn loves children," Earl Roy said to me. He had been at the hospital so infrequently during the winter season I felt a stranger in his presence.

Lori turned away, but her children ripped into packages without bothering to first remove their coats. Mrs. Donlin opened a hall closet and pulled out shopping bags stuffed with even more lavishly wrapped gifts. "Don't think your Mom-mom went and forgot y'all." The children shrieked like hyenas as they dove into the latest haul.

"If only their Pop-pop was here ta see." Mrs. Donlin dabbed at her eyes with a lace handkerchief she pulled from the sleeve of her rose pantsuit. "Has it been two whole years since he passed?"

Earl Roy opened his mouth to speak but she answered for herself. "Why yes it has, two years exactly." She counted it out on her fingers. "He took the stroke jest after Lori left Earl Ro-ee and moved our grandbabies up ta Baltmur."

"I believe you're right," Lori said sweetly. "And Earl Roy and Adella Dawn had become friends just two years before that."

Lovey's face flushed the color of her polyester pantsuit. But Adella Dawn's expression betrayed no emotion.

"Shall we move to the living room?" Earl Roy said with his best Harvard manners. "Pat shouldn't be expected to listen to our family history in the front foyer."

"Yes, of course," his mother said. "My culurd's in the kitchin cooking so she couldn't be here ta see y'all in." She took my arm to escort me to the next room. "Docter Donlin Senior always loved havin' his little nurses over." She tried to smile at me, but her loss of facial movement pulled her upper lip back into its familiar snarl.

"Thank you for inviting me, Mrs. Donlin."

"Oh, please, call me Lovey." Her eyes were teary once more. "Docter Donlin Senior gave me that nickname back when we were jest little cousins playin' tagether."

We escaped the blue flocked wallpaper for an identical pattern in a brilliant rose the shade of Lovey's pantsuit. The living room carpet and velvet furniture were the same, with pink satin pillows propped carefully against the back of the French Provincial sofa with white wood. I felt as if I had stepped inside somebody's uterus.

"Anyone care for sherry?" Earl Roy stood at a glass and chrome table covered with an array of crystal liquor decanters. A carved decoy of a mallard duck sat at one end of the table, and at the other a set of praying hands painted to match the room.

"Well, maybe because it's Christmas an' all," Lovey said. "We usually don't indulge," she said in the direction of the sofa where Lori and I sat. "Although I do like ta keep it around for company."

"Sherry would be fine," Lori said.

I could not take my eyes off the crimson praying hands. They looked like the nuns' in my dream.

My head hurt and my stomach rumbled so loudly I was certain everyone could hear. But even with the horrifying nightmare, my mind had not deserted my body, for which I was deeply grateful.

Adella Dawn served the sherry in delicate crystal glasses resting on a wooden tray which had ducks carved into its surface. She dipped low before each of us, providing an unrestricted view of stand at attention breasts beneath her gold lame dress.

My hand trembled slightly as I reached for the glass. I was hoping its contents would calm the network of nerves on high alert throughout my body. I managed to get the dainty vessel to my lips without spilling and took a generous swallow.

"Is something wrong?" Lovey asked.

The sherry was stuck somewhere between by throat and stomach. I was going to throw up in Mrs. Donlin's uterus.

"Why don't I show you to the bathroom?" Lori said.

I was in the bathroom only seconds when the sherry spurted into the turquoise commode. Lori held my head while I continued to retch.

"I'm so sorry," she said. "I shouldn't have made you come."

"I hate sherry," I managed to get past the burning in my throat.

"Maybe I should take you home. I could come back later for the children."

"It's O.K." I wiped my mouth with the damp cloth she handed me. "I think I can make it if I stay away from alcohol."

I rinsed my mouth in a turquoise sink the shape of a sea shell and sank to the plush turquoise carpet to rest. Columns of bubble-eyed fish increased and decreased in size on the wallpaper as they stacked up toward the ceiling on a pink and turquoise background. A pair of ceramic praying hands sitting on the back of the commode looked as if a turquoise Jesus was rising up out of the tank.

"Here, put this on your forehead." When Lori bent over to hand me a cool cloth, a diamond pendant slipped from beneath the collar of her dress. I reached a hand up to it.

"What's this?"

Lori's face was radiant. "We didn't want to make a big deal of it. Jeff gave it to me last night after the children went to bed."

"And...?"

"It's not what you think," she said. "Jeff was married once before. He doesn't want to rush into another commitment."

She sat down on the edge of a turquoise tub. "I need time too. I made a vow when I divorced Earl Roy that I would never remarry."

There was a knock on the door. "Is everthang all right in there?" Lovey asked. "Dinner's near ready."

"We'll be right out," Lori called. She tucked the pendant back beneath her dress.

When we returned to the living room I nearly swooned from the heavy odor of food. "Sorry I held you up," I apologized.

"Oh, you didn't a'tall," Lovey said as she ushered us into the dining room next door. She went back to the living room to call the children, who were playing with their loot in the foyer.

I was seated across from Adella Dawn, with Earl Roy on my right and an unused place setting to my left. "We always set a place for Jesus," Lovey explained. "To remind us he is always in our home."

I found myself grateful to be sitting next to The Lord as the meal progressed. My insides were in such turmoil I took little of the food passed to me. But next to Jesus' empty plate mine looked full.

The maid kept my glass filled with ice water, which I sipped at each time a dish of sauerkraut, sausage dressing or candied sweet potatoes came my way. There were also platters of turkey, fried oysters, raw oysters and sticky corn fritters.

Adella Dawn talked about a crystal social, the affluent version of a Tupperware party, she had recently hosted. "I swear, It's all so temptin' I end up buying half of it mahself." She looked at her husband, seated at the end of the table next to her, and giggled. "Earl Ro-ee is about ta make me stop hostin' parties."

Earl Roy smiled indulgently at his present wife, then returned to watching his former. Lori wore a soft green dress I had never seen before. On anyone else it might have appeared plain, but the color matched her eyes and made her blond hair shimmer.

"Did Hope Taylor ever come ta one a' your parties?" Lovey asked.

"Honey hush, she don't go nowheres but that graveyard." Adella Dawn took a surreptitious wipe at her nose with her linen napkin, then used it to dab daintily at her lips. "Or else she's home makin' those statues that are downright sinful."

"Everone of 'em naked as a plucked chickin," Lovey said.

"Hope likes to sculpt," Lori told me.

"Really? She's never mentioned it."

"Y'all know her?" Lovey asked with her penciled eyebrows climbing up her forehead.

"Not very well." I did not wish to encourage the conversation.

"Land child, no one knows her well, least of all poor Zebediah." Lovey helped herself to more mashed potatoes and topped them with sauerkraut and gravy. "I never did understand him marryin' her. "'Course he didn't have all his senses comin' outta that Jap prison."

"Korean," Earl Roy corrected.

"Chinamen jest the same."

Lovey forked a raw oyster. "Hope never did mix much with people, even when Adam Lee was alive," she said after allowing the slippery morsel to slide down her throat. "Neither nor went ta church." Her fork harpooned another oyster. "She started comin' ta church with Zebediah when they first married, but that didn't last."

"Well, how could she go ta Sunday service?" Adella Dawn asked. "She don't own but pants an' them long sleeved blouses she wears summer an' winter." She turned her attention to a bowl of okra swimming in butter and scooped a good portion onto her plate. "Don't you jest love Redfield china?" she asked as she passed the bowl across the table to me. "I do believe Mother Donlin has the prettiest set on the ahlund."

The dishes were covered with lavender flowers and leafy green vines. "It's very colorful," I said, and passed the bowl across Jesus' empty plate to Lori.

"I see y'all are wearin' an Alyce Anne," Lovey said to Lori. "She makes sech pretty dresses."

"I got a whole closet full a' Alyce Annes," Adella Dawn said eagerly. "But Earl Ro-ee likes me ta wear somethin' flat out wicked oncet in a while." She ran a finger teasingly along her low neckline.

"Lori, that color is very becoming on you," Earl Roy said. "I seem to remember that dress." Billy looked up from his plate at his father. He was spending far less time at his house now that the family was on Oyster Island most weekends.

"I guess it is kind of old," Lori said, ignoring the looks she was getting from Earl Roy's second wife.

"My, if Docter Donlin Senior was jest here ta see all these people gathered 'round his table," Lovey said with a sigh. "And little Earl Ro-ee sittin' there in his daddy's chair all grown up."

I studied the room while the family eulogized its departed member. The antique-white walls and draperies were as subtle as the remainder of the house was outlandish.

"Now mother, don't start crying in front of our guests," Earl Roy was saying. "Life is for the living."

Lovey touched her lace handkerchief to her eyes, then tucked it back into her sleeve. "Life is for the living," she repeated as she snarled fondly at her son. "I don't know where y'all come up with sech pretty sayings."

Earl Roy fidgeted with the long strands of hair sprayed and sculpted over his crown. He was almost as bald as his mother.

"Everyone ready for dessert?" Lori was determined to wrap up the meal and make her escape.

"I'll call my culurd." Lovey rang a tiny silver bell next to her plate, and the maid responded with a cart laden with sweet potato pie, apple fritters still smelling of the fat in which they had been cooked, and pecan pie that wept a thick syrup. Silver bowls of freshly whipped cream sat at each end of the cart.

"I'll just have coffee," I said when the maid pushed the cart to me. "Although everything looks delicious," I added when she looked disappointed. I wondered if she was from Colored Town, and what her family was having for Christmas dinner.

"That's how you keep thin as a twig," Lovey said to me. "Y'all don't eat enough ta keep a grasshopper alive."

Peggy smiled across the table at me. The children had been unusually quiet during the meal, scooping in food at a rate that rivaled their grandmother.

"I'm goin' ta be downright sinful," Adella Dawn said as she helped herself to a piece of both pecan and sweet potato pie. "I've bin saving up for this for a month."

Jesus didn't have any dessert.

When I reached for my coffee, my unsteady hand splashed some out onto the saucer. I abandoned the coffee and tried conversation. "This is an attractive room." It was the first opportunity I had to genuinely compliment my hostess.

"Honey, hush!" Lovey said with a wave of her hand. "This is what the builder did whilst I was tendin' ta Docter Donlin Senior. He took his stroke right in the middle a' buildin' this dream house." Her eyes misted and Earl Roy cleared his throat emphatically. "I'm goin' ta redecorate right after the holidays," Lovey said with forced cheerfulness. "I already have lavender wallpaper the shade of my dishes all picked out.

An' a deep purple rug ta set it off."

Lori was getting anxious to leave, but her children were busy sampling everything on the dessert cart. "How's Senator Taylor's campaign for Congress going?" she asked.

"Looks like he'll make it with no trouble," Earl Roy replied.

"Hen Fishback's already plannin' on how ta get him into the White House itself," Adella Dawn added proudly.

"Wouldn't that be something!" Lovey clapped her hands like a child. "A Christian in the White House, and an ahlunder ta boot!"

"Too bad that wife a' his never gave him a son ta carry on his name oncet he's famous," Adella Dawn said. "Earl Ro-ee an' me are hoping to have us one raght soon."

The stiff, white tablecloth rustled suspiciously as her hand reached under the table. Earl Roy jumped ever so slightly.

"Hope couldn't help having a miscarriage," Lori said. "And they do have Allison."

"But she's not Zebediah's own," Lovey said. "Though he treats her like a fairy princess."

As soon as the children put down their forks Lori announced it was time to leave. "I have company waiting at home," she explained.

"Your house painter?" Earl Roy asked. We had observed his new Mercedes driving past the house while Jeff and Billy were painting.

"Jeff said he only paints houses for people he likes," Billy said. He was watching his father for a reaction, and when he got none he twisted the knife another turn. "And he doesn't just like Mom," he said with no trace of island accent. "He likes all of us."

Lori smiled across the table at her oldest child.

"I'm pleased to hear that, William James," Earl Roy said in a tight but gracious voice. "Very pleased."

Then the final turn. "My name is Billy."

"Time to gather up your presents," Lori instructed before any more could be said. "And tell everyone thank you."

"Can I stay with Dad awhile longer?" Billy asked.

Lori was as surprised by the request as Earl Roy. "It's up to your father," she said after some hesitation.

"That would be wonderful," Earl Roy said under Billy's steady gaze. "But I'm afraid I have to go to the hospital to see a patient." Billy's reaction was amused rather than hurt.

"Do y'all havta run off so soon?" Lovey asked when Lori started to get up. "I hardly ever see my grandbabies with you traipsin' off to Erystchur Ahlund ever weekend."

"I'll stay with you, Mom-mom," Brendan offered. Lovey opened and closed her mouth several times but no words materialized.

"I think Mom-mom is tired after so much company," Lori said.

"I'll drive over to the hospital with you," I heard Adella Dawn tell her husband as we walked to the front door. I could not imagine what patient he had to see when he had not done a case in weeks.

"I might be late." Earl Roy picked up several of the children's gifts to carry to Lori's car. "You stay here with mother so she won't be alone on Christmas day." His wife did not look happy.

"God, am I glad that's over," Lori said as soon as we were in her station wagon and headed out the gates of Heavenly Acres. "That's the last time I'll inflict that on myself. Or anyone else."

"Does that mean you'll be giving up your Alyce Anne dress?"

"Old habits," she said with a laugh. "I don't know why I thought I still had to please Earl Roy's mother."

"Dad's going to see his new girlfriend," Billy said from the back seat. "She works at the hospital."

"How do you know that?" Lori's voice held none of the bitterness it usually did when discussing her former husband.

"I heard Adella Dawn yelling at him the last time I went to their house. I saw the new girlfriend," he continued. He held his hands out a good distance from his chest. "She has bazookas out to here."

"Billy!" Lori could not help laughing.

"Her name's Carol Faye."

Reba, wearing the new suit, shirt and tie Lori and I had given her for Christmas, waited until the first dinner settled before serving the one she and Jeff prepared. She smelled of celery, sage and cinnamon as she bustled about supervising the setting of the dining room table we used as infrequently as Lori's good dishes.

I was so relieved to be out of the Donlin's house I actually felt hungry. And I was happy to see Andy, even though I had hoped earlier that he wouldn't make it through a snow storm in Baltimore.

Soon to complete his physician's assistant program, he talked medicine with Jeff during most of the meal. When their conversation lagged, Reba filled it with plans to begin renovation of her properties as soon as her daughter could move from Chicago.

"I'm gonna fix those old heaps up something fine and sell them to all those rich doctors I used to wait on," she said. "Make 'em pay through the nose." She looked quickly toward Jeff. "I don't mean doctors like you, now. You'll never be rich the way you take oysters and crabs for payment." I could tell Andy was impressed.

"I hope you make a ton of money on your properties," Jeff said.

"I don't want Reba to leave," Peggy said in a wavering voice.

"Neither do I." Brendan looked like he had when Lori made him get rid of his turtle.

"Now don't go getting all upset on Christmas," Reba admonished. But the mood at the table had dimmed perceptibly. "I need to do something besides sit in this house all day with neighbors that won't let me get a breath of fresh air. Time I got busy."

"If you go back to Baltimore someone might hurt you," Peggy said.

Reba reached for her hand and squeezed it. "I won't be living where I did before, sugar. I'll have me a place fit for a king."

"We'll still miss you," Lori said.

Reba let Peggy's hand go and excused herself to go check on the progress of the pumpkin pies she had already removed from the oven.

CHAPTER TWENTY-NINE

Lori refused to attend the hospital's traditional New Year's Eve party, to be held at the home of Earl Roy Donlin. I was sleeping on the floor most nights because my back was so bad, but Skipper made it clear our boss expected one of us to show up.

"What about you?" I asked.

"I'm on call."

"Good excuse."

"Hasn't failed me yet." Skipper's tan was fading.

The party began at eight, but I didn't leave Lori's until past nine, wearing a black mini-dress Peggy helped me find in the mall. The exterior of the house was identical to Lovey Donlin's red brick colonial, the interior similar. Adella Dawn, in a red sequined gown with a long slit up one side, greeted me at the door. "I'm so glad y'all could come." She took my coat and put it in a hall closet.

Adella Dawn showed me to a living room filled with enough people, booze and polyester to be a sales convention. Carol Faye stood at the center of a crowd near a table covered with liquor bottles and a huge punch bowl, no doubt from one of Adella Dawn's crystal parties.

"Punch?" asked the man at the table when I approached. I nodded and he handed me a delicate cup that matched the bowl.

"What in the world is this?" The concoction hit my stomach like an incendiary bomb.

"Ladies' punch," the bartender said with a wink. "We put a little somethin' in it so's the ladies have a good time."

I moved into the throng, ditching my cup on the first available table. Carol Faye, squeezed into a fuchsia gown with tiny rhinestone straps straining to hold up her breasts, waved me into her circle of male admirers dressed in leisure suits and pastel shirts. They watched raptly each time Carol Faye's laughter set her bosom bobbing.

Another woman near the group wore an identical gown, but in bright green. "This is Doris Yvonne I'm always talkin' about," Carol Faye told me as she motioned her friend to her. "My very best friend from nursin' school." I shook hands with Dr. Arst's young wife.

"Haven't we met before?" she asked. "Y'all seem right familiar."

"I spoke to you when I called from the delivery rooms."

"Lord love a duck! Don't tell me about them danged delivery rooms! Docter Arst no sooner starts gettin' romantic when that danged telephone sets ta ringin'!" She smiled at the men around her. "Good thang he can work fast is all I got ta say."

The group all laughed, and Carol Faye's breasts bobbed like giant yo-yos. Dr. Arst might have enjoyed the sight, but he was occupied with a nurse even younger than his wife on the other side of the room.

I circulated through the crowd until I was sure Earl Roy had noted my presence. I began making my way toward the hall closet to get my coat when I heard Hope calling my name from across the room.

"Come sit with me awhile," she said when she reached me. "I'm tired of pretending to enjoy myself." She wore a long sleeve, floor length ivory gown, her copper hair done up in a royal crown of braids.

"I was just about to leave," I said.

"Please stay a little longer. I have no one to talk to." She looked toward her husband, who was with Earl Roy and Hen Fishback. He managed to talk while still keeping his wife in his field of vision.

"I guess I could stay awhile," I said above music blaring from speakers the size of refrigerators. I spotted Dolly packed into a Hawaiian muumuu, marooned on a loveseat without her recovery room stool.

"Let's go someplace where we don't have to shout."

Hope led me to Earl Roy's study just off the main room. It was strikingly unlike the rest of the house, paneled in expensive walnut. Matching floor to ceiling book shelves covered two walls. French doors led to a patio and large swimming pool covered for the winter.

The furniture was burgundy leather. Earl Roy's Harvard Medical School diploma and his certificate of anesthesia residency from Massachusetts General hung above a roll top desk. A National Rifle Association plaque hung next to an enormous, glass-fronted gun case.

Hope sat on a leather sofa holding a cup of ladies' punch that appeared untasted. Her eyes held their usual sadness, but tonight they also seemed weary.

"Have you been here long?" I asked when I took a seat in a wing-backed chair opposite her.

"It seems like forever." She appeared uneasy, and I looked to where she took furtive glances beyond the double doors leading to the living room. Zebediah still had her penned within his visual corral.

The senator was very much the politician in his dark suit, red tie and stiff white collar constricting his bulging neck. His hair, freshly cropped in white-wall style, matched his chest out, shoulders back, military stance, as he talked to Earl Roy and Hen Fishback.

"They're talking politics," Hope said.

"How's your husband's campaign coming?"

Hope seemed indifferent. "Quite well, I guess."

Zebediah's cousin, Reverend Taylor, joined the group. Hen left to refill their glasses and was quickly swallowed by the crowd of people who stood a foot or more above him. I heard Earl Roy asking the reverend about the progress of his Buy a Brick for Jesus drive.

"If the Lord sees fit," the reverend said, "we'll be in by spring." He put a hand on one of his cousin Zebediah's square shoulders. "And we'll kick off our crusade against baby killin'."

When Hen returned with ladies punch for the reverend and what looked like straight Bourbon for him and Zebediah, the conversation turned to hunting. "Where's that new gun your wife gave y'all for Christmas?" Zebediah asked Earl Roy.

"Raght in here." Earl Roy led the group into the study, each of them giving Hope and me a perfunctory nod. Hope seemed to fold in upon herself when Zebediah passed by, like a flower that closed whenever in shadow.

"Here she is," Earl Roy said as he carefully removed a gleaming shotgun from his gun case. "Sweet as a virgin."

Zebediah took it and squinted down its sights, pointed directly at his wife. Hope's light skin became even paler.

"Must be nice havin' a woman who appreciates a work a' art like this," Zebediah said while still sighting down the double barrels at Hope. "I have ta keep mine all shut off in the back room."

Hen appeared nervous watching Zebediah aiming at his wife. "Whatever it takes ta keep the little lady happy," he said with a wink, or perhaps a blink, in Hope's direction.

Zebediah handed the gun to Earl Roy and took his drink back from Hen, who seemed always at his side for such duties.

"Oh that don't make her happy," Zebediah said with a look in Hope's direction. "I haven't figured that one out yet."

Hope's hand jerked involuntarily, and she spilled the ladies' punch she was holding into the lap of her ivory dress. Zebediah shook his head as she hurried away to deal with the spreading pink stain.

"I can see we got 'r work cut out for us," Reverend Taylor said. "A wife and family's important oncet you start talkin' White House."

The men had rejoined the party in the next room by the time Hope returned. "I don't think it will leave a stain," she said, brushing a hand across the damp spot on her skirt.

"I really need to get going," I said.

"I can probably leave, too." Hope looked to where her husband was slamming back Bourbons as fast as Hen could scurry to and from the bar. He no longer seemed to care where his wife was. And Earl Roy had disappeared, allowing me the perfect opportunity to escape.

My coat was easy to find in the hall closet, but we were having trouble locating Hope's. "I think I put it back in me and Earl Roy's little love nest," Adella Dawn said when she saw us searching.

She smiled seductively and headed down the hallway. When Adella Dawn opened the bedroom door she let out a scream. Seconds later Earl Roy came running out of the bedroom zipping his fly.

"What kinda' slut are you, layin' with my husband in my own bed!" Adella Dawn shouted as Carol Faye hurried down the hall after Earl Roy. One of the rhinestone straps on her dress was broken and she struggled to cover her bouncing breast. She was barefoot and Adella Dawn came behind wielding spiked silver heels she threw at Carol Faye but missed. "You git outta my house, you...you big knocks!"

The crowd in the living room was so engrossed in the party, which had steadily increased in decibels, only Lovey Donlin appeared to hear her daughter-in-law's shrieks. "Don't go makin' a big fuss now," she said as she wrapped her arms around the now sobbing woman. "Earl Ro-ee was jest havin' a little man fun, that's all."

The Reverend Taylor left the party and came to Adella Dawn's assistance. "Come let us talk with the Lord," he said while he helped Lovey half carry the hysterical hostess into another room.

"Let's get out of here," Hope said. "I can get my coat later."

"I'll drive you home," I said when we were outside. Hope was shivering in the winter air, and I draped half my coat over her.

"My house is closer than your car. Let's make a run for it."

We ran down the street like young girls, joined together by our shared coat and laughter. "I don't know how I'll be able to keep a straight face when I see Earl Roy or Carol Faye at work," I said.

"They'll pretend it never happened, just like they always do."

We were shaking from the cold when we got inside Hope's house, to which I had never been invited. "Come with me to the kitchen," she said after hanging up my coat. "I'll make tea."

I followed her to the back of the house, which was red brick colonial the same as all the others. But the interior walls were white and the furnishings a haphazard mixture of old and older.

"This is beautiful." I was examining an antique corner cupboard in the kitchen. Like the furniture, the china behind its glass doors was an eclectic mismatch of patterns.

"Zebediah would prefer a set of Redfield China and a house full of French Provincial," Hope said from the stove. "We've never been able to agree, so he does his entertaining at his place in Annapolis."

I heard music and footsteps overhead. "Is Allison home?"

"Up in her room." Hope poured water into a teapot at a long harvest table made of burnished cherry.

I rubbed a hand over its edges, worn smooth by years of use. "What a lovely piece."

"Antique hunting is one thing I indulge in. At least I used to." Her expression became worn as the table. "I don't do much anymore."

I liked Hope better when we were silly little girls running down the street. "You really should have a set of praying hands," I said as I looked around the kitchen.

Hope laughed. "I haven't been to ceramics since you quit on me." She sat down at the table after first pouring jasmine tea into fragile oriental cups with no handles.

"I think I started collecting antiques in an attempt to create a past," she said. "I grew up in a series of foster homes after the orphanage so there were no family heirlooms, or relatives for that matter. Adam Lee was the first real family I ever had."

She swept a hand over the table. "I like this table because I can sit here and imagine all the people who have gathered around it over the years." Her elbows rested comfortably on the smooth wood. "Going into a regular furniture store is like going to a new foster home, everything so new and unfamiliar."

I noticed a photograph of a woman and child taken sometime in the twenties or thirties hanging on the wall next to the china cabinet. They stared with serious expressions at the photographer, their hair perfectly combed and their clothing starched stiffly.

"Who are those people?" I asked.

Hope looked, then laughed. "Oh, I have this thing about mothers and their children." She rubbed a hand along the edge of the table. "I can't stand going into an antique shop and seeing beautiful portraits of women who worked so hard to make their children perfect for a photo, then it ends up in a shop with strangers who don't care."

She looked shyly at me. "Sounds pretty silly, huh? At least Zebediah thinks so."

"Actually, I think it's nice that you rescue them."

Music from Allison's room drifted down to us. Edith Piaf was one of my favorites, but the soulful strains of the French cabaret singer known as the Little Wren were hardly what I would expect a teenager to be listening to. "Does Allison speak French?"

"She's taking it at school. If Odie and his crowd don't run the teacher off."

I did not want to talk about the goings on at the ceramic shop. "Lori tells me you sculpt."

"Some."

"Could I see?"

"I'm really not very good."

"Please?"

Hope went to a door opening off the kitchen and turned on a light. The unfinished room I entered smelled of damp clay and solder.

"I like to work with iron." She rubbed her hands together, producing a rasping sound. "But it makes my hands so rough." We wandered through the studio where several more portraits of mothers with children hung. "Zebediah hates my sculpting," she said. "He'd prefer I go shopping with the ladies."

There were several nudes, and a bust of a woman with such rage in her face I had to look away. A two-foot bronze of Allison was on a table in the center of the room. She walked along as if at a beach, her hair billowing out behind her. "This is so real I can almost feel the wind," I said as I moved around the elegant bronze.

"Most of my work is of Allison." Hope trailed a hand over a piece of her daughter as a baby. "She doesn't like to pose anymore."

When we returned to the kitchen, Allison was at the refrigerator pouring a glass of juice. She walked back across the room looking the same as the statue with her hair fanning out behind her.

"How was the party?" she asked at the door.

"Awful," I said. "You didn't miss a thing."

"I'm sure I didn't." She turned to her mother. "Are you going to show Pat your husband's studio too?" Her manner was challenging.

"I don't think Pat would be interested." Hope spoke in a subdued voice, looking down at her roughened hands.

"How do you know she wouldn't?" When Hope did not respond, Allison turned to me. "Come on, Pat. I'll show you myself."

I looked to Hope, who hesitated a moment then motioned me ahead of her out of the room. We passed through the dining and living rooms, with scattered photos of women and children, to a door at the far end of the house. Allison opened it, inviting me inside with a bow. "I present to you the great museum of Senator Zebediah Taylor."

Realistic models of fighter planes hung from the ceiling on wires and disarmed grenades served as paper weights on a large mahogany desk. A pair of worn but spit shined combat boots rested at the base of a brass pole holding an American flag. Photographs of young men in combat attire, Zebediah among them, covered the area behind the desk.

Along the back wall of the spacious room was a glass fronted gun case even larger than Earl Roy's, and inside it dozens of firearms polished to perfection. An NRA plaque hung near the case. Beneath a portrait of a much younger Zebediah in Marine dress blues was a bronze plate: Muskrat Marsh War Hero, Honorary Fire Chief and Sheriff.

I was finding the room unbearably hot. "What's the matter?" Allison asked in the same defiant tone she used with her mother. "Don't you like the senator's hobby?" I thought it a strange way to refer to the stepfather who had raised her from childhood.

"No, I don't," I said, looking squarely at her.

Hope spoke in an anxious voice. "Zebediah wouldn't like it if he came home and found us in here."

Allison trilled her high bird-song laugh. "You know those good Christians won't crawl home until the last bottle of booze is gone."

"Allison, please."

The young girl flounced out of the room and back upstairs. Hope carefully pulled the door closed after us. "He really doesn't like anyone going in there," she said as we returned to the kitchen. "He would prefer to keep all of his things out here. But I detest guns."

"Hope, how long was Zebediah a prisoner of war?"

She was surprised. "Why do you ask?"

"That room of his." The one thing I had allowed myself to watch on T.V. was the return of P.O.W.s from North Vietnam. The men hobbling down the stairs of military transports to be wrapped in the arms of their grateful loved ones were nothing like Zebediah. Their hair was white, their backs bent, and when the cameras caught their eyes, you knew they were people who would never glorify war.

"He was captured just three weeks before the big prisoner exchange between North and South Korea," Hope said as we sat back down to our tea. "Zebediah was freed in less than a month."

It was not for me to judge whether three weeks in captivity qualified one to be a war hero; a lot of horrible things could occur in less time. But Zebediah's military bearing and gun collection were now easier to understand.

"I've been wondering about something," I said tentatively. "Do you think Allison might be closer to Zebediah if she wasn't always hearing about her birth father?"

Hope hesitated. When she spoke it was in a flat voice.

"I don't expect you to understand some of the things I do, Pat, but I have my reasons. Allison loves to hear about Adam Lee, and she needs to have that connection in her life. We both do."

"But you're remarried. Life goes on." I sounded like Earl Roy.

"I do what I must, Pat. Please leave it at that."

Hope poured fresh tea and fell silent, her hands wrapped around her cup as if trying to warm them. "Adam Lee was my first love, just like your Dan," she said finally. "He is the only person I have ever known who truly cared that I was happy. And the only one who made me so." Her face took on an amused look. "I used to tease him that Allison should have been twins because we always made love twice." She blushed when she realized what she had said.

"I think that's nice."

She got up to clear the table. "Zebediah will be home soon."

I did not miss the unstated message. "I guess I should be heading home," I said, looking at my watch. "Hey, it's midnight."

We embraced and wished one another a happy New Year. "Maybe you could come another time when we can talk more," Hope said. "Zebediah will be returning to Annapolis right after the holidays."

"I'd love to."

I left her at the front door, looking like one of her statues in her long dress, and stepped out into the frigid January air of 1975.

Music and laughter came down the street from the Donlin's as the partiers rang in the new year. I stood there listening on the front walk until I became aware of another sound; Hope was shouting at Allison above where I stood. I turned to look up to a lighted window where the music of Edith Piaf filtered through the glass.

"You didn't have to take Pat into that room!" Hope yelled. A single silhouette moved across the room and the music increased in volume. "I need one friend, Allison, just one person I can talk to!"

The music grew even louder. "Be sure to keep your door locked!"

I realized that Hope was not angry, she was shouting through a closed door. "No matter what you hear, don't unlock it!"

CHAPTER THIRTY

Three months later my back deteriorated to the point that my left leg and foot felt constantly on fire. And I could not take pain pills strong enough to eradicate it while I was responsible for patients under anesthesia.

Jeff Wells, at Lori's request, did a series of tests which showed a herniated disc in my lumbar spine that was putting pressure on the sciatic nerve running down my left leg.

"You also have bone fragments," Jeff pointed out on the x-ray he was showing me. "You didn't tell me you had an injury."

He did not wear a suit like most doctors. His clothing was casual, but his manner professional.

I told him about being accidentally kicked in the back by a pair of combat boots going full force into a bunker to escape a rocket attack. "I hurt a lot, but we had so many casualties I kept working."

"Well, that noble, but rather foolish, decision has caught up with you." He gave me the option of being admitted to Fishback Hospital and put in traction to relieve the herniated disk problem. "But I think you're headed for the O.R. sooner or later to have the disk and bone fragments removed. And I suggest you do that at a larger hospital, like Filmore in Baltimore."

I did not wish to be admitted anywhere, especially Filmore. "I'll try the traction," I said.

Earl Roy was the first to visit me in the hospital. "Think you'll be up and around soon?" He scratched at his beard, which remained a series of unconnected patches across his cheeks and chin.

"I hope so." It was the first time I had been hospitalized and I was not happy with the role of patient.

He took off his surgical cap, and the long strands of hair he combed and sprayed up over his balding pate stuck out from the side of his head like taffy pulled too thin. "We need you at work."

"He's having to do your cases," Skipper said when he stopped by on evening rounds. "It won't hurt him to do a little work."

Skipper's scrub clothes looked as if he had slept in them. And the drawstring of the pants was a series of tight sailor's knots guaranteed to give the laundry department fits.

"I'm sorry you're having to take so much call," I said. His tan had now become an unhealthy jaundice.

"We managed before you, and we'll manage until you're well."

Lori visited whenever she could and Andy telephoned, but most of the long days and nights I spent alone. If one had to be in a hospital, however, Christian was not a bad choice.

Call lights were answered promptly and the nurses still made rounds during the night, the same as I had been trained to do. The first two nights I feigned sleep when the nurse shined a flashlight on the wall above my bed, shedding just enough light down on me to see if I was sleeping. On the third night she came closer.

"Miss Walsh," she whispered. I kept my eyes closed and concentrated on making my facial muscles relax.

"I know you're not sleeping." The jig was up, I opened my eyes.

"It's hard to sleep in a hospital," I said. There was not only the recurring dream of Dan, I had a new nightmare of being in a plane crash where I was trapped in the wreckage. When I woke with pain ripping through my back and leg, I discovered I was trapped in the wreckage of my own body.

"Let me get you something." The nurse was gone before I could object.

She held a medicine cup containing a sleeping pill out to me, but I did not immediately take it. "You need rest," she insisted.

When I woke, I was startled to see it was light outside and breakfast trays were being carried into rooms. It was the first time in years I could remember sleeping through the night.

In Vietnam there had been the constant awareness of artillery, which kept the mind alert enough to distinguish between incoming enemy fire and outgoing friendly fire even in the midst of sleep. And after Dan's death the dreams began.

My body felt wonderfully refreshed, even with several pounds of weights pulling my lower torso away from the upper portion to take pressure off my misplaced disk. But I felt disoriented.

I was accustomed to all the night sounds: fire trucks and police cars rushing to calls, garbage workers rattling metal cans, followed by the whining sound of the rubble being compacted. I heard the street sweepers, the delivery trucks pulling into supermarkets, and newspapers hitting steps and sidewalks. On the island there was also the cackle of crated chickens being hauled to processing plants, and the grinding gears of trucks carrying away wet feathers and entrails.

Jeff came to see me on his way to surgery to do a hysterectomy. "I feel good," I told him. "Like I could go home."

He was not persuaded. "I'm going to start you on some physical therapy and see how you do."

His bedside manner was old-fashioned, giving me time to ask questions before running off.

I was so bored by afternoon I turned on the television mounted on the wall opposite my bed. After a few minutes of Windy Duckman showing how to build the perfect duck blind, I turned off the set.

The knock on my partially closed door was welcomed. "Come in."

Hope entered carrying a vase of fresh flowers. "I heard you were sick," she said. I was about to ask how when I remembered I was living in a small town.

"They're beautiful." I buried my face in the fragrant bouquet.

She placed them on my window sill and sat down in the recliner next to my bed. "I hate arranged flowers," she said. "Especially gladiolus. Adam Lee always said they belonged on a coffin."

I almost told her I had heard her say that the first time I saw her and Allison at the cemetery, but it was when I was eavesdropping on their conversation. "I feel the same," I said instead.

"So how are you?"

"Better. But I can't convince my doctor to discharge me."

"Don't be in too big a hurry," Hope cautioned.

We had been visiting for over an hour when Lori stopped on her way to the delivery room. Hope seemed genuinely happy to see her, and the two embraced while exchanging admonishments for not getting together sooner.

"I've been meaning to call," Hope said.

Lori said nothing of the incident at the firehall. "I've meant to do the same."

Lori asked how Zebediah's campaign for Congress was going, and Hope told her it looked as if he would be elected. I noticed there was none of the gentleness in her voice when she spoke of her present husband, as was the case when she talked about Adam Lee.

"Will you be moving to Washington if he wins?" Lori asked.

"He's had his own place in Annapolis ever since winning the state senate seat," Hope replied. "I expect he'll keep it the same."

Lori looked at her watch. "I need to be going. I have a first-time mom in labor who probably won't deliver till the wee hours."

At the mention of time Hope glanced at her watch. "Allison! I forgot all about her!" She grabbed her purse and started for the door. "She went riding with friends from school," she explained in a less frantic voice. "I told her I'd be home by five."

"Good heavens, she's seventeen," Lori said.

"I have to go." Hope's heels clicked rapidly down the hall.

Lori started to leave but paused to straighten items on my bedside table. "She should have taken Allison and moved away from here when Adam Lee died," she said. "She'll have that girl as strange as she is if she doesn't stop living in the past."

"Just because she cares about her first husband doesn't mean she's living in the past," I defended. "Their marriage ended because he was killed, not because they stopped loving each other."

"I know you've been to the cemetery with them," Lori said suddenly. "People talk. And I've seen you there myself."

"So what? I don't have to tell you everything."

"I'm just thinking of your happiness. And hanging out in a cemetery doesn't seem like the right direction to be headed."

"I think you're trying to tell me I should spend more time with Andy?" He had called several times since my hospitalization. "If it makes you feel any better, he's coming down this weekend."

Lori looked offended. "I'm not telling you what to do, Pat. But he is an awfully nice guy."

"I know, Lori." She left without further comment.

After ten days of traction and physical therapy, Jeff finally let me go home. As long as I avoided all strain on my back.

Reba had freshly baked cinnamon rolls waiting. "You're thin as a rail," she said as she generously buttered a roll and put it next to the coffee she poured for me. I knew Lori had not had an easy time by the missing strips of wallpaper next to the kitchen table. Neither Jeff nor she could make a decision about marriage.

I was happy Reba had put off going to Baltimore a few months. She wore her good suit, and had even put on her tie in honor of my homecoming. She bustled about the kitchen making a dinner of fish Billy caught from the second hand boat he bought with his house painting money. It was good to be back in the cherry red house.

Andy arrived on Friday afternoon looking fit and happy. He had passed his Physician Assistant exams.

"Where do you plan to work?" I asked.

"Nowhere for awhile." We were on our way to Seaport.

"I'm going to take it easy a couple of months," he said. "Maybe get a place here on the water."

He drove up to the boardwalk and parked my Mustang. "Want some caramel corn?"

We walked along the boardwalk eating the warm, sticky corn and dodging sea gulls that swooped down around us with their high-pitched begging. It seemed a long time ago that I had done the same with Lori's children.

"How do you stay so happy?" I asked Andy. He was laughing as he threw caramel corn to the sea gulls, teasing them by not always releasing it from his hand.

"I'm cheerful, not happy."

"What's the difference?"

"Happy's for yourself. Cheerful is for the people around you." He threw more caramel corn. "Aim for cheerful, Danang. It's about as close to happy as folks like us are ever going to get."

I took him to the small cottage I had rented a year earlier, and he fell in love with it the same as I had. Before we left Seaport he had paid a month's rent.

CHAPTER THIRTY-ONE

Reba's departure was difficult for all, despite our joy that she was recovered enough from her heart attack to begin developing the properties she worked so hard to acquire. The timing was especially bad for me, since my back problems had forced me to bed again after only two weeks of agonizing work. The rambling old house, absent the children and Lori from eight until four, was unbearably lonesome without the creak of Reba's rocking chair downstairs.

I was glad when Jeff dropped by to see me on his way to Oyster Island, where he was now doctoring one day a week in a rented house. "You need to go to Baltimore," he concluded when he checked the reflexes in my left leg and foot with a rubber hammer. "You have no ankle reflex and a pronounced foot drop."

I boosted myself up on my elbows and saw that my left foot was drooped over like a wilted lily.

"Filmore has the best neurosurgeons, and that's what you need," he said. "Or that nerve damage will be permanent."

"I don't want to go to Filmore. And I don't want surgery."

"It's now or later. And you'll be a lot worse off later."

I knew he had spoken to Lori when she came directly upstairs after work. "O.K., I'll go to Filmore," I said when she went to the foot of my bed and uncovered by droopy foot.

"When?" Lori demanded.

"Andy's coming Monday. I'll ride back to Baltimore with him."

Andy took his carload of possessions to the cottage in Seaport, then came to get me. I was in such pain I had to lie in the back seat for the ride to Baltimore.

Dr. McClain, the professor of neurosurgery, examined me soon after I arrived.

"Tell me when you first hurt your back," he said while he hammered my painful leg looking for reflexes that now did not exist. Several young interns and residents stood by with hands ready to take my anguish to a higher level.

"A few years ago." I hoped he wouldn't ask how.

"How did you hurt it?"

"I was on a civilian medical team in Vietnam. I got kicked in the back while diving into a bunker during the Tet Offensive."

Dr. McClain's eyebrows rose above the frames of his glasses. "What in the world were you doing over <u>there</u>?"

"Taking care of civilian casualties."

I wished I could have had Andy in the room for moral support. But I could tell by the way the professor wrote everything in my chart that my malady had enough challenge to qualify me for decent care.

For the next hour he and his students took turns pushing and poking at me like prospective car buyers. When they had all kicked my tires and slammed my doors to their satisfaction, Dr. McClain told me he agreed with Jeff's diagnosis of a herniated disk and bone fragments interfering with the nerves coming out of my spine.

"I'm amazed you could live with such a situation so long," he said. "I recommend a myelogram as soon as we can get it, and surgery if it shows what I think it will."

When does a neurosurgeon not recommend surgery, I thought to myself. "Can I take some time to think about it?"

"Of course." He left the examining room with his students.

I was admitted to a neuro ward, where my roommate was an elderly woman with a severe head injury. She spent the majority of time moaning and trying to crawl out of the bed she was tied to. I had not made a decision by the next morning, or the next.

"Finish your move to Seaport," I told Andy when he visited the third day. "I'll be fine here."

"I'll leave as soon as you get your back cracked." He looked at the moaning woman in the next bed. "Why isn't anyone checking on her?"

"They do, about once a shift." I wanted to be alone to lick my wounds, like a dog who crawls under a porch after being hit by a car.

"I worked here, Andy. They'll look after me." He was finally convinced and left for the island.

But the staff avoided our room except for necessities like vital signs, and it took forever for me to get a pain pill even though they were ordered every four hours. No one made rounds at night with a flashlight, nor did nurses stop by much during the other shifts. Pills and meals, that was it.

I required little care, but the woman in the next bed was left lying in her own body wastes while nurses watched heart monitors attached to critically ill patients. Or carried out a myriad of high-tech duties that had been pushed ahead of patient care. Nursing had become too sophisticated for comfort.

"I don't have any sick days left," I complained to Andy when he came to visit from the cottage in Seaport. "And I'm worried that my insurance won't cover all these tests they're doing." There was also the matter of my job, which Skipper was managing to hang onto by once more enlisting the help of Earl Roy to do cases during the day.

"Why are you worried about bills?" Andy asked. "The government has to pay them."

"Do you think they would?"

"Well you sure as hell didn't wreck your back Stateside."

A distant memory surfaced of seeing a doctor at the State Department when I returned home. "He didn't do anything," I told Andy. "Just told me to sleep on a firm surface and no heavy lifting."

"Typical government quack."

Andy's years of tangling with the bureaucracy of VA hospitals was appreciated when he telephoned Washington on my behalf. In two day's time, he had a ream of government forms for me to fill out.

I worked on the forms during the day. And at night when my roommate kept me awake with incoherent rantings.

It seemed she would just be settling down so I could sleep when a helicopter would come swooping in to land on the roof of an adjacent wing. It was transporting critically injured or sick patients to a special unit called Shock Trauma, and the sound of its rotors never failed to transport me back to the war. An involuntary surge of adrenalin would pump through my body to prepare for handling casualties, which later kept me awake.

Sophisticated Shock Trauma units were springing up across the country to care for patients previously considered unsalvageable. Their protocol was based totally upon medical information garnered in Vietnam, where rapid evacuation of victims by helicopter, and resuscitation by highly skilled teams of nurses and doctors, had proven successful in treating even the worst injuries.

It was one of life's ironies that medicine's greatest advances were made in the midst of war, where injured young men and women were excellent specimens to try out new drugs and procedures.

After a week of shoddy care and continued pain, I reluctantly signed the surgery permit. Dr. Ware gave the anesthesia himself to ensure no interns or residents were left alone to carve on me.

For all the thousands of times I had pushed the plunger on Pentothal syringes, I was unprepared for the rush of euphoria, or the freedom from pain. The next second I was awake.

"Take a big breath, Pat. Your surgery is over."

I saw two Dr. Wares standing over my stretcher.

Doctor McClain was there, too. "Wiggle your toes for me," he said. When I complied I could see relief in his face. "You were a mess in there. You should be feeling a whole lot better real soon."

"I already do."

He patted my shoulder. "Good girl. I'll talk to you later."

Andy was waiting in my room and stayed with me through the night to make sure I had adequate pain medication and did not have any complications that went unnoticed by the three nurses on duty. He also took care of the head injury woman in the next bed, who quieted whenever he touched her and talked soothingly, even though she appeared unaware of her surroundings. Hearing was the last thing to go in a critically ill or wounded patient.

Recovery was a bit slower than I anticipated. My left leg had forgotten how to function, requiring hours of physical therapy.

I walked between parallel bars with a full-length mirror at the end so I could see what I was doing wrong. But all I could see was some old lady stumbling along in my body.

Washington had yet to respond to the forms I had submitted for compensation. But Andy was confident I would be taken care of.

Reba made a surprise visit one afternoon in a new suit that fit perfectly, a soft cream colored shirt and silk tie. Her transition to male was so convincing I wondered if the contractors and building crews she now had working on her properties knew she was a woman.

"You're becoming a regular tycoon," I said while I ate a savory chicken salad sandwich she brought from a delicatessen.

"You should see the plans my daughter has for those old heaps of mine," Reba said with a laugh. "And the two of us living in a swanky place looking right out over the harbor so we can supervise the people we're paying a fortune to work for us."

"You deserve a nice place to live and to have Jackie with you."

"Now don't you go thinking I'm just sitting back having me a good time without remembering where I came from," she said in the deep, sharp voice she used to use on interns. "I got ideas all drawn up for a place for people bein' pushed out of their apartments. And a name for it too," she said in a gentler tone. "Dreamland."

Reba cleaned up the remnants of our lunch, discarding food she would never have wasted in her days of begging soup bones.

Lori came to visit as soon as she could get away from work and children. She filled me in on all that was happening on both Fishback and Oyster Island, saving the best news for last.

"I was planning to wait until you were home to tell you," she began. "But maybe you could use some good news now."

I was afraid to guess, lest I put a jinx on what I hoped for.

"Jeff has decided to set up a permanent practice on Oyster Island. He's going to build a clinic sometime this year."

"That's it?"

"And we're getting married."

The semi-conscious woman next door roused when she heard my whoop. "When's the big day? I want to be there."

"There's not going to be a big day," Lori replied. "We decided it would be easier on the children if we just went off quietly and married in the court house." I couldn't help my disappointment. "It's the way Jeff wants it. And I've already gone through all that cotton candy crap of a big wedding."

I was so pleased for Lori it did not occur to me until after she left to spend the night with Reba that I would have to find someplace else to live. Newlyweds living with three children would be trying enough, it was time for me to leave my adopted family.

Although I had participated in hundreds of resuscitations, I couldn't recall ever speaking to the unfortunate bystander, whose only crime was being unlucky enough to have a bed on the other side of a curtain from a patient who suffered a cardiac arrest. Such patients were generally treated as a nuisance by staff members responding to a CPR call, particularly in a teaching hospital where dozens of residents and interns crammed into the already crowded room.

If the roommate was unable to get up and leave, his bed was shoved up against the far wall to make more space. And there he must lie, listening to shouted commands without a sympathetic word.

When the woman in the next bed arrested in the middle of the night, I found that despite my years of experience I was as shaken as the hapless victims I once ignored.

Twenty people loudly shouted orders and reprimanded those not doing their job satisfactorily. I had to remind myself I was a patient while the anesthesia person responding to the emergency attempted to put in an endotracheal tube and repeatedly failed.

"Jesus H. Christ! You've put it in the esophagus again!" a male resident fumed. "Get someone down here who knows what the hell he's doing!" Dr. Rasheif emerged from the mob around the bed, and without noticing me, went to the desk to call someone from anesthesia. I had to fight my inclination to get out of bed and do the intubation.

But perhaps it wasn't so bad Dr. Rasheif happened to be on call. The elderly woman had tubes going in and out of almost every orifice in her body and shouldn't have been resuscitated anyway.

An anesthesia resident finally put the endotracheal tube in properly, but it was too late. Her heart refused to restart with several jolts from a defibrillator. I was relieved when everyone left and the body was finally removed.

The next morning a long envelope was delivered to me with the seal of the Department of State.

"The rules regarding compensation for illness or injury require the employee to report said illness or injury to his/her supervisor within forty-eight hours," the first paragraph read. "All appropriate forms must then be completed, in triplicate, and filed in the Office of Workers' Compensation within no less than ten days."

I had explained in my correspondence that all of the military hospitals around Danang were too busy with severe Tet casualties to do anything about an injured back. Besides the fact that I was a critical part of the small team working around the clock to handle the hordes of civilian casualties my hospital was receiving daily.

"The rules are very clear regarding medical compensation," a woman told me in a government monotone when I managed to get a call through to Washington. "Forty-eight hours was ample time to complete the forms and get them to your supervisor in Saigon."

"We were doing a hundred major surgeries a day," I protested. "And Danang was cut off from Saigon because of the fighting."

"Can you prove that?"

"The Pentagon can."

"That is a different agency than ours."

"It's the same government, isn't it?"

"Rules are clear. We have to abide by the same ones."

"You're telling me that people in the middle of a war have to follow the same rules as workers in downtown D.C.?"

"It's State Department policy, not something I made up."

"Look, I don't even remember seeing any of those papers you're talking about. We didn't have enough penicillin or oxygen at our hospital, why would we have a bunch of stupid government forms?" The other end of the line was silent. "Hello, are you there?"

"I'm here," the woman answered. "But I won't be if you do not refrain from referring to our government as stupid."

"But I wasn't told I had to fill out forms if I was injured."

"Ignorance is no excuse."

I calmed myself enough to let my brain take over instead of my mouth. "The doctor at Navy Hospital in Danang who did my departure physical failed me because of my back," I said calmly. "He ordered x-rays and I took them to the Workers' Comp doctor in your agency as soon as I got back to the States."

I could hear papers being shuffled. "There is a notation in your file that you reported here, but there is no official note written by the doctor. And even if there were, that still does not exempt you from filling out the appropriate forms at the time of injury."

"I was running triage! I had more to do than deal with ridiculous government rules!"

I was holding the buzzing receiver when Dr. McClain and his students came in on rounds. "Sorry, but I can't help you with that," the professor said when I told him what had just transpired.

My dragging left leg and foot drop were not improving as much as anticipated, and the frustration the neurosurgeon felt visiting a patient who refused to get well was evident in his expression. He looked at me like an old mistress he would prefer to forget.

"Maybe I shouldn't say this," he said anyway. "But didn't you ask for this by participating in the slaughter going on over there?"

CHAPTER THIRTY-TWO

"Pat, do you hear me?"

I looked up at a high ceiling with pipes crisscrossing it. "Where am I?" The words were difficult with my mouth so dry.

Lori leaned over the side rail and brushed hair back from my face with maternal strokes. "They had to transfer you."

I tried to lift one of my arms and couldn't. When I raised my head to see why, I found both wrists in thick leather restraints like those used in the electroshock lab.

My heart rate doubled, blasting blood through the tiniest of capillaries until my whole body pulsated with alarm. "Am I in psych?"

"It's only temporary," Lori said in a voice as distressed as mine. I tried to yank my hands free. "Please don't do that," Lori pleaded. "That's why they had to put those things on you."

"Get me out! Get my hands unlocked and get me out of here!"

"Please, Pat." I was trying to sit up with my arms stretched out to each siderail, and the pain it caused in my newly operated back was horrendous. Lori attempted to lower me back to my bed, but I resisted despite the pain. "You've had a bad episode of some kind. The doctors need to find out what happened so they can help you."

Jeff stood behind Lori. "Don't make things worse," he said in a calm doctor's voice which only made me angrier. "If you keep fighting like this, Doctor McClain will have no choice but to keep you here."

"Doctor McClain?" Suddenly I remembered the telephone conversation with the woman and Doctor McClain driving a wedge through my chest with his remark. "Where is he?" I demanded.

"He said he would be back later," Lori reassured.

"You blanked out," Jeff explained. "He transferred you here for evaluation and called Lori."

I fell back to my mattress. My mind had taken such complete leave of my body I not only had a missing gap of time I could not recall, but it lasted long enough for Lori and Jeff to drive all the way from Fishback Island. There was no hiding it anymore, the suction machine had sucked my mind completely from my body.

"Don't let them do shock treatments on me," I cried to Lori. "Call my family if you have to, but don't let them do ECT."

Lori dabbed at my eyes with a tissue wet from wiping her own. "Don't worry," she said. "You're not having any shock treatments."

"I prefer you let me make that decision." Dr. Frankfurt, in one of his expensive courtroom suits, had entered the room while Lori was speaking. If he remembered me from our days of sparring in the electroshock lab, he gave no indication. "I would like to do an assessment while she's lucid," he said to Jeff and Lori.

While I was lucid? Jesus, what had gone on while I wasn't?

"Don't go." I had Lori's fingers gripped tightly in one of my manacled hands. "Please don't leave."

"It'll be all right," she replied. "Jeff and I will be right out in the hall." She pried herself free of my grasp.

I began pulling against the restraints again. "I'm sure Doctor Frankfurt would let you out of those if you settled down," Jeff said. Dr. Frankfurt did not look pleased, but when I immediately stopped struggling he summoned a nurse who unlocked the restraints with a tiny key. She did not remove them from the room.

The professor pulled a chair to my bed. "You were discussing some correspondence from the government when this dissociative reaction took place. What was it that upset you?"

A dissociative reaction. My mind raced back to my psychiatric training, grasping for information I had not used in years.

"It wasn't just the letter," I said. "Doctor McClain said something extremely distressing to me."

There was a water pitcher on my bedside table and Dr. Frankfurt focused on it. "And what was that?"

I wished the water pitcher could answer. "I was in Vietnam." I waited for a reaction, but he continued staring at the pitcher, tapping a pencil against a chart he held in his lap. My very own psychiatric record. "You probably know I got hurt over there." He continued tapping while I related what had gone on with Washington and Dr. McClain's response to my rejection for compensation.

"So the government's refusal to take care of you is basically what this is about?" Dr. Frankfurt was making notes in my chart.

"They shouldn't just abandon me."

"You seem to harbor a significant amount of hostility," he said to the water pitcher. "Plus these feelings of abandonment."

My mind was back with me. It was time I started using it.

"I didn't say I felt abandoned. I'm just upset that the government won't give me the medical care I deserve."

"You've had a rather profound reality lapse. I would say that's more serious than just being upset."

"But I'm worried about whether I'll be able to return to work, and pay all the bills I'm running up." He undoubtedly had his meter running from the moment he was called, regardless of whether I could communicate. "I was injured while in the employ of our government."

"I understand that, but I would be inclined to believe your psychiatric problems are more deeply seated than a rejected medical claim." He was moving in on the suction machine. "Doctor McClain says you can continue your surgical recovery here," he said as he chicken-scratched something in my chart. "I'm going to recommend that you stay with us for awhile."

Lori and Jeff returned the moment Dr. Frankfurt left. "He's keeping me," I told them.

"I'm sure it won't be for long," Lori said. Jeff gave her a cautionary look. "Why didn't you tell me about these spells?" she said when I confessed about the earlier episodes. She sounded hurt.

"I was doing O.K. until the letter," I said. "And a cruel remark by someone who should know better."

"So McClain's a jerk," Jeff said. "We can get you another doc."

"And get me moved off psych?"

"I didn't say that." I was disappointed to see him hide within the safety of his profession. "I'll get you referred to someone else in neuro. But you need to cooperate with people here."

"I thought we would go over to Reba's for the night," Lori said later. "Unless you want me to stay." I knew her offer was genuine, but she looked and sounded like she needed a good rest.

"I'll be O.K." They started to leave, but Lori paused to open a set of heavy draperies. There were bars on the windows, and she closed them quickly. "Does Andy know where I am?" I asked.

"Not yet," Lori replied. "Would you like me to call him?"

"No. And don't tell Reba."

I lay staring at the steam pipes crisscrossing the ceiling all night, feigning sleep whenever a nurse or orderly came in to check on me. I not only had the suction machine to fear now, the electroshock lab was just down the corridor.

When I heard Al's voice I tried to hide my face. But he came over to where I sat gluing beads to an empty plastic milk container along with other psych patients. I prayed he had not come to take me to his lab.

"How are you, young lady?" He acted as if he saw former staff members transformed to part of the patient population every day. "Long time since I've seen you."

"I moved to Fishback I..." I dropped the paper cup holding my beads and they scattered all over the floor.

"Dumb shit," a grey haired patient across from me said. She was dressed like an aristocrat and had pampered skin. But the two words were the only ones she uttered from morning to night.

The occupational therapist came to clean up the mess so I wouldn't have to bend my painful back. "Didn't we promise not to say that any more, Mrs. Caslick?" she said to the woman.

"Dumb shit," the woman said again. Al smiled and helped pick up beads. When he finished he asked if he could take me for a walk.

"As long as it's not off the unit," the therapist told him.

Al's attitude was as gentle with me as it was with patients I had put to sleep in his lab. We walked only a short distance before he pushed open a door and motioned me inside. There it stood, looking dead-center at me. The electroshock machine.

I stood immobile in the doorway while Al went to a cupboard and took out something metal. I was holding my breath when he turned with an electric kettle in hand. "Coffee or tea?"

He sat me in a chair alongside the stretcher patients reclined on for ECT treatments. The cup of instant coffee he handed me begged for the companionship of a cigarette.

"We had to open this second lab to keep up with all the treatments Frankfurt orders these days," Al said. "I run the whole operation with the help of one part-time nurse."

"I never realized how scary this place could be."

He took a swallow of his coffee. "Are you afraid Frankfurt might order treatments on you?" His manner was matter-of-fact.

"I have him for a doctor, doesn't he order them on everyone?"

"Not all. But some people can't get better any other way."

I looked at the anesthesia machine. It seemed impossible that not long ago I was confidently putting psych patients to sleep.

Al sipped leisurely at his coffee, as if asking me what I was locked up in psych for was the furthest thing from his mind. "So where're you passing gas these days?"

"A little hospital on Fishback Island."

"That's nice. Beach weather will be here before you know it."

I steadied my coffee cup with both hands. "I suppose you're wondering what I'm in here for?"

His demeanor was kind but not patronizing. "Can't I make you a cup of coffee just for old time's sake?" he said with a smile.

For the first time since being transferred to psych I could smile back and mean it, not fake it for the sake of people observing me.

"I never thought I'd be back here," I said, looking around the lab. "At least not with this." I tugged at the hospital identification band around my left wrist.

"You know what they say, every good nurse and doctor needs an incision or illness."

"You mean I'm going to be a better anesthetist after this?"

"Unless you use the experience to make yourself unhappy the rest of your life." Al reached for my cup to refill it, but I refused, lest I grab the pack of cigarettes apparent in his shirt pocket.

"It's not so important what happens to us in life," Al said over his shoulder as he made himself another cup. "It's how we react to it that matters."

"You should have gone to medical school instead of nursing. You're a much better shrink than Frankfurt."

He laughed. "Maybe so."

I didn't really want to tell him about the suction machine. "The nurses will probably be looking for me," I said.

Al nudged me gently along, getting more information. "How'd you end up in Nam?" he asked when I told him how I hurt my back.

The door was slightly ajar and I could see Mrs. Caslick shuffling by. "I volunteered."

"Dumb shit," Mrs. Caslick said.

Al laughed heartily. I was surprised when I heard my own laughter echoing up to the steam pipes on the high ceiling.

We were out in the corridor when I asked if I could come again. "Of course you can, friend." Al put one of his solid arms around me.

There were two cards waiting for me when I returned to my room, one from Hope and the other from Andy. I opened Hope's first. Her handwriting was like the rest of her, smooth and artistic. "I've only just heard you were in Filmore Hospital, and hope you are recovering well from surgery," she wrote. "I've thought of you often lately. I take Allison to ceramics every Tuesday evening, and it's terrible not having you to talk to."

Andy's card was more difficult. "Lori says you don't want to see me for awhile. I hope I didn't do something to offend you."

He went on to say how much he was enjoying the cottage and the beach. "I watch the sunrise every morning without another soul in sight, just me and the gulls. You have to spend some time here when you're discharged. It's the perfect place to recuperate."

CHAPTER THIRTY-THREE

Three times a week I saw Dr. Frankfurt, who had a system of channeling patients in and out of his office via separate doors so the departing one didn't bump into the one arriving. For a profession that preached acceptance for mental illness, I found it hypocritical.

During the first several sessions Dr. Frankfurt sat taking notes while I rambled on about the hospital, our supply problems and the patients. "How are you doing with your anger against Washington?" he asked at the start of my second week.

"It's gone."

He stopped writing. "And how did that come about?"

"I was awake one night when something struck me. How can I expect fairness from a government that got us into Vietnam in the first place?"

He considered a few moments. "But you must also remember that going there was a <u>choice</u> you made freely," he said like my mother. "Women didn't have to go."

"Women have been serving in wars as long as men have been starting them," I said.

His expression was at first defensive, then the closest thing to a smile I had ever seen crossed his face. "Point well taken." Dr. Frankfurt was proving to be a much better psychiatrist than I had thought while working at Filmore.

In the next session he said, "Tell me what bothers you most about your Vietnam experience." I felt myself convulse inside. I could not tell him about the burned baby. That was a private pain I could not share. But he sat waiting, and I had another secret sorrow that was always in the back of my mind. I started hesitantly.

"There were patients who died that I might have been able to help. Sometimes I went to the beach or to a party while they lay suffering in filthy wards." He betrayed no emotion. "We were always there for surgery on new casualties, but the wards..." I couldn't bear to think of them even now. "If I had been older and wiser, I probably would have used better judgment."

"War is not for the old and wise. It is the young who must do the dirty work, as well as suffer the consequences."

"That still doesn't excuse me."

"But you didn't have the necessary supplies even to care for the casualties coming into your triage. What would you have used to improve conditions on the wards?"

It was something I had never considered. "I don't know," I said after some contemplation. "But I should have tried."

He was making it too easy. Going through war forced you to face your imperfections, and I was not about to reject the simple honesty I discovered about myself in Vietnam. I had worked hard most days, but I had also walked past abject misery on my way to indulge my own pleasures. Despite the compassion I demonstrated most of the time, I was still capable of barbarous indifference. An affluent physician was not the one to judge whether I had behaved humanely within the inhumanity of war. It was up to a higher power to forgive me, or to determine whether forgiveness was needed.

In the next session we discussed what sort of incidents triggered the dissociative reactions and ways to avoid them. I listened carefully, hoping he would discharge me.

It had taken days to summon the courage to telephone Andy at his cottage in Seaport. He drove to Baltimore the same day.

"They don't pay any attention to my bad back here," I told him. "It's like I didn't even have surgery."

"You haven't figured out that psych docs and nurses think the human body ends at the neck?"

Doctor Frankfurt made an early morning visit to my room at the beginning of my third week of confinement. "I'm discharging you," he said from the chair he had taken at my bedside. "You may leave as soon as the nurses get you ready."

"I'm really free?"

He nodded. "And now that you are discharged I would like to share some personal observations with you."

"To begin with, you are the first person I have cared for who is suffering from what we are calling Vietnam Syndrome." He looked directly at me. "You have given me a much better understanding of the problems of those who served in the war."

He put my chart down, got up and walked slowly to the window where he looked through the bars at the world beyond. "I have a son," he began with his back to me. "I wanted him to go to medical school, and he was well on his way."

He turned to face me looking strangely vulnerable. "Then he got mixed up in the protest movement at Columbia University, dropped out of school and spends his time roaming the country with people who live off the parents they're accusing of being capitalist pigs."

"Maybe he'll go back to school someday."

"My wife and I hope so. He's our only child."

I couldn't believe I was feeling sorry for Dr. Frankfurt.

"Anyway, what I am trying to say is that maybe you didn't make such a bad choice after all." He moved closer to my bedside. "When your children ask what you did in the sixties, you can tell them you went to Vietnam and took care of people who desperately needed you."

It touched me deeply. "It's very kind of you to say that."

He shook my hand. "Good luck to you."

Andy came to take me home looking fit and rested from his time at the beach. He carried my suitcase while I rode in a wheelchair pushed by a nurse. We were passing the huge statue of Jesus in the main lobby when Reba hurried by on the opposite side. She carried a bouquet of roses.

When I called to her she stopped to look around, but didn't see me until Andy waved at her. "Over here."

"What're you doing trying to sneak out on me?" Reba said as I got up from the wheelchair to accept her hug. "Lori's been telling me you couldn't have visitors anymore, but I made up my mind I was coming anyway." She gave the nurse pushing my chair a "so there" look.

"I had some complications," I said to Reba when the nurse left. "They restricted visitors for awhile." Andy looked puzzled.

I was telling myself I didn't want Reba to know about my emotional problems because I didn't want her to worry. But inside I knew that even with my medical training, I still felt the stigma of having been a psychiatric patient.

"You look wonderful," I said to Reba.

"Never mind me, how're you?"

"I'm doing a lot better."

"I hate to interrupt," Andy said. "But we'd better get going if you want to get to the beach in daylight, Pat."

"Thanks for the beautiful flowers," I said to Reba.

I felt like a caricature of Miss America as I stepped outside, hospital pale with my arms filled with roses. When a long, black limousine pulled up, I thought I might be hallucinating. Andy gave a whistle at the luxurious vehicle when the driver got out and held the door for Reba. "I don't park on no back streets anymore," she said with a wink. The windows were darkly tinted, but Reba pushed a button and the one next to where she sat glided down soundlessly. "You promise to call if you need anything?" she said to me.

"I promise."

"That old lady's a trip," Andy said while he helped me into my Mustang, which felt grander than any limousine.

When we pulled away from Filmore Hospital, even the run down row houses stretching in all directions looked inviting viewed from the other side of barred windows. My back and left leg still needed healing time, and I had a stack of medical bills to pay, but I was free of the government.

Andy adjusted my seat back when he saw me shifting around uncomfortably. "I understand the advantage of pain you told me about when we first met," I said. "It sure lets you know you're alive."

"At least old age won't be a surprise to us," he said. "We already know what it feels like to be decrepit."

I slept most of the way, having been deprived of sleep like people usually are in hospitals. Andy woke me when we were pulling into Muskrat Marsh.

"Would you like to stop at Lori's or go directly to the beach?"

I could see the big red house from the highway, sitting like a whore in church among its austere, white neighbors. It was too early for the children to be out of school, or for Lori to be home from work. And I had no idea what Jeff's new schedule might be.

"Let's go to the cottage. I want to see the beach."

"I've been talking to Jeff," Andy said as we headed toward Seaport. "He's building a new clinic on Oyster Island. And he's hoping to start one out by the migrant farms so he can treat the stoopers when they show up in May."

"That's nice."

"I'm taking a job with him."

We were passing the Highway Holiness Church and I looked for Hope and Allison in the adjoining cemetery, which was abandoned except for the birds. Reverend Taylor's Buy a Brick for Jesus campaign was succeeding; the new church had everything but a bell in its tower.

Andy was waiting for my reaction. "Are you sure you want to

live on this island?" I asked.

"I don't mind the rednecks, as long as I can have a place at the beach and work for Jeff." He sounded excited as he told me about the clinic on Oyster Island, which would have a small operating room for minor surgeries, a delivery room for Lori's obstetrical cases and an emergency room and day clinic where Andy would be in charge. Patients from Colored Town could take the mail boat to be seen in the clinic.

"We'll be practicing real medicine on people who really need it," he said. "Not the big business crap that usually goes on."

Andy pulled my Mustang up to the cottage. It was built just back of sand dunes now covered with tall grasses that waved in an ocean breeze. I sat looking at it, afraid it would disappear if I moved.

It was early spring, but the day was so balmy I sat in a rocker on the front porch. Andy stood looking out over the water with the wind blowing strands of dark hair loose from his ponytail. "Thank you for bringing me here," I said up to him.

"My pleasure, Danang."

"When will you start working with Jeff?" I asked after several minutes of quiet watching waves wash ashore.

"Probably when you go back to work." He pulled a chair up next to mine. "I thought you could spend a little time here, take it easy on your back by letting me wait on you."

Gulls swooped and cried in the salty air, some coming to rest on gnarled pieces of driftwood lying unclaimed on the deserted beach. I craved the rest Andy suggested, but I had to have an income.

"I need to keep my job, Andy. And my medical insurance."

He looked disappointed. "Well at least stay awhile," he said.

He fixed a special dinner of crab cakes and a bottle of wine. The surf rolled ashore outside the cottage as he held me in his arms. And this night there was no dream about Dan.

CHAPTER THIRTY-FOUR

My back had healed enough in psych to go back to work after two weeks at the cottage, but for only five hours a day and no night or weekend duty. Skipper had made arrangements for Getta Mae, a proud new mother, to help with call so he could ready his boat for summer.

Earl Roy was happy to have me back so he could return to coming into the hospital only when he absolutely had to. I was surprised when I met him coming down the surgery suite corridor dressed in O.R. attire when I stayed late to handle a case in O.B. with Lori.

"Who called you in?" I asked. I had come to the O.R. for equipment I needed in delivery. Voices could be heard coming from an operating room with a towel taped over the small window in its door.

"Doctor Arst has a quick little case to do," Earl Roy told me. "I thought I'd go ahead and do it while you were busy upstairs."

I started to open the door to see what the case was, but Earl Roy grabbed the handle. "It's contaminated," he said. "You can't go in."

I got the equipment I needed and returned to delivery, but the next morning I asked Skipper about Earl Roy's sudden devotion to work.

"That's a lot of b.s.," he said, laughing while we drew pentothal and other drugs into syringes for the day's cases. "These good Christians were probably doing one of their midnight specials."

"What's that?"

Skipper looked around to be sure no one was coming. "Abortion."

"You serious?"

"Arst does them and Earl Roy gives anesthesia. Hell, everyone on the island knows."

"Everyone but me."

"I didn't see any point in telling you."

"But Earl Roy says he's against abortion."

Skipper laughed. "And he also claims he's a great family man."

My surprise turned to curiosity. "Who's having the abortions?"

"A good share of them are from Zebediah's hot shot private school," Skipper said quietly. "Evidently, the young ladies are learning how to ride more than horses."

Lori confirmed Skipper's allegations when the children had gone to bed and I sat with her and Jeff over coffee at the kitchen table. "Arst and Earl Roy were doing abortions before Roe versus Wade."

It was hard for me to believe. "What a bunch of hypocrites."

"Not all the people," Jeff said. His clinic on Oyster Island was now operating three days a week out of someone's home. And an old house he rented near the migrant camps to serve as a clinic was already caring for stoopers arriving for the spring planting.

Jeff was not limiting his Fishback Island work only to migrant workers. Word of his expertise and low fees had spread so quickly through Colored Town, he now cared for nearly its entire population.

Lori and I lingered at the table after Jeff retired, talking like we had in old times. The wallpaper next to it had been stripped down to bare plaster, with no plans to replace it. In addition to a new clinic, Jeff and Lori were in the process of having a permanent home built on Oyster Island.

Lori picked at the edges of what remained of the wallpaper. "What about you and Andy, any plans for the future?"

"I don't spend much time thinking about the future."

"Then maybe it's time you start."

"Is this going to lead to a lecture about me going to the cemetery?" Lori had recently seen me there with Hope and Allison.

"I want you to have a life, Pat."

"Hope and I have a special relationship. It may look like we're crazy, but we're not." I laughed. "On the other hand, I did just get out of the loony bin."

"That isn't funny."

"You've been good to me, Lori, but you don't need to worry about me any longer."

I agreed to return to ceramics with Hope on the Tuesday nights I felt up to it so she would have company.

"We've not got much more ta go," Iris Irene was saying to the customers up front my second night back. "Soon's we get two hunert more we're shipping 'em down."

"They're talking about bibles," Hope explained. "They buy them for people in underdeveloped countries."

"I hope them natives in Hattie appreciate all our hard work," a customer said. "I'm near wore out from fund raisin'."

"Is it Haiti they're sending bibles to?" I asked Hope.

She nodded. "They choose a different country each year."

"But most Haitians are illiterate."

The grey ghost overheard us talking as he came out of the back room. "Y'all been ta Hattie?" he asked me.

"I worked at the Albert Schweitzer Hospital there," I answered.

"Tell me, did ya take the word a' the Lord down there or jest your medicines?" Odie's voice was so loud it caught the attention of the others. Even Crystal Lou stopped tormenting the shop cat.

"I was taking care of tetanus patients."

Odie's face took on the look of one about to embark on a crusade. "The bible says, 'He who wins souls is wise.'"

"Praise God," someone up front said.

Odie was watching me with a smile that appeared permanently affixed to his face. When I said nothing, he removed his hat and used it to slap dust from his clothes. When Hope and I were sufficiently polluted, he moved to the front of the room, made a brief phone call, then joined his wife who was with the customers around the stove.

"Y'all shoulda' seen him," Iris Irene said. "Brazen as all get out he walks right up to our front porch an' says ta Odie Luke, 'Mister, did you shoot my dawg?'"

"And that white whore waitin' on him in his car," Odie said.

"'You darned right I shot your dawg,' Odie Luke says ta him. 'An' if y'all don't get outta my yard, the next shot's headed your way.'"

"I tell you, that nigger turned heel an' run when I raised up my shotgun," Odie said with a laugh.

"My daddy shot the nigger's dawg," Crystal Lou said proudly.

"They're packin' ta leave," Odie said. "Even takin' the carcass 'cause they don't want it buried on the ahlund." He shook his head. "Leave it to a nigger ta cart off a dead dawg." The people laughed.

Allison left her classmates and came to sit next to her mother. "That's our French teacher," she said in a desperate whisper. "She wasn't at school today."

"I'm sorry Allison, but there's nothing I can do."

"Senator Taylor give us the nod ta take care a' things after the woman called them folks from the NAACP to complain about how her lover-man was bein' treated," Odie bragged as he walked slowly by us on his way to the back room. "The Senator don't like nigger lovers an' heathens takin' over this ahlund anymore than we do."

"I think we should leave," Hope said when Odie was gone.

"But you can't just let them run off my teacher like that." Allison continued to speak quietly, but her friends from the Freedom School were listening closely. "She cares about me, Mother," Allison said pleadingly. "French is my favorite subject."

"We need to leave," Hope repeated, gathering up her belongings.

"Sure, let him ruin every last part of my life," Allison accused.

Hope and I started for the door, with Allison reluctantly bringing up the rear. I had my hand on the knob when the door burst open and Reverend Taylor stood there clutching a bible to his breast.

He wore a frozen smile and his eyes shone as brightly as Odie's when sizing up a new female customer in the back room. The reverend's oddly upturned nose left his nostrils exposed in a vertical position, like a double car garage with both doors open.

"I hear y'all have bin ta Hattie," he said, much to my surprise. "Tell me, did ya do it for the Lord?" His voice rose with each word and his nostrils flared in and out with the exchange of air.

"I did it for the Haitians."

The reverend sucked in a long breath which made his nostrils close completely. "Jesus knows who walks among natives without spreadin' His word. He's watchin' now whilst you have the chance to right your sinfulness an' be saved."

"The Haitians need food and medicine," I said. "Not bibles."

"They're starvin' for the word a' tha Lord!" Reverend Taylor's voice boomed over me as if he was speaking from a mountain top.

"Excuse us." Hope took my arm to guide me around the reverend.

"See them walkin' away from the Lord!" he shouted. "The bible says, 'Be transformed by the renewing of your mind!'"

"Shoot their dawg!" Crystal Lou yelled.

"The bible says, the bible says," Allison imitated on our way to Muskrat Marsh, where I was spending the night with Lori. "Their precious bible has an answer for everything."

"Odie called him there to try to convert you," Hope said to me as she coaxed along the battered Volvo she refused to get rid of because it was the one she shared with Adam Lee. "They did the same thing to me when I quit going to church with Zebediah."

"They won't leave you alone as long as you live in Muskrat Marsh," Allison said from the back seat. "You're their new mission."

Hope invited me in for tea, but Allison went directly to her room. The strains of Edith Piaf floated down to the kitchen where Hope and I sat at her antique cherry table.

"You have to excuse Allison if she sometimes appears rude," Hope said. "She doesn't have an easy life."

"Good heavens, Hope. Didn't you just buy her a horse for eight thousand dollars?"

"Zebediah bought her that horse, not me." Hope's hands caressed the edges of the worn table. "I don't expect you to understand our life, but..." She paused to choose her words. "The truth is, Allison and I are leaving here as soon as she finishes school in May."

"You're moving to Annapolis?"

"I'm leaving Zebediah." She kept a wary eye on the kitchen door.

"Did you just decide this?"

"Things have been better since he began spending so much time in Annapolis and on his congressional campaign. But I never should have married him." Hope tried to pick up her tea, but it spilled out into the saucer and she set it back down. "I shouldn't involve you in this," she said anxiously. "I haven't discussed it with anyone."

"I don't mind."

"People on the island wouldn't understand. They adore Zebediah. You know what it's like being so in love with someone and then losing him, Pat. I thought I could recapture that with Zebediah, but he's nothing like Adam Lee."

A shiver seemed to pass over her body. "I was so alone, and Allison just a baby. I did waitress work, but without Adam Lee I was just another outsider on this godforsaken island." She spoke rapidly, trying to convince me she had no alternative. "Where do you go when you have no family, no friends and a baby to support?"

"It must have been awful."

"Zebediah was lonely, too, because of losing his sister and both parents. He kept telling me how important a family is, and how I shouldn't deny Allison the chance for one."

Allison's footsteps could be heard overhead, along with Edith Piaf. "She loved her French teacher," Hope said sadly.

"If things are so bad with Zebediah, why not leave now?"

"I'm not as brave as you, Pat," Hope said flatly. "Besides, it's important that Allison be allowed to graduate with her friends."

We sat in silence listening to Allison's music. "I can't confide everything to you," she said finally. "But her classmates are as vital to her as going with me to the cemetery and hearing of the love her father had for her."

The pain in Hope's eyes was intense. "I was forced to grow up without ever knowing my parents. Allison at least knows she was created by two people who loved and wanted her."

"But Allison must have feelings for Zebediah if she's been around him since she was a baby. How is this split going to affect her?"

"Believe me, the feelings she has for Zebediah have nothing to do with love, or family." I waited for Hope to explain, but she left me to my own interpretation. "I had a miscarriage shortly after I married him. After that I never tried again; babies should only be conceived in love."

She drank her tea with a steadier hand. "I love Jasmine tea, it reminds me of how Adam Lee and I used to dream of travelling through the orient."

I was not ready to have the subject changed. "Does Zebediah realize you're planning to leave?"

"No," she said with alarm. "He can't know yet."

"Hope, are you afraid of him?"

"What makes you ask that?" She kept her voice down, ever aware of Allison just a floor above.

"I overheard you talking to Allison one night."

Hope's face was concerned. "You heard what?"

"On New Years Eve, telling her to lock herself in her room."

She gave a nervous little laugh. "Oh, that. Allison sometimes walks in her sleep. I'm afraid she'll fall down the stairs or..."

"For god's sake, Hope, she's nearly eighteen."

"You just have to trust that I know what's best for my daughter."

"But you must admit you are overprotective."

Hope slapped the table. "I am not overprotective."

"I'm sorry, I didn't mean to upset you." Her perfect complexion was now a collection of red blotches.

"You meant no harm." Both of us were uncomfortable with the unexpected anger that had passed between us. "You can tell no one about my leaving Zebediah," Hope cautioned. "Not even Lori."

"I still think you should leave now. Why wait until...."

The music overhead stopped and Hope put a finger to her lips.

"I was just about to drive Pat home," she said when Allison came into the kitchen. "Come keep me company on the drive back." Allison gave her an exasperated look. "I don't want you here alone."

"I'll be fine, Mother. You'll only be gone a few minutes."

"Please."

Whatever problems Hope was having with Zebediah, it couldn't be easy for him living with the ghost of her former husband, I decided on our drive to Lori's. Or with the sullen stepchild in the rear seat who wasn't left alone when she was nearly a grown woman.

CHAPTER THIRTY-FIVE

Whether Reverend Taylor was too distracted planning for the anti-abortion protest to take place in Muskrat marsh on Memorial weekend, or preoccupied with trying to get the interior of the new Highway Holiness Church ready by that same date, he made no further attempt to convert me. And just to be sure, I gave up ceramics permanently.

Dolly spread word of my heathen status through surgery faster than I thought her wheels could carry her, which undid any progress I had made toward being accepted by the island staff. The silent treatment I was receiving from everyone but Skipper might have bothered me, had I not been having so much fun doing anesthesia.

Jeff was scheduling surgery at the hospital two full days a week, primarily on patients with Chicken Hand. He had developed a whole new procedure that would not result in the excessive post-operative scarring blamed for contracting the hand into a claw. The technique was so simple, the patients could go home the day of surgery, if they did not have to recover from a general anesthetic.

I asked Jeff if I could try axillary blocks. By injecting nerves in the underarm with a local anesthetic, the hand and wrist could be numbed for surgery without putting the patient to sleep.

We had used axillary blocks, and every other kind of local anesthesia, in Danang because of the chronically short oxygen supply to run our anesthesia machines. But Jeff was the first stateside physician who would allow me to do them.

"I could do these a couple days a week in my Oyster Island clinic if you would come to work for me," Jeff said as he sat down on a stool pulled up to the patient's outstretched hand.

"I'll think about it," I said to Jeff.

Getta Mae was coming back full time after Memorial weekend. Andy, now working full time for Jeff between his migrant worker clinic in Muskrat Marsh and the new clinic on Oyster Island, was pressing me to move into the cottage with him for the summer. Living at the beach and working with Jeff was becoming more appealing as the weather grew warmer. But it was trouble at Lori's that made me move.

Billy wasn't happy having Jeff as a stepfather, even though he received no attention from his own father. With the tension level in the red house climbing, it was time for me to be on my way.

"I would have to leave soon anyway," I told Lori when she asked me again to stay. She had carried my few possessions to my Mustang and we stood talking. Neighbors we still did not know watched from behind their window panes. "It'll be easier if I go now instead of waiting until you move to Oyster Island."

"Maybe things will be better there," Lori said. I could feel how disappointed she was that her new marriage wasn't going smoothly. "Jeff says I should back off, let Billy come to him on his own terms. But he's so hateful, criticizing everything Jeff says and does."

"Jeff's a big boy. He's not going to let a fourteen year old get the best of him."

Andy and I lived well, and my left foot and leg were strengthening from walking or playing on the beach. My feelings for him were not the same as with Dan, but in place of the passion I at least felt a sense of peace.

The serenity was threatened, however, when Hope and Allison made a surprise visit. "I wouldn't ask if I wasn't so desperate," Hope said to me. "It's just a few weeks until she graduates."

It was Saturday and Andy was working. Hope and I sat on the front porch of the one-bedroom cottage watching Allison walk along the sand. The teenager looked so forlorn I felt sorry for her, even though she had been rude to her mother before going off on her walk.

"She would have to sleep on the sofa," I said. "I'm not so sure Andy would go for that."

"It's only until the end of May." I could not ignore the pain in Hope's face. It couldn't be easy asking if her daughter could hide out in Seaport because of some disagreement with her stepfather.

Andy was not happy with the arrangement, but he soon became so taken by Allison he gave her a key to the cottage. She came and went at her discretion, with Hope driving her to and from school.

"No young person should be that sad," Andy said while we flew kites in a brisk Spring wind blowing off the ocean. Allison sat in a rocker on the porch after declining our invitation to join us. "She's just beginning life and already seems so weary of it."

"I wouldn't feel too sorry for her," I said. "She's probably pouting because her Daddy won't buy her another expensive horse."

Allison revealed nothing about her dispute with Zebediah. She listened to her records, or sat on the porch staring at the ocean. Her conversations with me consisted of just yes or no to questions.

I was glad she was gone to a friend's house for the weekend when events unfolding on the other side of the world took complete precedence in my life, as well as Andy's.

South Vietnam had been on its own since the last American combat troops were withdrawn in 1973. It had taken two years, but now North Vietnam was on the march. And whether it was due to inadequate supplies, as some in Washington argued, or because they had become too accustomed to letting American G.I.s do the fighting and dying for them, the southern forces were retreating as fast as the North advanced. The huge air base in Danang was abandoned, leaving a hoard of sophisticated planes, weaponry and radar to the North Vietnamese.

Andy sat with me in front of the television trying to spot a familiar face in the mobs running frantically through the streets. I looked for my former housekeeper and her children, and for the students I had taught anesthesia. I searched, too, for the nuns from the orphanage and the children they would surely take with them. They were all there, but indistinguishable in the surging multitudes.

"Why didn't I have the sense to leave an address at the hospital telling people where I could be located?" I said to Andy. "I could sponsor them into this country." The nuns at the orphanage knew of my whereabouts because of the money I continued to send them. But they had made no attempt to contact me during the present crisis.

"There's no way for them to get a message out in that chaos," Andy said. "They're all running for their lives."

I tried calling the Red Cross, which informed me refugee camps were teeming with people. There was no hope of finding individuals until things settled down, and even then I was talking about trying to find people shoved into camps already holding tens of thousands.

"Who would have thought it would end like this?" Andy said.

The Paris Peace talks had promised a peaceful and orderly end to the fighting. But like its beginning, the summation of our nation's longest war was a study in deceit.

Andy handed me a beer and the two of us sat drinking and watching. My friend was so caught up in the events, he had not taken time to remove his prosthesis after getting home from work, for which I was thankful. The scenes on T.V. evoked enough painful memories of my experience in a country now falling apart before my eyes.

In addition to the obvious confusion, there was a strangeness to the coverage. Unlike the previous ten years, there were no journalists in carefully pressed safari suits standing in front of burned out planes, piles of munitions, or body bags, mouthing carefully scripted reports. Nor were there elaborate production sequences alternating flawlessly between Saigon and outlying battle areas. The reports were tense and spontaneous; uneasy looking journalists were reduced to covering what was happening right before them, with no second takes.

"It's the first honest reporting the bastards have done in years," Andy remarked.

Andy's commentary as we watched the coverage became angrier with each trip to the refrigerator for beer. And I was becoming more and more annoyed at trying to follow it with his ranting. "I'd like to hear this," I said to him in the middle of one of his tirades.

"Why?" he demanded. "They're all dead meat over there any way you look at it."

As the North moved closer, the residents of Hue, and then Danang, piled into boats that looked ready to capsize, risking their lives and the safety of their terrified children to flee their beloved country with what few possessions they could squeeze aboard.

The coverage turned to Saigon, where Vietnamese clambered over one another to get on the last planes and helicopters departing Tan Son Nhut airport. Those Vietnamese being allowed orderly departure were well dressed and dignified, many of them the same people who, with the help of dishonest Americans, had stolen humanitarian aid destined for places like my hospital. The money they made selling it on the black market, often to the enemy, was now providing the cash necessary to bribe their way onto the air base. Or into the American Embassy compound, where helicopters took turns landing on the roof to pick up frantic passengers.

The black marketeers were not the only people being shown preferential treatment. The programming switched to Travis Air Force Base in California to show planeloads of arriving evacuees.

"Jesus, look at that!" Andy shouted. "They've airlifted Tudo Street into the States!"

A large military transport had just landed, and female passengers came down the ramp laughing and joking as they waved at television cameras. They wore tight jeans or mini skirts and spiked heels, the same as when working the red light district of Saigon. The money they commanded, along with the prominent American contacts they made, guaranteed them tickets to freedom.

Another plane landed with more prostitutes and members of Saigon's aristocracy, but a few peasants had somehow managed to slip on board. They carried ragged bundles of clothing and household items and wore expressions as confused and frightened as the fretful children they balanced on their hips.

Young Vietnamese men dressed in dark slacks and white shirts came down the ramp smiling with arms draped around one another. I had seen them strolling in Saigon, looking for entertainment while American G.I.s and Vietnamese peasants too poor to buy their way out of the military, slogged through snake infested jungles.

The coverage returned to Danang, where human waves surged toward the river. Overflowing fishing boats tried to push away from shore as still more passengers clamored aboard, or jumped into the water and held onto the sides. The Bamboo Hut where I went for breakfast with Dan on Sunday mornings flashed onto the screen and was gone.

There were brief glimpses of the house where I had lived upstairs from a Chinese family. It was pockmarked with bullet holes and barely recognizable with the crowds streaming past it.

I wanted to turn away but could not bring myself to do so. People who had witnessed the war from the comfort of their homes might be able to turn the dial, but Andy and I could not turn it off on the screen anymore than we could in our hearts and minds.

"No more for me," I said when Andy started again for the refrigerator. "I think we've both had enough." I had a headache, and my back was throbbing from tensed muscles.

Andy returned with a whole six-pack, weaving unsteadily on his prosthesis. "Well, I'm not finished," he said as he popped open a can and took a long drink. "I'm having one for everyone of the guys I saw die, and I still have a hell of a long way to go."

"Sit down, Andy, before you fall and hurt yourself."

He laughed drunkenly. "I wonder how the guys in VA hospitals are doing tonight." He dropped heavily to the sofa. "Guys missing eyes and faces, or half their bodies. It must be fun thinking about the body parts they left over there for no fucking reason."

"Please don't talk like that, Andy."

"All the little vets tucked snug in their beds while visions of suicide dance in their heads."

"Stop it."

He was quiet until President Ford came on the screen reading a prepared speech. "Listen to that fucking asshole!" Andy yelled. "Maybe it's the end for him, but it sure as hell isn't for over fifty thousand Americans who saw the end with their faces buried in a stinking shit hole, watching that pretty, pink foam called your body and blood blowing up around you in your own personal horror flick!"

The president finished, and the coverage returned to Vietnam. Tanks ground through the streets of Saigon, now being referred to as Ho Chi Minh City, with victorious North Vietnamese soldiers riding on them waving red flags with a single yellow star in the center. The streets were lined with stunned looking spectators, some of them holding small flags of the same design they waved back and forth like robots. One of the tanks smashed through the gates of the Presidential Palace, and the soldiers on it all cheered.

Andy held up his can of beer in a toast. "Here's to you gooks, and to all the poor bastards who got their shit completely blown away! April thirtieth, nineteen seventy-five, the day it all became worth it!"

The smiles of the triumphant North Vietnamese vanished in an explosion of glass and acrid smoke. The stench of burning electrical wire and tubes stung my eyes as I looked to where Andy's beer lay fizzing and popping in the crackling remains of his shattered television screen.

"Fuckers!" he screamed at the darkened set while I ran to unplug it. "Rotten, fucking fuckers!"

He was crying when I helped him outside and lowered him to the porch steps. "It'll be all right," I said. "It's finally over."

"I loved themmm! They were my brothers!" His body convulsed with grief as he got up and lurched around in wide circles on the sand. "I was their doc! I was their father confessor! And I got them killled! I got them all killled!"

"No Andy, you didn't." I was trying to catch him, to take him in my arms. But he pulled away, shoving me to the damp sand.

"When more than one got hit, I didn't know which to take care of first," he wept as he looked down on me. "I tried, I fucking tried."

Looking into his anguished face I knew that all I had suffered in triage, trying to decide which Vietnamese would be saved and which would not, could not begin to compare with the torture of making such decisions when the victims were fellow countrymen one had come to know as family. Andy lived, slept and fought with the men whose lives depended on him.

"They were only boys," Andy whispered as he dropped down beside me and let me put my arms around him. "Eighteen, nineteen. Hell, I was twenty-three and they called me the old man."

I could visualize the young faces of wounded G.I.s I saw at Navy Hospital, catalogued away in some compartment of my mind where they would be kept forever young. While spiders pressed webs into the faces of those who survived, as our hair turned the color of our parents' and our gait became unsteady, there would be a population of young men with crew cuts, boyish smiles and weary, old soldier eyes living somewhere beneath our outward signs of age, tugging at our emotions at unexpected moments when those around us might think it odd to hear a sudden gasp or sigh.

A full moon hung over the ocean and the surf lapped ashore in short, impatient little waves. Music played at a party down the beach, and a couple walking arm in arm along the sand paused to look toward the cottage, wondering why a man and woman sat holding one another and crying on this beautiful night.

"We're the lucky ones," Andy said as we helped one another up from the chill of the beach and walked toward the porch. "At least we weren't sent over there to shoot people." He kicked at the sand with his remaining foot. "Think about all the poor souls having to wonder tonight why they took another guy's life."

"Or a child or mother's."

The moon was high in the sky and waves washed rhythmically, one upon another, when Andy took my hands. "We can't waste the lives we were spared, Danang, or what we have together. Marry me so we can look out for one another and give something back to this world."

CHAPTER THIRTY-SIX

"I never knew what to do with these after the divorce." Lori held a black and white wedding day photo of her and Earl Roy standing at the top of church steps. "I didn't want to throw them away."

"Let me see."

She handed the photo to me, picked up a thick wedding album and began leafing through it. "I guess I could cut Earl Roy out of all of them," she said with a laugh.

"Your children might like them some day. He is their father."

"Good point." She packed the album in the bottom of a box. "They sure look happy, don't they?"

She was looking out her upstairs bedroom window, where the two of us sat on the floor amongst the clutter of moving day. Brendan and Peggy carried their boxes of treasures to Lori's station wagon parked on the front lawn with its tailgate open. Billy helped Jeff and Andy load furniture into a U-Haul truck backed into the driveway.

"How're things between Billy and Jeff?" I asked.

"Better since Jeff started teaching him how to run the boat." Lori looked at her son standing next to Jeff. "It won't be long and he can have an operator's license."

Jeff had purchased a used cabin cruiser to ferry patients from his Oyster Island clinic to Fishback Island after treatment, or for treatment which required hospitalization. He was teaching Billy to pilot the craft and bought him the blue and white captain's hat he presently wore.

"How do you plan to get that truck over to the island?"

"We have to unload everything into fishing boats," Lori groaned. "The people have organized a regular flotilla."

The Oyster Island clinic was giving Jeff and Andy many

patients, and enough deliveries for Lori to maintain her midwifery skills. The other clinic near the migrant farms was also running at full capacity.

"I wish you would change your mind and come with us," Lori said while we observed the activity on the front lawn. "Jeff would love to have you do anesthesia for him, and I could use you in O.B."

Although I had grown very close to Hope and kept in touch with Reba, Lori was my dearest friend. But I had borrowed her family long enough. It was time to establish my own life, whatever that might be.

"You're not going to marry Andy, are you?" Lori asked sadly.

"I can't. At least not now."

"Have you told him?"

I looked back to the window where Andy could be seen carrying two kitchen chairs to the U-haul. "Not yet."

"What's going to happen to you, Pat? I worry so about you." She scooted over to me on the floor and we sat hugging, like best buddies packing up to return home from summer camp.

"I need some distance from Andy to think things through. To see if we have anything more in common than a war."

I was determined not to make the same mistake Hope had, marrying someone to take care of me because I didn't know what else to do, or lacked the courage to try to find out.

"Don't take so much time deciding that Andy finds someone else," Lori advised. "He's a good catch."

"I know." But it was a risk I felt I must take. "I called Reba. She offered to let me stay with her until I decide what to do."

Lori was relieved I at least had somewhere to go. "Will you come visit us on Oyster Island?"

"I'll be there for steamed crabs at least once a month."

Neither of us noticed Peggy standing in the doorway until she spoke. "Isn't Pat coming with us?"

"No, honey," her mother replied.

"You get to have a room all to yourself again." It was difficult to sound cheerful. "Just you and your fish."

"I would rather have you."

I could not bear to see the truck and station wagon pull away. "I'll help them unload into the boats," Andy told me before I left for Seaport. "I should be home in time for us to go out for some dinner."

My eyes were red and swollen by the time I reached the cottage. I let myself in and headed for the bathroom, but as I passed the stereo I looked curiously at an Edith Piaf record playing. Passing the open door to the bedroom, I was jolted to a stop.

"Allison!" She jumped up from the bed, grasping at bedclothes to cover herself. A young man as tanned and naked as she did the same.

"Your mother!" he croaked as he stumbled into his swimming trunks. "Is she your mother!"

While I waited in the living room, Allison's companion bolted past me and out the front door without a word.

"I thought you and Andy were going to spend the whole day helping Lori move," Allison said meekly when she came out of the bedroom.

"Obviously." I looked toward the front door, left open by her fleeing boyfriend.

"He's a lifeguard."

"I am not interested in what he does for a living, I want to know what the hell he was doing in my bed?"

She pulled tangled golden hair back from her face. "Please don't tell my mother, it would hurt her so much."

"You should have thought about that a little sooner." I got up to close the front door.

"Please, Pat."

"Allison, you are only seventeen. Your father could have Andy and me arrested for contributing to the delinquency of a minor."

She came across the room with fists clenched. "Don't call him my father!" she screamed inches from my face. "He is not my father!"

Just as suddenly, she dissolved into tears. "My father is dead and buried in the cemetery," she wept as I held her. "He loved me and my mother; he would never hurt us."

"What do you mean, Allison? You need to tell me the truth."

She pulled away and went to sit on the sofa, still crying. "He's just so unfair to us. I want my own father back."

"Why don't you go to the bathroom and wash your face?" I said when her crying subsided. "I'll make us something cold to drink."

I heard the shower running while I made iced tea, feeling as much to blame for Allison's predicament as Hope. Hadn't I encouraged the visits to the cemetery by participating in them?

Allison was so confused she no longer knew where she belonged, or with whom, Adam Lee, Zebediah or some nameless lifeguard.

She came out to the front porch where I was watching people surf fishing. Her hair was freshly shampooed and her composure restored. "I'll move home and never come here again if you don't tell my mother," she said. "The Senator's in Annapolis for a whole month now. I can tell mother I came back because I got homesick."

She held the key to the cottage Andy had given her out to me.

"Allison, what did you mean when you said your own father would never hurt you?"

"Just the way Zebediah and I argue all the time," she said nervously. "We fight over the dumbest things."

"Does Zebediah ever hit you?"

"No, never."

"You're sure?"

"Positive. But my mother is going to leave him."

"I know."

After several more minutes of pleading, I finally accepted the key and agreed to keep her indiscretion from Hope. But I was not so sure I should have done so when I saw both of them two weeks later.

It was at an equestrian event in which Allison and her classmates were competing. I stood near a railing with Hope watching Allison go over jumps she had once taken with ease. She looked unsteady in the trim saddle, and her face was pale against her crimson riding jacket.

"She's under a lot of pressure," Hope said when Allison rode past us with her head bowed. Hope appeared as pale and fragile as her daughter. "Things aren't going well."

"Allison told me Zebediah was in Annapolis. Did they get into another row?"

"I can't talk here," Hope said as she glanced at other spectators standing near us at the rail. "I'll come to the cottage when I can."

I thought of them often during the following week. Allison was graduating from high school, and I was graduating from Andy.

"I'll only be in Baltimore," I said after telling him I was not accepting his marriage proposal. "We can still see each other."

"It won't be the same." We were walking along the boardwalk eating french fries sprinkled with vinegar. The beach town was gearing up for its annual Memorial Day invasion.

"Maybe I'll be back, Andy. But I need to be sure."

Andy looked at me with the confidence in his face I longed for. "Take as much time as you need, Danang, but I'll be doing some thinking of my own."

Hope did not come to the cottage, but she called to see if I would attend an abortion rally Zebediah and his cousin Reverend Taylor had organized. It would be held during the new church's dedication.

"The rally's the night before graduation and Zebediah's insisting Allison and I attend." Hope sounded exhausted.

"So tell him no. You're leaving anyway."

"If we don't go he'll spoil Allison's graduation. I know it."

"But why do you need me at the rally?" I had already told Hope I would be at Allison's graduation, and I didn't want to drive to Muskrat Marsh and back the night before. Especially since I had so little time left to spend at the beach.

"Pat, I can't stand the thought of walking into that church filled with people I despise."

"I'd like to help but..."

"Please, just this one last favor." She sounded like Allison begging me not to tell her about the lifeguard. "I haven't been able to tell Zebediah I'm leaving yet. I have to get through graduation and this church thing first."

"I guess I could go," I relented. "Andy will be working late tomorrow at the migrant clinic."

I was to meet Hope at the church, but when I slipped into the rear of the new building I did not see her in the congregation. I took a seat in the back where I thought nobody would notice, but I was immediately aware of someone trying to catch my eye. Dolly waved from an oversized lawn chair so like the one in her car I wondered if she had been transported to the church by a half dozen strong men, like an Egyptian Queen. Her jubilant smile made it clear she believed I had finally decided to join the fold.

Lovey Donlin was there, too, sitting between Earl Roy and Adella Dawn. I noticed Earl Roy surreptitiously looking across the church and followed his gaze to Carol Faye.

It looked as if the entire staff of Fishback Hospital was in attendance, including its main benefactor seated up front facing the congregation. Next to Hen sat Odie, holding a guitar across his lap. His shirt was the same as Zebediah's and those of three additional men, whom I concluded must be part of The Lord's Messengers.

Iris Irene, Crystal Lou and others from the ceramic shop were there, plus hundreds of islanders easily recognizable by their faded features.

The crowd stood and applauded enthusiastically as Reverend Taylor, beaming widely, strode to the pulpit of the new church and took the microphone. "My dear friends, we are gathered here to dedicate this great temple to the Lord, and to answer His call as soldiers of Christ." He paused while the crowd applauded again. "And as good soldiers, we must not only take on the evil of sin, we must slay it the same as the servants of Satan are slayin' innocent babies in each and every part of this great land!"

"Say it, Reverend!" someone in the crowd shouted.

"Killin' babies as we stand here now," Hen said from where he stood at the side of Zebediah.

Students from the Freedom School came up the aisle carrying dolls swaddled in blankets like newborn babies. The girls made noises trying to simulate infant cries, but sounded more like suckling pigs. I smelled a strange, yet familiar, spicy odor as they passed by.

"See them! Hear them!" The reverend wiped at his garage door nostrils, then jabbed the same finger in the direction of the girls. "God's own children begging for mercy!"

The students stood at the foot of the altar holding their bundles to their breasts while the reverend denounced nearly every politician in Washington. "Every heathin' must be driven from office and replaced with God-fearing men as the Lord intended!

"Hear, hear!" Odie shouted from where The Lord's Messengers sat.

At the reverend's command, the young girls opened the blankets to reveal naked dolls smeared with what looked like catsup. "God's creations torn from the womb!" the reverend exhorted as the girls dropped to their knees and loudly entreated his forgiveness. The girls wept real tears.

"We must join together in one holy crusade! And we must take that sacred crusade to our nation's capitol!" the reverend bellowed over the heads of the weeping girls, who still clutched their red splattered dolls.

"Amen!" Dolly offered from her lawn chair. "Praise Jesus!"

Zebediah Taylor joined The Lord's Messengers in a spirited rendition of the "Battle Hymn of the Republic" and invited the congregation to join in. When the singing ended, Zebediah took the pulpit.

"I tell you, my good people," he boomed over the microphone. "Unless we join with other Christians to defeat Satan, we all face eternal damnation." Zebediah's manner became soulful. "Women having babies scraped from their bodies are going to have to answer to those innocent little souls on judgement day, mark my word."

Dr. Arst popped up in the congregation. "I say it's time ta turn this country back to decent, God-fearin' citizens!" He swayed unsteadily as he turned to sit down.

"Amen ta that!" another man yelled. "The decent shall rule!"

"The bleedin' heart liberals have split this country wide open, leaving us in a deep dark valley," Zebediah continued in a somber tone. "But we, God's chosen people, know the way and the light out of that valley. And it is up to us to guide our less fortunate brothers and sisters."

He wiped his perspiring brow and looked heavenward. "Yea, though I walk through the valley of the shadow of death, I will fear no evil for the LORD is my shepherd."

The high school band began playing Onward Christian Soldiers in the background. Zebediah pounded his fist on the podium to punctuate the last points of his sermon.

"Unless we send Christians ta serve in the Supreme Court (bam) the House of Representatives (bam) the Senate (bam) and even in the White House itself (bam bam) we will have Satan serving in all of them!" (bam bam bam)

I was so caught up in the proceedings I did not hear the person at my side until she pulled forcefully at one of my arms. Hope Taylor, her long hair hanging wildly about her face, practically dragged me from the pew. The congregation was cheering and singing so fiercely nobody noticed Hope or me leaving.

"Hope, what's wrong?" I called as I hurried behind her toward her car.

"It's Allison," she said breathlessly. "She's very sick."

Hope dove into her Volvo and put it in motion before I had time to get both my legs in. I grabbed the door handle and pulled it toward me as we careened out of the parking lot and sped through town.

It was the first I realized Allison was not with her friends from the Freedom School. "Where is she?" I asked, still gripping the door handle as the car squealed around corners.

"At home." Hope was so distraught she raced through stop signs and red lights, barely looking for other traffic. We were crossing a busy intersection when a chicken truck bore down on us.

"Look out!" I shouted in time for her to swerve around it.

Hope blared the horn on her Volvo as we approached the entrance to Heavenly Acres, giving the guard only seconds to hit the button to open the gates before we crashed into their iron grillwork.

The front door of her house was hanging open, and Hope ran from the car and through the doorway while I struggled to keep up. "Up here!" she called from halfway up the stairs of her living room.

By the time I reached Allison's room, Hope was on her knees by the bed. The young girl was shock white and her breath was as faint as the violets on her coverlet and walls. There were more photos of mothers and children Hope had adopted from junk shops along the staircase and hallway, and a large one of Hope holding an infant Allison, which hung over the sick girl's bed.

"How long has she been like this?" I asked as I felt for a pulse in an arm hanging limply over one side of the bed. It was rapid and weak and her skin fiery hot.

"Last night," Hope replied. "No, the night before...I'm so tired I don't remember." She got up and paced, running a hand through disheveled hair I had never seen out of its braids. Her clothes looked like they had been slept in. She began to cry and dropped back to her knees at Allison's bedside. "Do something, Pat."

"The first thing she needs is to get her temperature down." As I pulled the thick coverlet off the feverish girl, she moaned and drew her legs up toward her chest, revealing a large red stain creeping out from beneath her nightgown.

"Oh God," Hope said.

"Call for an ambulance," I said as calmly as I could. "Then call the migrant clinic and tell Dr. Wells to meet us at the E.R. as fast as he can get there."

CHAPTER THIRTY-SEVEN

Zebediah would allow no one but Dr. Arst and Earl Roy Donlin near the ambulance while Allison was loaded into it. All of the island's volunteer firemen were at the anti-abortion rally when the emergency call went out to their pagers, and a large group of them were congregated on the front lawn.

"Don't you touch her!" Hope shouted at Drs. Arst and Donlin as they were about to get into the back of the ambulance with Allison. She tried to stop them, but Zebediah grabbed her flailing arms and pulled her away. "Get your hands off me, you bastard!" Hope kicked and clawed at her husband. "Get those butchers away from my child!"

I got as close to them as the struggle allowed. "Stop this, both of you," I ordered. "We have to get Allison to the hospital."

Hope was fighting to get free of Zebediah. "Get Doctor Arst away from her," she implored me.

But the ambulance was already pulling away with Drs. Arst and Earl Roy Donlin inside. "She's in shock," Zebediah told the growing number of spectators. "She doesn't know what she's doing."

Hope broke free of him and started toward her car. "Come with me, Pat," she called. "I need you to drive me to the hospital."

Zebediah came after us, his jaw set and his face florid.

"You come near me and I tell it all right here," Hope warned with the stance of a mother lion. He retreated without a word and walked to his Lincoln parked in the circular drive.

Hope was shaking so badly she held onto the dash while I maneuvered her aged Volvo across town. "They did it to her, Arst and Donlin," she said in a voice hoarse from screaming. "We have to get her away from them."

"Hope, you have to settle down and tell me what happened."

"Allison had an abortion," she blurted. "Doctor Arst did it and Earl Roy gave the anesthesia."

"Oh no."

Hope jumped from the car the moment I pulled to a stop in the emergency area of the hospital. Zebediah was already there and tried to get hold of her as she started for the set of automatic doors. "Stay away from me!" Hope was close enough that the doors opened. But when Zebediah pulled her back they closed. "Get your hands off me!" she screamed. "And don't you ever go near Allison again!"

The doors opened and closed as both Hope and I grappled with Zebediah. A nurse came to see what was going on.

"My wife needs sedation," Zebediah told her.

"Let her go!" I shouted at Zebediah. "Or I'll call the police!"

Zebediah laughed and motioned the nurse away. Hope and I were no match for his powerful arms. I ran inside to call security, but before I finished dialing Jeff and Andy came hurrying down the corridor. I briefed them as best I could as we went to Hope's aid.

The two men had to wrestle Hope free of Zebediah's bullish grip. Andy employed a diversionary tactic to get Zebediah's attention off her, but Zebediah took a swift kick at him. The look on his face was both pained and surprised as he connected with Andy's metal leg.

"Bet that hurt," Andy taunted as Jeff hurried Hope inside.

"Goddamned, long-haired hippie!" Zebediah shouted as he and Andy squared off, both limping. "Nothing but a yellow dawg loser from Veet Namm! I'll show you how it feels to be up against a real trooper!" Andy fought back until Zebediah knocked his prosthesis completely off, catapulting him face down on the rough concrete of the ambulance dock.

I was torn between helping Andy, or following Hope and Jeff.

"Go on!" Andy yelled to me from where he sat on the ground trying to reattach his leg while Zebediah wiped blood from a cut over his eye. "I'll be O.K.!"

I found Jeff trying to get information from Hope, who ran frantically from one E.R. examining room to the other looking for Allison. "My baby!" she cried. "Where did they take my baby!"

A confused E.R. nurse stood in the corridor. "She's not here. Docter Arst and Donlin took her raght through to the operatin' room."

Hope turned to me with stark terror. "They'll kill her."

My stomach churned, knowing Allison had become pregnant while under my supervision. And I had kept it from her mother. "Hope

I..."

"Take care of Allison." My fingers were nearly crushed in her strong hands. "Don't let them do anything more to her."

Allison was lying on a stretcher outside an O.R. when Jeff and I arrived. Earl Roy pushed the stretcher quickly into the operating room when he saw us.

"You can't be in here in street clothes," Dr. Arst protested when we entered the room after grabbing caps and masks. He was haphazardly dressed in O.R. attire, minus a mask, and was trying to set up instruments without benefit of a nurse.

"I'll take over now," Jeff said to him.

"This is my private patient." Dr. Arst's breath smelled strongly of alcohol, as it probably had the night he did the abortion. "You have no right to come in here an' take her from me."

"From what Pat's told me, the state medical board would agree I have every right," Jeff said as he pulled on sterile gown and gloves.

The elderly gynecologist had to lean on the instrument table to keep from collapsing, but Earl Roy was not so easily cowed. "Abortions happen to be legal now," he said in his Harvard English. "And the patient's father signed the surgery permit."

I had pulled a gown over my street clothes and was opening sterile packs of sponges and instruments for Jeff.

Dr. Arst rallied at Earl Roy's remark. "That's raght, her daddy signed the permit," he said. "We didn't do nothin' outside the law."

"Of course, I had no knowledge of these complications she appears to be having," Earl Roy added. "I only administered the anesthetic."

"Could we cut the bullshit long enough to save this girl's life?" I demanded.

Jeff took over at the foot of the table, and Dr. Arst left the room pale and shaken.

Despite an oxygen mask over Allison's face, her eyes were sunken and she moaned incoherently. I had seen enough victims of back alley abortions to recognize the symptoms of a perforated uterus.

Earl Roy had one I.V. running and was about to start a second when I moved to the head of the table. I started to push his hands away, then stopped. He was a well trained anesthesiologist, and Allison needed every bit of expertise available.

"I guess it's the least you can do," I said as he expertly slid a large intravenous needle into place.

I listened to Allison's lungs with a stethoscope to make sure she was exchanging air adequately. I was encouraged to find them clear.

"We need to get her to Filmore," Jeff said after quickly assessing the situation. "She needs a shock trauma team."

He was putting in sutures and packs to slow the hemorrhage while Earl Roy and I pumped blood and plasma and injected antibiotics. The evening supervisor was given the duty of calling Filmore Hospital for the Flight For Life helicopter.

A chopper sat in the parking lot with its engine roaring when we rolled Allison out on a stretcher. The Shock Trauma chopper was already on a call when Christian Hospital's request came in. This one was operated by state troopers with no medical expertise.

Hope's loose hair whipped in the wind of the prop-wash as we loaded Allison into the chopper, our heads down to stay away from the rotating blades just above. "You go with her!" Hope yelled to me above the noise. "I only trust you!"

The familiar thwack, thwack, thwack of the chopper blades had dispatched adrenalin to all points of my body, but it had also put out a call for the suction machine. I looked to Jeff for help.

"I have a patient in labor and Arst is in no condition to cover for me!" he shouted above the rotating blades. He pointed toward Andy, limping toward us with bloody abrasions on his chin and arms. "You and Andy go! This is right up your alley!"

"You have to save my baby!" Hope cried to me.

I heard her say it again as we rose into the night sky. My mind was slipping back to a place far removed from Fishback Island. I was racing over rice paddies and jungle.

"C'mon, Pat, let's get a tube in her." Andy was on the opposite side of the stretcher from me in the cramped compartment. "She's not oxygenating well at this altitude."

I looked down, expecting to find a Vietnamese, but the patient lying before me had a beautiful mantle of gold framing a face whose only color was a bluish tint around the mouth. This is Hope's daughter, I told myself, who got pregnant under my care.

A vision of Allison in the cemetery with her mother rose from the stretcher. "Show me how he danced with me."

"Take her lower!" Andy shouted through a window separating us from the cockpit. "The oxygen's too thin up here."

"Too many flocks of birds lower down!" the copilot shouted back. "They get in the rotor, we'll drop like a rock!"

Andy turned back to where I knelt over Allison, making no attempt to help her. "Do you want me to put in the tube?" he asked.

When I didn't answer he pulled an endotracheal tube and laryngoscope from a bag of emergency equipment I had gathered together while Allison was in surgery. I looked at the things in his hands, the tools of my trade I had used to save so many lives.

"You have to save my baby," I heard Hope say.

"I'll do it," I said, reaching for the endotracheal tube and laryngoscope. "We need air-conditioning. She's burning up."

Andy gave me a thumbs up signal. The blast of cold air made everyone but Allison shiver.

As soon as I had the tube in place, I wrapped adhesive tape around it and secured it to Allison's cheeks. As an extra precaution, I put another long strip around the breathing tube, then completely around her head so it would stand less chance of becoming dislodged while moving her once we arrived in Baltimore.

To provide Allison with maximum oxygen, Andy hooked the tube to a breathing bag attached to a portable tank. He could then force oxygenated air into her lungs by squeezing the bag at a steady pace, while I was busy giving I.V. solutions, blood, drugs, and checking vital signs. We were a team, an efficient, super-trained unit that had done this many times before in our separate but common lives.

"How's your leg?" I asked Andy when we had things as well under control as possible.

"Not bad considering it's on a yellow dawg loser." Despite the crisis in which we were presently involved, both of us smiled. "The look on Zebediah's face when he kicked my leg was worth the hit."

The helicopter barely set down on the roof of Filmore's Shock Trauma unit when the doors were thrown open and several pair of hands reached in to yank the stretcher out. "Watch the tube!" I said.

"Hey, we've done this before, lady!" said a man in surgery garb.

"So have we, Buster!" Andy shot back.

Allison was still in surgery when Hope and Zebediah arrived by car. The nursing staff would tell them only that their daughter was grossly infected from a perforated uterus; any further information would have to come from the doctors working on her.

I was surprised Hope had driven to Baltimore with Zebediah. But he did look much more in control of himself in a clean shirt and politician's suit and tie. There was a bandaid above his right eye, where Andy had landed a well aimed punch, and his swollen nose looked slightly askew. Andy turned and walked the other way when he saw Zebediah coming down the corridor several paces behind Hope.

"I have to talk to you," Hope said to me. She had taken time to

246

run a brush through her hair and secure it at the back of her neck. But she still wore the same rumpled slacks and blouse. Zebediah started in our direction and Hope reacted quickly. "Come to the chapel with me, Pat," she said loudly enough for him to hear. "I want to pray for Allison."

Zebediah gave us a suspicious look as we moved down the hallway toward a small chapel, but he did not follow as we entered the dim interior. I had to tell Hope about finding Allison with the lifeguard, and somehow apologize for waiting so long to inform her.

"I have to say some things while I have the courage," Hope said before I could get out a word. "Someone has to know in case something happens to me." She turned to face me on the wooden bench where we sat, and even in the chapel's subdued lighting I could see the terror in her eyes. "Zebediah forced me to ride here with him. On the way he threatened to kill me if I told anyone what he's done."

"Hope, you're so upset you don't know what you're saying."

She closed her eyes to summon strength. "I swore to him that I would take Allison and leave the island quietly without anyone knowing. He told me he would kill both of us if I did." She got up and paced in the narrow aisle between rows of benches. "It's not me I'm afraid for, it's Allison. It's always been Allison."

"But why would he threaten to kill you? Did he find out you were going to leave him?"

Hope sat down slowly, as if she had to consciously direct each of her joints to bend. "He raped her," she whispered as if in a confessional. "He's been molesting her for years."

I could feel the walls of the small chapel closing in, squeezing the breath out of me.

"When I found out he started the threats," Hope continued while I stared in disbelief. "He carried a gun everywhere he went in the house, from the kitchen to the bedroom, the bathroom, everywhere."

"But why didn't you go to the police?"

Hope looked at me as if I were speaking a foreign language. "Pat, you heard him laugh when you threatened to call the police tonight. He's an islander, the honorary sheriff, for god's sake."

I had to tell her now, before I lost my nerve. "Hope, I wanted to tell you before that..."

"Let me finish, Pat. Please." She got up to pace again. "I know I should have left the island long ago, but he told me he would track us down no matter where we went." She came back to the bench and dropped slowly down beside me. "I was so afraid for Allison. You have to understand how terrified I was for her."

I took hold of the roughened hands of a sculptor, now cold as those of a cadaver. Hope was choking on tears that ran down the back of her throat. I pulled Kleenex from my pocket and handed it to her.

"When I found out what he was doing...that he was molesting her, I never let her out of my sight again. I even made her lock herself in her room at night." She wiped at her eyes, which immediately filled again. "He promised me he would leave her alone. He made me believe it was safer to stay on the island than to leave."

She looked at me with the bewilderment of a child. "I didn't know what to do, Pat. And things were better when he started spending most of his time in Annapolis." She got up, but her legs refused to move her body forward. "I still planned to leave him for what he had already done," she said as she sank back to the bench. "But Allison begged me to let her finish school with her friends."

Hope must have been thinking the same thing I was as her shoulders collapsed inward. While Allison's classmates readied themselves for graduation the following day, her child lay fighting for her life in an operating room.

"She had so little to look forward to, her riding and school were her only happiness," Hope said in a barely audible voice. "I didn't want to destroy her any more than she already was by pulling her away from her friends. Or by making public what had happened to her." It was said with such conviction I almost agreed.

"But Allison wasn't happy. How could she be?"

"I know." The ache in Hope's voice was far more intense than what I felt in my back and leg from riding in the rough chopper. "I found out...discovered just a month ago that he was still getting to her." Hope had to put her head down on her knees to keep from passing out. "On nights he came home unexpectedly from Annapolis," she said when she could sit upright again. "She was letting him into her room while I was sleeping. That's when I brought her to your cottage."

This was too much. "But why would she let him into her room?"

"To protect me." Hope rolled up the long sleeves of her blouse to reveal scars and bruises covering almost every bit of flesh. "My legs are the same. And every other part of my body that can be hidden with clothing."

Other than her face and hands, I realized this was the first time I had ever seen my friend's bare skin. "He shot at me one night when I was in bed. He makes me sleep on the bullet hole to remind me of what will happen to Allison if I ever tell."

"And all this time I thought you were being overly protective. I never dreamed..."

"You had no way of knowing," Hope said kindly. "My life has become such a nightmare there are times when I think I'll wake up and none of it will be real." She looked down at her battered arms as if to remind herself it was. "I quit going to church when I couldn't wear dresses anymore. And when I could no longer stand the hypocrisy," she added bitterly. "The same cruel hoax I grew up with."

Slowly and haltingly she related how she had been sexually abused as an adolescent and teenager. "If we weren't in foster homes, the nuns sent us out to work for wealthy people who contributed to the orphanage. The women made us work like slaves, cleaning their houses and cooking for them, and their husbands were after us every chance they got. When we tried to tell the nuns, they punished us for lying about our generous benefactors."

"Oh Hope, I'm so sorry. I'm sorry for all of it."

"I never thought it would happen to my own daughter." Her vocal cords were stretched so tightly her voice was high and thin. "We were so happy with Adam Lee."

She wept inconsolably, filling the dark enclosure with the grief only a parent can feel for a child.

"I wouldn't have brought Allison into this world if Adam Lee wasn't so wonderful," Hope said when she could speak. "That's why I take her to his grave, so she will know that good men exist, and that her father was one of them." She looked away when she added, "The baby I lost, the one I miscarried after one of Zebediah's beatings, was better off not being born."

The story continued in slow, anguished fragments. Zebediah began beating Hope almost from the start of their marriage. Molesting Allison came later, when she was in her teens. He managed to keep it secret for awhile, but when Hope found out she began a constant vigil over her daughter. Zebediah kept his distance, until he found a way to use his deceitful tactics on both of them.

He told Allison he would not beat her mother if she unlocked her door while Hope slept, exhausted from trying to protect her child and herself from Zebediah and his guns. And Hope thought tolerating the beatings he continued to give her in their bedroom, or when Allison was not around, would keep her daughter from his sexual abuse.

"I hid the evidence," Hope said as she pulled up a pantleg to show me one of her battered legs. "I even hid it from Allison, thinking Zebediah would leave her alone if he could take his rage out on me."

Her body quivered like mine when I was on the railway platform. "He used us against one another to get his way with both."

"Hope, I...."

"I was so afraid he would hurt her if I tried leaving the island," she said. Hope's expression changed to one of a person who has just made an extraordinary discovery. "But when I was sitting by her bed tonight, watching her get sicker and sicker, I suddenly realized he was already killing her. He's been killing her for years."

"Hope please, you have to listen to what I have to say." I held both her shoulders, forcing her to look at me. "Zebediah may not have fathered the baby."

She listened quietly while I told her about finding Allison at the cottage. "She was already pregnant when I brought her to you, although I didn't know it," Hope said when I finished. "That's why she was sleeping with all those boys at the beach." I was surprised to hear there was more than one. "When she found she was pregnant, she didn't want to believe it was by Zebediah."

Her hands rubbed up and down her discolored arms. "She's a good girl, Pat. She only did that because of what she was going through."

"Oh Hope, you don't have to defend her to me. I don't know how she survived, how either of you did." I was so nauseated by what I was hearing, my battle with the suction machine seemed a triviality.

"You have to go to the police," I said firmly. "They'll believe you here in Baltimore."

The chapel door opened and a nurse looked in. "Mrs. Taylor?"

Hope nearly fell as she ran to her. "Is she all right?" she asked in a voice so terrified I was afraid to hear the nurse's response. "Is my baby all right?"

"The doctors want to see you."

I stood back from where the surgeons talked to Hope and Zebediah, but close enough to hear that Allison was in extremely unstable condition. They had done a hysterectomy and drained several abscesses caused by a metal curette perforating her uterine wall. But her heart had stopped on the table.

"She's a very sick young woman," the chief surgeon said with a grim expression. "I haven't seen sepsis like that since the old coat hanger days."

"But she's going to be O.K. isn't she?" Hope asked. "She is going to get better?" She had forgotten to roll down the sleeves of her blouse and Zebediah was staring at the evidence of his brutality.

"We won't know for awhile," the doctor replied gently. "Right now she's on a ventilator and her chances are not as good as we would like them to be." The physician caught Hope as her legs gave out.

"Get a wheelchair!" Zebediah called out. "Someone help my poor wife!"

Nurses brought a wheelchair and took Hope to an unoccupied cubicle in the Shock Trauma unit, where they sedated her and put her to bed. Zebediah went to the waiting room, which was fortunate for him. I had my eye on a nearby instrument tray waiting to be sterilized, and if there had been a scalpel on it I felt I could sever both carotid arteries with one slice across his flabby neck.

Andy stood at the far end of the corridor, as distant from Zebediah as he could get. I left him there when the nurses allowed me to go into Hope's cubicle for a few minutes.

"I'm going to call the police now." Hope's eyes opened.

She pulled herself to a sitting position. "No, not yet." There was absolutely no color in her face. "Let Allison get better first."

"This has nothing to do with Allison's care. There are doctors and nurses to look after her."

"But I would have to be away from her to file the report and answer questions. I can't leave her now, not even for a moment."

I wasn't about to be swayed as I had been by Allison begging me not to tell her mother about the incident at the cottage.

"Zebediah needs to be in jail," I insisted. "He could hurt you, and he could hurt Allison."

I didn't want to use the word kill, but what better way to make sure Allison would not be able to testify against him than by disconnecting the ventilator she was presently attached to?

"He can't hurt us while we're surrounded by people," Hope said, indicating the glass walls of the cubicles which put the entire unit and its occupants on full display from the central nurses' station. "I won't leave here, I promise you."

"You said he would kill you if you told anyone," I reminded. "And you've already done that. You told me."

Hope first looked surprised, then alarmed. "Pat, I want you to leave here without letting on that you know. I'll tell Zebediah we went to the chapel just to pray for Allison, he'll believe that."

The revulsion I felt for Zebediah overshadowed my fear of him finding out that I knew his despicable secret. I wanted him jailed.

But I knew from my medical experience that Allison's heart could stop again at any moment, and it might not restart this time. If that happened, it was imperative that Hope be with her.

"You can't just let this keep going," I said. "It's gone on far too long already."

"I'll have him arrested the minute Allison is out of danger. Please go back to the island for a few days, and then come back and we'll take care of everything." I looked warily toward where Zebediah sat in the waiting room across the corridor. "He isn't going anywhere as long as I'm here," Hope assured. "He's too afraid of what I might say or do in his absence."

When I passed the glassed cubicle where Allison lay, I knew it would be more than a few days before she was out of danger, if ever. She was not only attached to a ventilator, a myriad of other machines beeped, hissed and buzzed as a team of doctors and nurses worked frantically over her. Only the jagged blip of a heart monitor tracing her cardiac activity across a grey screen convinced me she was still alive.

Andy came to stand beside me, after first giving a loathsome look to Zebediah in the waiting room. "I don't know all that's going on here," he said quietly. "But that son of a bitch has to be brought to justice for letting Arst do this to her."

"Don't worry," I said. "He will be."

CHAPTER THIRTY-EIGHT

I kept my promise to Hope. But only because I was afraid telling Andy that Zebediah fathered the baby might put his life in danger, as mine would be if Zebediah found out what Hope confided in the chapel.

The story circulating through Christian Hospital was that Allison had suffered a ruptured appendix with resultant peritonitis. She had been taken to Baltimore because of the complication, and her devoted father was taking time from his busy campaign schedule to sit at her bedside. Dr. Arst was back doing cases as usual. The only difference with Earl Roy was that he was showing up for work each morning.

"Everyone knows it was a botched abortion," Skipper said. "But the good Christian code of conduct says they have to play along with their denial game, as they always do when one of them is found out."

"I can't stand looking at Arst or Earl Roy," I said. "I have to get out of here."

"Go if you need to. But Jeff's reported both Arst and Earl Roy to the state medical board. Something should come of it."

I told Skipper I wouldn't be staying the rest of the summer, even on a part-time basis. And because I could no longer keep up the charade, I told him about my dissociative spells.

I was proud of having faced down the suction machine in the helicopter, but the experience convinced me that it was dangerous and unethical for me to be placing patients in a potentially precarious situation without their knowledge or consent. The same ethics which prompted me to volunteer to care for wounded Vietnamese now persuaded me that I must leave a profession I had scrubbed floors to learn.

I realized something else in that helicopter working with Andy.

His skill was unquestionable, but I also saw how he looked at Allison with total compassion and love.

It was the same look I had seen in Dan's eyes when he played with children at the orphanage or his island. His connection to them was beyond politics or duty, and it was the biggest reason I loved him.

"You're still a good anesthetist," Skipper said. "But I accept your decision."

I stayed at the cottage, spending my time walking on the beach trying to figure out what I should do about Andy, and the situation with Allison. When I returned to Baltimore to confront the latter, Hope met me coming down the corridor of the Shock Trauma unit. Her hair was in its usual coronet of braids, and she wore a fresh blouse and matching slacks.

"Allison's going to be fine," she told me. "She's off the respirator and breathing on her own."

"Thank God." Filmore Hospital had worked another miracle.

Hope wore a frozen smile I attributed to a combination of fatigue and joy over her beloved daughter's improvement. "I was so afraid we were going to lose her," she said as we walked together toward Allison's cubicle. "But everything's going to be fine now."

I looked through the glass, expecting to see Allison well on her way to recovery. What greeted me could have been in one of my nightmares. Allison's eyes rolled crazily in their sockets, and saliva dripped from a mouth that worked constantly in grotesque, contorted circles. The only thing recognizable was the yard of golden hair fanned out over the pillow.

I turned to Hope, who stood watching her child with a brightness in her eyes as alien as the rigid smile on her face. "The doctors told you she would be all right?" I asked incredulously.

"We may be able to take her home in a week or so."

"We?" I looked toward the waiting room, where Zebediah sat with his cousin Reverend Taylor and several other islanders who had come to give moral support to their idol. Zebediah wore another of his dark suits, and a starched white shirt with florid flesh oozing over the collar. "Hope, why isn't Zebediah in jail?"

She kept her eyes on her child. I put a hand on her chin and turned her to me. "You promised you would go to the police, why haven't you?"

A sudden thumping sound caused both of us to return our attention to Allison. Her legs were slapping up and down on the bed, then her arms. The activity quickly progressed to a full-blown seizure, bringing staff running from all directions.

They had to bar Hope from the room as she tried to get to her daughter. As the staff attended to Allison while I held onto Hope, I knew that she was severely and permanently brain damaged. And I knew looking into her mother's eyes that she absolutely did not see that.

When the seizure abated, Hope began reciting in a monotone voice what sounded like a carefully rehearsed speech. "Zebediah and I have had several long talks, Pat. It would do Allison no good for me to be vengeful. She needs both of us to make her well again, and with the Lord's help we will do that."

She looked to where her husband and his cousin sat, as if to enlist their support. It was then that I placed the frozen smile and glassy eyes with which she greeted me.

"Now I know," I said as I looked into her face.

The smile left for a moment. "Know what?" Hope asked in her normal voice.

"That look, it's the same one the reverend wore that night he tried to convert me at the ceramics shop." And it was the same one he wore now as he looked triumphantly in my direction.

"Whatever are you talking about?" Hope asked with her frozen Jesus smile.

I took hold of one of Hope's hands and pulled her down the corridor, away from her husband and the reverend's watchful eyes. "Hope, you can't take Allison back to that island," I said quietly but forcefully. "And you have to have Zebediah arrested for what he's done to her."

"People have been coming from the island every day," Hope said in her born again monotone. "They've prayed with me and helped me see what needs to be done to get Allison well."

"Those people aren't looking out for Allison. They're just trying to save Zebediah's political career."

"You're wrong, Pat. Zebediah has openly confessed his sins and repented. He's promised to devote his life to Allison, and the three of us have been joined by the reverend to the Lord Jesus Christ."

Hope's smile was as bizarre as Lovey Donlin's snarl. "The bible says, 'If we confess our sins, He will forgive us and purify us from all unrighteousness.'"

I felt as revolted as when she told me about Allison in the chapel. "I never should have left you here with them," I said, though Hope did not seem to hear. "They worked on you the whole time."

Zebediah and his cousin were coming toward us. "No matter what you say or do I will not speak against my husband," Hope said urgently. "The two of us will take our baby home and care for her until she is whole again."

"Good morning," Zebediah said to me. "Nice of y'all to drive all the way up ta Baltmur to see our little girl." His eye was less swollen than when I had last seen him, but there were remnants of discoloration beneath it. His nose still looked slightly off center.

"The nurses tell us only family an' clergy can visit," the reverend said. His upturned nostrils, one of which was occupied, flared in and out with each breath. "Sorry y'all can't stay."

"Those rules don't apply to professionals," I said. "I accompanied Allison here on the helicopter."

He was deterred for only a moment. "'Deed you did. And we thank you for your good work." His expression became one of a child with a fistful of candy he does not intend to share. "But Filmore Hospital and the Lord are in charge from here on out."

"Praise Jesus," Zebediah said as he linked an arm securely through one of Hope's. "'Whosoever believeth in Him shall receive remission of sins.'"

"Now if you'll pardon us, the senator and I'll jest take Mrs. Taylor on back to pray over their precious daughter." The reverend took Hope's other arm and she walked obediently between them toward Allison's cubicle, like a patient emerging from the electroshock lab.

It was still daylight when I drove through Muskrat Marsh on my way to Seaport. Workmen were spreading white paint over Lori's red house, readying it for the new owners. The emptiness I felt was like the first weeks and months after Dan's death.

I had told myself back then that I would never get that close to anyone again; I would not set myself up for that mind numbing pain. And here I was, enmeshed in a dilemma about Andy, an entire family I had adopted and a mother and child caught in a tragedy I could not even think about without feeling physically ill.

I couldn't keep my eyes from the cemetery as I drove past the Highway Holiness Church. It was empty, but I noticed a large sign on the new church's side facing the highway, announcing an anti-abortion rally and march on Washington the following month.

Andy was not at the cottage, and I spent the afternoon walking on the beach and thinking. Nurses did not go to battlefields, but the battlefields came to us in unrelenting horror. In order to face new casualties each day I had stuffed away my emotions, pulling myself into a cocoon of nonfeeling, until the burned baby forced me out.

I could see Hope doing the same, retreating into a world of religion and simplistic answers she found safer than the one in which

Allison would languish hopelessly. She and Allison were both casualties of their own private war.

I was waiting for Andy on the porch when he came home from work at seven. He listened with his jaw set and eyes burning while I told him about Allison, and about Zebediah's role in her catastrophic situation.

"Someone should castrate the fucking pervert," he said. "Or throw his ass in jail so the hard-timers can take turns with him."

"Without Hope's cooperation it's my word against a popular state senator's," I said. "I could only repeat to the police what Hope told me that night. I witnessed none of it first hand."

Andy went inside to get a beer. When he didn't return I followed and found him sitting at the kitchen table.

"I have to find a way to help Hope," I said when he did not acknowledge my presence.

"Has it occurred to you that it might be crueler to bring Hope's mind back from wherever it's gone?" I sat down at the table. "So the born again jerks managed to brainwash her. Maybe that's the only way she can live with a child who will never be anything more than a vegetable."

I lay awake all night thinking about what he had said. By morning I was forced to admit he might be right, yet both of us were too outraged to let Zebediah get off completely.

Andy had to work on Oyster Island, but Jeff consented to see me at his migrant clinic the next morning even though his waiting room was full of stoopers and their sick children. "Arst got a slap on the wrist from the state medical board," he told me in the former bedroom of the rented house he used as an office. Several water colors he had done of Oyster Island decorated the otherwise bare walls, and new linoleum covered the uneven floor. "Earl Roy didn't even get that."

"We can still establish Zebediah fathered the baby," I persisted. "That should be enough for the police to at least investigate."

"If you're counting on the aborted fetus as evidence, forget it. I thought of that the night we shipped Allison to Shock Trauma, but the specimen never made it to the lab."

Every aborted fetus or any other piece of tissue removed from a patient in surgery was sent to the lab for analysis and safe keeping. "Arst or Earl Roy?" I said immediately.

"Probably both. But no fetus, no case against Zebediah."

"There has to be someone who could testify."

Jeff got up, moving in the direction of his jammed waiting room. "There is," he said, "if Allison recovers."

I did not discuss with Lori, Jeff or Andy the plan I came up with to get through to Hope. I bided my time, waiting for her to return to the island with her daughter.

"I was upstairs," she said when she answered the doorbell on the third ring. "Allison will be so happy to see you."

When she motioned me inside, I stepped into a room as startling as Hope's appearance. It was filled with white, French Provincial furniture resting on a sea of blue shag carpet.

"Do you like it?" Hope wore her frozen smile and a sleeveless dress like the one Lori had worn to the Donlin's Christmas dinner. But I was not looking at the dress, I couldn't take my eyes off the scarred arms and legs sticking out from it like gnarled twigs.

"I'm always bumping into things," Hope said when she saw me staring. "Zebediah teases me about how clumsy I am."

The dress was not the only change. Her long copper hair had been brutally shorn and what remained teased up into a pile of stiff curls.

"The house was a homecoming surprise for Allison and me," she said as she closed the door behind us. "Lovey Donlin and the other neighbors took care of everything."

I walked past the blue flocked wallpaper in the living and dining room directly to the kitchen. The antique cherry table and corner cupboard were gone, replaced by a French Provincial table and hutch with glass doors displaying a matched set of Redfield China.

I opened the door to Hope's studio and found only the lingering odor of solder and clay. "They cleaned it out for me," she said in an embarrassed tone. "I don't know why I did all those sinful nudes."

We returned to the living room, where I bumped against the glass fronted gun case from Zebediah's back room.

"Zebediah is so happy to have it out here where it belongs," Hope said. "It was selfish of me not to allow it before."

"Could I see your bedroom?"

There was a hint of curiosity in Hope's otherwise flat voice when she asked why.

"I'd like to see how they decorated it."

"Of course." She led me like a proud new bride up blue carpeted stairs and down a hallway covered with more flocked paper. Nowhere in the house were any of the portraits of mothers and daughters Hope had rescued from antique shops.

When she opened the door to her bedroom, I went straight to the bed and ripped the blankets and sheets from it.

"What are you doing?" Hope grabbed at the bedclothes, trying to put them back in place.

I yanked them away again and tore off the mattress pad, exposing a bullet hole with black powder burns streaking out from it. "Look at that!" I shouted. "That's what your good Christian husband did!"

Hope scooped up the pile of linens and frantically tried to cover the evidence. "That was when I wouldn't let Jesus into my life." Her speech was rapid as she climbed over the bed like a frightened child, wildly smoothing the rumpled linens. "The Lord punished me for not believing by almost taking Allison from me."

The hole was covered with a disorganized heap. Hope knelt next to it in her Alyce Anne dress and scars. "But I'm better now," she said. "And so is my baby. Jesus is in our lives and nothing will ever hurt her again."

I ripped the bedclothes off again and hit my hand so hard against the hole in the mattress my arm rebounded painfully. "Zebediah did that so you wouldn't report him for molesting your daughter! Stop denying what you know is the truth!"

Hope closed her eyes so she would not have to look at the bullet hole. Her hands were held in prayer, much like the ceramic ones on the bedside table painted to match the avocado green room.

"Allison got sick because I would not take Jesus as my personal savior," she said with her eyes still closed. "And Jesus punished me by making her appendix rupture."

"Oh, dear god." I sat down on the bed and Hope came to sit by me, taking my right hand in both of hers. Her hands felt clammy and I missed the roughness from her art.

"Please don't be so upset," she said when I began to cry. "The bible says, 'I the Lord will hold thy right hand, saying unto thee, I fear not.'"

I looked into the face of a woman who bore no resemblance to the friend I once knew. They had gotten to her while she was vulnerable, beside herself with worry and grief over her suffering child. Her mind had separated from her body the same as mine, but I did not know where her's had gone. Or if it would ever come back.

"Hope, Allison did not have a ruptured appendix," I said kindly. "She had an abortion." Hope looked away. "You told me so yourself the night we took her to Baltimore."

"But don't you see?" she said as she turned to me with her unnerving smile. "I was so confused by evil back then I didn't know what I was saying."

"No, Hope, you're confused now. Allison could have had a safe abortion in Baltimore, or a dozen other places. But Zebediah didn't want to risk his political career by taking the chance of letting anyone find out what he had done." Hope sat silently. "Doctor Arst smelled of alcohol the night we took Allison to Baltimore. He was probably drunk when he did the abortion, too, and pushed a sharp instrument through the wall of Allison's uterus."

"She had appendicitis," Hope said with the same rapid speech she used while trying to cover the bullet hole. "Her appendix ruptured and she got peritonitis, just like Zebediah and the reverend said. Jesus saved her when I embraced Him and asked His forgiveness. The bible says, 'For whosoever shall call upon the name of the Lord shall be sa...'"

"Shut up with that moronic 'bible says' shit!"

I picked up the set of avocado green, praying hands on her bedside table and held them out to her. "You used to laugh at these."

A glimmer of recognition briefly crossed her face, then was gone. "A friend painted them for me."

"One of your new Christian friends?"

I started to set the green hands back on the table, but a sudden impulse caused me to smash them to the floor. Hope jumped from the bed to gather up the broken pieces.

"I used to laugh at the Lord and His disciples," she said as she tried to fit them back together. "And He punished me for it."

She was still sitting on the floor, working over the shattered hands like a child with a jigsaw puzzle, when a gurgling noise caught her attention. She dropped the pieces and rushed out of the room.

I followed her down the hall to the daintily flowered room I had not been in since the night we took Allison to Shock Trauma. The neatly made bed still had the photo of Hope and her infant above it.

Allison sat in a reclining wheelchair next to the window, held in place by wide leather straps drawn across her twisted body. Bits of sheepskin protruded from beneath her buttocks to protect them from bedsores, and a catheter bag dangled from one side of the chair. Spittle ran from the corners of her mouth as it worked silently.

Hope wiped anxiously at the saliva, then turned on an electric suction machine to clear out what was choking Allison further down her throat. I drew back from the sound.

"She loves to look out the window," Hope said when the suctioning was completed and the machine turned off. Her Jesus smile had been replaced with one of genuine adoration as she looked at her child.

"Look, there's a robin," she said, pointing to a tree outside the window. "It's come just to see my beautiful girl."

I stayed back, observing them silently as I had the first time I saw them in the cemetery. Hope brushed Allison's lovely hair away from a face so small and wasted it was almost lost in the veil of gold. "I get her up right after breakfast so she can watch the birds, don't I Allison?" Her daughter's head rolled spastically from side to side, her face showing no sign of comprehension.

"I guess she just isn't up to visitors today," Hope said to me.

Allison's eyes rolled back in their sockets and she began to seizure, her legs thumping violently against the leather restraints as if trying to break free. Hope held onto her twitching arms and wiped at secretions rolling down her chin. "With the Lord's help we will have you well again," she said above the grotesque moaning and gurgling. She turned again to the suction machine and switched it on.

She was still talking to her daughter when I ran from the room, down the stairs and out the front door. I could hear the machine and Hope's loving voice as I raced along the highway for Seaport.

And somewhere, very far away but coming ever closer, I heard a baby crying.

CHAPTER THIRTY-NINE

Andy is helping me carry boxes. "I still don't see what the big rush is," he says. "You could stay and take it easy on your back. Just lie on the beach."

I haven't even looked outdoors the past twenty-four hours. I am too preoccupied with trying to keep my mind, hovering somewhere overhead, from completely deserting me before I get away.

"I have to go," I tell Andy again. "I have to leave this horrible island."

"It isn't the island that's horrible," Andy says. "Just some of its inhabitants, like anywhere else in the world."

He stands in the doorway of the bedroom where I stuff the last of my things into suitcases. "I love you," he says.

Don't answer him, the mind up near the ceiling tells the body below. Just take your things and leave. But Andy comes to me and holds me tightly. "I worry about you," he says. "Especially when you're so quiet."

A Glenn Miller song is playing on WGOD as he kisses my forehead, then my cheeks. Get away, my mind warns my body. Or you're on your way to Shake and Bake.

"Please don't," I say, but Andy continues to kiss my neck and down along my shoulder.

Suddenly the music on the radio stops. "Ladies an' gentlemen," a male announcer says in a somber voice. "It is my sad duty to inform you that the bodies of Senator Zebediah Taylor, Mrs. Taylor and their daughter Allison were discovered shot to death in their home in Heavenly Acres just minutes ago."

Andy nearly fell as I pushed him away and dove for the radio he had not heard. I tried to adjust the volume but only succeeded in knocking the radio to the floor, where it was silenced. "Hope!" I yelled as I ran for the living room and turned on the television Andy had bought to replace the one he destroyed.

He hurried after me. "What the hell's up?"

The television showed police trying to control a mob of onlookers already gathered outside Hope's house. Windy Duckman stood at the forefront, looking as shaken as the others.

"The bodies were discovered by volunteer firemen who went ta see why Senator Taylor didn't show up for a strategy meetin' regardin' the abortion march on Washington," Windy said into his microphone. As he spoke, three shrouded bodies were being removed behind him.

"Holy shit," Andy said.

"Senator Taylor was shot once in the head, an' his daughter the same," Windy said. "Then Mrs. Taylor turned the gun on herself."

"No! It wasn't Hope! It was Zebediah!"

"Quiet, Pat. We need to find out what happened." Andy forced me to sit beside him on the sofa while we listened. The evidence was overwhelming. Hope had killed all three of them.

"I thought I should let them be," I cried into Andy's shoulder. "I knew nothing could be done for Allison. And Hope seemed happy just being with her."

"You did the only thing you could," Andy consoled.

"I knew she was insane, but I never dreamed she would hurt her child. I still can't believe it; she adored Allison."

Andy held me tighter. "Don't blame yourself. It was completely out of your control."

It was the last statement that made me suddenly discover my mind was back. It was a bad dream, I thought with enormous relief. Just one of my nightmares.

But the television was on and a reporter stood on the front lawn of Hope's house. "The Senator was shot in his sleep," he said solemnly as an ambulance drove slowly away with its siren silent. "His daughter, who was seriously ill after sufferin' a burst appendix, was found in bed dressed in her riding clothes. And her mother, who brought this turble tragedy upon them, was by her side."

"Oh please no. Don't let this be real."

"There's something we don't know," Andy said as he continued to watch the screen. "Something that made Hope completely snap."

The new Highway Holiness Church could not contain the crowd

of islanders, and politicians who came from Annapolis. The funeral was held in the only building large enough, the town firehall.

Three coffins sat at the front of the room, Zebediah's draped with an American flag, and Allison's beside it covered with roses. Hope's was off to the side, adorned with a single spray of gladiolus.

I wanted to take them off, to push her coffin over next to Allison's and tell everybody that none of this was Hope's fault. But with the suction machine hissing a warning only inches away, I remained seated in the back of the hall with Andy, Jeff and Lori.

"We should have brought flowers," I said as more people squeezed into the room. "Hope hated gladiolus."

"We're here," Lori said. "That's what matters." She took one of my hands and Andy took the other.

Hen Fishback sat up front near The Lord's Messengers, an empty folding chair signifying Zebediah's absence. The group sang two songs before Reverend Taylor strode to the makeshift pulpit for the eulogy. The high school band played Nearer My God to Thee in the background.

"Who knows how long the evil was growin' in her before it rose up an' took her over," the reverend said as he looked toward Hope's coffin. "The only pity was her takin' the Senator an' his beloved daughter with her." Handkerchiefs were everywhere; Hen Fishback's small eyes blinked at the speed of light.

"But I say rejoice that the Senator an' Allison went straight ta heaven to be with the Lord!" The reverend raised his hands skyward, then toward the floor. "Whilst she went to her eternal damnation!"

"The bible says, 'For the wages of sin is death,'" Hen shouted out from the front row of the congregation.

"'But the gift of God is eternal life in Christ Jesus our Lord!'" someone added from the congregation.

"'The soul that sinneth, it shall die,'" the reverend proclaimed as he pointed savagely at Hope's coffin. "'The wicked shall be turned into hell!'"

"Praise Jesus!" a woman intoned. The band continued to play softly in the background.

"She was not one of us." The reverend's nostrils flared in indignation. "Though she deceived us into believin' she was whilst giving her soul to the devil hisself."

Odie dropped to his knees, loudly imploring the Lord to bring Zebediah back to life. When the miracle did not occur, he meekly returned to his chair.

The reverend's voice was mournful now. "And so we gather here today ta pray over a man who was sure to be our next Congressman, and maybe even president of this great land. The first true Christian in the White House."

Lovey Donlin shrieked her despair and was comforted by Earl Roy and Big Knocks. Adella Dawn was nowhere in the vast hall.

"Lord have pity on us!" Dolly cried from her lawn chair.

A man in a group of politicians, who looked completely out of place among the islanders surrounding them, got slowly to his feet. "We will never have another like him. There was only one Zebediah Taylor."

"Thank God," Andy whispered beside me.

The band finished Nearer My God to Thee, somewhere close to the same time, and began ruffling through sheet music in preparation for the next number.

"Yes, my friends, Zebediah was headed for greatness, an' this ahlund with him," the reverend continued mournfully. "And she took it all from us in one sinful night."

He looked again at Hope's coffin, shaking his head from side to side. "Only true Christians would allow her ta lay here in the same room with us after what she did."

"Amen," someone in the crowd said, and others repeated it like an echo ricocheting back and forth off the walls.

I started to get up but Lori stopped me. "A scene is exactly what they want," she said. "Then they could throw us all out."

I knew she was right by the looks being shot our way. I could not leave Hope in a room full of people she despised.

"An' so our dream dies with you, Zebediah," the reverend said as the band began God Bless America. "There will be no Christian ahlunder in Congress, nor in the White House. And there will be no one ta lead us in our holy crusade against those trying ta bring us to the brink of destruction by murderin' our young."

"Hold on, reverend." Hen climbed up onto his folding chair to address the crowd. "We got us a Christian ta send ta Washington, and there he stands, right there!" He flapped one of his wings in the direction of the reverend. "What better person than the Senator's own cousin! An' a preacher at that!"

Reverend Taylor reacted with shock. "Why I'm just a simple man of the cloth." But the turn of events somehow did not appear to be quite the surprise the reverend professed it to be.

The band had stopped playing, and for a moment the room was totally quiet. Then, ever so softly, Odie began picking out tentative notes on his guitar and singing, "Mine eyes have seen the glory of the coming of the Lord. He is...."

The remainder of the Lord's Messengers joined in, then Iris Irene and Crystal Lou. "...tramping out the vintage where the grapes of wrath are stored."

It moved out over the crowd, spreading to the side aisles and rising in timbre with each new voice. Lovey Donlin dabbed at her eyes as she stood with Earl Roy and Carol Faye. Others were getting to their feet.

"We can get the reverend into the seat in Congress Senator Taylor was surely goin' ta win!" Hen shouted above the singing. "And from there it's nonstop to sixteen hundred Pennsylvania Avenue!"

"It's Jesus calling you, Reverend!" Earl Roy was clapping his hands to the beat of the music.

"It's Jesus calling all of us!" Big Knocks added as she clapped along with the man who would finally provide her a home in Heavenly Acres.

Hen flapped his stunted wings so rapidly I swore I could see space between his feet and the chair on which he stood. The band, wanting to get into the act but not possessing the appropriate sheet music, began playing what it had next on its agenda, The National Anthem.

The brass section overpowered Odie's guitar and the crowd all stood to sing, hands held over hearts, "Oh, say can you see, by the dawn's early light..."

"Christ. It's a fuckin' campaign rally," Andy said.

Reverend Taylor stood looking out over his flock with a smile so wide his nostrils disappeared.

Andy left early the next morning for Oyster Island, where he would work in the clinic then spend the night at Lori and Jeff's. He told me the previous night that he was planning to build his own home there with the help of the islanders as soon as he had the money.

There was no formal goodbye, he just wished me well, got into his rusted car and drove away.

I was about to walk down the steps of the cottage for the last time when I stopped to check the mailbox, which never held any mail. There was a pale ivory envelope inside addressed to me.

The moment I opened it and saw the artistic penmanship I shuffled to the last page, confirming both my suspicion and fear.

My Dear Pat,

By the time you read this you will have been hurt far more than I ever intended to hurt anyone. I hate to put this burden on you, but someone must know the truth.

I am sorry I turned my back on your kindness when you came to me that last time. Please understand that I truly thought I was doing what was best for Allison.

I believed with my whole being that she would get well, or at least that's what I wanted to believe. Zebediah promised me he would devote every minute of his life to her and never harm her again.

He made me believe in the power of religion, that if I prayed hard enough and took good enough care of Allison, she would be healed. I still believe in the Lord's power, Pat. It is helping me do what must be done tonight.

I found him at her again. He went to Annapolis to tell his people he was giving up politics, or so he told me. He came home while I was sleeping. I was so exhausted from caring for Allison, and I didn't think I needed to lock her door anymore.

She had a seizure that woke me, and when I went to check on her I found him on top of her. He was drunk but he knew what he was doing. He told me Allison didn't realize what was going on so it no longer mattered what he did to her.

I made it to the rocker on the porch and drank in large gulps of air before I could go on.

I got him off her and into his bed. I prayed over him before I shot him.

Allison is all bathed and dressed in her riding clothes now. She was so happy when she saw her red jacket, I actually believe she was smiling. I held her and sang all the songs Adam Lee and I used to sing when she was a baby until she fell asleep. We will go together in the same bed so I know she is safe.

A dog and its master ran by on the beach. The owner was young and tanned like Allison's lifeguard.

Guns can be friends, Pat, just as Zebediah always told me. If he didn't have them in this house I wouldn't be able to send us to Jesus tonight.

I asked the Lord to forgive him for what he did to Allison. And for what he did to his sister long ago.

He confessed to me tonight that it was he who raped her. Joanetta Jean let an innocent man be hanged and took her own life rather than tell on her brother.

Reverend Taylor has known all these years and kept it secret.

That's the power Zebediah had over people, Pat, the same power that kept me from taking Allison and leaving when I knew I should.

This is an evil place. People deceive themselves into thinking they speak for God, when a merciful Lord would never wish anyone to suffer as Allison has. Zebediah destroyed my daughter to protect his political career, just like you told me. If he was truly sorry for what he did, he wouldn't have been at her tonight.

I cannot let Allison's torture go on any longer, and I cannot allow Zebediah to continue with his evilness. I pray the Lord will be merciful.

My only regret is that I did not have the courage to tell people on this island the truth about what happened to Allison, or to tell them what I think of them and their so-called morals. I once told you I'm not as brave as you.

It is time for us to leave now, and I must get this letter to the mailbox. I want to be sure Allison is sleeping when I send her to heaven.

She will be happy there with Adam Lee and the Lord, where no one can hurt her. My fate is not so certain, but I know you understand that I could not go on living without my baby.

Hope

CHAPTER FORTY

The wind blew all night. A nor'easter was moving in.

I sat alone at the kitchen table watching dawn fight its way into a leaden sky. The surf assaulted the beach outside the window where I held my long vigil, waiting for the suction machine to make its final appearance to claim whatever was left of my mind.

I had failed Hope, the same as the mother who abandoned her, and the nuns in whom she later placed her trust. Surely this was as terrible as leaving a burned baby to suffer while I went home to eat.

In my soul I knew that I should have stayed at the hospital with the child, I must have known it even back then. But I put my own comfort ahead of the baby, and I would carry the pain of that decision the rest of my life.

Hope knew, too, what she should have done when she first discovered Zebediah's abuse of her child, but she let him frighten her into staying on the island. When it finally all came apart, she chose to go insane rather than face what she had allowed to happen, even if unintended.

She learned helplessness in the homes of people who abused her, and at the mercy of nuns who refused to believe her. And she let that helplessness take over when Adam Lee died, marrying a man who subjected her and her daughter to years of brutality.

I learned my helplessness in war, fighting a government comprised of bureaucrats who did not care whether we had the necessary supplies to care for the patients it sent us to serve. In the end, I let a helpless baby suffer the consequences of that indifference.

The United States of America had gone into Vietnam with ideals noble only to itself, and the result was disastrous. Our nation had been torn wide open, rejecting much of what made us strong, but possessing nothing to put in its place.

Cracks in a sidewalk did not stay empty. Zebediah and others like him were weeds filling the void left by a nation in grief and disarray. Their message was supposed to be one of healing and restoration, but their actions spoke of intolerance and retribution for anyone who did not agree with their self-proclaimed godliness.

If the weeds were allowed to grow unchecked, they would eventually take over everyone and everything in their path, choking off freedoms we fought desperately to achieve, and strangling nonbelievers who dared to stand in their way. The weeds would become the harvest instead of the waste.

The storm had not yet moved inland when I drove into Muskrat Marsh and up to the courthouse. A butter glow of morning sunlight glinted off the majestic building's dome, sprinkling the lawn with shafts of light. I sat in my car looking at the magnificent White Oak where the man accused of raping Zebediah's sister had been hanged.

People would be gathering soon beneath its vast branches, drinking their morning coffee and commenting on the approaching storm. They would discuss the funeral and wonder how they would go on without their honorary fire chief, sheriff, senator and war hero. There would be speculation about Zebediah's considerable real estate holdings, which would now go to his only surviving relative, Reverend Taylor.

Zebediah and Allison's tragic deaths would be eulogized once more, and Hope condemned for her evilness. Someone would say again how Zebediah should have married one of his own.

Clouds were beginning to roll inland, transforming the sky behind the courthouse into an ominous gray. A rising wind ruffled the sheets of ivory paper in my hand as I walked with hammer and nails to the massive oak.

People were beginning to arrive on the courthouse lawn when I drove the last of the nails into the tree's broad trunk. A small knot of them gathered around it the moment I walked away, calling excitedly to others while they read. The crowd was swelling as I put my car into gear and drove away.

I scattered dune grasses and wild flowers I had gathered in Seaport on Adam Lee's concrete slab first. From there I moved to the grave of Zebediah's sister, Joanetta Jean, and did the same. Finally, I went to the freshly dug graves of Hope and Allison.

After tossing the wilted spray of gladiolus on Hope's over a nearby fence, I replaced it with more of the wild flowers and grasses.

The withered roses on Allison's grave went over the fence, too, before covering it with a bouquet of violets picked from a protected hollow, just before the sand dunes, which I had secretly admired all spring.

Zebediah's grave not only had fresh flowers on it, but dozens of small American flags stuck into the mound of dirt that would later be covered with a concrete slab like all the other graves. The flags whipped and snapped in the wind while I stood there, just as Hope's letter was undoubtedly doing in the growing gale.

A smile spread slowly across my face as I thought of the townspeople reading it. I had added only one thing to the bottom: "Vengeance is mine, sayeth the Lord."

Andy was about to pull out of the marina, headed for Oyster Island in Jeff's boat, when my Mustang wheeled up to the dock and I jumped out. He looked with both surprise and alarm as I leapt across the narrow expanse of water separating him from the dock.

"Pat!" He caught me in his arms as I catapulted aboard.

"I've spent too much time worrying about marrying the wrong guy like Hope did when she married Zebediah," I said as we regained our balance. "And not enough time remembering how she married the right one when she chose Adam Lee."

Andy let out a laugh as he held an arm tightly around me and steered the boat toward the channel. "You're something, Danang."

THE END